RELATIVE
FORTUNES

RELATIVE FORTUNES

A JULIA KYDD NOVEL

MARLOWE BENN

LAKE UNION
PUBLISHING

Published by Lake Union Publishing, Seattle
www.apub.com

Amazon, the Amazon logo, and Lake Union Publishing are trademarks of Amazon.com, Inc., or its affiliates.

ISBN-13: 9781542005210 (hardcover)
ISBN-10: 1542005213 (hardcover)
ISBN-13 9781542091695 (paperback)
ISBN-10: 1542091691(paperback)

Printed in the United States of America

First edition

For my father, Peter Beckman

[The suffragette] is a woman who has stupidly
carried her envy of certain of the superficial
privileges of men to such a point that it takes on the
character of an obsession. . . . What these virtuous
beldames actually desire in their hearts is . . . that the
franchise of dalliance be extended to themselves.
—H. L. Mencken, 1922

CHAPTER 1

Two bankers—one gray and stout, the other pink and merely soft about the jowls—conferred in low voices outside the office door, flicking pained glances through the window's gold lettering. Julia smoothed the gloves across her knee to feign indifference and watched from the shadows of her hat brim. It mattered to her what the men said, and also that they not realize how much.

They stepped back into the room, closing the door with a solemn click. The older man settled behind the desk, and his colleague sat in the remaining client chair, beside Julia. She was flanked.

"It's a privilege to meet you at last, Miss Kydd," the older man said. "I remember your father well, and of course your brother has been a valued client for years. This bank and the Kydd family have enjoyed a long and cordial relationship, as you know."

She blanched at talk of satisfied generations. Trouble, then.

"Naturally we'd like to help," he went on, stroking his jaw as if to coax forth a kinder way to phrase what must follow, "but I'm afraid what you ask is impossible. While it's true the account is registered in your name and technically the money is yours, the terms of the trust prohibit release of funds to anyone other than the trustee or his assigned proxies. Not even to you." He forced a cough. "Particularly not to you. That's rather the point of a trust, after all."

Julia recrossed her legs. She pointed out that she was no longer a child. In less than three weeks, her twenty-fifth birthday would render the issue moot. "I've lived independently in London for some time now and am quite capable of managing my own funds. If Philip were available, I'm sure he'd authorize this, but he's not, and frankly I'm in a bit of a pinch."

Was she sure he'd cooperate? Ten years her senior, her half brother was a virtual stranger to her. They shared a name and a father but little else. If not for the small oil portrait over the library mantel, she might not have recognized him at their father's funeral. She was six, and he, studied from behind the folds of her mother's skirt, was a silent, taut-limbed youth summoned home from boarding school. Then he was gone again, until her mother's death seven years later upended everything. Julia had been pitched into Philip's last-resort care—or, more accurately, his legal jurisdiction. Their only filial touch had been an awkward handshake on signing her guardianship papers. From that moment on they'd been bound by a contract, nothing more.

For the past decade Philip had been little more than a distant signature, each month releasing the funds from the account that enabled her life to proceed. She had no reason to suspect he now intended to embarrass, much less impoverish, her, although the fact that he was legally entitled to do so (for seventeen more days) chafed at her dignity. Dignity, however, was the least of it. A dark troll of doubt stirred again in her mind: Wasn't this—control of her own money—the very issue that had dragged her back to New York?

Philip's note, folded over the toast rack on her breakfast tray two days ago, had merely said he'd "toddled off to Philadelphia," with promises to return in time for their appointment next week with the lawyers to resolve the questions he'd raised about her inheritance. Until then, he'd written, surely she could amuse herself? Julia was to enjoy her reacquaintance with the city. The new Matisse watercolors at the Pryor Gallery were particularly fine, and Stokowski was conducting Glière's

Third on Sunday at the Aeolian. As if she too could simply wave a hand to invoke subscriber's privileges or flick a finger for an account to be billed. For a man it was easy. Honor among peers was enough. Philip's elegance fell to him on credit, no vulgar cash required.

The younger banker swung his knees toward her. "We might be able to help in another way, Miss Kydd. I could advance you a small sum off the books, as it were. It's a kind of gentlemen's arrangement we occasionally offer our best clients, as even the most provident among us are occasionally caught up short. Say, twenty dollars? To be repaid at your brother's earliest convenience. He and I are lunching together next week, as it happens. That would be soon enough."

How droll. He would consider her an honorary gentleman for a day or two. Their little secret. Very modern. "I require at least fifty," Julia said. "As I told you." Most men she knew would ask for twice that and beam at the adventure of such thrift.

He puzzled at her obstinacy. "But—"

"May I apply for a loan, then? I clearly have the means to repay it and will accept whatever interest you must charge." She lifted her chin. Pride cost nothing.

The men's eyes reconvened. Lips were rolled, sighs suppressed.

"That's impossible too, I'm afraid. It's simply not done, Miss Kydd. No reputable bank in this country will lend money to a woman without the cosignature of a male relation. You must be reasonable."

The younger man tried again. "But your problem is so easily solved. A brief note would do. Philip can even telephone, if he speaks to one of us directly. We do sympathize, Miss Kydd."

"Trust your brother, my dear," his colleague added. "He'll look after you, decide what's best. I'm afraid there's nothing more we can say. You must understand."

Julia understood. It was they who failed to grasp the situation. She simply sought to withdraw a modest sum of her own money. She needed their services, not their sympathy. The more solicitous (and adamant) their manner grew, the more her cheeks began to burn.

She stood, and both men scrambled to their feet. "I see," she said. "I'd hoped for a more enlightened response, but it appears my faith was misplaced." Misplaced and outright trampled.

Her dignity, however, would not waver. She strode out through the bank's vast marble lobby. Her steps echoed beneath the high vaulted ceiling, gilded with the fortunes of prosperous men, and no doubt with the fortunes of women too—women like her, from whose feeble judgment and impulsive sentiment their money was so zealously safeguarded.

She continued down the steps into the mild September sunshine, ignoring the doorman's low whistle. She intended to march clean out of view, gaze high and shoulders back, beyond any shadow of those massive pillars and all the "simply not done" nonsense they supported. Instead she was forced to stop, stalled by a pebble under her left foot. Her shoes were made of a smooth kid leather dyed to match her dove-gray frock—pretty things but also a hobbling nuisance, intended for indolent afternoons at the card table and strolls through smart galleries, not rough Manhattan pavements.

She freed the stone and calculated: sixteen blocks. Difficult but not impossible. She turned left, took two steps, and paused. On reconsideration she reversed course, 51 percent certain the route to Philip's apartment lay to her right. Without the money she'd intended to collect, all hopes of moving to a hotel were thwarted, and she had no choice but to return to his so-called hospitality. She began to walk.

Two weeks, she thought. Maybe three. Certainly within a month it would all be resolved, and she would be steaming toward home again, perhaps even already back in her lovely flat in Shepherd Market. By then her housekeeper, Christophine, would have dry proofed, cleaned, and laid in the shiny new fonts of Garamont due to arrive from France any day now. She had barely demurred when Julia decided to turn the flat's small dining alcove into her printing studio, stationing the heavy oak type cabinet in the window bay so that during the long, close labor of letterspacing a line of caps, she might look up and rest her gaze on Green Park's distant overstory. Shortly before she'd had to sail for New York for this one last tangle with Philip, Julia had christened that alcove and all within it the Capriole Press, *her* Capriole Press. She'd produced only one official title so far, but it had pleased some of London's most discerning collectors, and it was enough. It made her a publisher.

Julia produced her books by hand, in necessarily small editions, planned and executed with a care that made her enterprise more important, not less. At this point Capriole was mostly still a vision in her head, a jumble of possible new projects combining texts, illustrations, papers, inks, and more. But that vision, awaiting only the funds to be unlocked on her birthday, was her future. Just thinking about it kept her stride steady and her pace brisk (despite a complaining whisper from her left heel), as if she could walk straight there today.

"Julia!"

A month ago she might have flinched at such a squeal, but now the sound of her name exclaimed in pleasure—or spoken at all, to be frank—was cheering. A silver motorcar glided to the curb beside her. "Where's the fire? You look like you want to get there yesterday."

Julia bent to the lowered rear window and greeted her friend.

"What luck," Glennis said. "Hop in."

Julia hesitated. Luck? She doubted it. Glennis had likely wheedled news of Julia's banking errand from Mrs. Cheadle, Philip's housekeeper. Glennis Rankin was an old school friend, half-forgotten until wild coincidence had jostled them together again last week on the crossing from England. Given Julia's long absence from the city and now Philip's neglect, Glennis was also Julia's sole acquaintance in New York. Chums for a single year when they were fourteen, they'd grown quite different in temperament and taste in the intervening decade. Glennis was still almost childlike, eager for a romp and a laugh, but her exuberance wasn't the problem. The problem was more embarrassing.

Glennis simply exhaled money. Successive evenings of chasing her restless fancy, abandoning twenty-dollar bottles of dubious champagne in one club after another, had reduced Julia to her present predicament. She could still afford her friend's company, barely, at least for another few weeks, but not without refreshing her supply of ready cash. She murmured as much as the motorcar pulled smoothly into traffic.

Glennis scoffed. "Easy. I'll float you. And anyway we can start at my sister's party tonight, and that won't cost a penny. Viv made me promise to kick things up if it gets dull."

And so it was settled. Julia sank back into the upholstery and accepted the prospect of yet another evening of her friend's cheerful meandering, which suited her perfectly at the moment. She needed distraction, any lark to get her through until the lawyers could resolve Philip's qualms. Another few idling weeks, she hoped, and she could recommence her real life, unencumbered by his oversight or anyone else's.

Until then, she would entrust her hours to Glennis's frivolity. Once again tonight she'd lead them everywhere and nowhere. New York had changed in the five years since Julia had left for Europe's fresh horizons. After dark in this new Manhattan, one party simply melted into the next. She'd seen it in London too, the endless searching for some new diversion—silly or vacuous or even dangerous, it didn't matter—anything to avoid thinking about all that had been lost in those muddy trenches.

Every night was the same. Whether stalking a saxophone's wail or tumbling out of a taxicab at a half-remembered address, one kept moving in the quest for somewhere the sidecars were safe, the chatter amusing, and the hours quick to pass. New York seemed full of such sanctuaries, given the right sort of knock and moneyed smile. On both scores Glennis's did nicely, which was a blessing, really, as Julia had just two dollars and sixty-four cents to her name.

CHAPTER 2

Julia followed Glennis into the front rooms of a spacious apartment somewhere in the East Eighties. She relinquished her wrap to the waiting maid and surveyed the smoky crowd. A sluggish knot of guests stood ravaging canapés by the piano, barely lifting their faces to inspect the new arrivals. Glennis shrugged off her sister's greeting as she peered down a shadowed hallway. Over the jittery bray of a phonograph, she demanded, of no one in particular, to know, "Is Russell here?"

Her talk all afternoon of a man named Russell had been interminable. She'd raptured at everything from his taste in neckties to his nile-green Jewett, apparently ranking him high on her list of prospective last-chance husbands. Never mind that they'd spent the past two nights on the trail of another elusive candidate named Warren, a Wall Street up-and-comer with a powerful devotion to Glennis when he could get away from his dishrag of a wife in Hoboken. The ever-resilient Glennis had shrugged at each disappointing prowl through another murky room, and off they'd gone again. Glennis knew a great number of places to look for whatever or whomever she was after, and Julia was content to trail in her wake, paying the fare every other time they alighted somewhere new. As long as she was able.

Glennis lifted two drinks from a passing tray and gave one to Julia. "Dreadful. No one here but wholesome, bloody strivers. Nothing we can do about that. Let's finish these and push off. I'll say you have a headache. Tab's on me tonight." She fiddled with her frock's shoulder strap and jerked her wrist toward her mouth in a clumsy bottoms up signal.

Julia agreed with a hasty gulp. What made some parties effervescent and others a sludge of misery? There was a sour whiff of boredom here on both sides of the canapé trays and cocktail shakers. Little wonder Glennis was already keen to soldier on.

But downed gin and a swift getaway were not to be. Glennis's sister lifted the phonograph's needle. Vivian Winterjay stood across the room in a spotlight of wary silence, mustering one of those small, composed smiles meant to carry one through any occasion—the bare-knuckle refuge of impeccable breeding. Her party was clearly not going well, not well at all, yet her fair features glowed serenely in the lamplight. It seemed fate had lavished the family beauty on Vivian, leaving only scraps for the younger Glennis, and a discreet swell of expectant maternity only deepened her radiance. A special treat was waiting, she announced, and they were all to proceed through to the dining room. She gestured to a pair of varnished oak doors as her eyes swept the room, enforcing the invitation with a jaunty smile. They pinned even Julia for a moment. Glennis could click and nod herself into a frenzy gesturing toward the exit (and she very nearly did), but to turn and leave at that moment would be unspeakably rude. They had no choice but to refresh their drinks and join the shuffle into the dining room.

Waiting at the head of the table sat an aging woman with tar-black ringlets and a wobble of white skin from chin to collar. Hands upturned to either side, she said simply, "Madame Sosostris, at your service."

A séance, then. Neither special nor a treat. In London séances were such exhausted party fare that Julia knew several young people who would revolt at this moment, upsetting the plan with brutal mockery.

These guests settled meekly into place around the table: either the game was less commonplace in New York, or they were simply a tamer lot. One hour, Julia calculated. No hostess on earth could hope for more.

The slap of dark was absolute, prompting a few seized breaths and a cluck or two of laughter. At the first shiver of blue light, someone gave a sporting whistle of appreciation, but that was all. There were no gasps or clutches for another's hand. The tiny light swayed above the table like a trapeze in search of its artist before swooping low in a staccato frenzy, sparking flickers off cocktails, brilliantined heads, and the tablecloth's embroidered sequins and mirrors.

"Poor thing needs a drink," Glennis said into Julia's shoulder. "Awful jimjams."

The jittery light sprang to the ceiling and stilled, a resting hummingbird.

"Who's there?" Madame prompted in a low rumble.

They waited. A muffled clatter and plaintive "Oh, for the love o' Mike" seeped through the wall from the kitchen. Snickers traveled the circle of hands, emerging in Mrs. Winterjay's soft sigh of irritation.

Still nothing. The swish of stockings as legs were crossed. A cough muffled into a lapel. Another rustle. The partiers were already restless. Spirit lights, if that was all they were to get, were as old as ankle-length hems. Julia revised her estimate of time remaining: ten minutes.

The light vanished in a wash of cool air. Glennis resettled her fingers in Julia's palm. "Now we're cooking," she said under her breath. "Make it a good wow, Madame Sosostris."

That preposterous name again. A snigger from across the table suggested at least one other person got the joke, if that was what it was. Perhaps Madame had read Mr. Eliot's thrilling poem herself, though more likely someone had suggested the name's susurrant riches to her. No matter—it added a fresh tweak to the routine. Occult thrill making must be hard work, and anyone plucky enough to tread those waters deserved a bit of indulgence. Julia gave Glennis's thumb a squeeze and resolved to see the silliness through.

Madame began to make low cooing sounds. "I see a child," she said. "A tiny child. He seems to be searching for his mama. Has anyone here lost a little one?"

A woman's fingers twitched in Julia's left hand. In a rattle of bracelets, she jerked it toward her bosom. Julia twisted to ease the angle of her elbow, pulled painfully toward a gullible nest of grief and crepe de chine. The woman began to cry.

"It's your sweet little cherub, Tillie," murmured Mrs. Winterjay. "What does he say to his mama, Madame Sosostris?"

Was she daft? Others shifted uneasily too. Only the most hardened cynics or willful innocents might wish to hear more; the poor mother clearly believed her child's spirit was near, and the silliness had turned excruciating. Julia's chin sank in dread of what must come next.

"He says nothing. Only silence, the silence of a small heart no longer beating."

In the appalled quiet that followed, Tillie bounced Julia's hand down onto the table. There was the creak of her chair, a stumble, a smothered sob.

"Poor old girl."

"Lousy luck."

Indignant voices barely bothered to whisper. The hapless séance seemed about to end, but Mrs. Winterjay's sharp indrawn breath signaled her resolve to continue. Someone slid into the vacant space beside Julia and groped to resume the circle. A man's fingers gave hers a friendly swipe.

"But he's with Jesus, dear. I'm sure he's happy," Mrs. Winterjay said as she tried again, inquiring whether anyone else had a loved one on the other side they'd like to summon.

Silence. Julia cringed. No London hostess would dare to utter such a heartless question. Even in America, didn't they all have someone dead in the poppy fields of France or Belgium or any of a thousand freshly swollen graveyards? She resented the sting of Gerald's face, so needlessly summoned. Its features were fading now but still dear, as only a first lover's could be. Did Glennis have someone? A brother, a lover, a friend? She must. They all had someone.

"Anyone?"

Julia heard the soft clack of Mrs. Winterjay's pendant earrings and imagined her head moving from side to side, desperate to stir something, anything, out of the sullen darkness that had become her party.

Madame's breathing shifted to a pulse of shallow grunts. Another chair scraped across the carpet—was someone about to leave? Julia unkinked her legs and prepared for an unpleasant end to the failed séance. She tried to recall where Glennis had suggested they might go next. She'd rattled off possibilities into her compact mirror in the taxicab between blots of Cherry Kiss, but Julia could remember only the Metamora, on West Forty-Fourth, and the Lido-Venice, closer by on East Fifty-Third. One place was as promising as any other in Julia's blurred sense of clubs and cafés and cabarets. She too had been born in New York, but Manhattan had become almost unrecognizable to her after five years abroad, its landmarks distorted in the hot shimmer of new energy. Her mother would have reveled in the city's youthful plunge into recklessness after the war; her father would have retreated deeper into his walnut-paneled midtown clubs.

"Wait." Mrs. Winterjay stilled the squirming. "I believe she has someone."

Madame gave a breathy gust. "So sad, so sad. I see a woman. A lonely woman, lonely and sad. She's weeping, weeping."

"Swell. Sounds like loads of fun," a low voice interrupted. "How about an Indian princess or one of those Egyptian—"

"She must be lost, poor lamb. She's departed this world but cannot find her way to the next. Who could she be? Someone's wife? Daughter? Sister? Friend?" Madame paused to weigh the group's returned attention like a ripe melon. "I see her now. Lovely eyes, orbs of sapphire they are, bright with—"

Pain shot up Julia's wrist as Glennis crushed her hand. "Naomi!"

Glennis's scream walloped Julia's heart and unleashed an answering chorus of cries and bellows. Julia may have contributed to the mayhem herself. She'd never heard a real scream before. Corkers from the stage, of course, and squeals at parties and regattas and the like but never a genuine shriek of terror and never at such close range. It launched knees into table parts and sent liquor splashing over skin and silk. Profane oaths escaped left and right, high and low. From crashes and thuds in the blackness around her, Julia guessed more than one guest had swooned dead away.

Above it all rose Mrs. Winterjay's voice, calling for Mary to get the lights. A murky rectangle appeared as the maid swatted through the bunting and punched at the wall switch. She stood astonished, a pink gingham oven mitt over her left hand, the aroma of hot cheese straws floating in from the kitchen behind her.

The partiers scrambled to repair the damage. Women's hands swarmed, straightening straps, righting twisted jewelry, and adjusting skewed hats. Men brushed at their jackets and trousers to blot the gin and whiskey deposited there, shaking olives and lemon curls out of their cuffs. Those at the table had fared marginally better in that none had actually fallen to the floor, though some would sport ugly bruises from the table legs, sharp and faceted as Greek columns.

Julia checked her right knee, fearing a gash and ladder in her stocking. The bump was red and sure to swell, but the silk had held. Thank goodness for French quality. The puddle of brandy in her lap was a disaster, however, even if her neighbor's handkerchief helped a bit. The dress was likely ruined. At least it wasn't one of her better frocks. *Quel dommage!*

Amid the commotion Madame Sosostris stood blinking. This time nothing could corral the guests back into their seats. Her portion of the evening's entertainment cut short, albeit with a satisfying thrill, she looked pleased and not a little startled. With a nod to their hostess invoking balance of payment—well earned, her glance crowed—she gathered up the voluminous gray tablecloth, stiff and crumpled as an elephant's hide, and disappeared through the kitchen door. The cloth trailed out behind her, tiny mirrors winking like dolls' eyes.

Mrs. Winterjay bent toward her sister. "For pity's sake, Glennis. It's a *party*."

Black streaks wicked out across Glennis's cheeks. She ground a knuckle against her lip as Mrs. Winterjay apologized for the outburst, explaining that their sister, Naomi, was alive and well. She'd seen her herself that very morning. She urged everyone to return to the living room, where ham biscuits would soon be served. And more music, please. She took hold of a fellow's arm and nudged him in the intended direction.

A handful of guests obediently moved off to start up the phonograph, but others exchanged glances and slipped away toward the hall and an artful exit. The chap whose fingers had met Julia's and whose handkerchief she still held caught her eye, one brow flexed in mute query. *Care to come along?* She'd have liked to reply with an eyebrow of her own and to whisk her handbag, shawl, and overwrought friend out the door with him, but Glennis's face told her they couldn't leave yet, and Julia gestured as much. With that he was borne away by a sinewy female in ecru chiffon. Perhaps they'd see him later at the Metamora or Lido, but Julia feared not.

Mrs. Winterjay eyed the exodus, reaffixed her smile, and hurried after her guests, one arm calming the mound at her waist.

"All that stuff about blue eyes. I swear I saw her." Glennis's own eyes were the color of an August sky, immense with agitation. She had pushed aside guests' wraps to sit on the Winterjays' bed and wait for her brother, Chester, to return her call. Naomi lived, it seemed, in a basement apartment beneath the family home. Chester had made a frightful stink about going downstairs to check on her, Glennis said, but it couldn't be helped. She couldn't bear another moment of not knowing. Her headpiece, a beaded bandeau of jet and crystal, listed over one ear, flattening her sparse bob like a fallen egg custard. She rocked a thumbnail in the gap between her front teeth. "Queer old Naomi. I hardly know her; that's the rummy thing."

Julia had witnessed such tumult before. Glennis was what their teachers had called excitable. Her mind leaped to fantastical conclusions, often on the skimpiest of evidence. She relished drama, especially with herself at center stage. At school Julia had soothed over many of her friend's outlandish notions—which soon had dissolved into good-natured shrugs once common sense prevailed.

"I take it Naomi is another sister?" Julia asked. She'd long ago forgotten whatever she once knew about Glennis's family, except that she too was a tardy caboose born half a generation behind her siblings. Until last week's chance meeting on the *Majestic*'s promenade deck not an hour out of Southampton, Julia had neither seen nor thought much of Glennis Rankin since the year they had both been gangly girls marooned at that stuffy school in Vermont. She recognized little things about Glennis that once annoyed her—the two-second delay before she laughed at a joke, her tendency to blurt first and blush second, her fondness for finishing other people's cake—but now those qualities seemed amusing, even endearing. And through six transatlantic days and now several long Manhattan evenings of Glennis's chatter mostly about fiancés, in hand and prospective, they'd discovered a new affliction in common: a difficult older brother. Julia righted the crooked headpiece and dabbed her friend's face with a wet cloth, though there was little to be done beyond plenty of fresh powder.

Glennis crushed out her cigarette and dropped both hands into her lap to pester her rings. "She's ancient, Julia—forty, I think, more like an old maid aunt or something. But when I was engaged before, the first time, and I needed a, a thing—" Her eyes jumped to Julia's. "You know?"

Julia nodded. A dutch cap, to prevent babies. She'd forgotten how girls in America could speak boldly about many things, swearing like sailors over a spilled cocktail or early curfew, yet fumble so shyly about matters of sex. Puritanical roots ran deep here. As if in illustration, she noticed several copies of a magazine called the *Woman Patriot* stacked beside the Winterjays' bed. The top issue promised shocking details on rampant moral perfidy among New York's unmarried women—who had sex, it seemed. Shocking indeed.

"Naomi helped me get one," Glennis went on. "Can you believe it? Queer old Naomi, who hasn't even had a boyfriend in donkey's years. She said it's better to be modern than rich, and when I told Archie, he said, 'What's better than both?' I couldn't believe it. Archie a card? Still and all."

Despite endless dithering about Russell or Warren or whether to make do with her English fiancé, Archie Allthorp—dull as mud but obscurely titled—if nothing better came along soon, Glennis could say the most remarkable things. As her company was Julia's best hope of diversion during her stay in New York, this occasional drollery was a welcome discovery.

Glennis's grin faded. Twenty minutes had passed since she'd roused her brother with a tearful demand that he check on their sister's safety. Music and occasional laughter drifted down the hall as the remaining partiers gamely carried on. She grumbled another lament about the apocryphal Russell and lit another cigarette. They smoked in fitful silence, watching the telephone beside the bed.

Julia's thoughts veered to her legal appointment on Monday morning. Philip's quibbles were so ludicrous they hardly deserved attention, but even so they began to chew at the usual spot beneath her ribs. She wrenched her mind forward to more pleasant prospects for that afternoon.

If the meeting went well, as by rights it must, she might pay a visit to the Twelfth Street book dealers. Before she'd left London, her beau had asked her to track down a copy of Bruce Rogers's latest typographic bonbon, *The Pierrot of the Minute*. Not for himself—fortunately, David's taste ran to more robust material—but for one of his clients. She could telephone the august Grolier Club about it if necessary, but she preferred to get the little book from a dealer to avoid mustering the admiration its publishers would naturally expect. Beyond that, she'd snap up any French pochoir editions she might see, though there her hopes were slight. American bibliophiles were said to be insular in their tastes, not to mention prudish. No matter how exquisite those finely stenciled illustrations, their mildly risqué subject matter likely rendered them taboo.

She felt an urge to sashay into the hushed quarters of the all-male Grolier—past the doorman's alarmed "Members only, miss! No ladies!"—and waggle a proof of her new Capriole pressmark under their noses. They'd no doubt start at Eric Gill's engraving of a young she-goat au naturel (Julia herself!), then sniff and turn her away, but she'd have issued her warning salvo that at least one woman intended to storm (someday) that most distinguished bastion of book collectors. What better way to announce her publishing ambitions to the book-loving world?

The telephone rang. Glennis seized it.

Julia was prepared for another wail—whether of relief or indignation, she suspected it would sound the same—but instead Glennis gave a kind of moan, a muted cry more aghast than astonished, the panicked wilt of a flower thrust through the oven door. This was a sound Julia had heard before, the first flinch from death's indifferent touch. More articulate than any sob, it chilled her scalp. She froze, a rabbit beneath the hawk's shadow.

By the time Mrs. Winterjay arrived, Glennis could speak only in spurts. Bobbing her head up and down from Julia's lap, she choked out that their sister, Naomi, was, in fact, shockingly, impossibly, dead. "Dead for hours!"

Mrs. Winterjay stared at the mucus-smeared face keening in Julia's arms. One hand caressed the swell at her waist as the other muzzled her jaw. Fragments of prayer leaked through her fingers, begging mercy for the poor soul, the poor, innocent soul. With a shudder Mrs. Winterjay wiped her eyes and murmured that the family needed to go there at once. She looked lost, bewildered about how to proceed, as if grief and instinct could take her no further. She brushed past Julia, unseeing, wondering if someone should summon her husband.

Julia had no answer, and none was expected. What could anyone say? The séance had been a game, an interlude of party nonsense. Surely Glennis knew better than to believe the tired old hokum, yet how readily her imagination had leaped from that ridiculously rumbled "orbs of sapphire" to her sister's face. And now—an unspeakably cruel coincidence. Julia shivered. Spirit lights jerked about by secret wires signified nothing, but death was very real.

Glennis's mouth fell open, strung with saliva. Powder clung to the fine hairs below her ear, over the sheen of perfume dabbed there hours ago. Her childish gaze darkened, aged with something new: fear. Julia had thought she knew all there was to know of simple Glennis, but she was wrong. Even Glennis's voice was different, low and bitter. "He killed her."

Another cold finger slid down Julia's spine. She had no idea what Glennis meant or who *he* could be. This was shock speaking, not reason. Six years since death's long romp across Europe, and still young people everywhere were caught short by its caprice. All that carnage and still they whimpered about fairness, about meaning. They told themselves the war had finally trounced their parents' palaver about good and evil, called its bluff, spat in its eye, but in truth they were like children under the bed, with their endless cocktails and games and parties, singing hoarsely with eyes squeezed shut. When death found and pulled them out, as of course it did, as they knew it would, it still helped to call it—or some nameless *him*—evil.

Mrs. Winterjay's guests hurried to be gone. One after another they came to the bedroom for their wraps, murmuring averted sympathies into gloves and sleeves and compact sponges. Julia hastened to join the exodus, resigned to returning to Philip's guest quarters at this early hour. She slipped away to fetch her shawl and handbag.

The maid was collecting cocktails abandoned on the mantel. Julia bent to retrieve her bag from the foot of the bookcase where she'd stashed it, beside an appalling gilded buckram set of sermons. With the idle carelessness of one who thinks herself alone, the maid stretched a yawn into a groan, glanced into the hall, and drank the dregs of an abandoned highball. She lifted another glass to examine its red-stained rim and floating cigarette. To no one but the night, she muttered, "Ain't the first party that wicked Naomi Rankin's made a pig of, is it?"

CHAPTER 3

Two days later Julia stood beneath an ornate iron arch over the drive to the Rankin residence, Glennis's note tucked into her handbag. Its fragrance of violets had overwhelmed Philip's vestibule yesterday as it waited for Julia to return from the Pryor, where the new Matisse watercolors were, she begrudgingly agreed, quite wonderful. In a large looping hand, Glennis had begged Julia to come to a memorial service for her sister. *It's beastly*, she scrawled. *They can't wait to bury her, as if they're glad she's dead!! You must come and help me bear it!!* Julia silently forgave the several exclamation points, fat as teardrops.

She strolled through an alley of crimson maples, their leaves beginning to smolder, and wondered again at the Rankins' strange haste. From what she'd gathered Friday evening, Naomi's death was at least untimely. She couldn't have been very old and apparently hadn't been ill enough to notice. Wouldn't they need time to accept the shock, perhaps grapple with its mystery? They did seem in an undue hurry to usher her along to her grave. Hardly the actions of a loving family, Julia thought. But then what would Philip do at news of her death? Or she at his, to be honest. As one who knew precious little about loving families, Julia was hardly one to judge the Rankins.

The drive turned, ending any suggestion of a pleasant garden. The house stood ponderous and angular, stone blocks the size of iceboxes piled three stories high in regimental symmetry. The old estate sloped away toward the East River and its willow-clogged bank. A battalion of rosebushes, blooms faded to cankered hips, marched beside the two paved tracks that led to the white-columned porte cochere.

She passed four parked motorcars. A driver's head jerked upright as her steps sounded on the gravel beside his door. Calmed by her unfamiliar face, he resettled back into the upholstery, arms folded and cap tipped over his eyes. She proceeded up the five wide steps and rang the bell.

A housemaid pulled open the heavy door carved with Celtic knot work, but before she could speak, Glennis bounded into view, her wide face suffused with the distress of a child whose nanny has strayed from sight. She pulled Julia across the hall, their shoes clattering on the waxed parquet, and into a small room that seemed to be some sort of butler's pantry. She elbowed the door shut behind them. "Oh, Julia, they're sweeping her away like yesterday's rubbish. It's ghastly. I'm the only one who even cares she's dead."

Julia found the handkerchief tucked into Glennis's sleeve and dabbed at her friend's wet cheeks, careful to dislodge as little powder as possible. "People mourn in different ways, Glennis. There's more to grief than tears, you know. I'm sure they care." The platitudes rolled out in smooth succession. Though predictable and perhaps mistaken, they were what one said.

Glennis frowned. "No, something's peculiar. They won't tell me what happened. Or even where they took her. I'm worried half to pieces, and they think *I'm* balmy."

"I'm sure there's nothing to worry about, Glennis. She was probably ill without anyone realizing it. I've heard of cases like this, when someone seems fine until the very end. Maybe it was a blessing, a sign that she didn't suffer much." Julia cringed at her further descent into clichés, but what else could she say?

Glennis gave a skeptical pout and patted at the back of her head. "Am I an awful fright?" Her hair was mussed, but otherwise she looked about as usual: plump, a little confused, and considerably younger than her twenty-five years. Julia shook her head *not at all* and gave Glennis's cheeks a brisk rub with her thumb.

"Come on, then. They're waiting. They don't know you're coming, and they won't like it, but so what?"

Before Julia could consider this ominous news—was she about to intrude uninvited upon a private affair?—Glennis tugged her across the hall.

The drawing room fell silent when they entered. Julia swallowed: her fear was confirmed. It was a very small, very private gathering, and she was not only unexpected but unwelcome. A handful of somber people eyed her from chairs pulled into a loose oval in the center of the room. There was no coffin, and there were none of the usual signs of mourning: no black buntings, no dark veils. A priest stood to one side, hands folded over a service book. In the awful quiet a middle-aged man with a horseshoe of graying hair stepped forward. His face seemed to not quite meet in the middle, leaving a flat stripe of bone between his eyes and a gap between two front teeth wide as spatulas. That and eyes the color of shallow water identified him as Glennis's brother, Chester.

"Everyone, this is my particular friend, Julia Kydd," Glennis announced. "You all have each other, so I asked Julia to come. Because I need her." Her nervous voice blared, and she clutched Julia's arm against her ribs, as if she expected her guest to be wrestled out of the room. Julia had a sudden notion of how strikers and suffragists must feel when facing down policemen.

Chester Rankin exchanged a long look with one of the seated women, a brunette with a stiff mass of marcelled hair, thin penciled brows, and shoulders so tense they raised faint welts in the black wool jersey of her dress. The woman considered Julia with red-rimmed eyes wide with disapproval at this blatant breach of decorum. Julia wanted nothing more than to apologize—she hadn't realized!—and creep away, but Glennis's grip and a fear of making things worse froze her in place. The woman seemed to reach the same conclusion: best to avoid a scene.

She dropped her chin and folded her hands in her lap, signaling reluctant forbearance. Glennis gave Julia a gleeful hug before her brother gestured curtly for another chair to be positioned behind the circle. He motioned Julia toward it and steered Glennis to sit beside him.

The service was brief and formal. As the priest intoned the sonorous language of the Book of Common Prayer, Glennis worked her handkerchief, but the only sound of weeping came from a gaunt, plain woman sitting, like Julia, apart from the others in a straight-backed chair. Two graying braids circled her head, and a strand of imitation pearls skimmed the collar of a brown wool dress at least five years out of date. Julia guessed she was the family's old nanny, fetched from an obscure Brooklyn boardinghouse.

The formal liturgy ended, and the priest closed his book. "Dr. Winterjay?"

A younger man rose from beside Glennis's sister Vivian with a sad smile that suggested he understood the ways of the world but loved it anyway. He looked to be a professional man of some sort, perhaps a promising scholar or judge, the kind of man whose easy manner and handsome face encouraged trust and caused young girls to giggle. Something about his earnest yet worldly smile also made Dr. Winterjay look, eerily, a bit like Julia's beau back in London. David too could both admire and tease in the same glance, inviting one into the intimate game that was modern gallantry.

"Ahhh." Winterjay expelled a long and meaningful syllable. "Naomi." His wife's pale-blue eyes—clearly the family's distinguishing feature—filled with tears at the sound of her sister's name. "Naomi was not an easy sister to love."

Julia blinked but kept her head still. Had he misspoken? Surely the *not* was a slip. She sneaked a glance at Mrs. Winterjay, expecting to see her eyes widen in a wifely signal of the gaffe. But she merely gazed at her husband with a leaden expression.

"Naomi was—" Again he paused. "Naomi was a difficult woman. She chose a life of turbulence and discord, and we have all been buffeted by the powerful storms into which she sailed. We have all suffered on her behalf, sensitive to the stings and humiliations which Naomi herself scorned. None of us was spared the acid of her tongue or the harsh judgments she delivered upon those she found wanting."

Julia fought to keep from squirming at this litany of misdeeds, hardly the usual talk of funerals. Was anything too awful not to be forgiven, or at least overlooked, on such occasions? Even the worst villain's faults could be veiled in euphemism and blandishments. She hazarded another furtive survey of the room, baffled by the docile quiet of the other listeners. Why were there no coughs, no jiggling feet, no whitened knuckles of suppressed alarm? Every face was lowered, every jaw rigid. Each man sat with arms tightly folded. Clearly this harsh assessment came as no surprise, but was it shared or merely endured?

What on earth had Naomi Rankin done to warrant such reproof? She must have been difficult indeed. But why then was Glennis so determined to lament her? The set of Glennis's shoulders, as round and rigid as last week's bread, gave no answer.

Winterjay went on, settling into the confident cadence and timbre of a high-church cleric. "And yet Naomi was also a child of God, whether she liked it or not. We must pray for her soul, not with less charity because of the pain she caused, but with more. We must remember what made Naomi in many ways a remarkable woman. She fought for what she believed would make our nation better. She railed against injustice as she perceived it. We may not share her convictions, but we must honor her zeal." He beseeched mercy for her troubled soul and prayed finally that she be delivered into her savior's merciful hands. The mourners added a ragged echo of *amens*, some sharp as kicks, a few measured and moist.

No sooner had the last sound died away than Chester stood and clapped Winterjay's shoulder. "Right. Now we leave her to the Lord."

As others also rose and reached for embraces, Julia turned to slip away without further embarrassment, but Glennis hurried over and gripped her elbow. "You have to stay. I won't let them make you go. Something's muzzy here, and I don't like it. You're clever; maybe you can understand what he's up to."

She was speaking in riddles again. Whoever *he* was, up to something muzzy or not, this was not the time to discuss it. Julia wanted nothing more than to leave the Rankins to their own peculiar and distasteful way of mourning. But before she could think of a civil way to extract herself without triggering more loud entreaties, Glennis whispered, "And look. Over there. It's *Russell*. Russell Coates. Our lawyer."

The elusive Russell: one of Glennis's quarries, the object of the fruitless search that had ended so abruptly Friday evening. He seemed unremarkable from across the room: well-dressed, thinnish lips, short-cropped wiry brown hair graying at the ears. His outstretched arm tracked the spines of leather-bound octavos shelved beside the fireplace. Julia itched to peer over his shoulder. Her favorite sport on earth was scanning another's library, for editions as much as titles. She knew Coates was a collector from the way his hand slid over the corded backs: light, sensuous. Yet it moved without discernment, drifting from habit more than pleasure. He looked lost in brooding thoughts far from the morocco beneath his fingers. Julia knew that trick. She'd used it herself many times to avoid unwelcome small talk. Beautiful books could be like nursing infants, handy for ensuring solitude: on glimpsing a bibliophile in commune with a book, most people smiled and tiptoed the other way.

"That's Nolda, Chester's horrid wife," Glennis went on, "and the old man is Dr. Perry. He used to be our family doctor. Nice and all, but shaky on his sticks, if you know what I mean." She referred to the tense brunette and an elderly man who, despite a tic that puckered the corner of his left eye, beamed about the room at no one in particular.

"And that's Miss Clintock." Glennis nodded at the woman Julia judged to be the retired nanny. "She's Naomi's companion, I suppose you'd say. They worked together and shared the apartment downstairs, though—"

"See here, Glennis," Chester said, interrupting her hasty survey.

Nolda Rankin joined her husband and finished his sentence, her tone just skirting rudeness. "It's time to discuss family matters. In private. I'm sure your friend will understand."

Julia did understand. More than that, she preferred to be well clear of an occasion not only private but evidently rancorous. Happy families attracted visitors; warring ones repelled them. She was about to excuse herself with a vivid apology when Glennis said, "No! You never tell me anything. You treat me like a baby. I deserve to have at least one friend here who knows what I'm going through."

"For pity's sake," Nolda said in a quiet hiss. "Pull yourself together. My ten-year-old has more self-control. This is no time to argue. Just do as your brother—"

"I will not!" The petulant shout quieted the room. "You're not my mother. I won't let you make Julia leave."

Julia had a sudden memory of Glennis's tantrum the morning she'd been told to clean the school lavatory basins, stained where she'd dumped a forbidden jar of beets. She'd bellowed defiance then too, to the head girl's shock and (impotent) fury.

The others abandoned the pretense of not watching. Julia lowered her chin but understood that no posture could save her from the embarrassment about to unfold. Why on earth was Glennis insisting she stay?

"What about them?" Glennis swung her arm toward Dr. Perry, Russell Coates, and Miss Clintock. "You let them stay."

Vivian Winterjay broke the awful silence. "I suppose there's no great harm in it, Chester," she said gently from across the room, fingering a gold cross that hung from a chain at her throat. "Glennis is taking this very hard. I'm sure Miss Kydd can be trusted, Nolda. She's Philip Kydd's sister, you know. Her people are top drawer. She'll understand the need for discretion." Poised at her husband's side and now free from the strain of the other evening's curdled party, Vivian was clearly the beauty in the room, in a refined, candlelit sort of way.

Chester and Nolda Rankin exchanged another exasperated look. "You must understand our situation, Miss Kydd," Nolda said. "This family has had a great shock, and these are delicate matters. Extremely delicate and trying."

Julia would have sworn over her firstborn if it would have eased the awkwardness, but before any such assurance was required, Glennis flung a triumphant arm around her. "Yes!"

Chester choked in irritation. "Then let's get this over with. Everyone, sherry in here." He crossed the room to push apart a pair of sliding doors. A maid jumped away from the dining table, cowering behind a fistful of cutlery. "Another place. Now!"

She fled with a nervous bob.

The old doctor exclaimed cheerfully about his failing joints as he labored to his feet. Glennis ran to join Russell Coates, nudging against his flank to be led into the dining room. Miss Clintock stepped back to let others pass. Trailing the procession, Julia resolved to ignore any future pleas from Glennis Rankin. Someday, she told herself, this might make an amusing tale. She craved a sidecar.

The maid scurried to rearrange table settings and chairs. Nolda Rankin instructed her to add a place for Julia beside Miss Clintock at the farthest distance from herself and her husband. As soon as the last fork was laid, the mourners sat, and a platter of sherry glasses circled the table. Chester raised his glass. "Naomi," he duly muttered. "Rest in peace."

Miss Clintock reached for her cloth, and Glennis sniffled, but the moment passed calmly.

Chester watched the maid retreat to the kitchen. "We can't talk during the meal," he said, arcing his jaw toward the door, "but as soon as it's over, we have serious business to discuss."

Everyone stared.

"Oh yes. Naomi has managed to pull off one last little trick. Pardon my French, but it's one holy hell of a mess."

The door swung open, and a silver soup tureen arrived.

CHAPTER 4

Whatever the Rankins served for luncheon that day, Julia did not taste it. She managed a few bites of each course during the interminable hour, but her thoughts alternated between how soon she might slink away and what Naomi could have done to provoke such an ominous pronouncement. Each time a course was served or dishes cleared and the service door settled shut, someone would beg Chester to explain, and each time the door swung open again as, palms flat across the starched linen, he silently refused.

At last the custard dishes were removed and a decanter of port delivered. The maid retreated for the final time with explicit instructions not to interrupt for any reason whatsoever. Cheeks pink with curiosity, she nodded and was gone.

"Please, Chester," Vivian said the moment the door settled into place. "For heaven's sake, what's this about?"

"Perry will explain."

Dr. Perry blinked and nodded. He unleashed a sticky cough that required a search for his handkerchief. "I'm afraid the situation is more complicated than we may have implied," he said. "When I arrived late Friday evening after Chester telephoned, I found that Miss Rankin was, as he feared, clearly dead. The cause was plain to us both, unfortunately." He massaged his eyes before resuming, each word slowed by lips stiff with age. "An empty tube of morphine tablets lay in her lap.

A few could still be detected, partially dissolved but not swallowed, beneath her tongue and on her lower lip. Quite simply, I'm afraid the poor woman took her own life."

He dropped his chin, mouth pressed into a flat line of dismay, as if he considered her act a personal affront.

No one spoke. Nolda turned a stony face toward her husband, who sat tapping his glass of port in a steady dirge. Vivian's hand rose to the cross at her throat. Edward Winterjay bowed his head. Russell Coates cleared his throat behind a tight-gripped napkin. A low gurgle tracked Glennis's slow comprehension of the news. Miss Clintock sat motionless.

Suicide. No wonder the Rankins had resisted Julia's presence. Suicide sharpened the sting of death, adding its own layer of torment to any bereavement. Most families would feel some guilty shame at its tacit message of failure, and a socially prominent family could face crushing judgment and scandal. Julia knew only one suicide, her sweet but haunted Gerald, whose horror at surviving when his trench mates did not proved more than he could bear. His family had worked strenuously to hide the truth from their friends and neighbors. Julia had hated their ruse, hated its antiseptic rinse of Gerald's pain, but had been powerless to stop it. Although his death had been more than three years ago, the ache remained.

"This is shocking news, unutterably sad," Winterjay said. "And I fear there are dreadful ramifications. It means her immortal soul is in peril. Those who turn a violent hand upon themselves forfeit the sanctity of Christian committal. Our service may be void."

Silence. Was this why the priest had been so hastily dismissed?

"Surely that's the least of it," Nolda said.

"It also presents a more immediate problem," Winterjay said. "Father Sterne no doubt expects a private burial at Saint Stephen's tomorrow, in the Rankin plot. I, for one, have serious qualms about that now, and Father Sterne will definitely balk."

"Dear Lord," Vivian said. She spread her hands across her abdomen, her gold hair falling forward to obscure her face.

"Naomi wouldn't care in the least what became of her remains," Winterjay said. "But her parents would take the sacrilege very seriously. I doubt they could overlook the church's strictures on the matter."

This time the silence lasted so long that sounds of the household drifted into the room: a chiming clock, irritable voices and clattering pans from the kitchen, a telephone bell quickly answered.

"Think of something, Coates," Chester said. "You're supposed to have answers."

The lawyer spoke without lifting his eyes from the table. "I believe a cemetery on Long Island offers cremation services."

"Repulsive practice," Chester said. "But I suppose she's left us little choice."

Dr. Perry raised his glass with a feeble hand and tasted the port. Smiling his appreciation of its rich flavors, he seemed unaware of the tension in the room.

"Naomi once lectured me at great length on cremation's merits," Nolda said. "It's an abomination, but in this case it might solve our problem. We wouldn't desecrate the family plot, and we'd be honoring her wishes."

"And there'd be no questions. No one would be the least surprised for Naomi to flout all Christian decencies," Chester said. "That's settled, then. Thank you, Nolda. Sensible as always. Coates, make the arrangements. Frankly, I don't give a peeled fig about Naomi's soul. She can sort out her own troubles for once. We've got bigger problems."

Nolda flinched at her husband's candor and twitched her eyebrows in Julia's direction. "Miss Kydd knows better than to repeat any of this," he growled with a warning glance down the table. Julia met it with, she hoped, no betrayal of the distaste she felt. Glennis was right to be upset. Her suspicions before the service seemed more credible every minute.

"I'm sorry to be so blunt," Chester continued, "but there's no time for sugarcoating. We have to face the facts. If the press gets wind that Naomi killed herself, they'll feast on it for weeks. We could be in for no end of nastiness."

Nolda's mouth sagged in the panic of one about to be sick. "He's right. The newspapers will be brutal. The mockery she's brought upon us has been awful enough, but I couldn't bear their smug pity as well. I just couldn't bear it."

Winterjay reached over to comfort her. She gripped his hand and peered into his face. "It's the family I worry about. We adults could endure it—heaven knows we've been through so much with her already—but think of the children. Yours are young still, Edward, but our boys are teased horribly at school about their ridiculous aunt. Young people can be so merciless. I won't have it. I won't. There must be something you can do."

Coates fidgeted with his salt spoon, pinching its tiny bowl between his thumb and forefinger. "Are you absolutely certain it was suicide, Chester? The notion staggers me. It's the last thing I'd expect from her. Could you be mistaken? What exactly happened here that night?"

Chester shrugged. "Since when was Naomi predictable? I didn't see it coming either. But I had to go down there after Glennis telephoned late, scaring us half to death. She made God's own fuss about seeing Naomi's hocus-pocus spirit at Vivian's party."

"I was worried," Glennis said, her first words since entering the dining room. It was a glum statement, the listless effort of one who is seldom consulted. News of Naomi's suicide seemed to have taken all the fight out of her. "Maybe I didn't exactly see her spirit, but something made me afraid for her."

"It seemed such a foolish concern," Nolda said. "I saw Naomi that morning, leaving the house. She looked miserable but no more than usual." She gave Miss Clintock a hard look. "And there was no sign of anything amiss when we left the house that evening."

"Fortunately we'd been at the theater with the Swetnams, and I was still dressed when Glennis telephoned, so I went straight down," Chester said. "Imagine my shock when I saw Naomi lying there on the sofa with a compress across her forehead and that empty tube in her lap. With those pills stuck to her lip, I got the idea pretty quick of what she'd done. I called Dr. Perry and waited for him to come. That's it."

"That's it? *That's it?*" Glennis repeated the unfortunate phrase. "Doesn't anyone care? First our sister is dead, and now you say she killed herself. She must have been horribly unhappy, and no one gives a good goddamn about it!"

Nolda's palm struck the table, rattling the tiny port glasses. "This may be a terrible time for us all, but I will not have profanity in this house. Control your mouth or leave the room."

Splotches bled across Glennis's cheeks and throat.

"It's not a matter of caring," Winterjay said softly. "Naturally we care very much, Glennis. But we need to understand what happened."

She ground her lips between her teeth.

"Was the door locked?" Coates asked.

"It was," Chester said. "I used the stairwell key. The outside door was locked too, but not chained. Miss Clintock used her key to let herself in later."

Everyone turned toward Alice Clintock. She refolded the napkin in her lap.

"I'm sorry, Chester," the lawyer persisted, "but I must ask. Did you touch anything?"

"Only the empty morphine tube. And I don't appreciate your tone, Coates. Dr. Perry can confirm everything I've told you."

Dr. Perry maneuvered his bulk away from the table edge. "Oh yes. Chester was naturally shocked and troubled, but all in all, he behaved sensibly. Once I confirmed what was sadly obvious, we had a brief discussion about how to proceed, and he convinced me about that too. It was only reasonable."

"About how to proceed?"

Julia could only admire the steadiness of Coates's voice.

"We had to think," Chester said. "Make some decisions right away. I knew we'd be swarming with newspapermen as soon as word got out."

"That's what I don't understand," Glennis said. "If she killed herself, why haven't the police and newspapers already been here?"

Chester grimaced.

"It's the obvious question," Coates said. "We'd all like to know."

"And I'm getting there, if you'll stop interrupting me." Chester flicked his wife's hand from his coat sleeve. "While I was waiting for Dr. Perry, I began to think maybe the situation wasn't so straightforward after all. For one thing, there was no note."

Several people started at this news, and Alice Clintock brushed at fresh tears. Glennis shot Julia a quick look down the table. *I knew it!* her glower said. *He's up to something.*

Julia kept her face still and looked away. Glennis's galloping imagination would only make things worse. Chester Rankin did seem to be a nasty man, but Naomi's death clearly caused great problems for him. Why would he do anything to invite the disaster he now lamented?

"Odd," said Coates.

"Well, it's true. I looked everywhere but didn't see one."

Glennis squirmed. Dr. Perry's wavery voice anticipated her objection. "I may be old, Glennis dear, but I know a narcotic overdose when I see one."

"Yet a suicide requires—" Coates began.

"Not only was there no note," Chester said, "but she was stretched out on the sofa like she was ill. I remembered all those abominable headaches she's complained about for years and got to thinking maybe that's what happened. Maybe her old brain finally had enough and just blew a fuse. She'd been looking peaky of late. Nolda remarked on it the other day, and Naomi's friend here confirmed she'd gone off her feed. Isn't that right, Miss Clintock?"

The brusque demand clarified why the poor woman was present.

"She suffered from digestive trouble," Alice Clintock said, "in times of stress."

Chester barked out a derisive laugh. "I'd say she thrived on stress. Certainly served us a steady diet of it. Just tell them what you told me, Miss Clintock."

The woman dabbed her nose. "I came home that afternoon to find Naomi resting. She said she felt ill, and her head was pounding. We both knew it was from the worry. She struggled terribly, you see, with the strain of trying to manage our work with so little money." She sent Chester a look that blistered with reproach but was unable to deliver it higher than his vest buttons.

"I expected her to pull herself together, as she always did, but instead she begged me to go." At the rustle of confusion, Miss Clintock explained. "There was an important meeting that night, you see, at the Union—our office. We'd scheduled it months ago with the state leadership of the NWP. The National Woman's Party? It was imperative we attend, only she said she didn't feel well enough. She insisted I go alone, without her."

She lifted her eyes. "I'd give anything to have borne her misery for her. You must understand that. Naomi was everything. She was the one who belonged at that meeting, not me. Had I known what she intended—forgive me—"

Her pain was excruciating to hear. Julia swallowed. Vivian wrapped both hands around her husband's forearm. Glennis gave a single dry sob.

"So you see," Chester said, "things were not so clear cut."

Coates turned. "What do you mean?"

"I mean I don't think she intended to kill herself. I think it was an accident—unfortunate, certainly, but not necessarily, in the strict legal sense, suicide. Tell them, Doctor."

Dr. Perry stared at Chester. "Didn't I say? Oh yes. It's not uncommon. She died by her own hand but accidentally. It happens when patients are confused or distracted, usually by pain. Severe headaches can be excruciating, you know. They don't realize how many tablets they've taken. Unfortunately, doctors see it more than we like to say. Oh my, yes . . ."

"Dr. Perry agreed," Chester said loudly, over the old man's fading mumble, "the overdose could have been an accident. And since there was no proof she'd planned it—we both looked for a note but found nothing—that's what he put on the death certificate."

Good Lord, Julia thought. Glennis might be simpleminded and prone to wild fancies, but that was better than this sly sophistry.

"Is this something different?" Vivian asked slowly. "Are you saying it's *not* suicide?"

Chester gave a smug nod. "Let's just say when someone's already ill, an overdose doesn't necessarily have to be declared a suicide. At least not in the sense that involves the police. Of course, she may have known exactly what she was doing, but no one beyond this room ever need know that. What's important is that Dr. Perry saw fit to file the paperwork in a most discreet manner. The medical examiner's office was satisfied, and the business was filed away this morning."

"That's wonderful!" Nolda could not smother her joy.

Miss Clintock fingered her collar.

"Can she be buried, then?" Coates asked.

"Oh dear," Vivian murmured when no one else spoke. "I'm not sure God would put such a fine distinction on the particular"—she moistened her lips—"degree of her sin."

Chester nodded. "Quite right. If she preferred cremation, who are we to say otherwise?"

Nolda draped her napkin over her smile. "Brilliant. Simply brilliant."

"We still have to tell people she's dead," Vivian said. "We must put something in the papers."

"Do we have to say anything at all?"

"She was too well known, Nolda," Chester said. "People will ask. Reporters will hound us for details. We have to know exactly what to tell them."

"You have something in mind?" Winterjay asked. Of course he did. Men like Chester would have a story all planned out.

"This is how I see it. Naomi neglected her health. We all know she never rested in normal ways. When and what she ate I have no idea, but she was such a scarecrow it couldn't have been much. Plus you heard Miss Clintock mention those headaches. She let herself get run down. I think we could simply say—accurately enough—that she died after a brief illness."

Chester pushed his stubby palm in the air to stay the first words of disbelief. "Who knows? The way she was going, an early grave was inevitable. Maybe she was more ill than anyone knew. Maybe she was about to die anyway, and those tablets just got to her first. In which case, what can it hurt to rearrange the timeline a little? You read about this sort of thing all the time, especially with unnatural spinsters who eat like birds. Dr. Perry says it's possible."

The old doctor nodded. "Possible," he echoed.

"Perfect," Nolda said. "Solves everything."

Everything, Julia thought, that might inconvenience or embarrass the Rankin family.

"But we have to agree," Chester persisted. "Everyone here must swear to it."

"A brief—and sudden—illness," Vivian said, trying on the phrase. So benign. So discreet. The euphemism hung in the air as artfully as a string of pearls lifted from its velvet box.

Alice Clintock fingered her cuff. Glennis's mouth puckered. The course of the conversation clearly did not suit her, but before she could object, Winterjay spoke again.

"Call it what you will, you're asking us to lie, Chester. That's no light matter. But I suppose there are times when the full truth is neither necessary nor kind. As long as the family knows what happened, what the public is told is of minor consequence. And your scheme leaves attention focused on Naomi's life, not her death, which is important here. I won't knowingly deceive others without just cause, but this does seem a wise solution, in the end."

"Beautifully put, Edward," said Nolda. She reached again for his hand.

"So do we all agree?" Chester asked.

Did they have a choice? A trickle of murmurs loosed his first smile of the day.

"No!" Glennis's fist landed on the table. "I don't. You make me sick. First you worm things around so maybe it wasn't *real* suicide. Then you cook up some bilge that she was going to die anyway. Our sister dies—she kills herself!—and all you care about is how it might look in the papers. Naomi was too smart, too serious, to make a mistake like that. I think she knew exactly what she was doing, which means she had a reason. A reason! And the most obvious reason is right here in this room." She swiveled toward her brother. "You did everything to make her life hell, Chester. Admit it. You hated her! Now you can't wait to burn her up and throw away the ashes."

She lurched away but too late. Chester caught her arm.

"Let me go!" she screamed, and Chester slapped her hard across the face. Julia pinched her wrist to stop a gasp.

Glennis stilled instantly. Her eyes found Julia's. Do you see? *Do you see?*

Oh yes.

"Let her go." It was Winterjay. "This is not the time for tempers."

Chester neither released his sister's arm nor eased his grip. "You will not leave the table until you agree. This is no game, Glennis. You know I mean it."

Glennis froze, her shoulder twisted awkwardly by the hand clamped above her elbow. "I hate it," she conceded in a fierce whisper, "but I agree."

The fingers edged apart, and she pulled free. She'd won the earlier skirmish of wills, but on this Chester's greater strength would not be denied.

Nolda released a deep breath. "All right, then. I'll take care of getting something into the papers. If I wait until tomorrow afternoon, there'll be nothing until Tuesday morning, which gives us another day of privacy and peace. I don't think it's necessary to send for the boys, as we've already had a service, and there'll be no burial. You'll see about that cremation business, Russell?"

Coates nodded.

"I'm afraid we'll have to carry on with the Children's Aid charity gala next Saturday," Nolda continued, glancing at Vivian, "as invitations went out under our name. We're in mourning now, of course, but it's too late to cancel or reschedule. I'm sure Clara Swetnam can take over greeting duties, and I'll ask—"

"Are you sure there wasn't a note?" Glennis's voice spiraled.

"For pity's sake!" Chester banged down his elbow. "I told you, no."

He looked straight at Miss Clintock. "At least not when I got there. We have only Miss Clintock's word for what happened before."

The woman twisted her napkin in her lap, but otherwise she met his scrutiny with admirable composure. "Naomi was alive when I left her," she said. "But I too wonder that very question. I really would have expected . . ." She pressed the mangled cloth against her mouth.

Chester made two distinct sounds. "No. Note."

Glennis erupted. "I don't believe you."

Her chair fell over as she jumped out of his reach. She threw down her napkin and ran toward the other end of the table. "I bet it said how you drove her to it."

Almost as brutally as Chester had seized her, Glennis pulled Julia from her chair. Julia's napkin went flying, and her shoe caught the side of Miss Clintock's calf.

"That's practically murder!" Glennis shouted.

The maid, Deborah, stumbled to catch her balance as Glennis flung open the door to the hall. Julia heard only the shatter of dropped crystal before it slammed shut behind them.

CHAPTER 5

Their heels echoed up a broad flight of curving stairs. Glennis did not release her hold on Julia until they were locked inside a large, violet-scented bedroom. "Glennis, really," was all Julia could say. Her wrist was reddened and painful, and she rubbed it with dismay. Never in her life had she been so tugged, pulled, twisted, dragged, pinched, prodded. She would have bruises upon bruises if she stayed within range of Glennis's grip much longer.

"I'm sorry, but you see how they are. I'd scream if I had to stand it another minute."

"You did scream."

Glennis smiled. "Maybe I did. Chester makes my blood boil."

"You virtually accused him of murder."

"Oh, who knows? I'm positive he drove her to it. Isn't that about the same thing?" She kicked off her shoes and flopped onto her bed.

After the dark paneling of the windowless hallway, the room dazzled Julia's eyes. White satin covered a large bed mounded high with glossy pillows and scattered with lingerie. Tall windows on either side were draped with stiff white damask, gathered with gold-braid loops: meringue soldiers standing at attention. The carpet was littered with shoes. A gilt-framed Boucher reproduction hung above a white French provincial vanity and triptych mirror. Incongruously, it was flanked by colorful posters of Léon Bakst's costumes for the Diaghilev Ballets

Russes. An empty martini glass and the current *Vogue* lay on the floor by the bed, beside a filled ashtray.

Glennis sprawled back, her legs dangling over the foot of the bed. "Where do they get the bloody face to stitch up some bunk about how she 'died tragically, in the bosom of her family'?" She affected a mournful bass voice remarkably like her brother's. "*We never know when the good Lord will call us home.* They'll shake their heads and say, 'It's too, too sad, even if her ideas were terribly shocking,' and then she'll disappear, forgotten. It's horrid. Filthy horrid."

She was right. It was horrid. Julia removed a pink chemise and crumpled stocking from the seat of a white slipper chair. She'd been too quick to dismiss Glennis's account of her family's sangfroid as yet another histrionic exaggeration. With callous efficiency, the Rankins had translated their sister's misery and death into their own problem of appearances, but then the living always had the last word over the dead.

"What on earth did Naomi do that was so terrible? I've never heard anyone described with such veiled—and open—antipathy. Was she truly as wicked as your brother suggests?" The question had been burning in her mind since Dr. Winterjay's strange eulogy.

"Chester's hated Naomi for years. I can tell you stories that would make your hair stand up."

"But why? A feud of some sort? Strong disagreements?"

Glennis let out a schoolyard whistle. "I'll say. The whole family fought, about politics mostly, but everything else too. I can't remember when they weren't mad as blazes at each other."

Julia considered this, wondering what might drive one to value some political stance above family peace. "Politics? That's all cigars and backroom deals, as far as I can see. Corrupt or dull as dishwater. I can't imagine caring enough to let it ruin your life. Was Naomi some kind of radical?"

Glennis shrugged. "I guess. She was a bigwig suffragette, you know. Until my parents died, she lived in Washington, and I hardly ever saw her, though once I snuck off to hear her at a rally in Albany. It was exciting, all that whistling and cheering like she was a film star, but I didn't understand the first thing of what she said. Something about Tennessee and President Wilson being a big lump about the vote." She shrugged again, with an expression of blank boredom that Julia recognized from their school days of conjugating verbs.

The subject of women's suffrage was no more scintillating to Julia. By the time efforts to ratify the Nineteenth Amendment had reached their fever pitch near the end of the war, she'd cared only about finishing school and escaping to a fresh start in Europe. Although she'd never admit it, elections did little to inspire her confidence in democracy. She supposed women voters would do no worse than men, but she also doubted they would do much better. Of course any woman who wished to cast a ballot should have the right, but like most young people she knew, Julia didn't see how voting made much difference. "Your parents didn't approve?"

"They couldn't abide her ideas, not just about voting, but about Jews and labor unions and socialists and I don't know what all. But what really steamed them was how she actually tried to get in the newspapers. When something didn't strike her as right, she'd shout about it from the rooftops. The worst was when Vivian was in the papers too, only arguing on the other side. Sometimes there were photographs of both of them on the same day." Glennis rolled her eyes toward the ceiling, as if words could not express the resulting upheaval. "Eventually Viv got married and settled down but not Naomi, and since Chester took over, it's been much worse. Like the bust-up after Naomi went to the bank and lectured the whole board of governors. It about killed Nolda. She must have had ten sherry parties afterward to smooth the waters."

Too bad Naomi couldn't lecture Julia's bankers. "What do you mean, Chester 'took over'?" she asked.

"He and Nolda moved in here after my parents died. Right from the start they tried to force Naomi to stay out of politics and especially to stay out of the newspapers. He did everything in his power to make Naomi obey. You saw what a bully he is. Now he's bossing me around too. He thinks he's in charge because I don't have a husband to keep me in line."

"How Victorian." It made no sense. Julia understood better than most how an older brother's oversight could chafe, but surely that was a function of being deemed too young to manage for oneself. Naomi was a grown woman, a good fifteen years older than Glennis. "Why did she—why do you—let him push you around?"

"I haven't told you? On the ship?"

"Told me what?"

Glennis laughed. "Did I actually keep it secret? Chester makes such a stink about privacy that I suppose I kept quiet, but now I don't care who knows. It's awful. The worst problem in my whole life."

"What is?"

"Our father's will. It's positively medieval. I swear it's to blame for Naomi's death, one way or the other. He set it up so that we daughters can't inherit directly. Ever! The money's there, in our names, but it can only come to us through our husbands. Until we marry, Chester controls it. If something happens to him, my uncle George is in charge, and after him, my cousin George Junior. You get the idea."

Julia shuddered. "That's outrageous." At least—she resolutely believed—her own father had intended all his children to inherit straight away once they came of age. Little as she'd known her father, she'd never regarded him as the problem. Philip was the problem.

"He thought women don't have good heads for money and business. He said we'd either spend all our money or lose it to some shyster."

The same vexing nonsense that had stymied Julia at the bank. Why couldn't women vote about that? If women could vote to change how fathers and husbands and brothers—and patronizing bankers—treated them, if they could vote to outlaw that condescending presumption of "knowing best," Julia would be first in line for the ballot box. "Is that why Naomi didn't simply ignore Chester and do as she pleased?"

"He said he'd cut her off without a penny—of her own money!—if she insisted on the same allowance my parents gave her. He said she could either find someone to marry her and get him to dish out the money, or she'd have to move back home and live in the housekeeper's apartment downstairs on whatever allowance he decided. That way she wouldn't have many expenses, and he could keep a close eye on her."

"She accepted those terms?" A ghastly scenario. Medieval indeed. But why would Naomi accept her brother's onerous restrictions, given the obvious alternative? It was easy to marry for convenience, fashionable even. Resourceful women without means of their own had been doing it since the dawn of time. In fact, wasn't that old bargain what most marriages were about, in the end? Julia couldn't imagine the resolve required to forgo a fortune merely to defy a bully. What strength, or madness, did that require? For the first time since hearing the name in Glennis's dreadful scream, she regretted not having met Naomi Rankin.

"I thought she was managing," Glennis said, "despite all his rules, but I suppose she just couldn't take living in a cage like that. I hate that Chester got the best of her. I'd give anything to telephone the *Times* and tell them exactly how he treated her, but he'd cut me off flat, without a bean. I'd have to come stay with you and your brother, or we could pool our pennies and go live in one of those hotels for impoverished ladies."

Oh Lord. Imagine the two of them sharing a flat. "He hounds you too?"

"All the time. That's why I'll probably have to marry Archie. Chester told me before I went to England last spring that it was the last trip he'd allow. If I didn't settle down, he'd declare me a spinster and make me stay home and do good works with the Miriam Maids, that sort of thing. So now if Warren won't heave-ho his wife or Russell doesn't perk up soon, I'll be stuck with Archie. He's my last chance. I know he's a damp old trout, but he's invited to good parties, so it won't be that bad. I've considered stinkers way worse than him. Plus, we made a sort of deal. He can keep his drafty old pile in the country and his dogs and all, and I'll get a smart flat in London and can spend my money without Chester *or* Archie having much say about it. Flaming hell, Julia, I'd marry Mervin—his stupid spaniel—if it would get Chester out of my hair."

This all tumbled out as Glennis sat upright, her normal cheerfulness returning. Wedding business was, after all, why she had returned to New York. From those long, endlessly embroidered monologues on the ship, Julia recalled that—barring late-developing better options—Glennis intended to make arrangements for a spring wedding in Kent. Presumably she'd initiate new financial arrangements as well. No wonder she was so eager to be a bride.

Julia unfastened her shoes and tucked one leg under her skirt. "What a nuisance brothers are."

"At least yours is handsome, Viv says." Glennis's tone shifted as a new thought formed. "Maybe I could meet him? Wouldn't it be a hoot if the cards fell right? We could be sisters."

Julia suppressed a laugh. "Your brother's a menace, but mine can be a real twit too."

"Why? What's he done?"

Julia sighed. How to explain what still seemed such a needless fuss? She answered as briefly as she could. "He's challenging my inheritance. He claims I'm not actually included in our father's will. The notion's preposterous, of course, but a dreadful bother all the same. We're meeting with the lawyers tomorrow morning."

"Why does he want your money?"

Of all the questions that might fall from Glennis's lips, this was the one Julia had most pondered and knew least how to answer. Philip's motives remained utterly baffling. He'd explained only once, in a glib note last June maintaining that an intriguing legal enigma had turned up, as if her half of their father's money were a plaything for idle speculation. *Nothing personal,* he'd insisted. But still the mystery plagued her. Sometimes she imagined his apparent life of ease was a sham disguising secret debauchery and debt. Or perhaps he was driven by simple greed, whether for money or the power it bestowed.

A third alternative was more painful to consider because it was more plausible: spite. He'd been just eight when his mother died. How must he have felt when his father left soon afterward for Europe, returning two years later with a beautiful young foreign bride and new baby already on the way? Philip had been shipped off to school in Massachusetts before Julia was born, and he never again lived under the family roof. Of course, by the time Julia was old enough to remember, neither did their father.

Glennis fell back across her bed, shoulders buoyed by the mounds of white pillows. "I bet you could marry just about anyone and chuck your brother forever."

Julia smiled. "I plan to part ways with Philip at the earliest possible moment but not by getting married. I'm not the marrying sort, Glennis. I doubt I ever will be."

It was simply true, more recognition than resolve. As far as Julia could see, marriage meant trading freedom for security, a dubious bargain at best. A wife relinquished everything in exchange for whatever her husband chose or bothered to provide. The sheer caprice of it pinched Julia's breath. Nothing but a man's honor and good fortune stood between his wife and hardship. Julia's parents' short marriage had been unhappy, but her father could escape into the world for solace; her spurned mother had been trapped at home, isolated without friends, family, or social standing. Julia had shared that genteel exile; it was all she knew as a girl, long before she understood its nature. No, the risk of being left powerless should affection sour was simply too great.

"Not ever?" Glennis exclaimed. "That's exactly what Naomi said. How can you be so thick? Don't you want babies? What about when you're old and wrinkled? If you're not married by then, you'll be stuck for sure. Like Naomi."

Julia waved away the shrill concerns. She generally avoided any thought of those distant decades. If she'd learned one thing in her twenty-five years, it was that the future was a bust idea. Hadn't the war's high-blown talk of a bright future made a terrible hash of things, especially in Europe? The past was dismal and done with, beyond repair, but the future might not exist at all. What future awaited those millions who'd marched off to fight for honor and glory—noble ideals that died quickly alongside them? No, the present was all you had. Best to seize happiness and meaning where you could. She had no plans to get old and wrinkled. It would happen, or it wouldn't. If it did, she'd worry about it then.

"But you must have boyfriends," Glennis said. "You must get mobs of proposals. Aren't you tempted?"

It was inevitable. After all the hours they'd spent together during the past few weeks, the conversation was finally turning to Julia's private life. She considered how to dispatch the question without inviting more, much preferring to observe the spectacle of others' lives than reveal her own.

"I like my life the way it is. I have an arrangement back home in London. With a lovely man. We understand each other perfectly."

Glennis crossed her arms to wait for the details. She would not be put off.

"It's not that interesting," Julia protested, but Glennis rolled her eyes in such comical rebuff that Julia sighed—*oh,* for a sidecar—and said, "His name is David Adair. He's tolerable looking, rich enough, and rather amusing. That's all, really."

"Don't be ridiculous. Who is he? What does he do?"

"He owns an art gallery in Chelsea. Do you know the Brille-Adair, in Cosgrove Mews?" Glennis frowned, uncertain but eager for more. "He has splendid friends, artists and writers mostly. And he throws wonderful parties." The drivel sounded brittle even to Julia. "We have a lovely time together."

"So he's your boyfriend?"

Glennis's earnest curiosity was so old-fashioned, so American. She might have been a maiden aunt fishing for secrets. "We have an understanding," Julia repeated. When she saw this remained opaque, she thought for a moment of how to explain discreetly. "We're both adults, with our own households. It's an open arrangement. You know?"

Glennis faltered. "Sort of."

"No promises, no expectations. We're both free to come and go as we please. Generally we choose to be together, but if and when that changes, we agree to part as friends. It's quite simple and deliciously free." The arrangement was mostly tacit, but for the past year or so since meeting after a rather daring production of *Salome*, it had suited them both nicely.

"Maybe I did meet him. Archie took me to a swanky party in Mayfair. There was a David, tallish, very posh, dishy accent. Is that your David?"

"Let's not say mine, but I suppose it could have been him."

"Must have been. But he was divine. Why in the world wouldn't you snap him up?"

Julia felt a scrape of irritation. This was the kind of thinking she'd moved abroad to avoid. Glennis hadn't heard a word of her attempt to explain, instead translating *handsome* and *rich* into *husband* as quickly as one of Jane Austen's calculating mamas.

"I mean it. Why don't you marry him?"

The answer was the single best feature of her understanding with David because it freed them from the tyranny of that very question. As long as the prospect of marriage hovered over every dance, every drink, every kiss and cuddle, romance was vexed with strategic maneuvering as complex as any dance steps. How many couples married simply to escape the constant bother? Julia suspected sheer fatigue accounted for more weddings than all the red roses and boxed chocolates in Christendom. It took considerable effort to resist those pressures to conform.

"I told you, I'm not the marrying sort. And even if I were," she added to forestall Glennis's objections, "I doubt his wife would approve."

It had been too tempting—though perhaps she should have sprung her punch line a bit less bluntly. Glennis's mouth opened with a pop. "Julia! That's terrible. Immoral. You're just dallying with the poor man."

Immoral? That was rich. Julia reminded her of last week's hunt for the elusive married Warren.

"That's different. He wants to marry me as soon as he can get her to shove on."

Julia left the obvious unsaid as a soft rap sounded on the door. "Glennie?" It was Edward Winterjay.

Glennis flounced off her bed and trotted to the door in her stockinged feet. "Are you alone?"

"Open the door, please."

She pushed back the thin bolt, and he slid inside, holding a half-full sherry decanter and two small glasses. "I thought you could use a little stiffening."

He lifted his arms out of the way as she embraced him with embarrassing fervor. "Thanks heaps, Neddie. You're too plummy for words. Why can't I have a brother just like you? I swear Viv gets all the luck."

He extracted himself and handed the decanter and glasses to Julia with a wink. Glennis tugged him to sit beside her on the bed, but he hesitated, twitching aside a crumpled pair of pink camiknicks with a roguish smile. She clucked and swept her underthings to the floor.

"I can't stay, kitten," Winterjay said. "Vivian and Nolda are going over details for the benefit, and it's best if they don't know I came up here. I just wanted to tell you to tread carefully. Your brother is in a terrible temper. You'd be wise not to provoke him any further."

"But you heard—"

He tapped a forefinger against her lips. "No, Glennis. Listen to me, sweetheart. Chester's under a great strain just now, but please, you must trust him. He's only doing what's best for everyone."

Trust your brother, my dear. The words echoed in Julia's head. *He'll look after you, decide what's best.* The refrain sounded everywhere. *You're a girl,* it said. *You need looking after.*

"Not best for Naomi," Glennis grumbled.

Winterjay quirked his head in disappointment, as if she were a pouting child.

"He doesn't own me!"

"Glennis." Winterjay spoke sharply. "I'm serious. I understand you're upset, as we all are, but Chester is in charge here, and he's dangerously close to losing patience with you and your reckless talk. You know what that means. You know what he can do."

She began to protest, then stilled as Winterjay pressed a second fingertip to her lips. In its wordless linger Julia sensed the more visceral warning. It worked. Glennis stifled whatever protest she had been about to utter. Winterjay cupped the back of her head and gave it an affectionate waggle. "Good girl. Let it go. Don't make Naomi's mistake." He rose and slipped from the room as deftly as he had entered, smiling in quiet conspiracy to Julia as he eased the door shut behind him.

Glennis reached for the glass of sherry Julia held out. "That's all you need to know right there," she said, her voice small and flat. "Be a good girl and button it. I've heard it a hundred times, Chester bellowing about how hard it was to keep Naomi *quiet*. He actually used to drown her out, pounding on the piano keys when she was arguing about something. He wouldn't stop until she did. If she made even a single peep, bang! A fist on the keys. No wonder she couldn't take any more."

Julia's spine tightened. She saw Gerald's tear-streaked face, his father singing a hoarse "God Save the King" at the top of his lungs. Whenever Gerald had tried to speak of the hellish trenches, his father had badgered him to stand to attention and join the raucous din.

Julia set down her glass. "And yet she did make a peep, didn't she? Isn't that what suicide is, in the end, one last cry to be heard?"

Even after the horror of Gerald's death—his thin body hanging from the conservatory rafter in his parents' country house, where they'd sent him to "stop moping"—his family still refused to recognize his ordeal. They blamed incompetent doctors, faulty medication, bad dreams. Silencing his message to trumpet their own, they declared him a war hero, a patriot proud to sacrifice for king and country.

"I suppose." Fresh tears glazed Glennis's eyes. "And she'd have been trying to say something big, Julia, something important. Only now Chester's made sure we'll never know what. He's a pig, and I hate him, but you heard Edward. There's nothing I can do."

Winterjay's warning had conquered Glennis's defiance far better than Chester's angry slap. She spoke through her teeth, as if those fingertips still hovered across her lips, resigned to enduring whatever it took to get her to that wedding next spring. It was painful to witness. Julia knew little about Glennis and far less about Naomi, but she did know about powerlessness. She remembered the shame that had flooded her own cheeks just a few days ago, when Philip's careless departure left her without means to pay for her own taxicabs, much less meals. The trouble Philip caused her was not deliberate (she trusted), but its difficulty was very real nonetheless. How far worse to suffer willful humiliation.

"You can find out what really happened to her," Julia said. "Not that bunk Chester wants you to believe."

Glennis's wide forehead rucked in a familiar frown. She finished her sherry in one go and plunked down the empty glass. "I don't see how. He'd squash me flat."

"Not if I help you. He can't cut me off."

Beneath the peevishness flickered Glennis's returning indignation. Her voice rose. "You would? Really?"

Would she? Julia wondered at her impulsive offer. By rights (and good manners) the mysterious nature of Naomi Rankin's death was none of her concern. Until two days ago, she'd never even heard the name. But something about the woman's story moved her, stirred her sympathies. Julia knew what it was to be dismissed as "difficult," her desires deemed inconvenient, her skills and judgment thought incapable of governing her own life. As a female she had to wait four years longer for her inheritance than Philip, who came into his share at twenty-one. Only his signature, not hers, could secure her flat in London. She could vote now, yes, but the choices were likely still two men, both insisting they knew what was best for her.

Like Glennis and Naomi, Julia knew what it was to have dependence imposed on her. Julia's despot had been relatively benevolent, but that made Philip's power over her no less rankling. She felt a frisson of sympathetic outrage. Her grievances were minor compared to Naomi's, but they spurred fresh interest in the woman whose fate she might have shared. What drove Naomi to pester her family, and apparently the world, so loudly and persistently? What drove her ultimately to take her own life?

Suicide. Wasn't that finally what pushed Julia to seek Naomi's truth? She'd been powerless to challenge the lies that obscured Gerald's death, but perhaps she could do for Naomi what she couldn't do for him. Helping Glennis discover the truth of Naomi's death could never right Gerald's injustice, but it might ease the pain that still swelled each time Julia remembered it. There might be nothing to discover, or they might fail in the effort, but she had to try. Maybe together she and Glennis could achieve what neither could alone. Wasn't that the message women like Naomi preached? That together muted voices might make themselves be heard?

Julia finished her sherry and took two ten-dollar bills from her handbag. She handed them to Glennis, who stared in confusion, then waved them away. She'd forgotten, of course. To her it had been a trifling loan, hardly worth the fuss, but to Julia paying her own way was important. She'd left a note about the problem for Philip on the hall table, and he'd laid out ten neat bills for her to find this morning, with a hasty *mea culpa* scrawled across the verso of her note. So easy a gesture, so small a matter—for him.

She sorted out her legs and stood, straightening her frock. Her unpleasant business with him loomed tomorrow, and it was time to gather her thoughts for that. She hoped the others downstairs were now gone, implicated as she was—however unwillingly—in Glennis's rebellious exit from the dining table. "I must be going now, Glennis, but yes, of course I'll help. If there's anything to be learned, we'll find it together."

At the door she turned to receive Glennis's grateful embrace and was nearly knocked off balance by her friend's breathless squeeze.

She'd forgotten about Glennis's fearfulness. She clung to Julia now, just as she'd clutched her arm when facing her family downstairs. At school they'd been misfits together—both new girls, neither popular nor pretty—but Julia had long since grown into her own best friend, her own champion and defender. Not Glennis. Despite her nightly social rounds, Glennis was still afraid of being alone. No wonder she fretted so much about marriage. She wanted desperately to belong to someone, someone whose arm would always be hers to hold. Lacking a husband, she needed Julia to be the next best thing: companion, confidante, friend. Julia was touched and a shade alarmed. Not even David expected so much of her. Not even Christophine. In that moment she felt the immense loneliness of that frothy white bedroom.

Julia held her friend a beat longer than was customary before easing free and stepping cautiously into the hall. Her shoe crunched on something smooth. Beneath it lay a wrinkled beige envelope. Glennis tore it open and held the note out for them both to read: *Miss Rankin, I would be grateful if you could come to the Empire State Equal Rights Union, on lower Broadway, at your earliest convenience. I need to talk with you in private, quite urgently.* It was signed *Alice Clintock.*

CHAPTER 6

The long-awaited appointment with the lawyers was delayed again. Julia could only watch as the firm's secretary resettled at her desk and raised her voice above the din of quarreling motor horns in the street below. "Mr. Van Dyne sends his apologies, but asks you please to wait a few minutes longer." This time she offered no consoling smile—the only hint of annoyance at Philip's third inquiry.

Julia unfolded the newspaper across her lap. The delay left her in a difficult position. She had trouble reading the tiny brevier type but preferred not to use her spectacles in public. She checked the seams of her stockings, adjusted the drape of her skirt, and tried again to consider the patchwork of headlines. Early September, and already the papers were a snooze of candidates' speeches and party rallies in Albany or Cleveland or New Orleans, enough to weary the staunchest of citizens. She couldn't imagine how anyone endured the eternity until elections. Coolidge or Davis? Roosevelt or Smith? This man or that man? The '24 election meant nothing more to her than rank upon rank of gray newsprint faces. She masked her face in civic absorption and studied her half brother from the shadow of her hat brim.

Sprawled sideways across the opposite chair, Philip sent a stubby pencil swishing over the sketch pad on his knee, pausing only to flick smudges across it with the side of his little finger. He propped an elbow against the chair's back cushion and settled his chin on his knuckles.

The past hour they'd spent together in the taxicab and this reception lounge—their longest stretch together in more than ten years—had convinced her the man was a kaleidoscope of postures: motionless, then a slithery blur. Agile as an acrobat, he could shift from one pose to the next like Nijinsky himself. He had the shoulders and grip of an athlete but affected utter lethargy. He was as likely to collapse into a chair as to sit in it, to slump against a wall as to stand upright.

The pencil paused, and Philip's eye rose fractionally to study her left foot. He flipped to a new page and began a portrait of her shoe. How apt that the dart of his hand across paper was the most animated thing about him. His signature was all she really knew.

When the lawyers' official summons had reached her last June, of course it had been alarming. Three days later Philip's personal note arrived, apologizing for the bother and dismissing his challenge as a mere formality, a tidying up of some inconsistency or ambiguity. He said only that he'd found a "spanking fine conundrum" that ought to put the lawmen through their paces, as if they were languishing horses in need of a good gallop. He'd been courtesy itself, inviting her to be his guest when she returned to New York. *If a chap has only one sister,* he wrote, *he might as well get to know her before she flies the ancestral coop.* Of course she would go. To defend her inheritance, certainly, and for the last chance to know the man who not only held such power over her but was also her closest kin.

The wait grew. A few minutes stretched to another twenty. Julia examined her manicure, refolded the newspaper. Philip's dark eyes rose and met hers. One cheek twitched in camaraderie at the shared tedium before he lowered his head and resumed sketching. On impulse Julia leaned forward. "A friendly proposal?"

His pencil paused, but he didn't look up.

"If this Van Dyne fellow doesn't appear in the next five minutes, how about we simply talk this through? We're both adults now. Surely we can sort it ourselves."

He smoothed his hair back from his face. A long strand sprang free and returned to its perennial place, a black stiletto against his forehead, tip buried in his right brow.

"Philip?"

Head still down, he added a swath of charcoal, three quick smears, and said nothing.

Again? For the second time since her arrival, he'd cut her flat. Not ten minutes after wrestling her luggage down the hall to his guest quarters, Philip had turned on his heel with a backward wave as she began to thank him. Her gratitude had sputtered into astonished silence. His manners were as quixotic as his posture.

Amazement again hardened into caution, and all sprouts of filial armistice shriveled clean away. Fine. Business, then. Fourteen more days until her birthday. Years of childhood solitude had grown into what she called freedom, and her taste for it was both deep and determined. If he preferred a fight, he would get one.

At last a distant door squeaked, and a young man approached. Freckles mottled his face, and dark-auburn hair lay in waves spreading from a part down the center of his scalp. He wore a brown suit half a size too large for his shoulders, but when he gathered up his modest stature to greet them, she saw he was at least her age, possibly closer to thirty. Van Dyne introduced himself with a smile as soft as his voice, making him not at all the sort of legal man she had been braced to confront.

He escorted them down a corridor of paneled cherry doors with engraved brass nameplates to the last door on the left, a scuffed wafer of birch with ESSEX J. VAN DYNE typewritten on a card slid into a small enameled frame. Judging from the space he proposed they squeeze into, Julia suspected the label had once read BROOMS. Had she crossed the Atlantic only to be shunted to the office dogsbody? Surely their business warranted more gravitas. She balked in the threshold, and Philip stumbled to avoid treading on her heel.

"Tripping not allowed," he said. "Nor poison darts or knuckle-dusters."

"I understood there were to be three arbiters," Julia said. "To ensure fairness?"

Van Dyne slid past her to his desk. "The active senior partners, yes." He motioned her to the room's only armchair, and Philip and the secretary, Miss Baxter, took the remaining seats.

Donning round tortoiseshell eyeglasses, Van Dyne became a red-haired Harold Lloyd. He spoke in a rush of words that sounded painfully rehearsed, which perhaps explained the delay. "We here at Feeney, Churchman, Kessler, and Rousch"—Van Dyne pronounced the firm's name with a melodic bounce—"are pledged to consider this matter with utmost impartiality. This morning's session ensures you both fair opportunity to speak and to address each other's arguments." He looked at Philip. "Soberly, I trust. This is a serious matter."

Philip's chin sagged in a comical show of bland affront.

"Once today's transcript is added to the file," Van Dyne continued, "they—I mean, we here at Feeney, Churchman, Kessler, and Rousch—will review all the documents most carefully." Once begun, the recitation of names could not be halted, and it spilled forth like a troupe of dancers taking a bow. His cheeks colored.

"A paragon of judicial scruple," Philip said. He perched sideways in his chair, one elbow hooked over its back.

Julia's nose flared. Why did he talk such piffle? Van Dyne, however, gave Philip a look of such deep gratitude for the frivolous reassurance that Julia uncrossed her legs, alert as a garden rabbit. Were they acquainted? They must be; she would not mistake that flash of familiarity. Van Dyne would not be involved in the judgment itself, but even so, any slant in Philip's favor was hardly cricket. She shifted forward, heart beginning to pace warily in her chest.

The firm's proposal of internal arbitration had seemed reasonable last spring. For two generations Feeney, Churchman, Kessler, and

Rousch had handled all Kydd family affairs, including Julia's, and no one wished to make the quarrel, if that was what this was, public. And yet and yet. There was still time to march to the nearest magistrate's office and demand a judge and formal hearing instead.

"We've made every effort to ensure a fair and thorough procedure, Miss Kydd."

Nervous hesitation lifted Van Dyne's statement into a question. He must have sensed her new misgivings. She looked away, unable to think with all four of those eyes pleading at her. Her gaze fell on an unframed etching of an old woman's hands that was tacked to the back of the door. It resembled one of Dürer's studies, but these surging veins and outsize thumbs evoked less piety than poke-in-your-eye defiance. Interesting. And recently done, she guessed, noting the inky residue on Van Dyne's right knuckles. So he was an artist—and a fairly gifted one, to judge by the etching. She rearranged her gloves across her knee. Fiddlesticks. If the man had art in him, as it seemed he did, how could she not give him a chance? Rash or not, she'd agreed to this arbitration. So be it. They had promised strict impartiality, after all. She edged back in her chair, dipping her hat in (tentative) acquiescence.

Van Dyne aligned his pen and letter opener. "So. As we all know, Miss Kydd will soon turn twenty-five. Although the terms of your late father's will are somewhat ambiguous—"

Philip coughed at the euphemism, and Julia's jaw stiffened. If anyone had cause to mock the careful caution of *ambiguous*, it was she. Philip was the one who had manufactured confusion where none existed.

Van Dyne reddened and began again. "Under the extreme circumstances that arose in November of '13," he said, "it was agreed that Philip Kydd would act as guardian for his half sister until she reached twenty-one and as trustee of her estate until she either married or turned twenty-five, whichever should occur first. While that arrangement was admittedly hasty and expedient, we believe it's been satisfactory, considering it was devised under duress."

More prepared prose, tepid and precise. Julia willed the fingers gripping her handbag to relax. She would not so much as blink. Those extreme circumstances, as Van Dyne described her mother's death, still tightened her throat.

She had been stretched out reading *Lorna Doone* under the coverlet when Christophine had knocked on her bedroom door. Her gentle hesitation had brought Julia's head up in suspicion. "Miss?" Christophine whispered. "We—" Her voice disappeared in a choke. *We?* Christophine and old Timkins, the butler, were waiting in the hall. Timkins held a folded telegram, which Christophine took and cupped to her throat like a wounded thing—a small dove tucked beneath her dark chin—as she explained in her lilting Caribbean Swedish English that Miss Lena, Julia's mother, had been struck down and killed by a motorcar in Stockholm. She'd left in a scrambling hurry the month before, called home by her brother's sudden illness. There'd barely been time for a brief, distracted goodbye, a kiss Julia had tolerated with a resentful shrug because she couldn't go too. Timkins stepped back respectfully and swayed, fists by his sides, as Julia furiously denounced the telegram's lie, then sputtered and finally quieted into a mute and dry-eyed terror. Christophine had wept for them all that night.

Van Dyne lifted a document. "The crux of the matter lies here, in Milo Kydd's only known will, deposited with the senior Mr. Kessler on January 28, 1890. It states simply that his fortune is to be entailed equally upon his beloved wife, Charlotte Vancill Kydd; his son, Philip Oswald Vancill Kydd; and any future issue yet unborn."

Yes, yes, yes. The beloved Charlotte and her bonny young Philip. Surely they'd all memorized the passage ages ago. At last the moment seemed ripe for Julia to speak. "Precisely," she said. "Simple then and simple now. Our father's will was grounds for the arrangement made eleven years ago. Surely it still pertains. According to its terms, I'm due to take full control of my inheritance on my birthday, two weeks from today."

For a moment Philip's gaze sharpened into focus. His head sank fractionally to one side, and he seemed to assess her with fresh interest. Intrigue, even, as if finally noticing she was no longer a tongue-tied girl with stubby braids and scuffed knees. Then the droll mask returned, and he clapped twice like an enthralled child. "Sensibly put and succinct to boot!"

However annoying this outburst, Julia hastened to echo it. "Excellent, then. As we agree these objections are nothing more than a baseless nuisance, I'll rebook on the next available sailing home, and our paths will part forever. Nothing would make either of us happier, I'm sure."

Another keen look crossed his face, and Julia wished she could seize hold of its mercurial intelligence. In that instant he was a man she could talk to, reason with. But again that discerning flicker disappeared, and instead Philip gave a flamboyant sigh. "And waste this morning's expedition?" He pulled a gold cigarette case from his jacket pocket and swung it in a lazy arc toward the others. "I spent half an hour getting this cravat to behave. Might as well take a stab at defending said baseless nuisance. It'd be a pity to have dragged you hither for anything less. How'd you put it, Jack, the nature of that arrangement? Hasty and expedient, I think you said."

Jack. The hairs on Julia's arms rose. More than acquaintances. They were good friends by the sound of it. She must be vigilant.

"The thing ain't so simple, you know." Philip lit a cigarette and drooped back into his chair to address the lawyer. "I wasn't much more than a pup myself at the time. I hardly knew the girl, but I did what was asked of me." He exhaled a perfect O of smoke. "I doubt she's had cause to complain."

True enough. For years the bank directives and holiday deliveries had arrived promptly, though rarely with more than a few scrawled words. Until she'd turned eighteen, she'd been the subject of his duty-bound attention—arrangements for stuffy boarding schools and dreary summer camps and tours, not to mention the various "mature gentle-women" engaged to monitor her general welfare—rather than its object. If not for Christophine's companionship, Julia would have lost entirely the cheer of loving arms, fond smiles. Those years had taught her well: to rely on herself—not hired overseers and certainly not her remote half brother—to shape her own mind and aspirations. Philip's greetings, arriving like clockwork at each birthday and Christmas, wouldn't total a single page.

"I've never complained," Julia said. "You're the one who raised this absurd business."

"Absurd? Is it?" Philip gestured to the papers on Van Dyne's desk. "May I?"

Van Dyne handed Philip the two typed sheets of his formal chal-lenge, which he studied. Maybe he was thick after all. This would be risible were it not so irksome.

"It gets going somewhere here, I think." Philip tracked a paragraph halfway down the first page, then read from it aloud: "Eleven years ago it would have been churlish to press my misgivings about the arrange-ments made for my half sister's keeping. But accepting that responsibil-ity did not mean accepting its addled logic, then or now."

He scanned ahead. "Milo Kydd's will now deserves more calm and deliberate examination. Note it's dated just a year after I was born. It fairly reeks with a proud papa's vision of a brood of Vancill-Kydds to follow. He refers specifically and solely to my mother. It's safe to infer that by future issue he means their children, theirs together."

Safe to infer? More like convenient and profitable, for Philip. Any necessary inferences had been drawn years ago when these very lawyers concluded that "future issue" included Julia. She recrossed her legs and drew breath to contest his facile assertion, but before she could, Philip resumed reading aloud.

"Milo Kydd did not die suddenly. He had ample time to get his papers in order. If he wished for my half sister or her mother to receive a share of his estate, he would have made those wishes plain. But he died leaving unaltered a will that did not mention, much less provide for, Lena Jordahl and her daughter."

"That's hardly—"

Philip silenced Julia with a raised palm. "My father had six years to name them in his will. He did not. Why? There's no mystery to it. The marriage was a disaster. Of all the rash things he did after my mother died, marrying a foreign girl half his age was surely the most foolish. Within a year he virtually lived at his clubs, in obvious misery and profound regret. His unchanged will confirmed what was plain to see: the marriage was dead. One must presume he wished to erase it, to expunge it—"

"Of course the marriage was unhappy." Julia's words sailed, startling the pen in Miss Baxter's hand.

A foreign girl. The epithet stung. Though rarely summoned into conversations and more rarely still admitted, Lena's memory still scraped a tender nerve. However much Milo may have rued their ill-suited marriage, it was Lena who paid the greater penalty. To now blame her for that folly was intolerable.

Julia regripped her bag and steadied her voice. This was too important to let anger shrill her words. "How could it have been otherwise? My mother had more life in the tip of her finger than that old man ever dreamed of." She tapped her forefinger to her thumb. "Yet the fact remains they were married. Unless you plan to claim that Milo Kydd was not my lawful father—which he most certainly was—this is a complete waste of time. I am every bit as much his legitimate heir as you, Philip."

A daft look of pleasure flooded Philip's face. His fingers fluttered a lazy dismissal: thin and lithe, fluent as doves. His little finger curved up—inquisitive? mischievous? droll?—as the others floated in a languid palmward curl. She'd seen it a thousand times before, at her own arm's length as she examined her hands for traces of ink missed by the printer's pumice. Was the gesture another legacy from their distant father?

"There's no question of your legitimacy, my dear," he said. "Only the old boy's wishes. If I may?" He scanned the document and continued reading: "It is significant that Lena Jordahl made no claim for herself or her daughter at the time of her husband's death."

Julia again drew breath to answer, but Philip's low voice bore on. "Apparently she saw the absurdity of such a claim. Not only were they estranged as man and wife, but she had money of her own. This is significant. The terms of Milo's will are predicated on my mother's fortune being entailed elsewhere—neither I nor my prospective siblings could hope for anything from the Vancill line. It seems to me the maternal situation bears some consideration, as it was in his mind when he dictated his wishes."

Philip laid down the sheets and turned to Julia. "I'd forgotten about that point, but it's a good one. Let's be reasonable. Yes, I accepted the expedience of footing your childhood bills. It was easier than trying to tap into that distant Jordahl money, mired as it was in Swedish barnyards. But really"—he exhaled a soft whistle—"there's enough to keep you comfortable. Now that you're grown and living on that side of the pond anyway, why haggle over the modest Kydd stash?"

This stung. "We may be a far cry from Rockefellers, Philip, but our father's fortune is ample enough. We can both live on its income, and like you, I depend on it."

Script forgotten, he parried back, "That's not true. Unlike mine, your mother was rich."

"You know perfectly well my mother's wealth was in land, which in any case reverted to her brothers after she died. I can't ask—no, beg— my uncles to break up their holdings so my pigheaded brother might steal my inheritance. It's unthinkable. Impossible."

Philip settled back, a new cigarette cradled between his fingers. "As trustee in the matter," he said to Van Dyne, "I assure you the Jordahls may be dull, but they're provident to the hilt. They could readily muster an allowance more than ample for my half sister's needs."

What new arrogance was this? Proposing she forgo a lawful inheritance to rely on charity instead? Presuming to know her financial *needs*? Julia fought to remain cool. This was important. She had Christophine to think of. Christophine had always been far more than a maid to Julia, especially in the hard years after her mother's death. She'd been just fourteen, a bright and eager waif by all accounts, when she left Saint Barthélemy with Julia's parents after their rather bohemian wedding at the Jordahl home near Gustavia on that tiny Caribbean island. Christophine was Julia's nursemaid and companion, growing into more of a surrogate sister or aunt and then into the essential manager of all that made Julia's domestic life proceed smoothly.

"You know nothing of the sort, Philip," Julia said. "I'm sure my household costs no less than yours. My need is not one jot less than yours."

"In household expenses, perhaps not. But you're spared a man's responsibilities of business and family. Furthermore, you hold the trump card." He surveyed her, his head quirked to one side as if she were an array of cufflink options. "I don't doubt you'll snare a rich husband. You'll have plenty of money to foot even the steepest milliners' bills." He eyed Julia's hat. "For what else is a female's fortune really required?"

Julia steadied her expression. Of one thing she was certain: the future she envisioned for herself, however vaguely, included no husbands, snared or otherwise. Her chin rose and twisted slightly, the better to display Mme Hamar's beautiful felt cloche with its pleated rosette of lettuce-colored faille ribbon nestled over her left ear. She owned others like it, finer even, and every one not a bit of his business. "While questions of need may amuse you, Philip, they're irrelevant. A will is a document of rights."

Miss Baxter rustled, and Van Dyne's chair squeaked. Duty bound him to inform Philip that Julia was right, he said, and all discussion should be limited to the documents at hand.

"Oh, naturally. And their context." Last salvo away, Philip's spine dissolved into another genial curve. He hoisted an ankle onto his knee, exposing a lavender stocking the exact shade of his amethyst tiepin. Julia wanted to despise his sartorial impudence, but the color very nearly matched the shade of her favorite silk pyjamas.

She held her tongue, letting his prattle dry to nothing in the little office's somber air. Philip had had his farce of a debate, but her words carried greater weight; let them conclude the meeting. Her position was the sound one, grounded in both precedent and logic. And it was fair. In the end that was her reassurance. Justice was on her side. It would see her through. Confidence. Confidence would carry the day.

Van Dyne measured the silence that followed. At last he unhooked his spectacles from his ears and dismissed Miss Baxter with a relieved nod. The partners would try to reach a judgment quickly, he promised, possibly as early as next week.

Philip unfolded himself from his chair, demurring that there was no need to rush. "Not bad for a first sibling squabble," he said, "though regrettably late in the game. Nothing like a brisk thrust and parry to get the color up."

Was he going to thank her? Wipe the sweat from his brow and praise her worthiness as an opponent? As if the past hour, the past week, the past few months since word of his objections arrived had all been some great sport? Before Julia could muster a retort, Van Dyne hurried to preempt it. "He's teasing you, Miss Kydd. You have to understand he's—"

"An utter lamb, capering for your amusement," Philip said. "Mild as milk." He selected a cigarette from Van Dyne's extended case. "They say the patch up afterward is twice as fun. Swords into swizzle sticks and all that? Lunch at the Pomeroy, on my nickel?"

"Do join us, Miss Kydd," Van Dyne said as he leaned close to light Philip's cigarette. A wry smile passed between them, and the younger man colored.

Blood rushed in Julia's ears. She wanted nothing more than a swift exit out of this office and into the reviving autumn sunshine for time alone to consider the morning's assertions, but the sight of Philip and the young lawyer relaxing into each other's company kicked all such thoughts out the window. Whatever these two had to say to each other, she wanted to hear it—and intervene if necessary.

"I suppose I could spare the hour," she said. "And it's Julia, please. *Jack.*"

CHAPTER 7

"Heads down," Philip said into a glass of claret. "Wright is on the move."

It was too late. He pushed back his chair and rose to greet a small man with a razor-honed Vandyke beard weaving toward them through the Pomeroy's crowded dining room.

Identified only by a small brass **P** above the buzzer, the Pomeroy occupied the third floor of the Hoskins Building. It was a hive of downtown Manhattanites, most of them feasting on liquid offerings. Drinks were served in their proper glassware; a clientele of judges, attorneys, and city officials, plus generous bribes underscoring that they served only members' own liquor, spared diners the usual Volstead farce of teacups.

The Pomeroy's bustling trade fueled a dull roar in the vast low-ceilinged room, a din Philip had twice already lamented. There was no need to mention that if not for Julia, he and Jack would be lunching peacefully at the Hogarth Club, which, like most such clubs, forbade females. Julia too left unsaid her fervent wish to be elsewhere. For the first time since arriving in New York, she missed David. She missed his mild, effortless company—demanding nothing and offering nothing beyond whatever shared pleasures might arise, in and for the moment only.

Even if Philip and his guests had been inclined to chat, they'd scarcely have had the chance. Three times in the past twenty minutes, a different young woman had ambled by to purr some vacuous remark in his direction. Each time he shooed the lady on, and each time she departed on a glissade of delighted affront. Wright was their only gentleman visitor and the only one to sink into the vacant chair. He spun the wine bottle around to read its label and signaled the waiter to fetch another glass.

Wright greeted Philip and Jack with a grunt, but he fixed his sharp brown eyes on Julia. "Where've you been hiding this morsel, Kydd?"

"Under my roof, if you must know."

Julia's throat burned at the rakish innuendo, though she relished the fellow's start.

"The lady is my sister," Philip said. "Cheering news for sybarites like yourself but stultifying to me."

"Hardly original, Kydd. At least choose a brunette." Wright's leer was creepish but his skepticism understandable. Julia's fair coloring shouted of her Swedish mother, while Philip could pass for a sun-browned Greek. Only lean frames and a left-handed grasp of the world suggested they were even partial siblings.

"She really is his sister," said Jack. "Half sister, at any rate. She's visiting from London."

Wright shrugged and filled his glass.

"Julia," Philip said, "manners compel me to inform you this is Willard Wright. An acquaintance of Van Dyne's who fancies himself a popular novelist." He watched Wright's show of tasting the wine. "What brings you out in the harsh light of noon, man?"

Wright glanced at Julia. "The scenery."

She inclined her head. Perfect flummery. She'd met a hundred Wrights before. Men like him loitered in restaurants and theaters and concert halls everywhere, each dispensing the same dreary arrogance disguised as compliments.

"Saw your piece on Stieglitz in *American Mercury*," he said to Philip.

"A trifle."

"Certainly. But Mencken must have thought it tolerable. It was a thin issue, with summer holidays, but still."

"Indeed."

"Any news on the sleuthing front?" Wright asked. His beard jutted in a sarcastic smile.

Philip winced. "Good Lord, no."

"No fiendish murders? No lovers' quarrel gone horribly wrong?" Wright persisted, elbows on the table, as soup arrived.

"You're a ghoul, Wright."

The man's small teeth gleamed. "I'd make you famous, you know. Just imagine, an insufferable ponce—a *clever* insufferable ponce—sniffing out criminals. With my pen and your nose for mayhem, readers would lap it up; you can't imagine the depths of literary taste these days."

Philip snapped the air with a violent flick of his napkin. He divided the remaining wine among Julia's, Jack's, and his own glasses. To Wright he said, "Alas."

Wright ignored the slight and buttered a slice of bread with Jack's knife. "Just as well. Indifferent vintage."

"Wright's got a point, Philip. Folks are mad for detective stories nowadays," Jack said, undeterred by Philip's frown. "You squared that business with the bank bonds in a flash. I could help, make sure he gets it right."

Wright smiled. "There's a thought. I could use a nom de plume, write as if Van Dyne's telling the tales. He could be your very own Dr. Watson."

Julia listened to this remarkable exchange with growing impatience. What on earth were they talking about? She put down her spoon with more force than she intended.

Jack apologized. "It's an old dispute, I'm afraid. We go round and round with it every time our paths cross. Wright here has a notion of writing detective novels—"

"For ready cash," Wright interrupted. "Bags of it, I hope."

"And he wants to model his lead character on Philip. Your brother's solved a few puzzlers for the police, and Wright thinks they'd make good stories. Philip detests the idea, though frankly I don't see any harm in it."

"This sleuthing twaddle is beginning to annoy me," Philip said, fixing Jack with a meaningful stare.

Refreshing as it was to see Philip back on his heels, Julia shared his irritation with the term, shouted nowadays by cheap magazines everywhere to sell cheap novels. She didn't particularly care if Wright's literary aspirations poached upon Philip's so-called deductive exploits, but she did agree that—for those bored with séances and scavenger hunts—"sleuthing" reduced to a game the serious work that she and Glennis had solemnly resolved to do. Their investigation might not involve theft or murder (Glennis's hyperbole aside) or even probably the law, but it was nothing to joke at. Naomi Rankin deserved, if not justice, then at least for the truth of her fate to be known.

Remembering her promise to help Glennis lifted Julia's spirits. It made a welcome alternative to all things Philip. But before Julia could investigate anything, she needed a better sense of Naomi. What kind of woman would push pills into her mouth so quickly that she had no time to write a note? Or write last words so troublesome her brother would steal them? Julia glanced about the table: these men must move in the Rankins' circles. Their gossip was a perfect place to begin.

"Speaking of mysterious deaths," she said. "I had a brush with one the other evening. I went with Glennis Rankin to a party, and bang in the middle of an ordinary séance—you know, spirit lights and the maid set to thump the walls—my friend uncorks a yowl about seeing the spirit of Naomi, her older sister."

Jack stirred to speak, but Philip brushed his sleeve. "Curious. Go on."

"By all reports the sister was as alive as anyone, but Glennis made a frightful scene. Imagine the shock when we learned the sister had indeed died. Poor Glennis went all to jelly, and really, who can blame her?"

"You say this dead woman's name is Naomi Rankin?" Philip asked.

"I believe so. Do you know her?"

He tapped his forefinger against his chin. Neither Jack nor Wright spoke. "She's rather well known. As is the whole Rankin clan, for that matter."

"I barely know Glennis. Who are they?"

A waiter replaced their soup dishes with plates of *aubergines à la turque*. At Philip's nod he opened a new bottle of wine and refilled their glasses—including Wright's, when he thrust it forward.

Julia ate three bites, laid down her fork, and gave her brother to the count of twenty. Then fifty. Another fifty. He ate with ludicrous care. "So? What don't I know about the Rankins?"

"Ask Wright. He's a student of the moneyed classes, particularly the females."

Wright protested. "Not those females."

"They're an old family," Philip said, "bigwigs in the city for decades. Banking and before that some upstate industry, one of the mills, I believe. But it's the current generation that entertains the locals. Your chum may lead a life of dull respectability—at least I've not heard of her—but the older sisters set the bluenoses sniggering with joy. Nothing regales them better than scandal among their own."

"There are three siblings," Jack said. "Or four, adding your friend, who must be considerably younger. Both parents died some years ago, soon after the war, I think. Chester is the oldest. He married Edgar Branston's daughter. You know, chief of medicine at Saint Bernadette's Women's Hospital, the fellow who wrote the book on modern obstetrics. Chester and Nolda Rankin spend half their lives on benefit committees and charity boards."

"Flinging about money and power," Philip said.

"Avoid their table at all costs," Wright said. "Rankin's a bore, and his wife's a regular Xanthippe."

"It's the two sisters who divert us," Philip continued. "Naomi's the elder. She's a leather-lunged suffragette, always up to some high jinks or other. Poor Chester goes positively gray in the gills each time she's front-page news. Lately she's been organizing rallies and what all to elect women into public office."

"To elect lady lunatics," Wright said. "Noisy and grim, the lot of them. They stomp their feet to cheer Mrs. Sanger and Comrade Debs and cry out for free love, as if any man would go near them. It's unspeakably bilious. Giving women the vote was the biggest squall yet of democratic tommyrot. Americans seem to think if you accumulate enough ignorance at the polls, something intelligent will result." He emptied his glass and set it down with a thud.

Philip's hand curled around the wine bottle. He gazed mildly at Julia. She returned his silent aplomb. No wonder he detested the man. What did it take to get rid of him?

"I met the other sister, a Mrs. Winterjay," Julia said, ignoring Wright's diatribe. "The party was at her home last Friday evening. She seemed pleasant enough."

Philip waited as the plates were cleared. "Ah, well, there's the joke. Vivian Winterjay, née Rankin, has political itchings of her own. The good Mrs. Winterjay leads a placard-toting swarm called Wives and Mothers First. They insist God and country, not to mention husbands and children, depend on ladies' domestic prowess. For every racket Naomi Rankin made demanding women get the vote, young Vivian offered up a dozen sweetly tempered reasons why they should not."

Wright laughed. "There you have it—two poles of womanhood in one family. Naomi Rankin and Vivian Winterjay may be sisters, but they couldn't be more bitter enemies, at least when it comes to politics. What a chuckle. Down to the mad glint in their eyes, they even look alike. Vivian's the finer specimen, though, I must say. As women go."

He paused to assess Julia with the frank air of the connoisseur.

Her jaw edged higher. *Ignore the swine. Even a blush rewards him.*

"Her husband's not a bad sort," Jack said. "He's headmaster at Saint Catherine's, and there's talk he may soon be vice chancellor at Barnard." Julia's guesses had not been far off.

"Winterjay's decent enough," Philip agreed. "More than once he's smoothed over family dustups in public. He'll go far, given those pacifying talents." He waved away the sweets trolley. "He's honed them to perfection. The sisters have been at it for years. One yearns to stride the halls of Congress; the other jiggles babies on her knee. One blasts from the news pages of the *Times*, the other coos from the color section of *Society Gazette*. They're well-matched foes." He smiled. "Just imagine the ennui if the Rankins ever came to peace."

And yet with Naomi dead, the rancor had seemed only to deepen. Julia couldn't imagine Glennis much further from peace with her family.

Wright's interest had wandered. He pushed back his chair. "Ducky chat, as always. Pleasure to meet you, Miss Kydd." Julia's cool nod was wasted as, glass in hand, he moved to join a pair of diamond-wristed women being shown to a nearby table.

Philip waited ten seconds before clucking softly. "That, *ma petite soeur*, was one of the most noisome men in my acquaintance. Why Jack tolerates his company is beyond me."

"He's an important critic," Jack said, "and he knows the best gallery owners in town."

"He's a mean drunk who lives off lonely widows and gullible girls."

"I can hardly snub him. He lives above me in the Belleclaire."

Philip ignored Jack's protest. He drew out his silver case and offered it around.

Julia gladly accepted a cigarette. Whatever his faults, Philip smoked Régies. "How do you know the Rankins?" she asked.

"Hard to miss them," Philip said. "Rankin and Winterjay turn up everywhere. They're both on the symphony board this year. I suppose the wives circulate wherever ladies pass their days, though both love a society crush. I knew Mrs. Winterjay when she was 'that lovely, lovely Vivian Rankin,' as my aunt Arlene called her, badgering me to join the queue. The lovely, lovely Vivian still has a following, mostly young female acolytes, but there's no shortage of smitten cubs, either, although her glow is decidedly maternal these days. Winterjay basks in it, as you might imagine, what with his wife a veritable *Überfrau*."

An unsettling image of Vivian Winterjay as a young Brunhilde stirred Julia to ask, "What about Naomi? Did you ever meet her?"

"Regrettably, no," Philip said. "Our paths didn't exactly converge. She was forever declaiming at anarchists' rallies or shouting up police stations from here to Albany." He refilled their glasses. "It's amusing no end to imagine the Rankin dinner table en famille. Makes our little set-to look like a nursery tiff."

Julia sipped her wine. If only he knew how close to the mark he was. So far everything accorded with Glennis's account of the feud.

"And now you say Naomi Rankin is dead." Philip swirled his wine. "Curious. There was nothing in the papers this morning."

Dead and as mourned as she ever would be, possibly already turned to ashes. "Tomorrow, probably. I expect the family's still in shock," Julia said. "It certainly rattled Glennis."

"Curious," Philip repeated.

"Curious in what way?"

But Philip only shook his head, eyes narrowing in thought. They smoked in silence until Jack leaned back and pulled out a watch. He returned it to his waistcoat with a grimace and said he had to get back to the office.

Philip noiselessly sparked his thumb across his fingertip. A waiter appeared with a slip of paper whose claim he accepted with a wiggle of blue ink, unaware, Julia mused, how simple that gentleman's prerogative made such matters. "This office business is a damn nuisance," he said. "Can't the excellent Miss Baxter shuffle those legal tidbits on your behalf?"

"She can do everything I do and better. But then she'd get my paycheck too."

"Codswallop," Philip said.

"Legal work bores me to tears," Jack admitted to Julia. "I'd rather be drawing, but that barely pays for cigarettes, much less rent. Kessler was good enough to rustle me a job, and I can't appear ungrateful."

"Kessler the lawyer?" Julia said. "I thought he retired ages ago."

"He did and promptly scarpered off to Florida," Philip said. "Jack means his son, T. Edgeware Junior. Young Eddie strayed badly and became a policeman, though he's assistant commissioner now, which eases the family's pain a bit. Did I mention he's my uncle?" He laughed. "Mine, not yours. He married my mother's sister, dear batty Aunt Arlene."

Julia turned toward Jack. "You're an artist?" A talented one, she'd already surmised from the etching in his office. She wondered if he was equally skilled with other forms of printmaking. She had a particular fondness for wood engravings, as they paired exquisitely with type printed on damp paper. In quiet moments on the ship (when Glennis was distracted by a handsome golfer from Cornwall), she'd begun plans for a small French-fold edition of a Siegfried Sassoon poem to christen her new fonts of Garamont, which Deberny et Peignot assured her would arrive by the time she returned. If Jack Van Dyne seemed interested and capable, and if he proved genial in the next few weeks, she might enlist him to produce a frontispiece. It would be a coup if Capriole could debut an American artist before any other London private press knew of him. Once her funds were secure, she could pay him well, and other commissions might follow.

"A thwarted one, but yes, I like to think so. Kessler disagrees."

"Eddie likes his art with at least a century's patina," Philip said. "He can't see much point to Jack's squiggles. Only think what he'd say to detective stories."

He eased Julia's chair away from the table, still talking to Jack. "Can't you creep away to see the Monets with me at the Ruel-Durand this afternoon? I'll hire you myself for watercolor lessons." He paused. "The moment my new inheritance rolls in."

She spun around. "You bloody rotter!" They had been conversing as civilized peers, if not mature siblings, and he queered it all with a poke at her most unfunny predicament.

Jack fumbled to his feet with a look that said, *He's hopeless. Ignore him.*

Philip made a show of repentance and settled Julia's cape over her shoulders. It felt like a shroud, as heavy as the prospect of the coming days marooned in his company.

CHAPTER 8

Much as Glennis would have liked to grab a hat at first light Monday morning and rush to lower Broadway to learn what Alice Clintock had to say, she could not. Firm protocols of bereavement and a frenzied encampment of journalists trapped her inside her home. Twice before noon on Tuesday, when news of Naomi's death became public, she telephoned Julia to describe the hordes shouting questions and thrusting cameras through the iron fence. During the night, she said, the house had been swathed in black bunting like Queen Victoria herself. Chester hired private guards with black armbands to escort deliverymen to and from the service entrance so none of the household staff would need to leave the premises. She was a prisoner, she wailed. Worst of all, Wall Street Warren had telephoned to say his wife was away in Pittsburgh for three whole days.

Glennis's confinement stalled Julia as well. At least she was spared the prospect of Philip's company when the telephone bell woke her on Tuesday—obscenely early, before light—and was followed by footsteps and men's voices. "Out," was all Mrs. Cheadle would say when she brought in Julia's first coffee. Something hush-hush with young Mr. Kessler and the police. Julia decided to explore the city on her own, see where her footsteps led her. She rose, bathed, and was fastening her shoes when Glennis's first call pulled her to the telephone. Over her friend's lament, a squall of rain against the library windows dashed all notions of neighborhood wandering. Julia resolved to pass the day in improving solitude—as she suggested Glennis might, prompting a snort. First, however, the morning papers.

The official obituary, appearing only in the *Times*, was brief, discreet, stoic. Describing Naomi Rankin's political work as "an ardent engagement in civic concerns," the family—Nolda, presumably—announced simply an unexpected death at the too-young age of forty "following a brief illness" and their wishes, in accordance with the deceased's, for private services. No mention of burial. Despite the announcement's brevity, or because of it, journalistic fervor on other pages and in other papers flew in all directions. Some writers insisted they weren't surprised at her death, as Naomi's speeches had long suggested she was unwell. Others painted her a martyr, sacrificing health and life itself to tireless striving on behalf of oppressed women everywhere. Still others claimed her political agitations proved too strenuous, her death ironically confirming the weakness of her sex after all.

When she'd read all the pontificating she could stomach, Julia gazed across her bedroom at Michael Arlen's new novel. She'd started *The Green Hat* three times but found the characters too annoying to endure. She was determined to read it, though; Arlen (as Mr. Kouyoumdjian called himself) was a neighbor and nodding acquaintance she was bound to see when she returned home, and she couldn't keep professing her intentions to read the blasted book much longer. It had become another unpleasant task for her trip.

She read two more paragraphs before her attention floundered. She laid the book and her spectacles aside and pulled from her trunk a handbound solander case wrapped in black flannel. Here at least her mind could dwell for hours. The flannel protection was more sentimental than warranted, as the box bulged and creaked with all the hallmarks of amateur craftsmanship: corners fat with excess linen, hinges that rubbed, air bubbles trapped under both thumb-stained pastedowns and a distinctly crooked front cover sheet of Cockerell marbled paper. She'd made the box four years ago, one of her first bookbinding projects as a student at Camberwell. Before sailing she'd added her new pressmark as a label, making the box a traveling case for her fledgling Capriole Press. The pressmark launched her venture with flair, featuring a decidedly warm engraving of a lissome young goat frolicking in a glade of book-leaved trees. She was a Kydd, after all, caprine through and through.

Inside were two glassine-wrapped copies of each of her first three productions. Sized alike, each fit in the palm of her hand: a tall twelvemo folded down from a single Barcham Green sheet, printed in half sheets on her small Albion handpress. The first would always be dearest: Gerald's *Three Sonnets*, each poem begun in the war and completed at Julia's urging, between bouts of the sweaty tremors that would finally claim him. The poems were no match for Rupert Brooks's or May Cannan's, but they were honest and the one fine thing that remained of Gerald's shattered life. The typography was too grand and overreaching for the simple poems, Julia could see now, and the only illustration was a clumsy fleuron construction shamelessly modeled after Bruce Rogers's *Ronsard* to frame the title and colophon, but she loved the little book regardless. However heavy-handed its design and flawed its execution— she now saw every blurred counter, the inelegance of its letterspaced title, the blotchy inking—it was the first book produced entirely by her own hands. It would always hold a tender place in her heart, entwined as it was with the memory of that fine and gentle man. She had worked madly to finish the printing and bind a copy (quarter calf over poppy-red French silk boards) before his tenuous peace crumbled away. He'd cried to see it—they both had, and that was what made it dear, even though in the end it had not been enough to save him.

Next, in a somewhat slapdash effort to fill the months after Gerald died, had come *Gruff*, the old Norwegian folktale of three goats who outwitted a troll. Her mother had often recited the tale in a heavily accented rollicking gait, ignoring Christophine's murmured concern that bedtime stories ought to be sleepier. Julia had used hand-me-down fonts of Caslon primer (wiser this time, choosing a text to suit her types) and added Hester Sainsbury's three simple white-line woodcuts, done in a single afternoon in Julia's dining room studio. The resulting chapbook was satisfactory but still a dilettante's bit of frippery. By the time it was finished, her tastes and skills were ready to move on. Her affections as well.

Julia held her third book and silently thanked David for introducing her to the writers and artists who'd made it possible to take Capriole into the world that mattered. Too bad he regretted the consequences. He applauded Capriole as a charming pastime, seeing her printer's smock as a kind of shepherdess costume: quaint fun. But last spring when Capriole had caught the attention of men of substance, including some of his associates and clients, it left no doubt that she planned to do more with her days than gossip and luncheon and had more on her mind than frocks and parties. David's dismay was quite real—and quite irrelevant.

For all but the most fanatic collectors, this third book was her first true imprint, the piece that announced Capriole's rise from juvenilia: *Wednesday*, a four-page, nine-sentence reverie about clouds, more or less, that Mrs. Woolf let Julia print to debut her first foundry fonts of Baskerville. She'd ordered a font of the beautiful italic caps in double pica for the title, so large she set the word in three justified lines down the page, ending in that fine fellow of a cap *Y*, doffing his hat to whatever unlucky character had to follow him in the line. The book's jewel, though, was Eric Gill's full-page engraving, a sweetly sensuous image that bore no relation to the text. (What image could?) If Mrs. Woolf minded, she never said; certainly no one else did. Except poor David, on discovering his shepherdess had muscles, means, and a very modern head.

The esteemed typographer Stanley Morison had been down at Ditchling when Julia took Gill his copies, and both men praised it with gratifying warmth and less gratifying surprise. Morison paid her five pounds for a copy. (She'd been flummoxed when he asked her price; Capriole was a private press! Her naivete prompted a cool laugh, droll remarks about collectors, and the banknote, with advice that thenceforth she take nothing less than a tenner.) Within the week he'd shown it round, and all thirty-two remaining copies (she held back five) had sold. Requests continued to arrive from collectors claiming they were out of the city that week, or the wife's surveillance of the book budget had only just lapsed, or one of the other familiar laments that circulated endlessly among bibliophiles.

Julia examined her treasures for the thousandth time, seeing their flaws (not so many, really, considering) and loving them not a shred less. She was glad for their company, even if it might have been mad to bring them to New York—as gifts, she'd thought, if the right moment arose. Glennis was now the only possible recipient, but she would have no idea what to make of the paper's feather-thin deckles and the Irish linen hand stitching. Or, heaven knows, of Mrs. Woolf's musings and Gill's nymph and satyr.

The afternoon dragged by in idle ideas for text and artist pairings and restive layout sketches, equally hypothetical and outlandish. As her next book project was still uncertain, Julia could do little until she returned to London. May Sinclair had offered a set of poems that would suit, but she refused to be paired with Gill's images, and Hester was busy on other projects. David Jones and Paul Nash were possibilities for engravings—but likely beyond her reach. Julia could only tinker and bide her time, sketching ever more frivolous thoughts for Capriole ephemera.

After dinner she was desperate for diversion, but all that came were more calls to the telephone for Glennis's lamentations and visits from Pudd'nhead and Pestilence, Philip's two elderly gray tabby cats. They looked like ordinary barn cats—short-haired, scarred and scuffed, missing a tooth or notch of ear—but were both friendly as kittens, defying their frightful names. (*But literary!* Philip had protested when she said as much.) Settled across her lap and against her hip, the cats brought a drowsy calm, which mercifully hastened the day's end.

By Thursday, the prospect of another long rainy day was even more intolerable. Again Philip was gone before Julia rose, leaving the day's papers in a disheveled heap. She smoothed the sheets, hoping some new light had been shed on Naomi Rankin's queer death. She scanned page after page but found nothing—as if Naomi had vanished from memory after two days. Instead headlines trumpeted news of the sensational murder of Dorothy Caine, a pretty blonde artists' model dubbed "the Broadway Belle" for her roles in stage revues. The police were tight-lipped about the investigation, but Assistant Superintendent T. E. Kessler assured the public the assailant would soon be brought to justice. Julia pushed aside the sprawl of newsprint and poured herself fresh coffee. If the killer qualified as "fiendish"—Philip's supposed sort of criminal adversary—this would explain his unnaturally early morning departures.

Julia resented facing another idle day alone while her nominal host (*Stay at my flat,* he'd said. *Call it a last fling at this sibling business*) careened about the city in pursuit of some clever quarry, abandoning her to ennui. He knew she was no vapid squealer. Why hadn't he invited her along on the adventure? The man infuriated and intrigued her. No sooner did he sketch a study of sleeping Pestilence than he pitched it into the waste bin when Julia admired it. He mocked her taste one moment (as if she'd brought Mr. Arlen's book for pleasure) and applauded it the next, dashing to the piano to play her favorite of Satie's *Gymnopédies*. He seemed to be leading her in some strange dance, gliding toward civility, then shying away with sharpened elbows.

The day yawned before her. She listened, hearing only the crackle of politicians' cant on Mrs. Cheadle's radio set in the kitchen, before slipping down the hall and into Philip's library, his private sanctuary.

She understood why he preferred it. It was a beautiful room, lined with bayed cases of mahogany. French windows opened onto a wrought-iron balcony overlooking a leafy courtyard. Two chestnut leather armchairs flanked a broad fireplace and mantel. A permanent depression in the seat nearest the fire told her where Philip liked to sit. She could picture him, brandy in one hand, cigarette in the other, a book abandoned across his knee. She imagined a sordid sheik novel or treatise on phrenology. Neither seemed likely, but both fit her mood, and she forced them into the scenario.

She moved to the nearest bookcase and scanned the usual meat and potatoes of any library, the sensible shelves of histories and biographies and science, the interminable Dickens and Trollope and windy Russians. Like a truffling boar, she quickly found the prizes. Her *Oh!* lifted both cats' heads. Who would have guessed that Philip owned a copy of the Ashendene Horace in its original vellum binding or Charles Ricketts's *Cupid and Psyche*, with all those lush engravings? He seemed to favor the private presses of the nineties with their decadent poets and illustrators. Julia preferred more modern fare, but she understood Ricketts's many-tendriled appeal. Fathoming Philip's interest was more difficult. She moved to other cases, more surprises.

It was some time before she realized why the collection was eerily familiar. What a clot she was. Of course. Much of it was from their father's library. After Lena's death Philip had supervised the sale of the family home (torn down now) and most of its furnishings. Philip allowed Julia to keep what she wished from the library—she'd selected a quarto German incunable with picaresque woodcuts and the prize little Aldine sixteenmos (none of which she could read, then or now). Precocious if eclectic taste, she thought smugly, for a thirteen-year-old girl. Apparently Philip kept for himself the English private press material: the two Kelmscotts, a few minor pieces from the Doves Press, and the Eragnys. He'd added the lovely Vale *Danaë*, which Julia took down merely to breathe in its mournful vapors, and a swathe of trifles from the Bodley Head. So Philip was a Beardsley man. Intriguing.

She unfastened her shoes and stretched out across the Chesterfield sofa. Mrs. Cheadle brought in a plate of apple slices and a wedge of Stilton—when persuaded it truly was all Julia wanted for luncheon—and another pot of coffee. She pulled the draperies and started a fire in the grate. Julia had to insist she was no invalid—please, no blanket and pillows—before the good woman would leave her in peace. She suggested the kind housekeeper might try restoring her burgundy shawl, badly wrinkled after lying for hours in the seat of the captain's chair, where Glennis had flung it before Naomi's service. Made of fine Egyptian wool embroidered with an intricate pattern of amber beads, it would have to serve Julia on further occasions during her stay.

Feeling like a pampered odalisque (albeit in a lemon shantung morning frock), Julia again surveyed the room. She admired Philip's taste in art, even if she didn't precisely share it. He owned a first-rate Braque watercolor, several abstract modern photographs, and a series of Sargent pencil studies that David could sell at a breath-catching price. The African tribal masks flanking the French windows were stunners, peering down at her like some ancient brooding jury. Crimson wallpaper glowed through their round eyeholes like patient volcanoes.

Julia found herself musing at the two oil portraits above the mantel, painted in the style of Sargent but signed by an artist she did not know. Both were of Philip's mother, Charlotte, a Mediterranean beauty looking regal but weary. In the painting on the left, an infant who could only be Philip slept in her arms. There had been other pregnancies and at least one other baby, Julia knew, but none that lived more than a few days. A young version of Milo beamed from behind Charlotte's chair.

Philip favored his mother as much as Julia resembled hers. Neither bore much trace of their father. Except for the hazel tint Milo's brown eyes had stirred into Julia's blue ones and the toasted shade of her hair, as if he'd been a passing flame that singed her Nordic coloring, Milo Kydd had disappeared completely from this earth. There he stood, beaming but already transient. Julia's memories of her father grew even fainter.

Had Philip known him any better? Growing up, Julia had sometimes pondered her mysterious half brother, wondered about his childhood, so separate from her own. By the time Milo returned to New York
with his Swedish bride, he'd missed two of his son's birthdays. Worse,
Lena had confided, he'd reveled in her flourishing pregnancy, bringing
her posies and pillows a dozen times a day. Little wonder Philip would
have none of either mother or child.

Had Milo ever tried to rekindle some connection to his son? If she
knew, Lena hadn't said. She did believe with a certain relish that her
husband kept a "special friend" in the Belafield Hotel. She'd told this to
young Julia one day without a trace of distress, and the idea had made
Milo more interesting to them both. By that time he'd become little
more than a dutiful but absent curiosity.

Julia tried to stir memories of the one Christmas afternoon Milo
and Philip had spent with their stepfamily. She was five. Both father
and son had been cool, with manners that bristled, and had watched
the clock. Thinking on it again, Julia hoped her father did have that
mistress, someone whose arms would have welcomed and warmed him.
But what of Philip? Was there any warmth for him, then or now? The
man gave no clue.

The other portrait above the mantel was of Charlotte alone, framed
alike but painted some years later. Here she looked less pinched, more
lively. Had life with young Philip rendered her last years a bit more gay?
Julia studied the woman's almost impudent expression.

"She's a tyrant, you know."

Philip's voice boomed from not two feet behind her. Pudd'nhead
leaped from her lap. Julia steadied her coffee cup, grateful for the saucer,
and lowered both to the table beside her elbow. "I beg your pardon?"

"Aunt Lillian. The formidable lady you're contemplating."

"Your aunt?" Julia looked again. That would explain the differences.
She felt a pang of regret, realizing that she had hoped Charlotte had

found some happiness late in her short life. But it was Charlotte's sister, apparently, who eyed life with a glint of mischief.

Philip helped himself to an apple slice. He pitched Pestilence from his armchair. "Lillian Lapham Vancill, oldest of the legendary Vancill sisters. Spinster extraordinaire. She lived with us when I was young and stayed with me while Milo went flitting about the globe after my mother died. She was a threat to polite society even then. Seventy-one now and a frightful virago." He gave a good-natured shudder. "Frightful."

He licked apple juice from his lower lip. "Would you like to meet her? I'm due in her parlor for tea at five. Meeting you would positively light up the old girl."

"With contempt?" They both knew the Vancill family had nothing but scorn for "those Jordahl creatures," as Julia had overheard herself and her mother described as she listened through the upstairs balusters after her father's funeral.

"True enough, at one time," Philip said. "But old Lillian may surprise you. Lord knows she surprises me. Please come. Your Rankin chum must be in mourning, so I know you've nothing else to do. Come. Let's wave the white flags and give it a go. I promise you won't soon forget a Thursday tea with Aunt Lillian."

Julia frowned at this blithe overture of sibling accord, so lightly made. But her empty calendar offered no resistance, and frankly, she was curious. She sighed and rose languidly to hide her glad relief.

Aunt Lillian lived in a third floor walk-up flat on West Seventy-Sixth. The building was caked with soot and the cramped lobby lit by a sole light bulb. A sullen woman whom Philip greeted as Nancy showed them into a sitting room bursting with outdated furniture. Green velvet draperies, worn to threads at the hem, were closed, and a fire and three candelabras blazed, giving the place not only a theatrical brilliance but also instantly tropical temperatures. Julia shed her shawl and gloves in the breathless heat. As she laid them aside, she noticed the shrine on Lillian's mantel: photographs of Philip at a succession of ages, his bronzed baby shoes, and a monogrammed silver rattle. Amid the clutter stood a half dozen gilt statuettes, trophies from the Gotham Park Fencing Association, each engraved with Philip's name. "Vice of my youth," he said into Julia's ear.

"You're a fencer?" It explained his martial metaphors.

"Dilettante. After Milo left, the old gal dug out her foils and taught me herself. We had some fine parries back and forth across the library, I can tell you, though usually she skewered me like cheese. Why she keeps these old baubles, I can't imagine."

Lillian Vancill made the imperious sound of a neglected duchess. She sat in a purple velvet chair with oak armrests carved into gargoyles. Birdlike, her legs dangled above the faded carpet. Her hair was the color of granite, marcelled in tight ripples across her skull. A cherry-red flannel circled her throat. She dismissed Philip's remark on it with a bony shrug. "Catarrh, nothing but a blooming nuisance." She fastened her rheumy eyes on Julia like pincers.

"So you're the menace?"

Philip spanked the top of her head. "Call her Julia, you old lobster."

He directed Julia to sit on one end of a shabby green sofa and settled himself at the other. "Aunt Lillian is convinced you mean to abscond with my fortune," he said. "The thought of thwarting you keeps her alive."

Where would she get that idea? Julia wondered darkly. It was a blatant distortion—outright reversal of the truth, in fact. She smiled politely at her nemesis.

"Don't simper, girl," Lillian said. "Charms don't fool me." Her dislike was very real, and Julia's discomfort turned to irritation. The woman was old and possibly ill, but Julia had little obligation to humor her and none whatever to endure her hostility.

"You're being a bore, Aunt," Philip said. "Julia is my sister and our guest. If she can be civil, so can you."

Lillian's face creased in fifty places. "Where's our tea?" she shouted.

Nancy pushed open the door with a cart. She transferred a tarnished tea service and plate of ginger biscuits to the table without a word. Lillian's hands, thin but contorted, gripped the leering heads on her chair. They were the hands in Jack's etching, identified by the gold ring on her twisted little finger. Lillian made no move to pour, apparently testing Julia's breeding and manners.

"Shall I?" Julia duly said.

"Don't be absurd." Lillian jutted her chin at Philip, both sparse eyebrows raised. "Took me years to train him."

"I warned Julia you're a tyrant," Philip said, pouring out three cups with dripless skill. "I also said you'd amuse us, so you'd better snap to, old girl."

This abuse delighted the old woman. She needled him about marrying soon, while "something tolerable" might still have him. This led to a blistering catalog of vices to blame for his bachelorhood: indolence, gluttony, loose morals, disrespect for the elderly, squandering of good family money. Each tirade provoked spirited objections. Julia sat back and sipped the weak tea.

"I'm sure you devoured the obituaries this week, as ever," Philip said, finally changing the subject. "Did you see that Naomi Rankin died?"

Lillian exclaimed that she had. "Shocking. Lamentable."

"I mention it because Julia has a glancing connection to the business. Turns out the youngest Rankin sister is one of her chums."

Lillian turned her gaze to Julia, and for the first time it was not entirely venomous. "Did you know Naomi?"

"I'm afraid not. I barely know her sister. We were in school together for only a year."

"Too bad," Lillian said, as if Julia had failed in some profound way. "Naomi had more spine than a herd of giraffes. I liked her a good deal."

"Aunt Lillian was heartbroken when she couldn't chain herself to the courthouse railings with Naomi and the others," Philip said. "Her

87

wrists would fall right through the manacles, and she'd be sent home to bed."

"For whom did you vote in the last election?" Lillian demanded of Julia.

Surprise sent a bite of stale biscuit down the wrong pipe.

Lillian watched Julia cough like a stevedore. "I hope not Harding," she said. "That trussed pig."

"I was abroad," Julia croaked.

"Well, Debs could have used your vote. I had to wait sixty-seven years to cast my first ballot. Haven't missed an election since. La Follette needs me now. I intend to keep at it until I'm a hundred, to make up for wasted time." Lillian transferred her glower to Philip.

"Nothing would delight me more," he said, and Julia saw he meant it.

They both noticed that Lillian was tiring. With a flurry of goodbyes and Philip's attempt to kiss his aunt's forehead—countered with a feeble swat—Julia's acquaintance with the woman was concluded.

"La Follette, girl," Lillian shouted as they left. "Make yourself useful!"

CHAPTER 9

On the third day after news of Naomi's death broke, Glennis decided it was safe to leave the house. In a stroke of luck for the Rankins, scrutiny of their misfortune was nothing compared to the speculation that swarmed to the lurid Dottie Caine murder case. Without family or servants to ply for information and with members of the Empire State Equal Rights Union just as reticent, reporters' interest in Naomi's death faded as quickly as it had flared. Glennis's prediction was right: reduced to the sad demise of a troubled spinster, it soon drifted from public thought.

Alice Clintock hadn't been in the basement apartment since Naomi's service on Sunday, Glennis said, and she was dying to hear what she had to say. Julia gladly agreed to visit the Union with her. They met at a stationer's shop on lower Fifth Avenue a few hours later. Glennis said she'd met Naomi at that very shop last winter because it was near Mrs. Sanger's clinical research bureau, where Naomi had seen to it that Dr. Bocker fitted Glennis with a "thing." Apparently the business required much winking and dissembling because she wasn't married. It was all Glennis could bring herself to say on the subject.

Mourning did not become her. Glennis was dressed in a gray wool suit with fussy bands of black satin across the cuffs and pockets. Its ashy color drained the warmth from her complexion, and wispy hair escaped from all the wrong places beneath a too-large black straw toque. At

Julia's glance she prodded it into place and grumbled of Nolda's taste in hats.

"Miss Clintock will meet us there," Glennis said as they walked the short distance to the Union offices. "She wouldn't say a word on the telephone."

Their pace slowed as they neared the address. Each step took them farther from the Manhattan either of them knew. Julia had grown accustomed to the infernal noise of the city—motorcars and taxicabs tangling at every intersection, engines and laborers hammering together ever-taller buildings, voices bargaining and complaining in a dozen languages, children squalling, mothers bawling. Here, however, was another layer of commotion: a fog of smells, some enticing, some revolting. One moment they passed a bakery's cardamom and anise and the next a grocer's spoiled refuse dripping from boxes on the pavement. Glennis clung to Julia's elbow, chattering nervously.

They nearly walked past the Union, a small storefront between a kosher butcher's stall and a barbershop reeking of peppermint and alcohol. The Union's front window had been boarded over for some time, judging from the layers of white paint obscuring vandals' ire, likely as vulgar as the large *candle-bashers* scrawled in fresh paint across the lost messages below it. Julia pushed open the door and saw three women bent over papers spread across a table.

Alice Clintock greeted them while her companions hung back. It took Julia a moment to understand why they had retreated, and she cursed her thoughtlessness. Her frock—though one of last year's, a simple day dress of aqua wool jersey with a narrow front placard of mother of pearl buttons—was finer than anything these women could ever hope to own. The sheer French silk on her legs would cost them a week's wages at least; their dark cotton stockings sagged thread thin at the ankles. Julia pulled off her gloves when introduced and reached to find each woman's hand, hiding in the folds of drab serge skirts. Glennis fumbled to do the same.

"It's an awful honor, Miss Rankin," said the worker named Fern Gillespie, a short, round woman with pocked skin and appalling teeth, caramel colored and fissured. "Naomi was a saint to us, a saint. We adored her like our very own sister, and now here you are. Her real sister, I mean. It's just too horrible she's gone."

Both women's unpowdered, unplucked faces shone with grief. Clearly they loved Naomi. Glennis swallowed. After Winterjay's remarks and the family's open disdain for Naomi, talk of saintliness was a jarring shift. "I miss her too," Glennis said, a beat late.

"And her with her greatest glory still ahead," Fern said. "It's just tragic, that's what it is."

Glennis looked lost. She seemed to still be fathoming *saint*.

"Maybe you didn't know, miss. She didn't tell many. Soon as this election's over, she was going to announce herself a candidate for US senator. Wadsworth is up for reelection in '26, and we'd love nothing more than to give him the boot he deserves. He's no friend to women, that's for sure. Sooner or later there'll be a woman elected to the Senate, and no one deserved that glorious place in history more than our Naomi."

Glennis gave no immediate reaction to this news—things took time to sink in—but Julia couldn't check her surprise. Perhaps a woman senator was inevitable but surely a long, long way in the future. Agitating for the vote took boldness enough, but campaigning for office, and at such an ambitious level, would require herculean confidence and courage.

"You know how little patience she had for might-have-beens, Fern," said Miss Clintock, or simply Alice, as she insisted Glennis and Julia address her. "Naomi would rather we focus on the important victories she did achieve."

Fern scowled at this mild rebuke. Beatha, the more bashful colleague, asked if they'd like a cup of tea. Both women retreated to a sideboard at the back of the room, where a kettle simmered on a gas ring. Over the rustle of tea making, Alice thanked Glennis for coming.

"Many ladies of your set won't give us the time of day," she said. "Fern's right. Naomi was a saint here. She never took on airs. She always did what she could to make things better, for all of us."

Glennis glanced at Julia. "I didn't know Naomi very well. I'm sorry about that, especially"—her voice trailed—"now."

"I regret I didn't know her at all," Julia said. It was true. She was more intrigued than ever by the woman who could somehow provoke both her family's picture of a tiresome shrew and this portrait of exemplary kindness. "I understand Naomi was a suffragist, of course, but what did she do, exactly, to be so admired?"

If Alice was surprised or offended at this ignorance, she did not show it. Her plain face, younger than Julia had first judged, sparked with pride. "I hope history will make that better known, Miss Kydd. Naomi was a great champion of women's suffrage, as you say. Since that glorious victory, she's worked with Miss Paul to promote the new amendment for equal rights of every kind." She pointed to three framed photographs, slightly askew and filmed with dust, on the wall. "We call those our trophies. They remind us of Naomi's finest hours."

Glennis touched one of the pictures. "That's her."

Julia stepped close for a better look. Beneath Glennis's finger stood a woman little different from the dozen or so others lined along a pavement, all wearing sashes and flanking a tall banner that read *Mr. President How Much Longer Must Women Wait For Liberty*. A wintry White House loomed in the background. Someone had written in spidery white ink *Alice Paul and NWP picket, 1917*. It was the sort of lifeless photograph that made newspapers so dull. Julia pulled the acronym out of her memory: National Woman's Party, the organization planning to form some alliance with the Union. Naomi was to meet their representatives to discuss it the night of her death.

Julia studied the photograph, but it was too grainy to gain much sense of Naomi. She was tall. Even beneath a heavy skirt and lumpy coat trimmed with fur, probably squirrel, she looked thin. She stood with chin up, mouth firm, eyes fixed on the camera, unsmiling. Beneath a cumbersome wide-brimmed hat, her fair features marked her as a Rankin. She was fortunate to have shared Vivian's more regular features rather than Glennis's and Chester's sparse hair and wide-spaced eyes and teeth. "She seems a strong, determined sort of person," Julia remarked.

"Oh, miss, come see this one." Glancing at Alice for permission, Fern led Julia into a windowless office at the back. Glennis and the others followed. Against one wall stood a mammoth wooden desk, its legs dented from decades of heavy use. On it lay a large sheet of paper labeled *Sept* across the top and hand ruled into an appointment calendar filled with scribbled notes, numbers, and other jottings. It was the desk of someone hard at work, who'd perhaps stepped away to find a file or greet a visitor. One expected a cooling cup of tea or half-smoked cigarette nearby.

"I haven't had the heart to touch her desk," Alice said. She trailed a finger through the week's dust.

"Here." Fern handed Julia a photograph. It was smaller and cleaner than the others, more candid than the "trophies" in the outer room.

"That's the two of them, Naomi and Miss Paul. It was taken some time after the strike," Alice said.

"Force fed," Fern said. "Knobsticked."

Julia knew remotely of the hunger strikes, in both England and America, but the thought of suffragists starving themselves to protest their imprisonment had always been too grisly to ponder for long.

"Naomi?" Glennis's voice crawled with dread, either from fear of the answer or shame at the widening scope of her ignorance.

Alice nodded. "That fall in Washington they were arrested for obstructing traffic. False charges, of course. They were beaten and humiliated—oh, in dreadful ways." She folded her arms. "So they refused to eat. When they were too weak to resist, those jailers forced tubes through their noses and down their throats. They poured raw eggs into them each day."

"She said that tube was worse than anything," Fern said. "But she weren't about to knuckle under. Wouldn't give them the satisfaction. It killed a lady in England!"

Alice frowned at her colleague's enthusiasm. "They were tortured for three weeks, and every day our support grew stronger."

"Naomi was tortured?" Glennis dragged the brutal word into her vocabulary, a word as alien there as *dungeons* or *martyrs* or *knobsticks*.

"They endured and they won. They showed the nation we would not be bullied or silenced. Wilson announced he would support us after all, and Congress finally voted our way."

Julia gazed at the photo. Two women in white cotton shirtwaists, sleeves rolled to the elbows, and long dark skirts stood close together, arms around each other's waists. Neither wore a hat. A few loose strands of hair blew across Naomi's face. Both were caught in unguarded smiles, bright with some pleasure or amusement shared with the photographer. Across Naomi's skirt was inscribed *To Naomi, sister, friend.* The signature was large and clear. There was no date, but the clothing was several years out of fashion.

All her life Julia had heard the jokes about suffragists. At smart parties everywhere they were easy targets of ribald mockery. They were called failed women, or thwarted men, or even some unnatural third sex. But to Julia's eye the two in this photograph had a new and enviable kind of feminine beauty. One dark and the other fair, they glowed with confidence and strength. Passion shone in Naomi's eyes, reminding Julia of a scandal-be-damned Sargent portrait of a disgraced countess or adored courtesan. Naomi's defiant gaze would be impossible to forget once you had seen it. Julia regretted that she'd never get the chance.

Alice added, "You probably know the rest."

Glennis nodded vaguely. Julia doubted her friend knew and was certain she herself did not, but neither was inclined to reveal how blind she'd been to the whole business of women's suffrage.

Alice took the photograph and replaced it carefully on the desk. "You must be wondering why I invited you here. We ought not keep you waiting." After gesturing for Glennis and Julia to pull nearby chairs up to the desk, she instructed Beatha and Fern to go whitewash the front window boards. "We're a favorite target for the local ruffians," she said, "though fortunately it's only a nuisance. We're accustomed to the language by now, and the girls are dab hands with a paintbrush."

She closed the door and dragged over a third chair to sit beside Glennis. When Alice bent to unlock the desk's bottom drawer, Julia saw a faint scar through the corner of her lower lip and another behind her left ear, disappearing under the coil of her braids.

Alice pulled out a brown envelope. "It may be foolish, but I'm worried about these. They started coming about six months ago."

She upended the envelope, and several pieces of folded paper tumbled out. A few had been crumpled and resmoothed. Glennis unfolded one foolscap sheet. A short message read, *Watch your wicked tongue, Naomi Rankin. Your in for worse trouble if your not careful.* Not surprisingly, there was no signature.

Typed on what looked to be identical sheets of cheap paper, each made a similar blustery threat. The notes' very ordinariness made them seem more sinister, as if the trouble they promised were all in a day's work. Julia wondered at the mind that would harbor such animosity and then coolly go to the effort to announce it. Pure malice? On a second reading she noticed that none of the notes were specific about either Naomi's offense or her punishment. Perhaps the author intended simply to frighten her, not actually cause harm. More bark than bite?

Alice pressed both index fingers against her lips as she watched Glennis read. Her legs were tightly crossed, right foot bouncing in the air.

"She must have been terrified," Glennis said shakily.

Alice made a face. "Naomi? She laughed and threw them in the rubbish. I pulled them out and saved them, though, because I was afraid for her. I wanted to show them to someone in case something happened." Alice leaned closer and dropped her voice. "Maybe something did happen."

Julia shot her a sharp glance. Was Alice suggesting the notes had driven Naomi to take her own life? That Naomi knew the author and secretly feared whatever "trouble" they promised? This would mean Naomi's death had been deliberately provoked, orchestrated to drive her to administer her own fatal overdose. If so, the author was both cunning and exceptionally cruel. Julia hoped Glennis wouldn't think of any of this.

Glennis bit her lip. "What do you mean?"

Alice swallowed. "She's dead, isn't she?"

CHAPTER 10

"Oh!" Glennis's comprehension came as a small explosion. "You think she was murdered?"

The word shimmered, released like a malevolent genie. Julia couldn't suppress a sigh. She'd barely tamped back the sensational notion the other day in Glennis's bedroom; now it would hover and beckon each time they spoke about Naomi's fate. She wished she could have warned Alice of Glennis's eager suspicions, steered her from that needless touch of drama.

"What?" Alice reared back. "Oh no. She took those tablets herself. I only mean she didn't take them by accident. These notes show the kind of hatred she faced every day, enough to crush even a spirit as strong as Naomi's. It's a marvel she carried on as long as she did."

"Did you show them to the police?" Julia asked.

Alice shook her head. "Naomi would never allow it. The police are no help anyway. They blame us for any trouble. They call us hysteric crones or say it's our own fault for not behaving sensibly."

"And we can't talk to them now," Glennis said, "or Chester would boil me alive."

"There's more too," Alice said, "though it's only a feeling, a bad feeling."

Glennis cringed. "What?"

"Earlier that day we were here, alone, when a telephone call came in. Naomi answered it here in the office—I was in the outer room, repairing our placards, which get terribly battered, you know—and right away she got up and closed the door. I couldn't make out the words, though her tone was agitated. A few minutes later she came out with her hat on, saying she'd meet me at home later. And before I could say half a word, she was gone, with a sharp scold that her private business didn't concern me. That alone was mighty odd. But then she could sometimes be rude like that when things weighed on her mind. I forgave her and didn't think of it again until . . . after."

"You think the call was related to these threats?" Julia said.

"I don't know. She was upset. Like she was bracing for something bad."

"What time was this?"

"Morning. Before ten." Alice turned toward Glennis. "The more I think about those last hours, the more I believe she was planning it. And I was too thick to see the signs."

She thumped her palm on the desk, steadied a rolling pencil. "When I came home, she was curled up on the sofa, saying she didn't feel right. She asked me to bring her those tablets and a glass of water, and like a fool I did. But she took only two—I'm certain it was just two—then got up to dress and repin her hair. I assumed it meant she was feeling better and would go to the meeting. But at the last moment she lay down again and insisted I go instead. By then there was no time to argue, and I had to leave right away, or I'd be late.

"If I had any inkling that Naomi intended to take her own life, wild horses could not have dragged me away. You must believe that, Miss Rankin. I'd have borne any burden for her, any trouble, if she'd let me. I loved her, you know. Loved her dearly."

Glennis fumbled needlessly in her bag at this talk of love for Naomi. Fern and now Alice, more ardently. Julia had never heard Glennis use the word, and Winterjay's homily had mentioned nothing more than the astringent love of Christian duty. Glennis must have wondered, as Julia did, if Naomi and Alice had shared what Americans called a

Boston marriage, though Julia doubted Glennis would have the composure, much less the words, to speak of it. Most likely it was of no consequence, except to make Alice's grief more poignant.

"You say she was ill later that day?" Julia said. "In what way, exactly?"

"Indigestion. Stomach pain something fierce. She looked feverish too, though she dismissed it as bad plums."

"Why didn't you call for a doctor?"

"She insisted it was nothing. Doctors cost money, you see."

"But surely—" Glennis began. To one who'd never had a fleeting care about money, forgoing the comforts of an attentive doctor made no sense.

"Did you describe these symptoms to Dr. Perry?" Julia said quickly.

"Maybe I should have, but there seemed no point. It was plain to see what she'd done. That she'd been indisposed didn't seem relevant anymore. Naomi's trouble was in her heart and mind, not her stomach. That's what killed her, Miss Kydd, the constant worry. That's what drove her to do this terrible thing."

Over Glennis's whimper Julia posed the question bluntly: "So you believe Naomi had the courage, the will, to take her own life?"

Alice met it with a steady gaze. "Naomi lived with purpose, Miss Kydd. She wanted everything she did to *count*, which for her meant to ease suffering and right wrongs. If she felt she could no longer endure the misery of her situation, then yes, I think she'd want her death to mean something. Like with those hunger strikes. Sometimes death is the loudest voice you have."

Julia understood. She'd heard Gerald's last shout, even if his parents refused to.

Alice watched Glennis's head bob over her lap in quiet sniffling. "But I'm certain she would have left a message for us here at the Union. She had a notebook and pen—to gather her thoughts before the meeting, she said—beside her when I left. But when I came home and found

Mr. Rankin and Dr. Perry there, the notebook was in a strange place, on the pantry sideboard. She'd never put it there, you see. It's been worrying me no end."

"Chester." Glennis's face lifted. "I knew it. Was he horrid to you?"

Alice hesitated. "He was upset. We all were. I could barely fathom what had happened, why he was there, before he began asking me questions. He wanted to know about her headaches and didn't I think she'd suffered terribly from them, but when I saw the empty tube, I realized what she'd done. I also understood then how he intended to explain it away."

"He can be a brute. Did he hurt you?" Glennis asked. "Say something nasty?"

"He was upset," Alice repeated dully.

"You're too nice. He bullied Naomi, and he must hate you too. He did, didn't he?"

Alice answered with care. The subject was clearly a bitter one. "As you know, he was obliged to allow her a small stipend. It was her money, after all. Last fall he wrote up a special document spelling out exactly what he would and would not allow her to do with it. As if she were a child. He made her sign it, promising to abide by his terms or risk losing access to her money altogether. Oh, his terms were plenty clear, but they left her so mean a pittance that it's a marvel she managed at all."

"That's how he forced her to move back into the house," Glennis said.

"There was enough money to maintain a small household or to fund our work. Not both," Alice said. "So she agreed to live under his nose, literally, and used her monthly stipend to keep this place running. We pay our workers far too little, but we must pay them something. You can't begin to understand her generosity, Miss Rankin. She let me live in the apartment with her, even though I couldn't help with expenses. We ate mostly what friends brought us, women who can't give money to the Union but can spare bread and vegetables, and we did our own laundry and housework, to save money." She pulled a hand across her face. "I'll miss our little home."

"You'll stay, won't you, until you find another place?"

"No." Alice paused. "After the service, Mr. Rankin asked me to move out. Or, rather, he said I could either stay in or stay away once the obituary was published. I couldn't come and go. I had to be here, of course, so I left. He didn't want the newspapers to ask me—"

Glennis began to interrupt, but Alice added, "And he promised the Union a large sum, five hundred dollars, from Naomi's account if I told everyone here she died from a sudden illness and if we promised not to speak to reporters about her. It was hard, but for so much money I had to agree. He said he'll let me know when I can return to the apartment, after the attention dies down, to gather my things. I hope by next week or so."

"Do you have somewhere to stay?" The flare of her nose suggested Glennis was imagining one of the pungent doorsteps they'd passed on their way.

Alice gestured to a narrow cot against the far wall. "It's not bad. I can make soup and tea on the gas ring and wash up at the basin there. We often—"

At the sound of voices in the outer room, Alice spoke in a rush. "Miss Rankin, please understand me. I showed you these notes only so you'd know Naomi had reasons to take her life, reasons beyond her usual difficulties." She gathered up the papers and pushed them into the envelope. "I'm afraid I must ask a favor of you. I'm absolutely certain Naomi would leave a note. Your brother must have taken it away for some reason. If you could find it and tell me what she wrote—the part for me and the Union—I'd be forever grateful. It would mean the world . . ."

She gripped Glennis's wrist. "She'd want us to know exactly why she did it. She was so strong, so full of life. It would take something terrible, terrible, to defeat her spirit. I wish the world could know why too—know that her battle for justice finally cost her her life—but that's impossible now. Your brother has seen to that. But I want to know, and everyone in our cause who loved her deserves to know her sacrifice. That's enough for me."

"I need to know too," Glennis said. "If Chester's behind this, if he drove her to it, well, as soon as I can get my money out of his hands, I'll tell anyone who'll listen. He may have gotten away with murder, but that doesn't mean he can just waltz—"

The door opened, and Fern and Beatha crowded into the small room with another woman, a rosy-faced matron with a bosom the size of a bread box. Alice slid the envelope into the drawer and locked it as the newcomer engulfed Glennis with more wringing declarations of grief and sympathy.

Ten minutes later Glennis and Julia stood on the smelly pavement outside the Union. They retraced their steps to the stationer's shop without speaking, each absorbed in thought. As they neared Broadway, Glennis turned abruptly and said, "I've been to a place somewhere around here. I think I can find it. We need brandies."

It was six o'clock. They bobbed their way through workers streaming out of office buildings and shops and factories. In the second building they entered, Glennis searched until she found an unmarked third floor door that looked familiar. A man in shirtsleeves with oiled black hair answered the bell, sized up the chance that they might cause trouble and the probable extent of their money, and let them in.

A young man lay flopped over one arm of a sofa, too pickled to move or speak. Another man and two women sat beside him, bleating laughter. Glennis headed toward two stools at the other end of the room. "Martell brandies, if you have it," she told the man who'd admitted them. "Otherwise, gin rickeys with your best stuff."

Glasses of what was purported to be brandy arrived. One sip told Julia there may have been a splash or two of brandy in the vicinity, perhaps even of Martell, but something else predominated, and a heavy hand had watered it well. It stood to reason, sadly enough. Any place that would serve strangers, even poshed-up and thirsty-looking ones, must extract big profits to cover the risk.

Glennis wrinkled her nose. "Weasel pee," she declared before downing a hearty gulp. "Well, now we know. Something's skunky, and I bet a bank wad Chester is behind it. Alice is right. Naomi would never take those tablets by mistake. That means Chester stole her note. It's exactly what he would do. Because it said how impossible he made her life."

She shoved her hat back into place. "I still think he forced her to swallow those tablets. That's murder for sure."

The unhelpful specter of murder reappeared, settling comfortably on Glennis's shoulder. Julia ignored its grin and waited for Glennis's better nature and common sense to prevail. But it was left to her to point out, "We just heard Alice confirm how miserable Naomi was. If she's convinced of suicide, it seems fruitless to harp on about murder, Glennis, however much you'd like to indict your brother. And besides, he didn't go downstairs until after you made that scene at Vivian's party. By then she was already dead."

"So he went down earlier. Or Nolda did. She thinks she's such a cleversticks. The apartment key's at the top of the stairs. Maybe she did it."

For heaven's sake. "While Alice was there?"

"Oh, all right. But even if Chester didn't outright kill her, he did his best to make her life hell, and that has to count for something." She folded her arms, as obstinate as a four-year-old. Chester had to be guilty of something.

Julia rather suspected he was, but leaping to the most outlandish possibility only diverted attention from his less drastic suspicious behavior. "Let's get back to our real aim," she suggested. "We want to find out why and how Naomi died. Everything points to suicide, but then why was there no note? Alice insists she'd have left one. So I'll agree that Chester does seem intent on ensuring no one knows what really happened."

"I'm positive he trousered that note." Glennis downed the last of her so-called brandy and waited for its strange flavor to pass, making a face that mirrored her brother's moue of disgust.

"Very possibly. But I'm sure it's long gone now," Julia said. "He'd destroy it right away."

Glennis brightened. "Not necessarily. I bet he still has it."

The room was filling with boisterous young people, stenographers and clerks from nearby offices enjoying the first fruits of the week's paycheck. Julia set her untouched glass beside Glennis's. "Is that realistic? Why would he save proof of his own deceit?"

Glennis found money in her bag, too much, and tucked it under the glasses. "He's a banker, Julia, a glorified bean counter. He keeps everything, in triplicate if he can. None of us can sneeze without him writing down when the doctor came and how much the medicine cost."

"He keeps files?" An idea formed, risky but perhaps not impossible. "Do you know where? Any chance we could sneak in and have a look?"

"I know exactly where!" Glennis exclaimed. "Come over tomorrow, and we'll beard the old bully right in his study. With you there he can't roar at me. We might even find out if he sent those threats. I bet he did." She pinched Julia's knee with bruising joy. "This is going to be fun."

Julia turned away. She didn't have the heart to warn her friend that truth and justice might not fall neatly into their laps or that their search might not lead in the direction she expected. Of all they'd seen and heard that afternoon, one thing was lodged in Julia's thoughts like a thorn.

It was the one piece of Alice's story that made no sense. On Naomi's desk calendar someone had jotted a reminder for last Friday's meeting with the WPA, the fateful meeting Alice had been forced to attend alone. It was scheduled for eight thirty that evening. Unless Dr. Perry had been wildly mistaken, for some time before Alice had to leave the apartment, Naomi would have already been dead.

CHAPTER 11

"I don't believe you've met my sister," Philip said to the middle-aged couple about to join their table. "Julia, Eddie Kessler and my aunt Arlene."

The assistant police commissioner bristled at his nickname. His wife craned to present a cheek for Philip's and Jack Van Dyne's kisses. "Why aren't you shameful creatures dancing?" She reached for Julia's hand. "With so many young lovelies to choose from. Hello, dear."

The third Vancill sister, Julia cautioned herself, not taken in by the woman's strong grasp and twangy country voice, which brought to mind gingham picnic baskets and peach brown betty. Very unlike Lillian, the oldest sister.

"Exhaustion," Philip said. "All that vivacity wrings me out."

"Tosh. You'll never find a girl just sitting here. I know for a fact your mama taught you better manners."

"For God's sake, let them be," Kessler said. His wife quieted to a dimpling smile.

They sat at a round table toward the rear of a cavernous ballroom in the St. Regis Hotel. Despite lavish decorations, elaborate refreshments, free-flowing liquor, and a crush of wealthy New Yorkers in benevolent finery, the Children's Aide benefit gala was boring. That some of the gaiety and munificence would be dimmed when the primary hosts, the Rankin family, were in mourning was to be expected. Harder to bear for

Julia were Philip's and Jack's resolute disinclinations to dance. Barring the approach of a total stranger, she could only watch the swirling colors, stirred by tall black spoons, on the distant dance floor.

"I'd offer to stagger through the paces with young Julia here," Philip said, "if only to staunch her peevish sighs, but I shouldn't have a clue where to put my hands." He regarded her through a haze of smoke. "She puts a chap in a frightful corner with that indecent getup."

Julia smiled as if he'd paid her a lavish compliment. In a way, he had. He'd been fuming about her appearance, and particularly her gown, from the moment she entered the library to wait for the motorcar to collect them. It was a beautiful thing, her third-best evening frock, a Molyneux of tangerine chiffon. The calf-length hem was cut in points, each glazed in silver beads. A rolled edge of white velvet skimmed across the bodice and over each shoulder, converging behind in a deep V just below her waist. Julia adored backless gowns. Her preferred décolletage bared shoulder and spine, plunging not to bosom but to bum. Philip might grouse like an old fusspot about her choice in clothes, but most men concurred with David, who'd once declared her back, framed in flutes of satin or chiffon or crepe, *magnifique.*

"Seems peculiar," Philip mused, "what passes for ladies' fashion these days. Wasn't long ago a chap pined for a peek of the curvy bits, but a good square mile of cloth intervened. Now girls prance about in a few frayed handkerchiefs, and all we get is bone and gristle. Really, Julia, with a puff of beard and a head cold, you could pass for a lad. Can you honestly think that's to be paraded about?"

After her morning adventure with Glennis, she'd spent the afternoon at an uptown salon. Massaged, painted, and coiffed, she emerged with every inch rendered ready for display. Her hair was freshly shingled, the last few inches of fluff left behind on the salon floor. She found it delicious, head sleek as a seal's beneath pomade and a lattice of pearls. And Philip was dead wrong about her figure; these days curvy bits were for parlor dowagers.

Mrs. Kessler objected on Julia's behalf, as she was meant to. Her lecture on the male's responsibility to admire the female was interrupted by an old man with a pink skull and pendulous jowls: Mr. Rousch, Julia was informed, of the toe-tapping Feeney, Churchman, Kessler, and Rousch. One of the arbiters. He assessed Julia openly, giving no hint of whether he saw her as victim or interloper, before inviting Mrs. Kessler to dance.

Kessler flagged a waiter and ordered a fresh service of Courvoisier. "She's been full of beans all week. Muriel's expecting again. Arlene's off to Cleveland tomorrow, though what help she can be at this point I can't imagine. Just as well. I've been run off my feet with this damnable Dorothy Caine case." Kessler glanced at Julia. "Pardon, Miss Kydd."

Julia waved off the apology. "The papers say the killer has you outfoxed, Mr. Kessler. Is it true?" Apparently Philip's detecting acumen was not so swift and wizardly after all. He'd waved off her inquiries into the alarming headlines—*Killer eludes capture! Police baffled!*

"The usual flummery," Jack said.

Kessler drew heavily on his cigarette. "For once not, unfortunately. The victim's rooms were locked, Miss Kydd, and the doorman swears no one entered until the maid found her body the next day. It's the queerest thing."

"And yet there were—blast!" Philip coughed.

Willard Wright sank into Arlene Kessler's vacant chair. For the second time in less than a week, he joined Philip's table uninvited, though this time he came bearing his own glass, half-full of champagne. He tipped it toward Julia. "Dazzling as ever, Miss Kydd."

"We were just speaking of the Dorothy Caine murder," Jack said.

Wright's goatee spiked. "Delicious. Dead Broadway canary. Negligeed demimonde, midnight assignations, underworld johnnies. Grist for your crime-besotted brain, Kydd. Let's see you solve this puzzler."

"Don't be an ass."

"Locked rooms got you cheesed? Not enough bloody fingerprints?"

"They're making progress," Jack said.

"Half the force is on the lookout," Kessler said. "They're good men, well trained in sound investigative procedures. We'll find the devil."

"Oh, assuredly," Philip said. "Despite all that."

Wright leaned closer, wordlessly goading for more.

Philip eyed him with open dislike. "As I've said before, fingerprints, bloody or otherwise, have little to do with finding criminals. Modern coppers are so busy measuring boot prints and powdering crime scenes they overlook the only evidence worth considering."

Wright looked pleased at having provoked this little lecture. The others might have heard it many times before, but Julia felt obliged. "Which is?"

Kessler snorted and poured himself more brandy.

"The psychological," Philip said. "Subtle aspects of the crime's nature and execution—its distinctive signature, if you will. Determine that and you need merely find the person who matches it. Everything else is for convincing juries."

Kessler looked away with an air of benign endurance. Julia knew a hobbyhorse when she heard one, and this was clearly Philip's. It begged for a swat on the rump.

"But surely circumstances are powerful too," she said. "Any person can be driven to do a terrible thing if the situation is dire enough."

"The beloved motive? Right behind clues in a copper's heart. Just as useless and misleading. I'll grant you most crimes occur for some purpose, powerful or flimsy. I merely claim that how a crime is committed, its particular *style*, is what reveals the culprit's hand. Degas and Renoir could observe the same haystack, but their paintings of it would be discernibly different, regardless of why they wanted to paint the prickly thing. It's the same with crime." Philip scrambled to his feet. "Miss Schoenmacher."

A young thing in mauve satin, like a dozen beauties before her, swanned past their table in hopes of an invitation to dance. This creature was in luck—or perhaps not. Wright rose, circled her waist, and led her away.

They swerved to avoid the returning Aunt Arlene, who took a sip of her husband's brandy and told him he had to the count of three to get off his duff and dance with her.

Jack murmured something as the couple departed, and Philip answered with a canny smile. Off the two men went, just like that, down that private rabbit hole Julia had at first found alarming. Now, after witnessing the mundane drift of those conversations, they seemed simply tedious and rude. She cupped her brandy in both hands and held the fumes close to her face. Her thoughts wandered elsewhere until Philip reached over and prodded her. "Nothing more? My theory leaves you dumb with astonishment?"

Julia tipped her head, feeling the heavy swing of her aquamarine earrings. "Thinking. Of my friend's dead sister."

She had formulated the scheme last evening in the taxi heading uptown after their dubious brandy. Glennis readily agreed, telling Julia to come to the Rankin home before ten this morning. One way or the other, she'd insist Chester meet with her to discuss some urgent detail of her monthly allowance.

He'd rumbled in surprise when Julia followed Glennis into his private office, a book-lined room at the back of the house, overlooking the river, but accepted the story that she'd dropped by to borrow a bracelet for the gala. After quickly glancing around for a typewriting machine—and seeing none—Julia moved to the window, according to plan. While Glennis wheedled her brother to check the receipts, adamant that some dressmaker's charge had been paid twice, Julia gazed out over the back lawns. They spread downhill, toward a brick wall that ran the length of the riverbank. Someone had been raking there recently, clearing the season's first litter of leaves.

"At least look, Chester," Glennis pleaded, her voice ascending to a whine.

"For pity's sake." He dug in his pocket for a set of keys, then unlocked and jerked open a deep drawer. He pulled out a file folder and dropped it on the desk.

Glennis glanced over: *now*. Julia yelped astonishment, pressing both hands against the window glass. "No!"

Chester turned. Glennis ran to the window.

"A man, down there, by the wall, and he just went over. Like that." Julia snapped her fingers. "He was stretching to clip a branch, and then—whoosh. Heels over head. Gone!"

"Henderson!" Glennis's cry raised the melodrama quotient far higher than necessary. "He's been working there all week. Chester, do something!"

He rushed out, bellowing for help. Pounding footsteps disappeared down the corridor as Julia quickly closed the door behind him. Glennis ran to the open desk drawer and pulled out another folder bulging with papers. "I knew hers would be twice as fat as mine."

She spread it open on the desk and pawed through the sheets, disturbing their pristine orderliness. Julia saw Naomi's obituary neatly cut from the *Times*, pinned to a carbon typescript, and a series of receipts, including one from the Oak Grove Crematorium on Long Island.

"Look." Glennis held up a document with two signatures across the bottom, Chester's and Alice Clintock's. A quick scan confirmed what Alice had told them: his payment (termed a donation) of $500 in exchange for Union workers' refusal to speak to reporters about Naomi's death.

"It's got to be here," Glennis said, pushing deeper through the pile. "He's such a tidy old wart. Hey!" She pulled out a single sheet covered on both sides in distinctive script, a bold *Naomi E. Rankin* penned on the verso. "That's it. That's her writing."

The writing sloped acutely, hunkering forward across the page. Long narrow ascenders and descenders jutted into adjacent lines like ribbons in a wind. It would not be easy to read under the best circumstances, even with the specs Julia was loath to produce in public, and the note had clearly been written in haste, or perhaps in pain. Glennis tried to puzzle out the words.

"Esteemed readers," she read aloud and looked up in surprise. Had Naomi hoped the note would be published? Was there an envelope with instructions, or had she assumed Alice would find her body and understand her intentions? No wonder Chester intervened. There was no time to discuss it. Glennis squinted, sounding out words and phrases as they became clear, skipping over the rest. "Denied my birthright . . . outrage . . . under his feet . . . betrayed . . . cannot stop . . . justice . . . never defeat me . . . thousand righteous voices . . . this cruel abuse."

"Sounds like Naomi, all right." Glennis waved the note with unseemly glee. She rolled it into a tight straw and pushed it down the center of her bodice, right into her cleavage. Julia itched for a crack at deciphering it herself, but there wasn't time. "This proves I'm right," Glennis said. "Why would he take her note if he didn't have something to hide?"

Julia glanced out the window. Chester and a maid had reached the wall and hoisted themselves up to balance awkwardly on their waists, calling the gardener's name.

"He's concerned about scandal, Glennis," she felt compelled to say. "That's been clear from the start. It's possible he took the note only to persuade Dr. Perry the suicide was an accident and avoid inquiries. Shady behavior, I agree, but hardly nefarious."

"He's covering up his own guilt. I bet anything he sent those threats too." Glennis began to dig through the file again, searching for some evidence to further damn him.

Julia didn't like or trust the man any more than Glennis did, but rash accusations only weakened their position. "That's an awfully big leap."

"Not if he found out she was going to run for senator. Seeing Naomi in the news for months on end would positively destroy him. Oh!" Glennis's eyes widened. "I just remembered. Nolda and Viv are pals with Senator Wadsworth's wife. They're muckety-mucks in some big organization against the vote. Plus I think they're on the board of the *Woman Patriot*. They'd be almost as mad as Chester."

Julia agreed. Naomi's Senate campaign would be a powerful cause for family apoplexy, but sending her anonymous threats? It seemed rather draconian for a family that valued dignity and decorum above all else.

"Uh-oh." Glennis pointed to a man in belted overalls rushing across the lawn to where Chester and now three others were thrashing about in the riverbank's brush. "There's Henderson. You'd better scram."

Glennis straightened the gaping *Naomi* file and shoveled it back into the drawer. Moving to the window, she waved both arms in sweeping gestures of apology and relief as Julia hurried out, nearly knocking over Nolda in the hall as she rushed toward the taxi waiting beyond the front gate. Glennis would no doubt construct a fabulous explanation for the mistaken scare. Shadows of branches, an empty stomach, all those silly adventure novels. "That Julia," she'd say. "Such a goose."

Philip cleared his throat. More loudly he said, "Naomi Rankin, you mean?"

Julia looked up, startled out of her reverie. He was studying her face. The temptation was powerful. She'd dearly welcome a chance to discuss events and discoveries of the past several days with someone less giddy and hell bent than Glennis. Of Philip's quick mind and perceptive intelligence, there was no doubt, but could she trust him? Would he take her questions seriously or twist and distort them to suit his fancy? There was also the matter of respecting the Rankins' privacy. Given their duplicity, she decided she was entitled to some of her own.

"I attended the family memorial service," she said. "The situation is not as simple as you might imagine."

Philip's left eyebrow rose, and he glanced at Jack.

"Assure me you won't breathe a word of this, especially to your police chums. It's none of their concern or ever likely to be. Consider it merely, as you like to say, a conundrum. Promise me," she added, as Nolda Rankin had neglected to insist.

Both men nodded and shifted closer.

"All right, then. It's this. Naomi Rankin died of an overdose of morphine tablets. The family believes—or at least they assert—her suicide was accidental, and they managed to get the detail omitted from the public record. The tale in her obituary that she died of a brief illness was fabricated to avoid a scandal."

Philip sat back, cradling his brandy exactly as Julia had done. "And your reason for sharing this morsel?"

"There are differing accounts of the hours surrounding Naomi's death. The going assumption is that she succumbed to chronic pain and despair."

"Not to mention remorse for years of disturbing the nation's peace. That alone would stagger a lesser mortal."

Julia gave this remark the withering glance it invited. "Others think she was driven by malicious pressure. That she took the tablets but under coercion."

"Murder, then, by consent? How civilized. Any chance the fatal dose was actually administered by another? Or that she died from some other cause?"

"Impossible to know. They had her cremated."

Philip smiled.

Exactly. "So I find myself wondering how your precious theory might apply. Did Naomi freely choose to take her life, or was she, in effect, killed, manipulated by some powerful external force?"

Philip's cigarette smoldered close to his fingers. "Intriguing. Does my theory work in reverse? Can the nature of the crime—as the law insists we regard suicide—be deduced from the identity of the criminal?

Well, let's think. What do we know of the so-called criminal? In this case we know plenty." He ground out his expiring cigarette and lit another. "Naomi Rankin reveled in drama. She flung herself in the way of every billy stick and handcuff she could find, and yammered loudest when she could cry oppression. Just the sort of self-destructive traits that point to suicide. Afraid I'd put my money on that."

"But she endured great pain and degradation," Julia said. "She survived weeks of force-feeding during the hunger strikes. Doesn't that show a great tolerance of pain and a fierce will to live?"

"Or she resisted in order to spotlight the jailers' mistreatment. Classic suicidal psychology—dramatize others' abuse in the most graphic fashion possible. Naomi Rankin was nothing if not pleased at the maelstroms she kicked up."

This sounded like Winterjay's self-consoling eulogy. "That's vile, Philip. She could as easily be praised as heroic. The trouble with your theory is that it's all semantics. You see what you wish and label it to suit your purposes. Psychology, my foot. I don't know what particular menace coerced her, but it must have been frightfully powerful to defeat her will to live. So strong, in fact, that I suspect Naomi's death was closer to murder than suicide, regardless of whose palm carried the tablets to her mouth."

Julia paused. What had she just said? Did she suspect that? Hadn't she repeatedly cautioned Glennis against racing to that very conclusion? They were a long way still from knowing the true cause of Naomi's death. Chester's subterfuge to obscure that truth was hardly grounds for assuming she was murdered. Neither, though, did it preclude the idea. At this point all was still speculation, and as such, well then, yes, she stood by her words.

"Horsefeathers." Philip's face was radiant with delight. "You're merely back to the motives claptrap. Motives for suicide abound no less than for murder. We're all awash with motives for crimes of every stripe. Naomi Rankin's array must have been stupendous. What varies is how we respond."

"That's blaming the victim," Julia said. "It's appalling, the worst sort of—"

"I propose a wager." Philip set his brandy on the table. "If you can show she was murdered, I will abandon my objections to your inheritance. If not, if indeed she took her life willingly—with or without a collaborator—you cede it to me. Just between us. What say you?"

Jack launched himself forward. "You're mad! That money's nothing to joke about. You can't do this."

"What do you say, sister?"

"I'm thinking."

"Stop!" Jack hissed, bringing glances from nearby tables. His cheeks flooded to the beet-dark color of his hair. "Both of you. This is folly. Philip! Julia! Have some sense."

"Julia?"

"I accept." How could she not meet Philip's bravado with her own? Jack might be easily panicked into squeals, but Julia could match her brother's mettle ounce for ounce—that they were made of the same stuff was the whole point—and would deny him the satisfaction of so much as a blink. Another bluff move in his absurd game of sibling tug-of-war wouldn't faze her; she could sustain the farce as fearlessly as he. She had him dead to rights by law (yes, Jack, she knew); why cower from yet another facetious jest? This time she would play the game too, eye to steady eye.

"God Almighty!" Jack jumped up with more vigor than Julia thought him capable. He pulled her to her feet in the direction of the dance floor. "That suit's a legal matter. You can't simply wager it away. Before you slay each other like perfect idiots—" The thought sheared away as the Kesslers returned.

"At last, Jack!" Aunt Arlene exclaimed. "Thought I'd have to stick a pin in you."

She guided into view a young woman in a frock every bit as revealing as Julia's, but who had cleavage to speak of and a dress that did so eloquently. Mrs. Kessler nudged her forward. "Look who I found, Philip. You remember George and Clara Swetnam's youngest, Brenda?"

He graciously escorted Brenda Swetnam away toward the dance floor, hesitating not one jot about where to place his hand.

Jack was a different story. "The partners will never recognize this insanity," he said as he commenced a staid two-step.

"No matter. Philip and I have agreed."

The muscles in Jack's jaw twitched and stammered. His guiding hand hovered just above her back. Poor man. He couldn't quite bring himself to touch her *dos magnifique.*

CHAPTER 12

As their third dance slowed to an end, Jack's feet grew more cumbersome and his manners more noble. The poor man's energy was depleted, at least for Julia's company. She spotted the Rankins' table beside the central dais, where Glennis looked to be drowning in a squall of black silk and feathers. "Please, Jack. I must visit the ladies'. You should get back before Mrs. Kessler thinks we've eloped." At this he stumbled outright, and Julia turned to join the Rankins.

Weaving through the crush of couples, Julia saw Glennis twine her arm through Russell Coates's and move with him toward the refreshment alcove. She slowed, uncertain whether she should follow them or contrive some other errand, when she heard a low "Miss Kydd?" It was Edward Winterjay, beckoning from the Rankins' table with a two-fingered wave.

Vivian sat beside him, her back to the table, absorbed in conversation with three young women standing behind her. Nolda Rankin was seated at his other side, bent over his arm as if sharing some secret. At his abrupt rise to greet Julia, she stood too. Winterjay's invitation seemed an amiable courtesy, but Mrs. Rankin's coldly narrowed eyes as Julia neared made it clear she was, once again, not welcome. She eyed Julia's bright dress and shining, fresh-cropped hair. "Glennis is not available, Miss Kydd. I'm sorry to disappoint you," she said tersely, "but we're in mourning here. You young people may not fully grasp the gravity of our bereavement."

"I'm sure she understands, Nolda," Winterjay said. "I merely wanted to thank her for helping Glennis cope this past week. I believe we owe Miss Kydd no small measure of gratitude."

Nolda conceded with a brittle smile. "Yes, of course. We are grateful, Miss Kydd, for your comforting Glennis and respecting our privacy. You brought us up short last weekend, as you must know, and—"

"There's nothing to worry about, Nolda," Winterjay said. He wrapped an arm across her shoulders. She covered his hand with hers—acknowledgment? gratitude?—before moving away to settle beside Chester at the far end of the table, where in their solemn finery they resembled minor royalty receiving condolences from the long line of sympathizers.

Winterjay guided Julia into Nolda's empty chair, his hand warm against her skin. How refreshing, the confident touch of a man not the least flustered by the cut of her frock. In fact, he paid her the perfect compliment of an appreciative gaze. Neither leering nor fatuous, his was the sort of reassuring smile most young women might count on from an affectionate older brother or cousin.

"Glennis just left with Coates," Winterjay said. "She's dying to dance, but a stroll's the best she can do under the circumstances. I'm afraid I'm bound by the same stricture, or I'd have cut in on Van Dyne some time ago. I must be content merely to say you look lovely tonight, Miss Kydd."

Winterjay was handsome in the clean-jawed, clear-eyed way Julia preferred. He was roughly David's age: past the urgency of grasping, hot-breathed youth. When seen at close range, threads of gray showed behind his ears, and the grooves beside his eyes remained after a smile had passed. As with most men, evening kit became him enormously. Julia noted the smooth muscles of his neck and shoulders and smelled the bracing scent of shaving tonic. A skilled lover, she thought. She felt the twitching antennae of nearby females in the crowd; curious gossip— *Who is she?*—would fly soon amid the lipstick and powder in the ladies'.

"I meant what I said about the family's gratitude," he said. "Glennis tells me you've been a good friend to her this past week."

Did he know of their outing to Naomi's Union headquarters? Julia answered cautiously. "I think it pains her to realize how little she knew her sister."

Winterjay nodded. "For years Naomi was so busy with her work that none of us saw her much. She was rarely in New York and then seldom at home."

"I understand she was a woman of great passions."

He smiled. "Naomi was nothing if not passionate. She loved arguments—she invited them, relished them. As you may know, my wife disagreed profoundly with her, though in many ways their objective was the same. Most people failed to recognize that, unfortunately including Naomi."

He explained. "They're both great champions of women. As am I. My wife is as fierce an opponent of those who disparage women's gifts as Naomi was. They simply differed on what they thought the best course to pursue."

Vivian Winterjay stirred, and the circle around her receded. Before another could form, she laid a manicured hand on her husband's knee and greeted Julia. She wore a gown of midnight blue under black lace. Whether it was the dress or the intervening days, Vivian's pregnancy seemed more pronounced. One hand rested on the mound like a priest bestowing peace.

"I understand you're active in women's politics, Mrs. Winterjay," Julia said.

"It's a vital issue," Vivian said, "for all of society, not just women. And please, do call me Vivian."

"I take it you and Naomi were opponents?" Perhaps it was rude to force the issue, but Julia accepted the risk. This was important to understand.

Vivian smiled. "We agreed on several fundamentals. Our differences, however, were more lively. They were certainly better known. Naomi loved making scenes, the more public the better, a preference I found impossibly vulgar."

"I'd like to hear about those differences," Julia said. "If you wouldn't mind explaining."

Winterjay pushed away from the table to rest an arm across the back of his wife's chair. Had he heard the subject discussed a hundred times before? A thousand? Was the answer always unwavering, or did he listen for minor embellishments and variations?

"Not at all. Nothing would please me more," Vivian said. "It's simple, really. You see, Naomi believed equality was best achieved by eliminating legal distinctions between men and women. She thought women should be treated no worse and no better than men in all respects. At first blush this may sound fair and liberating, but in fact it would subject women to all sorts of new burdens and obligations. Would you have girls serving as soldiers and priests? Cutting timber? Digging mines?"

No reply was expected. She offered to send Julia a clipping of an article she'd recently published in the *Woman Patriot*. "I believe the natural distinctions between the sexes cannot be overturned. Rather than force women to compete with men on their turf, I want better recognition for the work we do best—making good homes for our families, raising informed and dutiful children, nursing the ill, and comforting the poor. Instead of hiring more girls into factory jobs, for example, we need to protect them from that crippling work altogether."

Julia nodded vaguely, trying to imagine what Alice or Fern or Beatha at the Union would say in response. Vivian's ideal posited every woman at the center of a home and family, presuming for her a husband (or father or brother) with an income sufficient to shelter her from need.

What of women without such a patron, either by choice or by fate? Or those whose menfolk offered not shelter but neglect or abuse? Naomi must have posed those very questions, challenging her sister at every turn. No wonder theirs was a fractious family. Naomi's own personal rejection of such "shelter" must have galled Vivian badly.

Vivian smiled again. "That's why I opposed the vote. I feel it's better to leave sordid civic and legal matters to the men, who are made of sterner stuff, and concentrate on those domestic arenas where we women excel. It's a more sensible equality, a social partnership really, with men and women contributing different talents."

She smoothed her frock over her abdomen, a large emerald wedding ring flashing against the dark fabric. "Naomi simply refused to see. She scorned the things I call blessings. I have everything she forfeited in life, you see. I have a husband who's widely regarded and eminent in his field and who's given me two precious children—soon three. She could win all the political battles in the world and still not have half so much to cherish. It made her bitterly jealous, though she'd deny it to the skies."

"Maybe not jealous, darling," Winterjay said. "Frustrated, yes, but I think she really did prefer her life to ours. She put a great store in her lady comrades."

"But how could she? I have to believe a true woman's heart beat under all that fierce talk. It pained me that she spoke so harshly of marriage, when living without it doomed her to such a barren life."

Barren? Alice and Fern and Beatha deemed Naomi's life purposeful beyond measure. Did Vivian consider Julia's life barren as well? What would she make of her beautiful, promising infant Capriole?

"Then we should admire her strength all the more," Winterjay said, "for what she sacrificed. She was in many ways a remarkable woman."

Vivian gave her husband's thigh a soft slap. "You keep saying that. I swear you're incapable of speaking ill of anyone, even someone who gave us as much trouble as Naomi did. But you're right. It's time to forgive our little skirmishes. She's my sister. How could I not love her in the end?"

"Even when I'm sloshed?" Glennis loomed behind her sister. She slumped forward, forearms denting Vivian's shoulders. Winterjay took the martini glass dangling from Glennis's hand and set it on the table, a full arm's length away.

"I want to meet that brother of yours, Julia. For a drink. Can't dance." Glennis scowled, boss eyed, at Chester.

"I think Glennis needs another parade around the room," Winterjay said, pushing back his chair. As he led Glennis away, she blew Julia a kiss and winked grotesquely at Coates, wondering loudly where her martini had gotten to.

Coates rubbed his arm where Glennis had gripped it. "She's a good kid, but I thought my arm was about to fall off. Winterjay's a sport to lead her round this time."

"We'll take her home soon, Russell," Vivian said. "These evenings are so exhausting."

Julia tried to smile but felt wretchedly unweary herself. After a dismal week of solitary evenings (Philip apologizing lamely each time he hurried out to meet Jack or Kessler, likely at one of their clubs), another night that ended before midnight was too disappointing to consider, especially dressed as she was. She was relieved, and a little alarmed that her thoughts might have been obvious, when Coates asked her to dance. Vivian shooed them off with a matronly blessing.

Coates had no difficulties with her dress. He was respectable on his feet, a pleasant surprise. Book men, in her experience, were seldom good dance partners. His conversation was blameless, polite, and respectful—restricted to territory they had both traveled countless times with countless partners on countless such occasions. Effortless and inoffensive, he spoke with the same deceptive detachment she'd observed as he surveyed the Rankins' bookshelves. It allowed him to move through the world while his mind remained masked, preoccupied with private thoughts. Julia didn't mind this retreat—she often indulged in its freedoms herself—but she did wonder at its cause. She detected something ponderous, heavy.

"I gather you're fond of books, Mr. Coates," Julia said. "I watched you after Naomi's service last Sunday. One bibliophile can usually spot another."

The mask disappeared. "Russell, please." He smiled. "I do collect. Modern firsts mostly, poetry, essays, some fiction. Conrad, Hardy, Stevenson. Americans too. Hergesheimer. Aiken. Elinor Wylie and Stephen Benét. I've kept up pretty well on Christopher Morley. He has scads of ephemera out there, but as he's an acquaintance, I get good leads. Do you know his work?"

Julia admitted she knew little of Morley (a darling of American collectors, for reasons that eluded her) and said her own passions ran more to modern fine printing. Not every collector cared for new books made to meticulous standards of handcraftsmanship, but enough did to embolden her to mention her own typographic venture. He'd never heard of her Capriole Press, of course, but his reaction—stopping midglide with a robust *how interesting*—sent her gabbling on about Baskerville types and Hester Sainsbury's engravings and the droll new kid-nymph pressmark she was eager to debut on her next chapbook, contents as yet undecided.

The pace of their dancing fluctuated wildly. His astonishment that a woman would launch a fine imprint was immensely gratifying. She wasn't alone in that endeavor but very near. Serious women bibliophiles were rare enough. He gaped, smiled, and mentioned that a younger subset of the city's Colophon Club was meeting next Thursday evening. Would she care to join him for an informal supper and incorrigible book talk? He could show her a bit of the city afterward too, if she liked.

The prospect pleased Julia absurdly, and she agreed with unseemly speed. They lapsed into a companionable silence. As the music slowed,

Julia thought quickly to bridge the interval to another dance. "Glennis tells me you've known the Rankins for years."

He nodded. "My father was old Alford Rankin's attorney and a close friend. I grew up with Chester and Naomi. There are gaps, you know. Vivian is some years younger than Naomi, and Glennis came along well after that. At any rate, we oldest three were once thick as thieves."

"I thought Naomi and Chester detested each other."

"Not until after college. That's when Chester went into the bank and Naomi marched off to Washington to change the Constitution. I joined my father's law firm and inherited the Rankins to keep me busy."

"And I'm sure they do." Julia phrased her next comment delicately. "They seem an interesting family."

He reared back to gauge this comment, then firmly resettled his hand as the orchestra resumed.

"The more I hear about Naomi Rankin," Julia added, "the more I wish I knew her."

Some moments elapsed. Perhaps she had penetrated to the source of Russell's disquiet. If he'd grown up as a second brother to Naomi, he must have known her far better than Glennis did. "She was extraordinary," he finally said. "Nothing ordinary about her."

"Was she outspoken even as a child?"

"She was always doing whatever was forbidden, especially if Chester and I were allowed and she wasn't. We tried our first cigars together. It nearly killed her, but she was not about to cough until one of us did. As soon as I gagged, she practically exploded, but then she declared it a kick and started keeping a stash in her bedroom, mainly because her father swore he'd thrash her if he ever caught her with a cigarette. She thought it was fine fun that he hadn't mentioned cigars and took to the things like a Tweed boss. That was Naomi all over." He laughed softly.

"You liked her?"

"Very much. But with time it got harder. She was always sparring with her father, and I had to please him, of course. Then she and Chester couldn't draw breath in the same room without one of them going into a rage. It was pretty grim for the rest of us."

"I did notice his temper."

"You mean the scene with Glennis? She chafes under his heavy hand, that's all."

"She told me about her father's will," Julia said to ease his burden of discretion.

"Wills often speak loudly from beyond the grave. But Glennis is a strong girl. She'll figure something out. In fact, I gather she already has."

Julia answered with care. "She is in rather a hurry to get down the aisle." Did Russell have any idea how prominently he figured in Glennis's efforts? At least occasionally. Her list of possible alternatives to Archie varied from day to day, with candidates rising and falling in favor on whims so comical, so utterly detached from actual romantic stirrings, that even Glennis laughed at every update. Russell Coates was currently in distant third or fourth place, trailing not only Wall Street Warren but a discarded former fiancé named Lyle, who was apparently rethinking his decision to pursue mission work in Madagascar.

"Have you met this Archie she's all loopy for?" he asked.

"Oh yes." Julia wanted to say more, to produce the usual bland compliment for Glennis's erstwhile intended, but she could not muster a single positive word. There were a hundred Archies these days, clogging the clubs and racetracks and weekend shooting parties all across England: minor aristocracy of the most depleted kind, with only crumbling estates and cobwebbed pedigrees to call their own. Not three wits among the lot. Dull as lemmings, and the most stupid were the most opinionated. At least Archie was too slack to have opinions. As one who smiled "righty-ho" at virtually anything one said, he wouldn't be bothered by what Glennis got up to. She was right: she'd quickly reduce him to signing over checks, probably from some distance away, and no doubt commence another list of favored admirers, fantastical and harmless as ever, to regale her new British friends.

A tremor at Julia's silence began deep in Russell's shoulders. "I see," he said. "A modern bride."

Julia leaned her ear against his jaw, blending her tremor with his, and her gown and salon extravagance began to do their work. She lost track of the Rankins and imagined—hoped—Philip and Jack had made their exit long ago. If Russell Coates had any other business to conduct that evening, it was abandoned. The dance floor grew less crowded, the music more pensive, the room more shadowed. Here was a promising fellow, she thought as they drifted in aimless arcs. A book man, that was the first delight. A fine dancer. Easy to talk with. Some sense of humor. And there was no denying the ageless conversation that had started up between her bones and his. She felt each rise and fall of his chest and the easy stretch of his fingertips as they slid beneath the rim of her dress. Just a fraction. Just enough.

Until, with a flare of trumpets and stage lights, the orchestra announced its evening over. To Julia's surprise, Glennis and Winterjay remained, alone, at the Rankin table. When Glennis began to wave madly, Winterjay caught her arm midair and guided it to the table. She was more sozzled than ever.

"You have a devoted friend," Russell said under his breath as they returned to the table. His palm lingered across Julia's back before he promised to telephone early in the week.

"Julia! I need to tell you something!" Glennis stood and pitched sidelong into Winterjay. "Isn't Russell dishy?" She swerved away for a wet belch. "So's your dishy brother. The dishy ginger one too."

It all returned to Julia in a whoosh. Naomi's mysterious death. Philip's claims to her money.

"Uh-oh." Glennis slapped a hand over her mouth and stumbled to untangle the hem of her frock from the chair's leg.

Pulled along toward the ladies', Julia had time for only a quick nod to the men. These were Volstead days. Everyone understood.

CHAPTER 13

A brisk tattoo sounded on Julia's bedroom door. One eye told her the light was still murky, the hour ungodly. Christophine? She jerked her head out of the pillow and collapsed back into the warm linen. New York. Philip. Monday morning.

"Pardon for the early hour, miss," came Mrs. Cheadle's voice from the hall. "Mr. Kydd said to rouse you. You've been summoned to the lawyer's offices this morning. Ten sharp."

This woke Julia. Cold legal reality dispelled the weekend's pleasure. So soon? Just one week? She'd expected they would need at least twice that to arrive at a judgment. Her feet churned to find her mules. She pulled the clock to her face. Eight thirty. She took the coffee Mrs. Cheadle handed through the door and clutched it as she thought of how to ready herself in a scant hour. This was hardly an auspicious start to the most momentous day of her visit, if not of her future life.

She had the satisfaction of reaching the vestibule first—bathed, dressed, and composed. She wore her favorite frock of apricot silk piqué with a panel of fine pleats along her left hip and, in perverse, vindicating (she trusted) logic, another felt cloche from Mme Hamar's shop. Philip appeared a moment later, no less confidently arrayed. He adjusted his necktie in the hall mirror, quirked a smile, and turned to her with an extended elbow. She took it coolly, and they descended together to their fate.

Jack was waiting in the reception lounge when they arrived. "They're ready," he said. "It took less time than anyone expected."

A valve stuttered in Julia's heart. Was this good news or bad? Jack's face was guarded as he showed them into a windowless conference room. Its only furniture was a large round table. The firm's three active partners—Feeney, Churchman, and Rousch—rose. The table was bare except for two plain envelopes.

Churchman spoke as soon as they were seated. "We understand you've made the trip from London solely for this purpose, Miss Kydd, and we naturally wish to inconvenience you as briefly as possible. But we want also to assure you both that, despite the speedy decision, we gave this matter of disputed inheritance our utmost deliberation. We reached a unanimous decision, which you can read in detail for yourselves." He gestured for Jack to hand Philip and Julia each one of the envelopes. She hated to see her hand tremble as she took it.

Philip balanced his envelope on edge across his knee. "Our hearts are aflutter," he said. "Can't someone just blurt it out?"

"Yes, of course," Churchman said. "You can read the full deliberations, but in a nutshell we found yours the position with better merit, Mr. Kydd."

Julia liked to think she made neither sound nor gesture, but later she could not be certain. Her face was as shadowed as her hat brim could make it, but even so she fought to govern every muscle that might betray her. She had understood there was always a slim chance this might happen, of course, and she considered herself prepared for even such a monstrous outcome. In that moment, however, she realized how utterly she had done no such thing. Her only consolation was in preventing others from realizing it too.

Churchman's voice resonated as if from a deep cave. "My younger partners have only a vague recollection of your father, but I knew him well. He came to Kessler Senior and me in the early days of our practice, back in the eighties, before you were born, Philip, and for a time his business was a mainstay for us. I remember the day he and your mother first brought you into the office and the care he took over that first will."

"First will? There was a later one?" Julia's voice was a masterpiece of dignity.

Churchman removed his spectacles and polished them with a handkerchief. "That question has haunted me for years, Miss Kydd. I worked with your father in early '06 during those last few months of his life. He wanted to make a few key revisions, which I'm not free to disclose. But when I brought him the final version to sign, he said he had some things to discuss privately—I assumed with his estranged wife, your mother—and he promised to get it signed, witnessed, and filed within the week. That was nearly a month before he died, so I naturally assumed he did so while I was away traveling in Virginia. I was as surprised as anyone when the only will we found in his papers after his death was the one from 1890."

"Which named only Philip," Rousch said.

Churchman frowned and repositioned his spectacles. "Your mother was gracious about it, Miss Kydd, remarkably so, I thought. She insisted it didn't matter, claiming she could provide for herself and for you through her own family's wealth."

"Until her death, in fact," Rousch interjected, "we all understood Milo Kydd's final wishes to be just as his will stated, with Philip his sole surviving beneficiary."

"The mystery of your father's last-minute hesitation seemed immaterial, yes," Churchman continued. "But when your mother died suddenly, not only intestate but abroad, it was of enormous significance. With war imminent we couldn't ship you off to relatives in Sweden, the family to whom her fortune reverted, and you were just thirteen, I believe, far too young to be left on your own. The Kydd family was not very sympathetic to your plight, I'm sorry to say, so we were in a proverbial pickle. That's when it was suggested, I forget by whom, that the somewhat ambiguous language of 'future issue yet unborn' might be construed to include you. Perhaps Milo felt it did, we reasoned. Perhaps that's why he decided revisions were not necessary after all. At the time, it seemed the only humane conclusion. We named Philip as your guardian and then trustee, and everyone was relieved to have you off our consciences, if I may speak plainly."

"Mr. Kydd's recent suit, however, allowed us to revisit the matter," Rousch said. The reminder of Philip's unprovoked assault stung, and Julia returned her gaze to her lap. "We did our best, despite the significant problem of some key documents missing."

"I don't believe we need go into that, Arthur," Churchman said.

Rousch ignored him. "I thought it prudent to send someone down to Saint Barthélemy to see if a proper marriage license could be found, but I was overruled."

At this Julia did make a noise, despite herself, as did Miss Baxter, who had slipped into the room with her stenographer's tablet. It was a pernicious old rumor, the insinuation that Julia's parents had not been legally married, stemming from their rather impetuous decision to take their vows in such relatively obscure, if lushly tropical, circumstances.

"Yes, you were overruled," Churchman said. "If I may continue? As I was saying, I knew Milo Kydd well and found him to be scrupulous to a fault. His will was much in his thoughts during his last months. He had both time and presence of mind to sign and return the revised document if he so wished. In the end, it's now clear to me, to all of us, that if he had intended to include Miss Kydd as legal beneficiary to his estate, he would have made that intention explicit. That he did not, that he left the earlier will unaltered, seems now the best possible evidence in young Mr. Kydd's favor. We are naturally sorry to disappoint you, Miss Kydd." The voice swung toward her. "We will do everything in our power to ensure a smooth transition for you." A low buzz circled the table, a despicable swarm of courtesy tinged with pity.

A smooth transition. That was rich. Julia lifted her chin. Did they expect gratitude for easing her plummet into poverty?

Philip tried to catch her eye. "Yes, thank you for your scrupulous work in this matter, which I'm sorry had to be addressed at all." Julia turned away at this appalling hypocrisy. "We appreciate your discretion and disinterest."

The buzz deepened into the usual commotion of men congratulating themselves. Julia rose and walked calmly from that stifling room, ignoring the outstretched hands, the consoling smiles. She reached the elevator before footsteps sounded behind her. She expected Jack, kind to the end, but it was Philip's voice that said, "Hold on half a tick. May I join you?"

She ground her thumb against the button to summon the machine.

"Damned awkward, I know, but we have a great deal more to discuss."

"Discuss? You have mocked, ignored, or challenged nearly every word I've uttered since the day I arrived."

"Not true. You must—" he began as the elevator arrived. Julia stepped inside, nodded to the attendant, and the gate clanked shut.

"I must find some air before I suffocate," she said. The door closed, all further solicitude stalled in Philip's silent, rounded mouth.

❧

An hour later Julia could not say how she'd arrived at the table where she sat, or even where in the city she was. All she knew was that through the street window the tea shop had looked commonplace enough, the sort of dim and listless place where she might sit in peace for however long it took to consider what had happened and what she should do next.

She pushed aside the untouched tomato aspic she'd ordered to justify her midday table and curled both hands around a teacup, turning the chipped rim away. The tea tasted like ditchwater, but that was the least of her concerns.

Everything, every single thing she'd believed about her life, had just evaporated like steam from an angry kettle. Without her half of the income from her father's estate, how was she to live? She pummeled the question over and over in her mind. She must face this disaster with cold, practical sense. Sentiment was pointless now, a luxury she soon could not afford. (*Luxury? Afford?* The old cliché's metaphor had never registered before, but now it stung.)

Her heart, however, outmuscled her will. To her surprise, she had fallen into a more devastating abyss: the certain knowledge, stark and utter, that her father had disowned her. There were no clerical errors, no oversights, no muddled semantics. She had been six years old, his only daughter, a child who dreamed of his lap, who memorized the smell of his smoking jacket that hung on a hook in the library, and he had chosen to erase her from his life. Julia's teeth dug into her lip, but it was too late. She turned to the dingy green wall, a blur of veined plaster, and wept. A jilted shopgirl could not have seemed more forlorn.

Fresh hot tea appeared by her elbow, with two clean if thread-bare napkins. She could not lift her head to thank the waitress, but no kindness had ever seemed greater. She was powerless until the anguish subsided.

No. She would not wallow. The faded green wall slowly emerged in dubious clarity, with its long-dried tea splats and tiny thumbprints of butter and jam. Enough of that. She had more pressing concerns.

By the time she set down the empty teacup, a vague outline of options had formed. Without her half of the Kydd estate, income from which she now received through Philip's trusteeship—for precisely seven more days—her financial situation was dire. She could not support herself, much less Christophine, on the occasional monies she received from her uncles in Skåne—a decent but unpredictable and wholly discretionary sum. All right then, what could she do?

She could protest the verdict. She could hire independent counsel and take the matter to the real courts for a proper judge to decide.

Possible vindication made this scenario alluring but only for a moment. With what funds would she hire this lawyer? The case would have to proceed in New York, and she could neither live under Philip's roof nor bear the expense of a hotel for the months, possibly years, a lawsuit might involve. Worst of all, a judge's decision might be no different. This was a poor option.

What about those Swedish farms? The land had belonged to Jordahls since 1753. Could she ask her three uncles to break up their holdings and sell some of it to provide her a sustaining income? Could she ask them to evict their tenants? The idea was repugnant. So was presenting herself on her relations' doorsteps as a refugee hoping for a place at the table. She set both possibilities in the category of *only if starving*.

Irony stung at a third option. She could marry. Philip's cynical suggestion the other morning in Jack's office was the most obvious and probably the easiest course, though more abhorrent for that reason. Was it just a week ago that she'd puzzled over Naomi Rankin's refusal to take a husband for financial expedience? Now she understood such reluctance acutely. That every day women everywhere faced this truth—that their best chance for a comfortable life depended on attracting a reliable husband—was no comfort. She tried to imagine herself emulating Glennis, affecting delight at every insipid antic of some Archie Allthorp. Perhaps she could thump Helen Adair in the shins and demand she divorce David. To be reduced to either absurdity was an odious prospect. In Julia's head a new small voice, the voice of a woman without money, scolded her for such arrogant niceties. Pride and a free spirit might be universally admired in a man, but they now joined the list of luxuries Julia soon could not afford.

Was independence a luxury reserved for the wealthy? With money of her own, freedom to live as she chose had been a privilege, she now saw, not the simple choice she'd so blithely pronounced it. Now she understood it was an either/or equation. She could be wealthy—by marrying well—or she could remain independent, so long as she could earn her own way. There was the true choice. Julia made pretty noises of being modern, but working to achieve what one valued was vastly more modern than exercising a privilege.

Could she, Julia wondered. Could she earn her own way? Naomi Rankin had managed well enough on her own. *(Well enough?)* Plenty of women chose to make their own course, to earn their own keep. Julia could seek employment. There must be something respectable she could do for wages.

The hours she loved best were those spent with her Albion and at the typecases, in the painstaking work that was her Capriole Press. But Capriole was unsuited for (and likely incapable of) producing reliable income. In fact, fine printing itself was another luxury, she realized with a sharp twist under her ribs, and one she could not afford to continue.

Her jaw stiffened at the prospect of conceding yet another cornerstone of happiness. It was usually a luxury, yes. But couldn't there be an exception? Surely a few fine presses came close to paying their way. Francis Meynell's Nonesuch showed promise in that direction (never minding the production compromises). The Gibbingses were determined to make a go of it with Golden Cockerel. What about those Californians Bruce Rogers spoke of? It would mean rethinking a great deal. She would need to work very hard, develop her skills (and get considerable help), take more courses at Camberwell, cultivate important authors and illustrators, lay in stock for sizable editions, find ways to catch and hold more collectors' eyes.

The list came to an abrupt halt. All of that took money. Without it, she had no hope of attempting to earn a living with Capriole. The days of patrons and benefactors were over. Her best bet in that vein remained the next-closest thing, a husband.

All right, she lacked the resources to make Capriole profitable. What else? Her education had been indifferent, designed mainly to ensure she wouldn't embarrass the family name—a name she'd now gladly forfeit in exchange for better schooling. She was passably knowledgeable about only two things, art and books. Perhaps she could get a job as a bookshop or gallery assistant. She pictured Elsa Mowrey and Martin Hepplewhite, David's assistants, and registered a new despair.

How had she not thought of it before? Employment of any kind would scuttle her understanding with David. He needed a lover with fine things and fine manners, someone who moved in the same effort-less circles as he did and whose flair and spirit would add luster to his own. Their affections were deep and sincere but also—mutually—opportune. The relationship would shift drastically if her wealth did not match his; it would founder by Christmas, she was certain, one of the many wreckages of her diminished state.

In truth any work she was fit for paid little more than a pittance and, to a woman, half a pittance. At best she might afford cheap tea, meat once a week, and a bedsit in Bethnal Green. The prospect was as bleak as marriage to a dullard like Archie.

All impulse to tears had passed. This was too important for self-pity. Marriage or employment? It came down to a choice between pragmat-ics and principles, between comfort and dignity. Had Naomi Rankin cowered in a dreary tea shop and grappled with this very choice? Could Julia also choose the harder course?

She recrossed her legs as a new thought occurred.

She tried to recall the exact terms of the wager Philip had proposed. It might have been a jest, but it had been offered and accepted, and she could hold him to it now. Jack's howl of protest was ample witness should Philip try to renege. If she could prove Naomi Rankin's suicide was in fact murder, Philip had promised to withdraw his claim to her half of their father's estate. She hesitated. Was this crass even to con-sider? No, she decided, the wager didn't alter her desire to discover the true story of Naomi's death. What harm could there be if now some more tangible consequences depended on the outcome? Naomi, Julia dared to believe, would approve.

It wouldn't be easy. Apart from Glennis's blind determination to blame Chester, there was little hard evidence to suggest foul play. And yet several details—the stolen note, Alice Clintock's schedule discrepancies, the anonymous threats, Naomi's erratic health and sudden illness—begged for explanation. Whether they pointed to murder, Julia couldn't yet tell, but she now had more reason than ever to find out. Winning the wager would not be an easy path to reversing her personal calamity, but it was relatively palatable and the only one to which she could devote immediate energies. It swelled into a great new incentive to learn the truth.

Julia turned to the wall to repair her face. She slipped a bill under the rim of her cold teacup. The waitress was helping two young mothers settle their children around a table. Julia gave her a small smile as she passed, pleased that she could thank her with a generous purse, as long as it was still hers to command.

Halfway down the street she found a hotel with a small but clean telephone lounge and asked to be connected to the Rankins' number. Glennis let out a boisterous cheer when Julia asked if she was free tomorrow to continue looking into Naomi's death. "You bet I am! What do you have in mind?"

In that instant Julia decided not to tell her friend her own disastrous news. Not yet. She needed all her strength for the task at hand; there was none to spare for weathering the hullabaloo with which Glennis greeted all news, good or bad.

Her idea was barely formed, but it might be enough to move them forward. At several points during the luncheon with the Rankins, Julia had wondered why Chester had called in old Dr. Perry that night. Why would he summon a doctor so clearly past his prime, if not to muddle the fellow's mind and trick him into not calling the police, as any clear-thinking doctor would have done?

"I have a few questions for Dr. Perry," she said.

CHAPTER 14

The next afternoon at two Glennis and Julia met on the doorstep of Dr. Perry's brownstone on East Seventy-Eighth Street. The house-keeper, a mature woman with a formidable Slavic accent, asked them to wait in the parlor at the front of the house. It was furnished with a magnificent burled walnut desk, two leather reading chairs, and a Bechstein grand piano. The piano was covered in a red brocade shawl and a dozen or more silver-framed photographs beneath a gleaming baroque candelabra.

Glennis was drawn to the photographs. In the largest frame, a mid-dle-aged Dr. Perry stood beside a beautifully dressed woman, flanked by what must be the young families of their children. From the remain-ing pictures Julia surmised the wife had died some time ago. In one a grandson, years older than in the family portrait, posed grave and proud in the military uniform of the Great War. Had he returned? The photographs held no answers.

Behind the piano hung a column of diplomas and certificates: Universitatis Princetoniensis, 1870; Johns Hopkins School of Medicine, 1875; State of New York Medallion of Distinction, 1891; Kennewick Prize for Esteemed Service, College of Physicians, 1904; President Emeritus, New York Metropolitan Medical Association, 1913. Other framed honors and tributes receded into the shadowed corner between two draperied windows.

Julia's attention moved to the surrounding bookcases like metal to magnet. It was a scholar's collection, not a bibliophile's, although the distinction could be small. Scientific tomes predominated, but she also spotted ornate cloth spines in faded colors, sentimental novels of the previous century—Fanny Fern, Mrs. Southworth, Mrs. Stowe. Julia drifted sideways along the glass-fronted cases, admiring a run of seventeenth-century Elzevir twelvemos and several shelves of eighteenth- and nineteenth-century continental editions, still the stuff of serious scholarship for those acute enough to read Latin, classical Greek, and German.

Julia was not among such readers. As yesterday's turmoil had reminded her, her education had been expensive but haphazard and "female"—meant to breed appreciation more than inquiry, competence more than command. Apart from a gloss of ornamental French, languages were not thought necessary. Whenever she saw books she couldn't read, like these, twinges of regret nipped at her like pinches from those smug Elzevirs. Now the pain was irrelevant. Better she had learned nursing or stenography.

Julia had literally grown up among books. Her father's library had been her earliest playground. Her mother believed in childhood freedoms (and spent long hours behind mysteriously closed doors herself), so Julia roamed unsupervised throughout the big house. She loved to elude Christophine by tucking herself inside an ancient lectern, often as not tented over Doré illustrations that sent her breath sailing. Those books—too valuable to be anything but sternly forbidden—were her best toys, leather boxes with moiré satin linings and woven silk headbands, baubles of color, pattern, and pictures. The words were pictures to her too, the harsh weave of barbed blackletters guarded by demons and imps, the heavy tread of Kelmscott romans, the filigree of Fournier ornaments and italics. As she grew older, those books had remained treasures but still for hands and eyes more than mind. Apart from those in English, she knew no more of the books' texts than had centuries of girls before her.

Dr. Perry's housekeeper led them down a hallway lit by electrified sconces into a small sitting room, where a powerful fragrance greeted them. In the windowed bay overlooking a garden of purpling foliage and rain-pulped dahlias stood a floral arrangement worthy of the Ritz lobby. The old doctor sat in a wing chair with one leg propped on an ottoman, a brown satin quilt across his lap. "They come every week, to cheer me," he said, waving a mottled hand toward the bouquet. "My wife always kept flowers in the house. She seems closer by with them here."

He apologized for not rising. His gouty leg was at it again, he said. He was forbidden to indulge in the cakes and tea sandwiches glistening from a tiered plate on the trolley at his side, but the girls, as he called Glennis and Julia, were to tuck in to the sugary pyramid. Glennis took two small cakes and set the translucent little plate on the table.

"We're sorry to come rampaging in on you like this," Glennis began, the slang sounding ridiculous in the hush of porcelain, silver, and hothouse freesias. "We were wondering, well, we thought—" She stopped, as if stricken by the amiable gaze of his dewy eyes. "We, that is, I, well, both of us . . ." She fumbled a glance at Julia.

"It's kind of you to talk with us, Dr. Perry," Julia said slowly, in full voice, and the old man's face relaxed. "We spoke with Alice Clintock last week. Naomi Rankin's flatmate? She's naturally quite upset. We hope you can help us ease her mind, if you'd be so kind, by clarifying a few matters that are troubling her. She's rather a nervous person, it seems."

Alice had expressed no misgivings whatsoever about Naomi's illness. She would probably be aghast that they were pestering the old doctor in her name. But it was too late to change course, and the impromptu ruse would have to do.

"I remember her. Poor woman." The doctor's words came with bursts of phlegm. "She was quite distraught."

"She told us she was too distressed the night you found Naomi's body to fathom exactly what was happening," Julia said. "We were hoping you could clear up a few questions for her."

He agreed to try. He sat back, fingers knit around his teacup, the saucer in his lap.

"It was late that evening, I gather, when you were called in?"

"Near midnight. Mrs. Lucovich had retired some while before. She usually brings my evening cocoa in about ten. Sometimes as early as nine thirty but rarely after ten. I don't sleep much anymore, you see, and find those late hours restful. I often read until my eyes tire."

"And that particular evening?" Julia said.

"I was sitting just here. I'd put down my book." He twisted to peer at the stack of books beside his chair. "Maurois's *Ariel*, a most enjoyable biography of Shelley, quite excellent. I was listening to the wireless program, a silly vaudeville thing broadcast from one of the cabarets. I remember wishing they would switch to music, maybe some nice Chopin or Schumann, something restful. Yes, Chopin, that's what I was wishing for."

"The telephone bell must have startled you?" Julia gently prodded a return to the subject.

"Oh yes. But as I say, I was awake. It took a few moments to reach it"—he nodded at the writing desk to his left—"but I tried to hurry, before it could disturb Mrs. Lucovich."

"What did Mr. Rankin tell you, Dr. Perry?"

"He was agitated, naturally, but he conveyed the details clearly enough. I knew it was a sad business right from the start." The old man turned to Glennis. "He said your sister had taken her life."

"Were you surprised that he called you? Not Dr. Pyle?" Glennis was blunt. Julia held her breath, hoping he would not take offense. Her next questions needed to find him in good spirits.

He chewed a mouthful of tea before replying. "I did wonder at the time. I've been retired a good eighteen years now, and Dr. Pyle handles the practice entirely. I assumed he was out on another call. If Chester had not told me Naomi was already dead, I would have insisted he telephone a younger man, probably Wendell Forsman or John Pugh, both excellent men not far from you. But as she was already deceased, and it was late, and I was awake and dressed, I thought I would spare those fellows and go myself. And with the nature of the trouble, I could see Chester was calling me because I know you all so well. He mentioned several times that it was a serious matter of some great delicacy. At any rate, I agreed to come at once."

Dr. Perry spoke slowly. Listening to him involved a great deal of patient sipping.

"When did you arrive?" Julia asked.

"Hector, my driver, brought round the motorcar. I should think I arrived shortly after midnight. Around then, at any rate."

"It must have been a shock to find Naomi like that."

"It's always difficult to find someone who had been so full of life. Your sister was very full of life, my dear," he said, turning to Glennis.

"Chester must have been in quite a state," Julia said.

Dr. Perry stared, sympathetic but puzzled. She was about to try another approach when he caught his breath and nodded. "Quite a state. He was pacing back and forth, perspiring heavily. I gave him two grains of Luminal to calm his nerves. He finally sat down and told me how he found her. But I could see for myself what had happened."

"You mean the morphine tablets?"

Another nod. "The empty tube was still in her lap, poor girl. The glass was right there too, with a little water still in it and some residue, probably a tablet that had fallen and dissolved. She was stretched out as if she'd made herself comfortable first. But it was plain to see what she'd done. The tube confirmed everything. It was a new Parke-Davis tube, containing twenty-five tablets. If she'd taken them all, it would make more than six grains total, far more than a lethal dose."

"And you saw tablets still in her mouth?"

"Yes, just inside her lip, and a few had fallen onto her blouse. She may have emptied the tube into her hand and tried to down them all at once. Sometimes people do that. I suppose they hope it will happen more quickly that way."

"Does it? Happen more quickly, with a single large dose?" Julia asked.

"No. One can just as easily swallow a few at a time, over and over. It only matters how many accumulate at one time in the bloodstream."

She hesitated. She'd already misrepresented Alice's concerns and now saw no alternative but to plunge further into deceit. In for a dime, in for a dollar. "Miss Clintock worries that Naomi suffered terribly before she died. Do you think she did? I mean, had she been violently ill, that you could tell? Nausea and fever and that sort of thing?"

"Nausea and fever? No, I saw nothing to suggest either one." Dr. Perry's forehead wrinkled. "No. I'm quite sure."

"You wouldn't expect them with a narcotic overdose?"

"Nausea and vomiting are not uncommon, though one can never say for certain. The usual thing is a metabolic slowdown as blood pressure drops and pulse and respiration slow. Most likely she would have slipped into a stupor. It can be a fairly peaceful death. I suppose that's why people choose it. Please assure Miss Clintock that Naomi probably suffered little at the end."

Julia thanked him. "Dr. Perry, you told the family she may have swallowed the tablets by accident. But if she took all or even most of them at one time, wouldn't that suggest deliberate intention, rather than an inadvertent overdose?"

His smile bore a practiced patience. "Not necessarily. Someone might be so desperate for relief they take a handful, and then another, without realizing what they're doing. It's not uncommon, sadly. And when Chester pointed out the absence of a note, I had to agree it was peculiar. It made accidental overdose seem far more likely."

"Peculiar," Glennis echoed under her breath. "I'll say."

Dr. Perry did not appear to hear, and Julia ignored it. They had reached the most delicate business at hand, and she needed to concentrate. She took a deep breath and tried to sound muddled.

"Dr. Perry, please excuse me for asking this, but Miss Clintock was wondering why you didn't order an autopsy. Isn't it the usual thing with a sudden or unexpected death?"

He drank the cooling remnant of his tea and lowered the empty cup to the trolley at his elbow. The saucer lay forgotten in his lap. A sigh whistled from his lungs. "It's usual, yes. But not mandatory, you see. Quite a lot is left up to professional discretion."

Hand shaking, he reached for his teacup. He peered into it for a moment, then looked up in confusion. Glennis refilled it.

Dr. Perry held the hot beverage below his chin. Almost a minute passed before he spoke. "When I suggested an autopsy was the prudent course in such situations, Chester expressed concerns. He felt it was plain enough what caused her death. He said the shock of her actions would be hard enough on the family, and an autopsy would only further distress his wife and young sons. Well, with the situation so clear, and when he reminded me about Naomi's terrible headaches and so on, I saw no reason to doubt the obvious conclusion." Dr. Perry took a sip of tea. "We decided an autopsy wasn't necessary, as there really was no question of the fatal overdose. Mrs. Rankin had already consulted her father, Edgar Branston, on the telephone, you see. Chester explained that Branston knew a great deal about Naomi's sort of troubles, as he specializes in complaints of women her age, and he felt the situation—her chronic difficulties and discomfort—supported indications of an overdose. Branston's quite a powerful force in medical circles, you understand. One word from him settles any dispute. I was happy to confirm his judgment."

"You also agreed not to summon the police?" Julia asked softly.

Dr. Perry considered, eyes on his knees bundled beneath the lap robe. When he looked up, he addressed Glennis. "My dear, you know how important family dignity is to your brother. As the oldest of you children and the only son, he's always felt an extra responsibility in that department. He was troubled by the prospect of intense interest, some of it no doubt prurient, in the particulars of Naomi's death. I've seen too often the needless pain police involvement can cause after a suicide. We all know how the newspapers can be."

"But I understood the law requires suicide to be reported," Julia said. Her knowledge was based on a few minutes' conversation with a distracted Jack, whose concerns at the time lay more with the movement of his feet and placement of his hands.

Dr. Perry shifted his weight. "Again, there is some room for professional judgment. The unexpected death of an otherwise healthy person, whatever the cause, certainly invites notifying the police. No question there. But it's different when an ill person dies. As I explained to the family, Chester persuaded me it was at least plausible Naomi's death was an accident."

"But not probable?"

"Oh, my dear young lady. I've lived too long to rack myself with such hair splitting. Does it matter? In the end I think not. To put it simply, Chester persuaded me that no good purpose would come from either an autopsy or involving the police."

His words hung in the scented air. Glennis shifted in her chair, and Julia prayed she wouldn't exclaim triumph, breaking his contemplation. The old doctor had more to say, she was certain.

"I did what I believed was best," he said. "When Chester asked for my help to ease the family's pain with this terrible thing, how could I refuse? He assured me the family would be told the truth, and you saw he kept his word there. So I told the medical examiner—Robert Spelzburg, a good fellow, friend of mine—it was a private tragedy, an accidental overdose. As it may well have been, don't forget. Dr. Spelzburg agreed, as a favor to me, to leave it at that. You Rankins have been good friends to this city. Neither of us saw any reason to prolong your ordeal."

He shuffled a hand toward Glennis, then dropped it to his quilt-covered thigh. "I know you grieve for your sister, my dear. But we must think of the family's suffering too."

Glennis tried to reassure the old man, but her smile was more of a grimace. Everything he'd said confirmed their suspicions of Chester's manipulation. Julia spoke before Glennis could blurt out something foolish. There was more she needed to learn.

"You've been very helpful, Dr. Perry. But I'm still a bit confused." She rubbed a round patch in the center of her forehead. "Miss Clintock told us Naomi was quite ill shortly before her death. Apparently she suffered severe stomach pain and a fever. This was before she took the tablets. Can a headache make someone that ill?"

The room was still except for Dr. Perry's heaving breaths. He leaned forward, tea forgotten, brows beetling. "No one mentioned this before. Stomach pain with fever? Chester mentioned only the headache. It certainly fit, as a reason for taking the tablets, I mean."

"What would cause—" Julia began.

"Migraine often brings on nausea. But rarely with fever and abdominal pain. Some sort of food poisoning? An intestinal virus? Any number of things might explain gastric trouble. Fever and a headache too? A brain ailment, an infection? I couldn't possibly say with any certainty."

Julia spoke as gently as she could. In for a dollar, in for a whole bloody inheritance. It was the principle of the thing she needed to establish, not firm fact. All facts had been destroyed in the crematorium. "It's a dreadful thought, I know," she said, "but Miss Clintock worries that if a few tablets were still on Naomi's lips, maybe she died before she could swallow them all. Maybe they hadn't yet entered her bloodstream. Maybe her affliction was so severe it killed her before the tablets could . . ." She let her voice trail away.

Dr. Perry pawed at the arm of his chair to pull himself up. Alarm aged him dramatically. "Abdominal pain and fever? Miss Clintock should have told me. If only she'd said something. This raises all sorts of questions. This is terrible. I must have missed something; I must have. I'm an old man. I shouldn't have gone. I see that now."

His distress brought a swift tread from the kitchen, and Mrs. Lucovich appeared. "Enough," she said, motioning Glennis and Julia to the door. "I won't have the good doctor agitated."

He raised a hand. "Thank you, but I'm all right. Please, Ermgard. Leave us." The woman muttered a foreign word and retreated behind the door, where no doubt she remained.

"This puts things in a very different light. I must consider the possibility she died from some other cause. A ruptured appendix. Some kind of toxic reaction, perhaps. Or tainted food."

He kneaded his right eyebrow with a gnarled thumb. "But evidence for an opiate overdose was very strong. I saw no reason to suspect anything else." It was a plea, a confession.

Julia eased up from her chair and took one of his hands, limp as laundry. "You have no reason to blame yourself, Dr. Perry. Miss Clintock was probably too upset herself to think clearly. You've been an immense help, and we're deeply grateful."

That was a profound understatement. He had just confirmed her theory that Naomi might have died before the tablets could kill her. That alone didn't spell murder, but it opened wide the gate to that possibility.

He blinked and kneaded her fingers.

Seeing color return to his cheeks, Julia risked her last but most crucial question. "One final thing, Dr. Perry. Are you quite sure she'd been dead for some time before you saw her?"

His voice quieted as he regained his professional footing. "Rigor was half or more advanced. Under the room's conditions that meant several hours. At least eight. More likely ten. She was dead before evening. Of that, at least, I am certain."

⁓

Alice Clintock rose so quickly from the Union's worktable that her chair fell over. She tucked a wrinkled handkerchief under her waistband and rubbed at her cheeks. She looked wan, but whether from the cares of Union business or the surprise of their visit, Julia couldn't say.

"We're sorry to interrupt," Glennis said. "Could we talk with you for a minute?" It might have passed for a casual overture, as they'd planned in the taxi coming from Dr. Perry's, if she hadn't added, "In *private*?"

Alice instructed the other women to continue folding the materials laid in various piles across the table—a newsletter, judging by the cheap newsprint and large grainy photograph of Naomi—and led Glennis and Julia to the back office. As soon as the door closed, she said, "Did you find it? Her note?"

Glennis handed her the letter they'd found in Chester's folder Saturday morning.

"I knew it," Alice said at once. "Does he know you found it?"

"No. You'll need to copy it so I can put it back before he sees it's missing. I would've, but there're too many words I can't make out."

Alice eagerly scanned the spiky handwriting. "I can't thank you enough, Miss Rankin. This means everything to me, to us. I know we can't publish it directly as she'd have hoped, but I can borrow her words to assure our friends she died a hero, concerned more for the cause than even her own health at the end. That ought to inspire women everywhere to join our fight."

Alice pressed the letter to her breast. "You've both been kindness itself. I doubt our paths will cross again, as I need to remove my last things from the apartment this weekend. Thank you for your help, most sincerely, from all of us."

She was right. It was hard to imagine where or when they might again encounter each other. Julia had to push ahead with her half-formed thought. "Alice, before we go, I wonder if I might ask a quick question. On the day Naomi died, did you feel peculiar too? I mean, were you ill?"

Alice moistened her lips. Once noticed, the scar at the corner of her mouth was prominent. She folded Naomi's letter and smoothed it against her hip. "What are you suggesting?"

"I'm simply wondering what caused her to fall ill that day. If she was prone to headaches, and to indigestion as you describe, why was it so much worse that day? Could something else have been bothering her? Something she ate or drank, perhaps?"

Alice studied the floor. "It's possible. I've gone over the scene countless times in my head, Miss Kydd, and I just don't know. To answer your question, no. I felt nothing unusual. But Naomi and I rarely ate the exact same meal even when we dined together. I'm afraid I don't know what she ate that day or even where."

Glennis began to shake. "What are you saying? Julia? Alice?"

"She's suggesting that whoever wrote those evil notes may have made good on the threats," Alice said. "It would explain Naomi's sudden illness."

"You mean she was poisoned?"

Julia steadied her friend's hands, cold as rubber. "It's a possibility. Maybe slim but we can't ignore it."

"He's a fiend!" Glennis stiffened. "And I'm next!"

Alice recoiled, unprepared for Glennis's abrupt leap into melodrama. Julia tried to reassure her with a quick look begging forbearance, but beyond that all she could do was embrace her friend with the usual tutting and shushing and lead Glennis back through the Union's front office in a clumsy waltz of apologies. They bumped against a table where a typewriting machine sat unattended—long enough to give Julia a close look at the crisp pica font, unlike that of the threatening notes, on a stack of prepared envelopes—and stumbled out to the street.

They were back in a taxi before Glennis spoke with any coherence. "I know it, Julia. I'm next unless we stop him. We have to get at her file again."

"Do you honestly imagine your brother would let me anywhere near his study after the goose chase I led him on last time? You'll have to be on your own for returning that note."

"Not that. You don't understand. For the proof. He'd keep the receipt. He keeps *everything*."

Julia sighed, weary of Glennis's Machiavellian mind. If only it could be so simple. Not even Chester would file a receipt for poison in his private folder labeled *Naomi*.

CHAPTER 15

"To new friends," Russell Coates said, raising his glass, "and endless evenings."

Julia dipped her nose into a halo of Cointreau. If only this one wouldn't end. It had begun at a fourth floor Village walk-up, where a party of Colophon Club bibliophiles was already in full flow. They were greeted by a fellow named Maurice Firuski. Wearing a white whale lapel pin and holding a martini in each hand, he nodded in lieu of a handshake.

"Ask him anything about Herman Melville," Russell said. "Or better yet, don't."

"And whatever you do, don't mention T. S. Eliot," added the young woman who had opened the door. She was striking in a forthright, unfussy way, with thick dark hair. Her dress was shapeless and office gray, the sleeves rolled halfway up her arms to expose fine wrists and a purple beaded bracelet. Her remark launched Firuski's tale (abbreviated by demand) of having been approached by Eliot about issuing a fine edition of *The Waste Land*—a coup to raise any publisher's pulse—from his Dunster House Press. But before Firuski could pounce, Horace Liveright got there first. And everyone knew the glow that cachet still gave the crafty old publisher. Another guest named Austen Hurd, who worked for Liveright, gave a riotous account of the firm's indecent celebrating. This prompted Russell to mention Capriole, Julia to beam, and someone to pour more martinis.

Yes, she did happen to have *Wednesday* with her—produced from its flannel wrapper—and yes, Gill's work was a stunner. And Virginia Woolf no less—brilliant! The partiers commiserated about the problem of authors, especially living ones. Among typophiles as she was, Julia could admit that the artistry of fine printing—illustrations, typography, papers, inks, bindings—was what interested her, though of course one needed a text with shoulders sturdy enough to support (and docile enough to accept) the fancy dress. Most printers fell back upon familiar mainstays whose authors wouldn't kick up a fuss. Dead, if possible. (Norwegian folktales or one's lover's poems, for starters. Julia was as guilty as any of them.) Much as Julia and most bibliophiles tired of fine editions of Mrs. Browning's sonnets or favorite Psalms, they could forgive any old-hat text if the edition itself sparkled with some fresh wit, beauty, or mastery.

The dark-haired woman was named Beatrice, or *Paul*, she said with a moue of mystery. She turned out to be a year younger than Julia but already in charge of the American Type Founders library in New Jersey. Julia began to tell her about Stanley Morison's scheme of reviving historical fonts for Monotype in London, but Bea (the third name given to her in as many minutes, this one by her taciturn and febrile husband, Frederique Warde, who never left his chair beside the liquor cabinet) already knew about it, having met Morison during his American visit last spring. It was soon clear that Mrs. Warde was the most knowledgeable bookman in the room. She talked of Updike and Rogers, Goudy and Rollins, and a type-and-lettering man named Bill Dwiggins whose work might outshine them all. As if they'd been friends for years, Bea and Julia began to trade the usual book-hound gossip, much of it merrily apochryphal: of misspelled vanity watermarks, of the binder who boxed up the trimmed deckles as per his client's instructions to save them, of the deluxe edition of *Song of Solomon* moldering in a Boston warehouse for want of a codpiece and wind-arranged tresses.

When time came for the evening's customary chili bean stew, kitchen-brewed beers, and poker, Russell and Julia said their goodbyes and headed downtown for a dinner of oriental delicacies. Overlooking mists of oil and steam, they perched on stools amid swirling sounds they did not understand and dishes too fantastical to recognize. Julia tasted a broth threaded with curd and citrus zest, a skewered red creature with limbs so strange it might have come from the moon, and morsels resembling nothing so much as insects from the alleyway. Some bites stung the corners of her mouth, others dissolved into a disconcerting jelly, and some yielded numbing flavors of anise, lemon, or coriander.

From there they taxied far uptown to a club where a turbaned Negro woman of immense girth, each breast the size of a wrestler's thigh, mewled one double entendre song after another. When a small orchestra at the back of the stage struck up in the new jazz style, Russell and Julia were sucked forward with the crowd onto the dance floor, then pinned in place by the gyrating crush. Julia's temples ached in the alchemy of sweat, gin, talc, hair cream, perfume, and smoke, mostly of the illicit variety. And yet how lovely, some dizzy part of her mind thought, that a random assortment of strangers, white and colored, whether in fur coats or patched coveralls, could share such intimate camaraderie. In London one took care to party, as to live and shop and work, within one's narrow slice of peers. Adventuring up or down the social tiers was a gamble; it could wreak wild amusement or intense mortification. Here mingling sweat and caresses among complete strangers was part of the excitement. This was what those bored Talbot Leaguers milling about the Winterjay apartment so restlessly sought but didn't dare pursue. Here lay the possibility of genuine clashing—clashing of minds and words and eyes and mouths and bodies that could destroy everything and reinvent anything. Here, beyond all borders of race and class, one risked new knowledge, new realizations. Thrilling. Terrifying.

As a thin yellow light from the stage warned that another show was about to begin, Russell and Julia wriggled free and moved on again through the moonless night, arriving at another dark cabaret back downtown, one of the city's countless refuges where a word and a bill ushered one into a cave of crowded privacy and expensive liquor. They paused to greet three men who nodded at them from a table near the empty stage. One of them was Willard Wright. He seized Julia's hand, stroking it with an unctuous familiarity slicked by alcohol.

"We're recovering from the philharmonic," he said. "The Franck D Minor, God help us. Frightfully sentimental, but what can one do in these mawkish times?"

His companions were a fat, dour-faced man Russell introduced as Henry Mencken and Paul Duveen, a large blowsy fellow with bulging teeth and white-blond hair. Both, he said, were bookmen of a fairly serious stripe. Their interest in Julia grew on learning she was a fine printer and proprietor of a new English private press, but before it could harden into the usual eye-glinting collectors' avarice, Russell made their excuses and led her farther into the shadowed club. They slid onto a velvet banquette.

Throughout the evening they had spoken of books, of London, of the Volstead nuisance, and of books again. Julia was happy, distracted. How blithely she'd once enjoyed such carefree hours. Stripped of their certainty now, or soon to be, she understood with fresh empathy how Glennis lived. In her new circumstances Julia too should now be humming with alert schemes. She too should be on the lookout for a prosperous husband. What about Russell? Should she set her cap for him, muscling Glennis aside in that pitiful old spectacle of rivaling misses?

The thought was repellent. Not Russell as a lover (no, as a husband—business before pleasure now) but the cynicism, the scheming. She pushed it away, at least for the short time remaining before her twenty-fifth birthday ended her Kydd income forever. Enjoy *this*. Here were pleasures to savor. Cointreau, Russell, the unfolding wonders of this new Manhattan. Absorb delight while she could.

And yet. Why concede her independence was doomed? The ruling had gone against her, but Philip's impulsive wager offered her a lifeline, however tenuous. She'd interrupted his breakfast on the library terrace Tuesday morning to declare as much. "You haven't impoverished me quite yet, you know," she'd said from the open French door. "You proposed a wager last weekend, and I accepted. As far as I'm concerned, it still stands. I intend to learn the truth about Naomi Rankin's death, and if I'm right about it, you agree to forfeit your claims to my money." It came out rather well: clear, calm, resolute. Best of all was Philip's stunned face.

But he recovered instantly, lifting his coffee cup in an assenting salute. "Brava," he'd said without, for once, a hint of guile.

Before her head could drift away on the fumes of the Club Noir, Julia leaned into the pungency of Russell's shaving balm and hazarded the night's most vital conversation. "Tell me about Naomi Rankin."

He drew back. Something clouded his eyes. "A curious request."

"The more I learn, the more I wish I'd known her. You said you were friends once. I'd like to hear more, if you wouldn't mind."

He sank back into the cushions, pulling Julia's shoulders with him. "All right." He took a long pensive breath. "Naomi was a bit like you. Not one to giggle and flirt and pretend she didn't understand. Even as a girl she spoke her mind. I remember once she refused to go to church because girls couldn't be altar boys. Her father finally picked her up one Sunday and literally carried her into the service, but when the music stopped, she yelled at the top of her lungs about how Saint Stephen's wasn't fair to girls. Old Alford nearly knocked her head off right there. Soon after that they shipped her to a school in Connecticut, and I only saw her at holidays. We were about twelve or thirteen then."

"A rebel."

"Mmmm." His eyes closed. "She felt girls' things were less fun, less important, less dangerous, less everything, than what boys were allowed to do. And generally she was right."

"Proud of her skinned knees and scraped knuckles? My mother had a bit of that in her. She once tried to teach me to smoke a cigar. I desperately wanted to like it but threw up instead."

The corners of Russell's mouth stirred.

"What about after you grew up?" Julia asked. "Were you still friends?"

He held a swallow of brandy in his mouth and stroked the length of her bare arm, shoulder to elbow to hand. "Oh yes."

He paused on the small knob of her wrist. She rolled her palm to slide her fingers through his. Why hadn't she guessed before? Glennis hadn't, she felt certain. "You were lovers?"

He carried her arm over the table to rest across his lap. "For a time. But in absolute secrecy. It seems comical now. Maddening at the time."

"Why secret? I wouldn't think she'd mind those old scruples."

"She didn't care two sausages about propriety. But she was becoming more involved in her politics, and I think I embarrassed her."

"Why? Did you oppose her?"

"I thought she was utterly right. It was a national disgrace women weren't allowed to vote. But beliefs were never enough for her. She needed action. As the movement gathered steam, it completely absorbed her. She'd have thrown herself in front of Wilson's train if she thought it would change his mind."

He filled his lungs and slowly released the air. "I couldn't understand that. She said I was becoming a typical male—that was an epithet—too lodged in my ways to see my own privileges. Clubby years at Yale and then law school, the waiting partnership with my father, the notion that politics happened between gentlemen in clubs or boardrooms or during country weekends. And she was right. In that world, shouting in the street was vulgar, bad form—*womanish*."

Vulgar: a denouncement always wielded by the strong against the weak, by the rich against the poor. Julia recalled the images of Naomi Rankin standing tall and fierce beneath a placard, the White House an anemic thing behind her. And Naomi's face, alive in laughter with her friend, arms cradling each other's waists, hair streaming loose. "Did you talk about marriage?"

Where did that come from? Was her mind already snaking toward the marriage snare at the end of every romantic story? Worse, was she prying into his past to pursue her own imminent interests? Before she could withdraw the intrusive question, he stroked her arm and said, "I did, sometimes, but Naomi wouldn't consider it. She called marriage legalized slavery. And then as things heated up in Washington, we saw each other less and less. When we did, we didn't talk much, if you understand. There was passion, certainly, but then she'd be off again to a march or a rally. I began to feel like her guilty secret, her vice. I was her partner in sin but not in life.

"It's a relief to talk about this, you know, now that she's dead. It was all a long time ago, and much has happened since then. I still prefer the Rankins not know, as they're my golden goose these days. Chester declared war on Naomi almost the day their father died, and he'd have me shot for treason if he knew I'd"—he kissed the tip of Julia's nose—"fraternized."

"The secret must have been hard to keep, working for the family like that. I can't speak for the rest of them, but I'm certain Glennis has no idea."

"Glennis has no idea of anything much of the time, bless her." Russell smiled. "No, she's a good kid. She was quite young when Naomi and I were most, what, involved, so she wouldn't have noticed anything. No one did. And of course we were still good friends. No one thought twice when we turned up together. With a passel of her friends, often as not, for chaperones. But it was clear our lives were going in different directions. My old dad began to nag me about marrying, starting a family. He's impatient for grandsons—even though, as you see, I still haven't obliged him."

Julia freed her arm to raise her glass. "A modern man," she said. "A kindred spirit."

"Modern," he repeated without her gloss of humor.

"What about recently? Did you see her much in the last year or so?"

"Some. After Chester forced her to move into that miserable apartment, she occasionally needed to escape from living in his shadow, so to speak. We'd head out to the country for a drive. She said it cleared her head. We'd have a few drinks, talk a little."

"And?"

He gave a short, harsh laugh. "And not much else. I admit I hoped she might want to rekindle things, but it didn't seem so." His face clouded. "There wasn't much chance to find out. Her flatmate, that Clintock woman, was like a jealous mother hen, jibing at me every chance she could. I don't know if it was me in particular she didn't like or men in general. I hate to say it, but she's the sort of crabbed creature who gives Vivian Winterjay's ideas some credence. Clintock can't hold a candle to Naomi as a woman."

"Her death must have come as a terrible shock."

"You can't imagine. And then when Chester said it was suicide . . ." Russell scrubbed his fingertips across his chin. "All he cared about was keeping it quiet and disposing of her body. You were there. I was simply the lawyer, an errand boy, nothing more." He put down his glass. "Enough of that. I want to hear about you. Your plans. What made you leave New York? What brought you back? Your life, your childhood. Who you are and who you hope to become. I want to hear whatever you'll tell me."

Julia hated such moments. Anything she cared to say rang hollow and banal. "It's a dreary story. When I was thirteen, my mother was killed by a motorcar in Stockholm."

Russell sucked in breath. "How devastating. Were you close?"

"We were."

Julia knew that expectant gaze. But how could she explain? Lena grew more beguiling and more elusive each year, glimpsed in the flickering kaleidoscope of Julia's memory: the glowing tip of her pencil-thin cigar on the balcony late at night, her penchant for trousers, her efforts to teach Julia and Christophine to ride a bicycle. Lena at the piano in the dark, drifting from Scriabin to Chopin to Satie. Her huge vases of lilies and roses, damask dressing gowns worn until dinner, colorful canvases on spattered easels, beds heaped with mismatched pillows. Lena had filled the space she was allowed to live in. It was shadowed, beyond society's gaze, but not solitary. Like Milo, she too had special friends. Julia knew well about locked doors and long excursions to the park. And yet, despite all Julia would never know about her mother, she'd never doubted that she'd been her mother's one ferocious love.

"And your father?" Russell asked, a quiet tap to dispel her reverie.

"My father had died years before, so my older half brother Philip—"

"I met him the other night. Interesting fellow."

"—was made my guardian. We hardly knew each other. He packed me off to boarding schools, and I seldom saw him again for any length of time until a few weeks ago. When I turned eighteen and he gave me more say in spending my money, I decided to put an ocean between myself and those years. I left for Europe as soon as the war was over and it was safe to travel, with no plans other than to live where and as I saw fit."

"You chose England?"

"I visited London, made a few friends, and decided to settle. Terribly desultory, I'm afraid." Her narrative, such as it was, faded away.

"And now you're here. For a good long time, I hope?"

"It depends." It was the best she could offer. How could she possibly mention the crisis with Philip and her vanishing income? It changed everything—her household with Christophine, her understanding with David, Capriole's fine start—and she didn't have the heart to describe what would soon falter and likely collapse. The future and the past conspired against happiness, she knew that; one must find it in present moments, however fleeting.

Russell fingered Julia's earring and then her jaw. Did he feel her pulse leap? Was he too slipping into that uncomplicated language of skin to skin? At the moment hers would happily follow his down that path, but her mind balked. If things were to proceed, which seemed both likely and desirable, she needed to speak now, before lines were crossed.

"I should tell you," she said into his temple, "Glennis still has doubts about Naomi's suicide. She's enlisted my help in asking some questions, and it looks as if her fears may prove justified."

Russell pulled back. "What do you mean?"

"She may not have killed herself. Something else may have caused her death." Julia hated how this must pain him. She feared he might be angry, resentful that an outsider knew more than he did about Naomi's last hours. She wouldn't blame him for cursing her and Glennis for their meddlesome curiosity.

He only lowered his head and shook it. "Oh, Julia." He gazed out toward the smoky lounge where a woman had begun to sing. "Here's a warning for you in return. Naomi's private life is no treasure hunt to go barreling through."

Before Julia could speak, he covered her mouth with his fingers. "Tread very, very carefully."

CHAPTER 16

The brush of knuckles against her door woke Julia on the morning of her twenty-fifth birthday. Anticipated for years, the occasion now soured her throat even before she opened her eyes. She sat up, sending Mr. Arlen's impossible novel to the floor for the absolute last time. Mrs. Cheadle knocked again and cracked open the door. At Julia's mumble she placed a pot of coffee on the dressing table and returned a moment later with a dozen Claudius Pernet roses in a cut-crystal vase. The note relayed Philip's good wishes and an invitation to meet him for champagne in the library at seven. Perfectly civil. As if his needless questions hadn't already smashed her future to bits.

Julia had managed to avoid him since she'd confronted him on the terrace almost a week ago. That evening she'd found a note balanced on her bedroom doorknob. Philip was a benevolent conqueror. He promised Julia's financial arrangements would remain unchanged until the lawyers drew up permanent papers. (How could that take more than ten seconds? Zero was simplicity itself.) He also reiterated his intention to take her to dinner and the theater on her birthday, a plan brokered last summer when it was clear Julia would have to celebrate the event in New York. The thought of such an outing now, when any celebrating would be his alone, was noxious, but he'd pressed the matter so relentlessly she'd finally agreed.

She spent the afternoon in a handsome but arctic library at the offices of the Pynson Printers on West Forty-Third Street. David had arranged a private showing of recent fine editions from the Californian private presses. The work of the Grabhorn brothers and John Henry Nash was stirring a buzz in London's printerly circles, especially after Morison's authoritative disdain, which had piqued Julia's curiosity. The shop's proprietor, Elmer Adler, met her with a correct but clipped welcome—clearly taking her for a tiresome female dilettante—and entrusted her to a solemn Miss Greenberg, who brought the volumes one at a time in silent progression. Miss Greenberg sat at a nearby table, ostensibly tending to catalog cards but in fact watching Julia's every move for breaches of bibliophilic decorum. It took no more than five or six books, each unwrapped from glassine wrappers by this hovering high priestess, to convince Julia that Morison was right: there was something overreaching and tasteless (*terrifying,* Morison had said) in those heavily deckled pages strutting the printer's initials. The color-besotted confections of neomedieval, or neorenaissance, or neorococo marzipan seemed more suited to a candy carnival than a library. After a second florid version of *The Sermon on the Mount,* she began to pray that *Californian* would not become synonymous with *American* in the realm of fine printing, or she would have to endure much teasing among her book friends at home. Surely there were printers in New York doing more interesting work, with their heads and hands in the twentieth century. Maybe Russell would know. She barely glanced at the last selection, Nash's slim and sanctimonious *Life of Dante,* before thanking Miss Greenberg and hurrying outside in search of warming sunlight.

What she found was wan at best, so she sheltered alone in a nearby hotel tearoom for as long as she dared before arousing suspicion or, worse, pity. First one hour, then a second crawled by until it was time to return to Philip's apartment to prepare for their dreaded evening. There was only one incident of interest. She had been quietly tracing the pattern of her table's wood grain when a handsome couple entered the lobby and approached the desk. It was Edward Winterjay and a young woman in navy linen and a matching cloche pulled low to shade her face. Winterjay's resemblance to David struck her again, the easy confidence of his smile and low timbre of his voice. He spoke briefly to the clerk and signed the register, and the couple disappeared into the elevator without looking around. The woman carried a small portmanteau; Winterjay had only his hat and coat slung over one arm. There might be a perfectly innocent explanation, Julia told herself in the worldly tone of one who knows otherwise. How commonplace. It happened every day, everywhere. Did Vivian know of her husband's afternoon inclinations? It was an idle question—not Julia's business—and she dismissed what she had witnessed as yet more knowledge not to share with Glennis.

With the help of a hot bath, her new Vionnet evening frock, and her favorite pearl and peridot earrings, she was determined to salvage the day. At seven she found Philip in his wing chair by the fire, deep in conversation with Jack. Both men rose to their feet, scattering cats.

Julia begrudged Philip a small measure of gratitude for inviting his friend along. Two weeks ago she had viewed Jack with wary alarm—rightly so, it turned out, given his firm's shocking decision—yet now she was glad for the kindhearted buffer of his company. He quickly assured her he'd played no role in last Monday's judgment and was as surprised as anyone by it. She acknowledged this with a fractional nod.

Philip had the good sense not to apologize. He busily opened the champagne, the 1920 Dom Pérignon cuvée Julia had seen the bootlegger's courier deliver earlier. He raised a glass and let the champagne's chatter spill over his carpet. "To Julia Kydd, *sans peur et sans reproche.*"

"Happy birthday," Jack said.

"Compliment excessive but accepted." She bathed her throat in the fine vintage and met Philip's gaze square on. Was he smirking or merely burgeoning with good fortune? All right, enough pretense.

"You should know I haven't been idle this past week, Philip. I fully intend to secure my inheritance by whatever means available. I won't let you gouge me with legal trickery."

"Excellent news," he replied. "Much better to prevail by one's own wits."

Jack was aghast. "Don't start that nonsense again. It's done, over. There's no point in starting another battle. Can't you two have at least one evening's peace together?"

Before either could answer, Mrs. Cheadle wheeled in a trolley of fragrant canapés. Julia's stomach made a rude noise, which brought on a cough. Philip handed her a plate with three circles of lobster paste on toast. "I take it you're on the trail of a villain?"

"It's nothing to joke about," Jack insisted. "If Julia found any sign of murder, the police would have to be involved. You both show an appalling sangfroid—"

"Bilgewater. We all know perfectly well that clever murders go unnoticed every day. The police bumble onto only the most maladroit cases. If she's right, this is not one of them. But then nothing was said of convincing the police, only me, and I'm a much more formidable judge. Julia, please. Enlighten us."

Jack stuffed an entire canapé in his mouth and wheeled toward the fire.

"It's early days yet," Julia said, settling onto the sofa. Pestilence curled against her thigh, purring. She guided the cat's sheathed claws away from her dress.

Philip dragged his chair around to face her, pitching Pudd'nhead to the floor. "Go on." Jack poked furiously at the grate.

She hadn't intended to confide her inchoate ideas to anyone, not even, not entirely, to Glennis. Least of all to Philip. But she was tempted. His observations might help her think more clearly, and better to hear his doubts and challenges sooner than later. His dark eyes waited, for once neither mocking nor superior. It seemed safe enough, if she were careful to draw out his thoughts while shielding her own. She set down her glass.

"You're still bound to silence." Both men nodded. "All right. In a nutshell, the family accepts Chester's claim that Naomi simply despaired of her life and chose to end it. He contends she took a fatal overdose of morphine tablets, if not on purpose, then by accident. It doesn't matter to him, as long as the newspapers don't know about it."

"The logical conclusion," Philip said. "You cling to more intriguing scenarios?"

"It's *too* logical, too tidy and conclusive. Conflicting details suggest she may have been murdered, by one of two possible means. Perhaps she swallowed the tablets but not of her own free will. Perhaps someone took advantage of her agony and administered them without her cooperation."

Philip lit a cigarette. "Or?"

"Or she took the tablets but died before they took effect. Meaning her death was caused by something else, likely the illness she suffered that afternoon, which there's reason to suspect was induced."

"Poison? How ghoulish."

"Maybe," Julia said. "She was in unusual distress that day, with fever and abdominal pain, and she was dead before nightfall. An unknown malady both sudden and acute points reasonably, I believe, to poison."

"Or to suicide. How do you explain the tablets?"

"A red herring, provided by the murderer."

"Do you hear that, Jack? She's been reading Mrs. Christie. I still think suicide's more likely, but my sister's ideas are more entertaining. Kessler's been asking the wrong Kydd for help. Julia's made more progress on her mystery than he has with that Dorothy Caine business."

A series of wavery Os rose from Philip's mouth. "All right, let's think. Criminal possibility one is chilling enough, but two is positively bloodcurdling. It suggests the overdose was a ruse, staged for others' benefit. Very curious. Why would someone disguise her death as suicide when scandal was more worrisome than the death itself?"

"Exactly." Julia took up her champagne. "Unless the truth was even more damaging. To the Rankins, with their great fear of family scandal, what could be worse than a sensational suicide?"

Philip chuckled, his chin bobbing at the ceiling.

She said it anyway. "Murder."

"Brava! Taking notes, Jack? This might make a pretty story for your friend Wright. If only Miss Rankin had waited, her final blaze of glory could have been bright indeed. Murder garners so much more publicity."

Julia finished the last swallow of champagne.

"And too bad for you as well, Julia. Do poke around, though I doubt you'll find anything to prove either hypothesis."

"She was planning a run for Senator Wadsworth's seat in '26."

Philip's eyebrows rose. "You don't say? The story gets richer and richer. Imagine the Rankins squirming through *that*. They'd flee en masse for the duration."

"It's a powerful motive for silencing her."

"Yes, though the prosaic obvious usually proves true. Old Chester may have outwitted Naomi in the end by hushing up the splash she hoped to make, but that makes not a whit of difference. Older brothers have a pesky way of prevailing, you know. But it would be in deplorable taste for me to mention it. More champagne?"

After saluting her disdain with the raised bottle, he replenished their glasses and insisted they finish the canapés. Mrs. Cheadle had fussed for days over recipes, he said, and had subjected him to three inferior practice batches since Saturday, with variations in the amounts of cayenne, mustard, and Worcestershire. Julia made a mental note to thank her tomorrow. It seemed time to move on, and she said so, rising carefully from under the cat.

"Unfortunately, there's been a change of plan."

Julia held her breath. Philip's surprises were rarely good. Jack studied his shoelaces.

"Aunt Lillian's nurse telephoned. Apparently the old girl sneezed twice and insists I come hold her hanky. I really must go see to her, but Jack here is on orders to squire you about town with all the manly charm he can muster. I apologize for the frightful timing—but you've seen what the old girl is like. I couldn't refuse. She'll be a bear, having to wait at all."

Jack's role became clear. He had been invited not as a kindness to Julia, to ease her awkwardness, but to solve Philip's dilemma. She swept her shawl from the back of the sofa and reached for Jack's arm, extended with alacrity. "Apologies for delaying you. We'll be off, then."

"Sorry it turned out like this," Jack said, more to Philip than to Julia. She wished he wouldn't sound so miserable. Had he negotiated a reward for the chore?

"Cheer up," she said. "I won't make you dance."

∽

It was barely past one when they returned to the apartment. Laying her handbag aside, Julia drew Jack close enough to invite a tepid kiss on her right cheek. He delivered it without even a brushing embrace. At that she dispatched the poor fellow, vowing to erase the evening from her memory. It burned like acid in her throat that a modern woman of reasonable health, wits, and appearance should be reduced on her birthday to a reluctant buss from a brotherly acquaintance.

She smelled it before she saw it. It would be excessive, of course, in proportion to its lateness. David was like that. Julia turned into the hallway to her bedroom and stopped short, alarmed at the sheer size of the floral delivery blocking her door. It dwarfed Dr. Perry's arrangement. White roses, perhaps three dozen of them, massed above a froth of baby's breath, ivy, and lady ferns. Tall blue flags and yellow gladiolas—she smiled at the Swedish touch—sprang from it like quills from a porcupine. It was beautiful, fragrant, and quite preposterous.

She had to crouch on hands and knees to drag the vase to one side to get to the door. Philip had it placed there deliberately, of course, and she half expected him to appear in the hallway to witness her groveling. Nose prickled in foliage, she found the card and sat back on her haunches to read it.

Inside the florist's envelope was a folded telegram. As David never wrote social letters, Julia had expected no correspondence from him. To be honest, she admitted rather guiltily, she hadn't much missed him. There had been a few occasions, of course, but fewer than one might have expected. But that was the beauty of their understanding, the freedom they both enjoyed and granted each other. With a fond tremor she unfolded the telegram. He didn't know of the disaster that could put the kibosh on their understanding, but for now she'd relish that ignorance. He was a charming man, a charming lover. She could—must—enjoy him while she could.

She read it three times before she was certain she'd provided the correct missing punctuation. No other construction was possible. *Darling,* he wrote. *Blissful birthday surprise Helen has better offer divorce imminent joy supreme return at once and marry your perishing David*

Julia's ankles wobbled. Her evening shoes were not meant for such a peasant's posture. She stood and leaned against the wall to read again the thunderclap in her hands. What madness was this? The second thought to race across her mind was, absurdly, the squeal Glennis would make on hearing it. Only third came a more reasoned, if cynical, reaction: Was this her salvation, the answer to her financial problems?

David's wife. For as long as Julia had known him, that was Helen Adair. They'd met once, when she and David ran into Helen and her companion, an Austrian named Rudolph or Rupert or Ruthven, at a supper club in Mayfair. They had a drink together. Helen was close to David's age, approaching forty, but she remained handsome in an athletic sort of way, with the strong shoulders and muscular calves of a tennis player. They'd married young and separated in mutual boredom a few years later. At first, David told Julia, they simply didn't bother with a divorce, but then they both found the arrangement oddly freeing. As long as Helen behaved sensibly and discreetly, he supported her in lavish style. Each enjoyed easy love affairs, unencumbered by expectations of marriage. That freedom was exactly what Julia relished too, and why David's proposal—no, his decision—that they now marry was so stunning.

Should she be glad? David was one of the few men who rarely bored or dismayed her. He was amusing, reasonably wealthy, well connected, even tempered, and a fine lover. But love in the marrying sense? They'd never spoken of it, and she was sure neither felt it, not honestly. Even so, a voice repeated her first coldly practical thought: marriage would certainly solve her looming financial crisis. David had plenty of money for them both, especially once Helen no longer had claim to his income.

Julia stared at the telegram. She knew well that sparkling glib tone ("perishing" indeed), but never before had it been addressed to her. She had always been in on the amusement, sharing the wink, not receiving it. This apparent offer of supreme intimacy instead opened a sly, calculated new distance between them. She felt whisked onto a dangerous dance floor, expected to match his complicated new steps, to parry romantic strategy with counterstrategy.

What on earth was behind this shift? What did he really want? Of course they were fond of one another, but neither had ever expressed the slightest yearning for a more fixed relationship. David loved the freedom a remote marriage gave him. Even if Helen had a better offer and now wanted a quick divorce, why suddenly thrust his arrangement with Julia into such upheaval? She felt a small stab of resentment, even betrayal. It had been so nice, so easy; why jigger that? The mere logistics of marrying—taking into account Christophine and their lovely flat—made her head spin.

Did he think she secretly pined to be married, that her claim of preferring independence was simply a brave front hiding private bouts of weepy loneliness? Did he feel her honor was now at stake, obliging him to make the proverbial honest woman out of her? As if their present arrangement did not already embody, to her mind, the perfect honesty. She hadn't thought him inclined to either strain of romantic condescension.

She'd have to inform him of her own calamitous news straightaway. Some men would balk, reluctant to take on a wife who'd burden their resources rather than expand them. David, though, might welcome her disaster. His generosity would be patient and reasonable and overpowering. David was a shrewd businessman; he used his considerable wealth to acquire what he wanted. That was why their present understanding was so perfect: neither had the upper hand, and neither was beholden to the other. Marriage would end that. A wife—the more absent and ambivalent the better—ensured his freedom but at the expense of hers.

Marriage would also end, however, Julia's very real threat of drudge and poverty. Her head throbbed. She frowned at the floral behemoth filling the hall. Its fragrance was suffocating.

She squeezed past, leaving the flowers to be dealt with in the morning. Perhaps Mrs. Cheadle would be a saint and move them somewhere more appropriate, like the lobby of a grand hotel. Groping for the doorknob, Julia knocked over an envelope balanced there. Without a hall table nearby, Mrs. Cheadle seemed to think this a handy place to leave messages. Another birthday surprise?

Inside the plain white envelope was a typed message identical to those Alice Clintock had dumped out onto Naomi Rankin's desk. *Stop sticking your nose where it don't belong if you know whats good for you.*

For heaven's sake. Julia's birthday, such as it had been, was well and truly over.

CHAPTER 17

Julia did not sleep well. At five she draped her burgundy shawl, the one crumpled beyond any ability to restore, over her shoulders, slid past the floral blockade, and made her way across the dark apartment in hopes of finding Mrs. Cheadle's first pot of coffee. Julia could smell it, so keen was her hope, but she was too early. She stared into the murky kitchen, wondering if she could manage to make tea, but was ashamed to admit she had only a vague knowledge of American cookers and might botch it spectacularly. (The kitchen was strictly Christophine's realm at home, territory ceded in exchange for Capriole's new studio.) She'd seen a faint hint of early light leaking under the library door and could wait there to ambush Mrs. Cheadle at the first clatter of a kettle.

Julia retraced her steps, silent as a thief, past the hall leading to Philip's bedroom at the other end of the apartment. The library would be chilly, but it offered better fare than the hopeless Arlen novel. She pushed open the doors and bit down on a cry.

Philip sat angled low in his smoking chair, pulled around to face a lively fire, whose light Julia had mistaken for dawn. Curled in the other chair, also angled toward the fire, was a woman. She was forty at least. Hair the implausible color of new pennies billowed down her back. They held cups and saucers—the coffee Julia thought she'd imagined. He was shirtless; she wore a man's dressing gown. The woman brushed Philip's arm, and his murmuring stopped. Following her nod, he turned.

"Ah." He set his coffee on the floor. "Good morning. You're up early."

Julia was too dumbfounded to reply.

He stood, spilling both cats onto the carpet. "May I introduce my friend Mrs. Macready? Leah, this disheveled young thing is Julia."

He wore black silk pyjama trousers knotted loosely at the waist. His bare chest was smooth and muscled, the physique of a fencer more skilled than the dilettante he professed to be. With a turban and glaze of oil, he could easily pass for Nijinksy in the firelight; Julia's initial comparison had been apt. Many would have found his appearance indecent, but she suppressed a smile. A Beardsley man was no more likely to simper in girlish modesty than she was.

The woman handed him the dressing gown draped over the arm of his chair. She held her own together at her waist as she crossed the room. Her hand was warm and carried a perfume Julia didn't recognize, more spice than flowers. "Happy birthday, Julia."

Who was she? Philip's mistress? Julia hoped he would have the tact not to say so.

"Mrs. Macready is an old and dear friend," he said.

"More dear than old," the woman clarified. Dark green silk rippled beneath the folds of her charcoal robe, its sleeves rolled into fat cuffs. She found the belt and secured it with a neat tug and loop. Each hand flashed with rings. "Would you like some coffee?" She gestured toward a white pot on the hearth tiles.

She dispatched Philip to the kitchen for another cup. "No need for alarm," she said the moment he was gone. "We keep to ourselves. He talks well of you, you know. No, really, Julia. He's quite sick about the will business and—"

This astonishing speech dissolved into a brilliant smile as he returned.

Julia imagined how foolish she must look, hair tousled as a school-boy's, shoulders slack beneath a wrinkled shawl, pyjamas billowing over bare feet. Philip's dark head, silhouetted against the fire as he bent for the coffeepot, suggested something safe to say. "How is Lillian?"

Mrs. Macready answered for him. "Hoarse as a crow. She can barely squawk, which frustrates her no end. Nancy says the house has never been so peaceful."

"I'm sorry to hear it," Julia said. "I mean that Lillian's ill." Philip filled the third cup and handed it to her.

"She asked again about your spat with Philip over his theories of crime," Mrs. Macready said. "It amuses her, and Philip reenacts it with great relish. He's quite a good mimic."

Julia said nothing at this predictable news of aunt and nephew's sport at her expense. With an enormous desire to be gone, she accepted the coffee and mumbled thanks in hasty retreat. By the time she pulled the library door shut behind her, they had returned to their chairs, legs again stretched toward the fire, feet mingling on the hearth, cats circling in their laps. The scene was every bit as unsettling as at first glimpse.

⁓

Julia walked around the side of the Rankin house, past the loggia shel-tering a black motorcar, through a honeysuckle arbor whose fragrance had passed, and down a flight of shallow brick steps to the basement apartment, where Naomi and Alice had lived. Movement at the bay win-dow overhead caught her eye: Nolda Rankin, watching her approach. Without looking up Julia edged nearer to the house, out of view.

Glennis opened the apartment door before Julia could knock. Alice stood beside a frayed velvet sofa, its seat cushions covered with a brown crocheted afghan tucked firmly into place.

"Look," Glennis said. "It was left in the letter box during the night. Alice got one too." She held out two typed warnings identical to Julia's.

Alice said hers had been tucked under a brick on the stoop, which worried her because few people knew Chester had finally allowed her to return to the apartment for a few days—against his better judgment, he'd said, and only until she could find another place to live.

An hour earlier Glennis had telephoned to say she'd offered to sort through Naomi's things, separating valuables the family should keep from things to be discarded or bundled for charity. Her voice jumpy with hope of clues to Naomi's last days, Glennis urged Julia to come and help. She said nothing about Julia's birthday or the business with Philip. Happy to keep her personal tumult to herself, Julia left without seeing or hearing any further sign of Philip or the phantom Mrs. Macready. If not for the cup and saucer she had returned to the kitchen, she might have thought she'd dreamed the extraordinary predawn encounter.

"I received one too," she said. "Philip's housekeeper said the envelope was pushed through the mail slot sometime before she retired."

"More threats?" Alice spoke through a cage of fingers. "Someone wanted to silence Naomi, and now they want to frighten us. They must be afraid we'll discover something. But what?"

Madame Sosostris could not have produced a better shivery gasp than Glennis's. Julia peeled off her gloves. "Maybe an answer will turn up among her things. How do you want to proceed?"

Glennis looked around, shoulders hunched, overwhelmed by the task, but before she could answer, Nolda Rankin emerged from a dark hallway behind them. "Don't spend much time down here, girls," she said. "The air's unhealthy, and I doubt you'll find anything to save. Some of the furniture might have another few serviceable years left." She looked about with narrowed eyes. "Most things, though, like this filthy sofa, are beyond disgusting. I want it hauled away and burned. It was a disgrace twenty years ago. The beds too. Strip the linens and leave them to be taken out as well."

"We're only looking for Naomi's personal things," Glennis said. "After Miss Clintock takes what's hers, no one cares what you do with the rest of this rubbish." She clearly resented her sister-in-law's meddling, though her rebuke also thoughtlessly scorned the place Alice called home. If Alice felt the sting, she hid it well. Her eyes flickered but not her expression.

In fact, the apartment was small and spare. The ceiling seemed to hover just above their heads, and it creaked when someone passed overhead. A musty smell put Julia in mind of root cellars and garden sheds. The only window was shadowed by the wide overhanging bay upstairs. Even with its starched cotton curtains pushed aside, it let in little of the day's sunshine and none of its autumn warmth. The seating area held only the sofa, a low table covered with pamphlets and papers, and an oversize rocking chair. At the end of a dim hallway behind the rocker was a door of rough-cut boards whose frame skimmed the ceiling. Its bulk suggested it connected to the basement and house above, not merely to another room in the dank apartment. This guess was confirmed when Nolda Rankin disappeared through the door as quietly and abruptly as she had come.

"Here's Naomi's room, though I doubt you'll find much of value." Alice led them to a windowless bedroom so small the three of them could barely crowd in. "She sold most of what she had. But almost everything in the apartment was hers. I brought only personal things and a roasting pan. If it were worth anything, we'd have sold that too."

Alice pulled a bead-weighted string to switch on a small ceiling light bulb. Their shins brushed against a narrow iron bedstead. Two fruit crates were stacked beside it, each filled with books and papers. On top sat a round clock and a lamp with an insect-stained cloth shade. Pushed against the foot of the bed was a pine bureau topped with four small framed photographs of Naomi with women Julia didn't recognize. The top drawer's pull had been replaced with a nail. A curtain of ticking covered the narrow entrance to what was likely a closet or recessed shelving. Except for a shapeless gray sweater and a Children's

Aid Society calendar, both hung on nails, the once-white walls were bare.

Glennis's face went slack with shock.

"I'll leave you to it," Alice said. Julia leaned her knees into the bed's thin mattress to let her pass. "I'll be packing my things across the hall."

"Dreadful," Glennis said. "I don't know if I can do this."

Julia eyed the moth holes and yellow stains of the bed's wool blanket, wondering when the linen had last been laundered. Fortunately she'd worn her oldest frock, expecting something like this. "It shouldn't take long. Just look through the bureau drawers and the closet. She may have a little jewelry tucked away. And keep an eye open for a diary or private keepsakes. If she had secrets, here is where they'd be."

Glennis sucked her lower lip. "Poor Naomi. I don't know which breaks my heart more, the way she died or seeing how she lived."

Julia gave Glennis's fingers a quiet squeeze for courage and went to sort things in the main room.

An old sideboard stood against the far wall. With a round claw-foot table and three mismatched chairs, the area passed for a dining room. In the sideboard's two top drawers, Julia found four cotton napkins, clean and folded, six partly burned candles, three pencils, mismatched sheets of paper of varying sizes, a pair of scissors with one of the points broken off, and a cigar box containing basic sewing and darning supplies.

Below the drawers, two shallow shelves held assorted crockery, none of it matching, and a tarnished pair of silver candlesticks. Julia placed the candlesticks on the table and moved on to inventory the kitchen: an old-fashioned sink, icebox, and oil stove in a grimy alcove. She found tin canisters of flour, sugar, and oatmeal; an unopened tin of lard; a packet of Uneeda biscuits; a white enamel bread box, empty; and a bowl of green pears. Behind a red gingham curtain in the cabinet were a squat white teapot; an assortment of dishes; a box of cutlery, its silver plate rubbed down to brass; and a chipped pickle crock holding utensils. Overhead stretched a thin rope with a dozen or so clothes pegs at one end. Everything told of a mundane and cheerless life. Just as well Glennis would not see it close up.

"We don't have much."

Julia wheeled so abruptly she nearly knocked Alice over. They both apologized as Alice filled the kettle. She lit the stove, set the pot on the water-stained wood counter, and measured tea from a small packet. "We've been here nearly a year," she said in answer to Julia's question. "Naomi took me in when I had nowhere else to turn."

This was the sort of phrase that Julia's London friends sometimes mocked, declaiming the lament in weepy falsetto voices from cheap novels left in subway carriages. Over her shoulder Alice gave a slant smile that promised to explain in a moment. Was this the endless chore of a suffragist, Julia wondered, to tell her story to curious ladies untouched by poverty or struggle? Told a hundred times, was it now polished smooth as stone? She waited, silent as the teakettle began to rattle and hiss.

"I left my husband in '16, more than eight years ago now," Alice said. "That's how it turned out, though I meant to return. I left a note and three fresh loaves of bread, plus a full pot of beans and a basket of apples, and I took my children to stay with my sister in Clarksville. Then I rode the train to Washington to walk that picket line at the White House. It was the most glorious time of my whole life, those three weeks."

Alice made the tea and carried the pot to the table. They sat across from each other and held the hot tea to their faces. "By then I knew I couldn't live with myself if I didn't go. I'd seen too many girls put to work so their brothers could get a few more years of schooling. Then those poor girls get auctioned off like slaves to husbands willing to pay for their upkeep, because their papas decide the poor things' wages don't cover the food they eat. Before they know it, those girls have babies of their own and worse work than most factory jobs, which at least give you Sundays off. If a woman gets fed up and wants better, or even if she tries to improve her lot on her own somehow, she's beaten for sassing off, and no policeman in seven counties will believe her story or help her even if he did."

Alice's gray eyes turned to flint. "Three weeks. That's all I was gone. I took just half of the money from the cigar tin and bought a train ticket and as many days in a rooming house as it would cover. But when I came home, he wouldn't let me in, wouldn't even talk to me. He'd already been to the sheriff, and do you know he had me declared unnatural, unfit to mother my own children, just for going off like that? Before I knew it, he'd divorced me, claimed I abandoned him with wanton intent. He married Sally Kraus soon as that ink dried, and neither one would let me so much as say goodbye to my children. Three boys I had—have—" She corrected herself fiercely. "Oldest was eleven, and my girl was the baby, just three that summer. She won't know me now, only the lies they tell her. My husband made good and sure I had nothing, not a penny, not a friend, not even my good name. Can you think what he tells my boys about me?"

Julia felt Alice's grip and saw her own arm stretched across the table, her manicured fingers covered by Alice's scarred and reddened ones. Who had reached for whom? Too stricken by the story to remember, she reversed their hands and stroked the older woman's knuckles.

"I near went mad," Alice went on. "Everything I ever knew was behind me, locked away. I had no choice but to start walking. Eventually I made my way back to Washington because that was where you wanted to be if the vote mattered to you. I washed dishes and ironed shirts in boardinghouses across Ohio and Pennsylvania, working my way east. That's when I knew the movement was going to be my life from then on. I could never start over with a husband and children again, not after what had happened. The party, the other women, they're my family now."

She slid free of Julia's hands to take up her tea. "When the war came and the men went off, a few of us found better work that wasn't just squab jobs, but they fired us as soon as the boys came home. Even if you could hold on to one of those good jobs, they paid you half as much as a man. Half. Or worse. There's no justice, Miss Kydd. I decided that if I was going to work hard and still scrimp for a meal and roof over my head, I might as well make sure the work had some reward to it more than measly wages. During the war I learned bookkeeping and clerking. That's what I do for the Union. I take notes at meetings, keep the accounts. I manage our financials, what little we have." Her eyes rested on Julia, but her gaze was elsewhere.

"When did you meet Naomi?"

"In Washington, the second time. I was poor as a church mouse, beholden to the charity of others. Those who had a bit didn't mind sharing with those who had nothing. Every one of us valued our sisters' stiff backs and aching feet as much as our own. It was sheer good fortune. Mine, anyway. Naomi and I were assigned to the same city block, so we marched together, back and forth with our banners and our signs, for nine days in the rain. There were others too, but pretty soon we got talking. I could listen to her forever. She knew women I'd only heard of—Alice Paul, Lucy Burns, Gertrude Pinchot. Naomi listened to me too, to what I felt and thought.

"That's when I understood Naomi was different. Other rich women fight with us, and they help in huge ways, but poor women know best what we're up against and why more than the vote has to change in this country if women will ever be as free as men. Rich women can join the marches and protests, but in the end they go home to hot meals and servants. Like I said, Naomi was different. She understood hardship because she suffered too. She said it was nothing to sacrifice a few privileges of fine living when others were sacrificing so much more. She said until we could all have proper meals and good doctors and opportunities to pursue our talents, she wouldn't enjoy those luxuries herself.

"Well, before that marching was over, I knew I wanted to work with her, for her. We both stayed on in Washington through that summer, and whenever she needed anything—a letter posted, a seam mended, her hair pinned—I'd take care of it if I could. I followed her to New York and helped set up the Union. I've always done whatever she needed me to do."

Alice leaned into the table, pushing her words toward Julia with a strain in her raw, lined face. "I loved her, Miss Kydd, like a twin of my very soul."

Nothing could have been more clear. "Her death must be terribly hard for you. I'm so very sorry."

"You can't possibly know." Her chin dropped, and Julia saw a thinning spot at the top of her head, where gray hairs outnumbered brown ones. When Alice looked up, she released a great breath. "Naomi had been troubled for weeks before she died. Not so much ill, not that I could see, but unhappy, worried. For the first time she raised her voice to me, sharp and hurtful. Something was wrong, but it was an awful secret even from me. All I could think of was those hateful threats. She kept insisting it was a private matter, that she could deal with it herself, and that I shouldn't worry. Well. It was agony to watch her suffer. Something was gnawing at her from the inside, like a vicious worm, and all I could do was save those notes and pray I never had to show them to anyone, because that would mean they'd finally driven her to desperation. And then that's what happened, my worst fear come true."

A loud thump sounded from Naomi's bedroom, then a muffled blasphemy. When nothing more followed, Alice went on. "Something made life unbearable for Naomi. She'd take her own life only if it was the last bit of freedom left, her last chance to strike back at what tormented her. I always thought it was mental torment, but I can't stop thinking about your notion that maybe someone used physical pain to drive her over the edge. If I knew what or who was behind it, I'd stop at nothing—*nothing*—to see him shamed for it. Only God can punish him now, but I swear I'd do everything in my power to make sure he has not one more minute's peace on this earth."

Julia's jaw ached. She willed her teeth to unclench. The tale was largely as she'd conjectured, but now her blood and muscles hummed with the horror that logical guesswork neatly elided. Outrage, frustration, pity, grief—it was impossible not to feel some inkling of Alice's anguish. After several moments she said, "You say *him*, Alice. Do you know something more? Or have suspicions?"

A vein throbbed in Alice's forearm. She brushed down her sleeve to cover it and fastened the buttoned cuff. Her hand shook. No doubt she'd shared more than she'd intended. "Him, her. It, they. I wish I did know, but I don't. I have my suspicions, of course, but they're ugly to say without any proof, and I won't. It would be un-Christian and unwomanly."

"You suspect Chester Rankin, don't you?"

"So does his own sister," Alice snapped. She bit down on her lip and swung her head toward the kitchen. "Here I've talked your ear off and kept you from your work. I'm late too. They're expecting me at the Union." She stood, bustling together the tea things. She paused before adding in a low voice, "But I'm grateful you heard me out, Miss Kydd. I wish you could have known Naomi. You'd have liked her. She was very different from her sister."

Alice glanced at Naomi's bedroom, where Glennis was thumping about, frowning at the inadvertent insult. Then she shook her head and carried the dishes to the sink. After dropping two pears into a string bag and calling a hurried goodbye to Glennis, Alice left the apartment.

Watching her boots clatter up the brick steps, Julia thought hard. She rose and moved quietly to listen at the door, where Glennis had gone silent. Before her resolve could falter—it had to be done, like it or not—Julia stepped across the narrow hall and slipped into Alice's bedroom.

The room was even tinier than Naomi's, scarcely more than a cupboard. A pallet on the floor sufficed for a bed, filling the room from end to end. In the corner three fruit crates were stacked, as in Naomi's room, as shelving. They held a few books, a hairbrush and three bone combs, a chipped saucer with a pair of plain earrings, and neatly folded underclothes. The bottom crate was filled with a mound topped by a folded cotton bedsheet. Julia's heart sank. She listened for a sound, half hoping to be driven from the room in a guilty panic.

But there was none. She knelt, careful to disturb nothing but the folded linen pushed into the crate's cavity. She laid it aside and uncovered a small typewriting machine.

CHAPTER 18

Julia carried the machine to the dining table, inserted a sheet of paper from the sideboard drawer, and advanced it over the narrow roller. Wincing at each snap of a key in the quiet apartment, she punched out the words and laid the sheet beside the note delivered to Philip's apartment last evening. The two typed texts matched exactly, calibrated to identical letterspacing. They matched in color too, each produced with a fresh black ribbon, and each featuring a clouded counter of the lowercase *o*, filled with ink residue, and a *y* with a scratched left stem. There was no doubt the threat she'd received had been typed on this machine. She'd noticed both damaged characters on the notes Alice had shown them at the Union; this machine produced them as well.

Julia stuffed the sheets into her handbag and returned the machine to its hiding place. Declaring her sorting task finished—other than the tarnished candlesticks, there was nothing the Rankins might want to keep or sell—she sat in the old rocker to think. A faded quilt draped over the chair's back and folded into a seat cushion made it surprisingly comfortable.

Why would Alice send anonymous notes to threaten her dearest friend? Her devotion seemed genuine and unshakable. Perhaps she'd hoped to frighten Naomi into caution. Perhaps she'd perceived an enemy and hoped the notes would suggest treachery to Naomi too. But why resort to subterfuge? Why not simply confide her suspicions?

Julia remembered something curious about the notes Alice had shown them: none were dated and, without envelopes, none were postmarked. They could have been produced years ago or recently—even after Naomi's death. That raised a new question: Why on earth would Alice fabricate a story of menace looming over Naomi?

And why would she now warn off Glennis and Julia? That was most puzzling of all. Alice had gone out of her way to raise alarms in Glennis's mind, to provoke questions about Chester's account of an accidental overdose. At every chance Alice had encouraged Glennis's suspicions; why would she now want to frighten her? To deepen those suspicions? All Julia knew for certain was that the machine that had produced the threatening notes was hidden in Alice's room. She assumed that meant Alice had written and sent the notes. Was she meant to think so?

Maybe Alice wasn't aware the machine was there. Everyone knew Chester had insisted she stay away from the apartment for several nights after Naomi's death. While Alice was away, he or someone else could have typed the latest notes and then hidden the machine among her things. To scare her? To incriminate her when it was found? Regardless, it must be someone with access to the apartment. Someone who could enter from the home above? Nolda Rankin had just demonstrated how easily it could be done.

Naomi's bedroom door opened. Julia quickly added her discovery to the list of things not to tell Glennis, not yet. She needed more time to ponder its implications, to see how it fit among the other unexplained oddments she'd noticed. If it fit.

Glennis flopped onto the sofa, dropping an old cigar box onto the squashed, afghan-covered cushion beside her. "Has she gone?" She raked her fingers into her hair. "Just as well. It's too much, Julia. I can't bear what I'm finding. Nothing makes any sense. Look."

Glennis handed her the box. Inside was a jumbled heap of folded papers. They seemed to be receipts bearing various letterheads, some ornate and effusive, others terse. Each listed one item cryptically described: *1 brlt gold & dmd; 1 ldys ring, sphr; 3 ivry combs w. prls; 3 dlx bks ½ moroc*; and so on, followed by a sum marked paid to N. Rankin. Paid to, not paid by.

"Naomi sold these things?" Julia lifted her voice into a question, but they both knew the answer. These were receipts for things Naomi had sold or pawned, probably when her reduced funds from Chester no longer covered expenses at the Union. They tracked her descent from affluence to poverty.

"I recognize most of it," Glennis said, voice sullen. "A lot was my mother's. Naomi was the oldest daughter, so she got the best jewelry and silver. I remember that sapphire ring. I thought it was the most beautiful thing in the world."

Julia thought of her own few treasures linking her to her mother.

"That's not the worst part. Some of this stuff disappeared last year. Chester made a big stink when his special edition of Lincoln's speeches went missing, all three volumes. He tried to whip a confession out of his boys. He was sure they took it, since they love that old war stuff."

Glennis dug through the pile in Julia's lap and pulled out *1 brclt, gold & gems, $75*. "This has to be Nolda's gold bracelet. Last winter she fussed us all to pieces when she couldn't find it. She dismissed one of the maids, sore as blazes when the girl refused to confess and return it."

Glennis pushed the receipts back into the flimsy box. "All that trouble and it turns out Naomi stole it. Well, we can't let Chester and Nolda know." She pushed the box at Julia. "Take it. Burn it or throw it in the rubbish, anything. Just get it out of this house."

It was hard knowledge for Glennis to accept, understandably so. These slips made Naomi real in a painfully new way. They were sad, mundane evidence that Naomi was neither a saint nor a harridan, as her public life led others to declare, but simply a woman driven to deceit and thievery by the all-too-ordinary realities of need.

To change the subject Julia said, "I found a pair of silver candlesticks that may have some value. Everything else should probably go to charity. Or to Alice, who seems to have very little of her own. I can't imagine how she's going to live." This was another dispiriting thought. She quickly asked, "Did you find anything to save?"

Glennis fell back hard against the sofa cushions, raising a puff of dust. "Save? You could say that. Come on. I'll show you."

The tiny bedroom was in chaos, with clothing strewed across the bed. Each bureau drawer was open, contents spilling out. Boxes lay on the floor in disarray. "Sorry for the dog's breakfast," Glennis said. "She had a few decent blouses and a good leather belt. But this is what gives me the flipping glooms."

She unfolded a cotton handkerchief. Inside lay a small apple-green bottle of Lalique glass pressed with an ornate vine pattern: Le Jade, the new Roger et Gallet perfume. "Lyle Curley gave this to me last year when we got engaged. I was sick when I couldn't find it. I didn't tell anyone because Nolda would go poisonous about the help again, but I was sure one of the day girls took it. That's when I had a better lock put on my door. And here it was Naomi all the time. As bad as a common thief. It's too horrible."

"Maybe Chester allowed her less money than you thought. She didn't exactly live high off the hog here."

Glennis kneaded her lips between her teeth, an unattractive habit. "I can see taking things from upstairs to sell, maybe. Chester's such a skinflint, and Lord knows he's crawling with it. Serves him right for being so tight. But my perfume? I thought she liked me. We were friendly, sort of, when we saw each other." Her voice hardened again. "But she took my perfume, just to have, not even to sell. I had to buy another bottle so Lyle wouldn't find out I'd lost it, and it cost me a fortune."

Julia doubted the expense had put more than a small dent in Glennis's budget. She probably spent more on manicures in a month. Julia took the elegant little vial and held it up. About a quarter of the precious liquid was gone. "I suppose Naomi liked nice perfume too, now and then."

Glennis's face fell like a soufflé just from the oven, from resentment to remorse. She had the most unguarded face of anyone Julia knew. "And here I am fussing at her. I'd have given it to her or bought her a bottle if I'd known. I would have, Julia. She should have told me she wanted it."

In a burst of generosity, Glennis took the bottle and pulled out the tiny glass stopper. She drew it behind each of Julia's ears, then remoistened and rolled it in the hollow of her own throat. A French parfumerie blossomed in the close room. "She must have felt like a boiled rag down here, knowing about all the nice things upstairs just sitting there, completely ignored. Chester's so stingy I don't blame her a bit for helping herself to a few of them. It still feels sneaky. I don't like that part, but who can blame her?"

Glennis rewrapped the little bottle and set it on top of the bureau. She sat down beside a loose pile of blouses. "A few of these might fit me. I'd like to have something of hers. Vivian might fit into the smaller ones, after the baby comes." She shuffled an inventory of the mostly white cotton blouses. "I didn't think to bring down a basket."

Julia pulled back the wool blanket and reached for the flat pillow. "I read this once in a novel. You can use a pillow slip to carry things. It's a zippy trick." Of course, in the novel it had been a trick used by zippy thieves. "You can—" She fell silent. The case was made of exquisite white silk, monogrammed with an ornate *R* in brilliant blue thread.

Wounded shock returned to Glennis's voice. "Nolda wondered where that went."

Julia shook the thin pillow out onto the bed. A few feathers drifted onto the piled clothing, but both women stared at a second surprise hidden in the shallow dent beneath where the pillow had been. Julia lifted and unfurled an ecru silk sleeping gown, its bodice of Calais lace still curved eerily in the shape of its owner's breasts. A glance at the side seam confirmed it came from Cadolle in Paris. With almost palpable clarity Julia understood the desire to slide into such pleasure at the end of a difficult day.

Glennis exhaled a soft sound, something between a whistle and a word. Again Naomi Rankin had eluded Julia. Here lurked yet another facet of the woman, one who even in desperation must have savored intense sensuous luxuries. Did Alice know this side to her friend? She must. What Julia knew of Alice slid further into the same shadowy thicket.

"Look," Glennis said, fingering the almost weightless garment. They saw careful stitches where it had been mended, where the lace had been reattached at the shoulder, and a ghostly stain at the hem. "It's old, but isn't it stunning?" She lifted it to her cheek. "I want to keep this. I'll never fit into it, but look how it's almost like she's still inside. It must have made her feel beautiful."

Indeed.

"Archie would faint dead away if I sashayed out in something like this," Glennis said, palm sliding across its shimmer. "He won't even let me leave the lights on. It might do him good, stir him up a little." She sighed. "I suppose your David wouldn't bat an eye. You'd look divine in a slinker like this."

Your David pinched Julia's breath. Such proprietary drivel was as naive as it was smug, but a prospective marriage would render the expression unwittingly ironic. To avoid Glennis's avid eyes, shining with curiosity, Julia folded and slid the blouses into the pillow slip. "Did you find a diary?" she asked, crouching beside the stacked fruit crates where Naomi kept her few books. She scanned the miscellany but saw only worn copies of common editions and thin volumes of polemical tracts.

"Just what's there. Nothing to write in. If she kept a diary, it's somewhere else." Glennis wrapped her hands inside Naomi's lingerie like a muff.

Julia sank to her knees beside the jumbled books. They might have no particular worth, but they were still books. She pulled them out onto the floor and replaced them upright in crude order of subject matter. In the bottom crate a fat, gilt-stamped clothbound Bible lay on its back. Ten thousand like it languished in secondhand bookstalls, the ubiquitous stuff of late Victorian Christianity.

"We all got one of those for First Communion," Glennis said, "from our uncle George. Mine has gruesome pictures. I used to like them but wouldn't care much for them now."

Julia lifted the large quarto, weighing its bulk. "Did you look inside?"

Glennis stared at her. Julia opened the front cover. Its several hundred pages had been glued together and hollowed out, leaving a cavity. Old Bibles were common candidates for homemade hiding places. It was another of the useful insights readers gained into the criminal, or at least the devious, mind.

Inside the Bible lay a thick paperbound booklet filled with the same handwriting they'd seen on Naomi's suicide note. Glennis made another inarticulate sound and reached for it. "Crikey." She rifled the densely covered pages between her thumbs. "I must have pudding for brains. I'd never've found this in a hundred years."

She turned to the last entry and brought it nearly to her nose, squinting at the crabbed, heavily pointed script. "It's hopeless." She slapped the little diary shut. "I just can't read this."

Julia fought an impulse to snatch the booklet from her. She wouldn't give up so easily. "Let me, then."

"No, she was my sister. I have to read it, and I will. I need to know what happened. Even if it means learning more terrible things about my family." Glennis pushed the diary into the pillow slip with the blouses. "But not now. I'll need a stiff drink to get through it. For courage."

A drink sounded like a capital idea to Julia too. As she lifted the hollowed-out Bible to return it to the crate, something rattled across the bottom of the secret cavity and caught on a small slip of paper. It was two pieces of jewelry, fastened together, an old-fashioned diamond brooch and a gold ring with a beautiful square-cut emerald. Along its inner band was inscribed *W. C. to M. L.*

Glennis examined them. "Not ours. Must be her latest loot, ready to pawn next. Guess I'd better take them. Call it evens for pinching my perfume."

Julia nudged open the little note, subduing an irrational hope that it might explain everything. But it was an ordinary appointment slip, confirming the next appointment for "Naomi Pearsall" with Dr. Cecelia Greenbaum on September 22 at five o'clock. This coming Monday. The doctor's Brooklyn address and telephone number were printed in Copperplate at the top. Conventional in every way. "Did Naomi ever use the name *Pearsall?*"

"Not that I knew. It's our mother's maiden name. Why would she do that?" As Julia silently wondered herself, Glennis added, "Who's Dr. Greenbaum?"

"No idea. Should be easy to find out, though. I'll look into it."

As Glennis gathered together Naomi's clothes, Julia sat back on the bed, forehead on her palm. She stared at the innocuous little paper. A doctor's appointment could be the answer to their questions. It suggested Naomi had suffered some health problem that she had concealed from Alice and her family. The words *next appointment* carried immense significance. If a previous examination had detected symptoms that pointed, in hindsight, to poison, that information could help confirm Naomi had been murdered. Glennis's suspicions would be vindicated, Naomi's memory would be redeemed, and Julia could sail home to London secure in a future of her own choosing.

If, however, Naomi had had a natural ailment, one that flared into an acute crisis that fateful day—well, it was very sad, of course, but also supremely disappointing. It would mean Chester's self-serving tale of "death following a brief illness" was on the mark after all.

His cruel stifling of every impulse that gave Naomi life and energy would pass unchallenged. And, short of accepting David's shocking proposal, it would be off to that bedsit in Bethnal Green for Julia. Everything depended on the nature of Naomi's complaint. On what Dr. Greenbaum said.

"*Ow*." Glennis turned to see what had poked her when she stepped back. It was a nail. Hanging from it was a gray cardigan, probably as Naomi had left it, shed carelessly, not knowing it would never again ward off the early autumn chill.

"Anything in that pocket?" Julia eyed the sagging square patch.

Glennis pulled out a wadded handkerchief, reeking of dried vomit, and dropped it in disgust. A second, reluctant search found two dimes and another slip of paper. She read it and tossed it into Julia's lap. "Looks like breakfast."

On it was written *5-9* followed by *Heacock special. One egg, scrambled. Extra salt. Black tea, no sugar, no milk. $40.14 paid in full.* It seemed to be an ordinary receipt, though the price was impossibly rummy. A slip of the pen, surely. Julia asked if she could take it and try to make some sense of it.

"Go ahead. Can't think how it will help."

Julia had no idea either. But thanks to years of living abroad, one possibility had already occurred: 5-9 could be a date, September 5. The day Naomi had died.

CHAPTER 19

The steps to Philip's apartment had never felt steeper than they did early Monday evening. Julia had spent the afternoon lingering at an obscure table in an uptown café, nursing a café au lait as she tried to wring clues out of the two notes they'd found hidden in Naomi's bedroom.

She tackled the breakfast receipt first. In all likelihood it was as ephemeral and banal as it seemed: cryptic from carelessness, not guile. Hundreds of diners dotted the streets of Manhattan, many of them serving breakfast fare innocuous enough to require only terse scratchings on simple slips of paper. Unable to spend endless hours on the pavement or hunched furtively over Philip's telephone, she despaired of ever locating the source of a "Heacock special." It was the suspicious price that lured her on. For three hours she conjured constructions so fantastical (and ridiculous) she couldn't bear to recall them—secret recipes for deadly potions, elaborate codes for poison formulas, and so on. Illicit drugs or chemicals might command such prices, but Julia's scant knowledge of pharmacology or even rudimentary chemistry made finding any correspondence between tea and poison impossible.

It was labor beyond her ability, and she conceded defeat. Praying for better luck with the appointment slip with Dr. Greenbaum, Julia moved on, in search of a quiet hotel with a private telephone lounge.

She placed the call to Dr. Greenbaum's office shortly before four. Identifying herself as Naomi Pearsall's secretary in a tremulous voice,

Julia apologized that Miss Pearsall was unable to keep her appointment that afternoon. Delayed in Albany at a meeting, she reported.

"Would she like to reschedule?" the receptionist replied, after an icy pause of rebuke for the late notice.

"I suppose it depends," Julia said. "I'm afraid I'm just the assistant here. The others are all in Albany, and I was only told they're delayed. Is it terribly important, you know, the reason for Miss Pearsall's appointment? Something serious, I mean?" She was fishing. Dr. Greenbaum's listing in the telephone directory gave no indication of her medical specialization.

Another pause, conveying more censure. "Details of patients' appointments are confidential, miss."

"Oh, of course. Oh yes, I see. Yes, certainly." Julia fumbled along, hoping to provoke either sympathy or exasperation on the other end of the line. "They don't tell me anything, you see, and I don't want to do the wrong thing. Is it crucial, do you think? Maybe we should reschedule for as soon as possible, in case it's really important?"

The receptionist's tone thawed. "Was Mrs. Pearsall experiencing any discomfort, do you know?"

"Yes, some, I think," Julia said. "She's been having headaches and tummy trouble, if you know what I mean. No one's told me anything more, but then that's the way it is around here. I suppose that's why she was seeing the doctor?"

The woman laughed. "Nothing too alarming then, dear. How about if we reschedule her for a week from Wednesday at three? Please ask her to confirm when she returns."

"Oh yes. I'll do that. Thank you so much. For understanding, I mean." Julia babbled gratitude to disguise her frustration. Not only was the receptionist scrupulously discreet, but Naomi's ailment appeared to have been utterly nonfatal. Whatever her complaint, it hadn't roused concerns or suspicions. Julia couldn't let her inquiry end on that discouraging note. She pushed her voice to a new and shameless register of forlorn. "It's just that I'm so worried for her."

The woman laughed again, more kindly. "I doubt there's anything to worry about, dear. It's quite common to experience a funny tummy, as you put it. But if she's worried, you can assure her the second trimester is usually much more comfortable."

"Oh, quite right. Yes, of course. Thank you so much." That time Julia's stutter was genuine. Her hypothesis of malicious cunning collapsed in a heap, wrecked by the most everyday explanation.

Naomi had been pregnant.

⌒

The telephone bell sounded as Julia stepped into Philip's apartment.

"That'll be for you, miss," said Mrs. Cheadle, materializing in the hallway. "Tiresome thing's been ringing me off my feet."

Gloves still on, Julia dropped her umbrella into the corner stand and hurried to the alcove where the instrument was kept. Her new knowledge complicated what she might say to Russell, but the prospect of hearing his voice was still cheering.

"Get over here." It was Glennis. "Dr. Perry's called a powwow. He says he has something important to say about Naomi. Hurry!"

Julia turned on her heel and was gone.

⌒

Heavy rain had carved braids of mud along the Rankins' entry drive. Julia stepped around the muck and mounted the steps to the front door. Out of the evening gloom, Russell appeared from the other direction. They exchanged muted greetings. "I have no idea what this summons is about," he said, "but if it's half as shocking as what I—" A wedge of light fell across them as a housemaid pulled open the door. "Fasten your chinstrap," he said into Julia's upturned collar as she preceded him into the house. She had a bad feeling she might need one. Whatever Dr. Perry felt compelled to tell the Rankins, she hoped it didn't include mentioning their visit.

The family was gathered in the sitting room much as they had been for Naomi's service, and Alice Clintock was there too, in a straight chair pulled slightly away from the group. Dr. Perry had settled into the oversize wing chair, this time with a needlepoint ottoman bearing his troublesome leg. Head down, fingers steepled against the bridge of his nose, the old man didn't seem to notice as the others assembled. Apart from the scrape of chairs across carpet and the old doctor's labored breaths, the room was thick with an anxious silence.

"So, we're all here," Chester said as soon as the maid closed the door. "You've given us quite a turn, Dr. Perry. What's so important?"

The doctor lowered his hands to his lap. "I owe you all a great apology, and I can't rest until I've made it. In my vanity I thought I could still perform the duties of a medical man, but I'm ashamed to admit I was not thinking clearly the night Naomi died. I overlooked, or rather I failed to consider properly, something quite vital. Something that changes everything about what I said before."

Chester gaped. "What are you saying?"

"Simply this, my boy. I now believe Naomi did not die from an overdose."

The silence swelled.

"You're saying it wasn't suicide?"

"What did kill her, then?" Russell demanded.

"Is it possible to know?" asked Vivian.

The doctor rubbed the long muscles of his gouty leg. "No, my dear, I'm afraid not. With her body cremated, we will never know the truth with certainty. Had I been thinking more carefully that night, I would have ordered an autopsy. I am very, very sorry."

Grateful as Julia was to have her suspicions confirmed, she'd never reckoned that her questions would provoke the good doctor to confess his failings to the Rankins. Now she prayed the old man would consider his conscience cleared and leave it at that. Any more honorable soul baring might expose her investigation.

"A few weeks ago you were certain the tablets killed her. How can you now say they didn't?" Chester demanded.

Dr. Perry heaved his frame toward Julia. "I have this young lady to thank for pointing out a perfectly sensible question. She and Glennis joined me for tea last week, and we had quite a chat. After you left, my dear, I couldn't stop thinking about your observation, about the tablets."

A fire began to lick about Julia's heels. As she feared, every eye was on her. Surprise burst audibly into indignation, then anger. Worst was Russell's hard syllable of dismay.

"What did Miss Kydd say?" Nolda asked, each word taut.

"She was puzzled about the tablets still intact in poor Naomi's mouth. Miss Kydd asked how quickly the tablets would take effect. I assured her it could be a relatively calm death, in which one first drifts into unconsciousness. The true upshot, I understood later, was that unless death had been nearly instantaneous, the unswallowed tablets would be gone, dissolved by saliva. At death, saliva production would cease and the tablets remain partially whole."

"Well, then—" Chester began, but the doctor swung his head to continue.

"She died, you see, before the tablets could do their work."

No one spoke or moved. Julia's breath felt pinned inside her.

Chester slapped the arm of his chair. "You realize what this means?" he shouted. "It means we were right. She ran herself ragged, too hard for too long, and it finally killed her. Just like we said. We've been telling the truth all along."

"Is this good news?" Vivian asked. "Can we put to rest those awful whispers about why she's not in Saint Stephen's?"

Wrath flared in Alice's voice. "She must have suffered terribly if it was something bad enough to kill her."

"But now we'll never know what," said Vivian.

"Something's not right here," Russell said. "It's bothered me from the start. Those tablets suggest she wanted to take her own life, but she'd know they take time. She'd have done something else, something quicker. Especially if she was in great pain, why mess about with tablets?"

His forehead furrowed as he worked out the gruesome logic. "More likely someone put them in her mouth. To make her death look like suicide. Or to make sure she died."

Oh, Russell, Julia thought. *Please, please hold your tongue. I can explain later. Don't put ideas into their heads, not before we know anything for certain.*

"You're saying someone else was involved?" In the stir, Julia couldn't be sure who spoke. The voice was a female's. Nolda? Vivian? Alice? Glennis?

"Someone manipulated her death?" Another garbled voice.

"Oh dear Lord, will there be an investigation?" Nolda said, her panic cutting through the commotion. She gripped Winterjay's sleeve. "This can't turn into another scandal. There must be a way to keep it private. Please, Edward, think of something. We can't let Naomi keep destroying our peace. It's too much."

Dr. Perry made a loud noise, not quite a cough and not quite a shout. "Please, dear people. Calm yourselves. You've been through enough already. Whatever killed poor Naomi has gone with her to eternity. The matter of her death is officially closed and will remain so unless you prefer to call it to police attention."

Nolda's relief was so sharply audible that there was no question of any such call.

"Wait." Glennis pounded her chair cushion. Hot color was splattered across her face and throat like drops of summer rain. "Someone forced Naomi to swallow those tablets when she was *dying?*"

This quieted the room. Alice fingered the beads at her throat and began to weep.

"How could anyone subject her to such a terrible farce?" Russell said.

"Who would do such a thing?" Vivian's pained echo hung in the air.

Russell stood. He reached into his coat pocket and pulled out a folded sheet of paper. "I have news too. It may very well answer that question." His next words followed like gunfire: "I learned today that Naomi filed a new will last year without consulting or even informing me. I knew nothing of it until my partner returned from Mexico and produced it this morning. It supersedes the will I read to you the other day. The new will changes everything."

"For God's sake, what does it say?" Chester demanded.

"As of October 19, 1923," Russell said, "Naomi bequeathed her entire fortune to Alice Clintock—" Harsh oaths sheared through this announcement, but he continued, reading from the document in his hand: "With the express stipulation that she is to employ the funds to advance the work of the Empire State Equal Rights Union. Should the Union cease to exist or deviate from its present objective, the funds are to support the operation of any organization, foundation, or enterprise Miss Clintock judges to best adhere to the objective of securing equal rights for women under the law. In gratitude for this stewardship, a generous retainer is provided for Miss Clintock for the remainder of her life."

Alice sat rigid, unbreathing. Julia felt her lungs contract. This did change everything, all she thought she understood about Alice.

"How dare you?" Chester swung toward Alice. "How *dare* you?"

"Subvert this family . . ." Nolda could only sputter, still clutching Winterjay's arm.

"You conniving, murderous snake." Chester crossed the room to where Alice sat. "You watched my sister die—holy hell, you probably hurried her along—and then you tried to shame us with that suicide farce. You weren't content to leech off her money while she lived; you made sure she gave you control of it. I swear you'll never see a penny. We'll crush you and your pathetic mob. Just you wait."

Chester's bent arms hovered at his sides, fists clenched. His fury misted Alice's face. If there was another noise in the room, Julia couldn't hear it, so loudly did the blood pulse in her ears.

"I swear I knew nothing about her will." Alice's voice shook. It took Julia a moment to realize she was trembling with outrage, not fear. "But I adore her more than ever for having the courage to change it."

Alice sucked two shallow breaths of air and unclamped her fingers from the chair. Her feet stirred as if she meant to rise despite Chester's looming bulk, but she either failed or abandoned the effort. "I'm the only one here who knows how she suffered and why. I loved her more than any soul on earth. If anyone killed her, it was you all, you hateful, hateful people."

Chester spasmed, and Julia threw an arm across her face as if the blow would fall on her. Winterjay and Russell lunged. Chester's shoulders came out of his jacket, but his fists were stayed. "Get out of my house," he shouted. "This instant. Get out and never set foot on my property again."

Alice slid her feet to one side and stood, gripping the back of her chair. Her eyes never left Chester's face.

"You can't!" Glennis jumped up. "Her things are here. You can't make her leave, not until she can take her things."

"Three days." Chester's voice went icy soft. "You have three days to get out of my house forever. Then if I ever see you here again, I'll have you shot for trespassing." He silenced Glennis's protest with a step toward Alice. "Get out!"

As if blown by the force of his anger, Alice fled.

CHAPTER 20

Glennis darted across the room and pulled Julia from her chair. This time she was only too glad for a hasty exit tethered to her friend's grip. At any moment someone—Chester? Nolda? Winterjay? Russell?—would confront her for stirring up this new maelstrom. She and Glennis slipped out as the others besieged Russell and Dr. Perry for something overlooked or misinterpreted, anything to blunt the double catastrophe. There was no mistaking their bleats of fury.

Glennis had prepared. After locking her bedroom door, she produced a silver bowl filled with shaved ice. She set it on the vanity table and drew from the cabinet a tall bottle of Dewar's and a spritzer of soda water. "I knew we'd need fortification," she said, handing Julia a heavily poured highball. "But I had no idea things would get this awful. Did Dr. Perry say someone murdered Naomi and then tried to make it look like suicide?"

Julia wrapped both hands around her glass. Good liquor would help. "Not precisely. He said she didn't die from an overdose of tablets. It leaves open the question of what did kill her, but it's too late for an autopsy to tell us."

"Which is a problem for us who want to know but a huge relief for whoever killed her. That much I get."

"If someone did kill her. That's still an *if*, Glennis. But yes."

"I don't think it's an *if* at all. If it wasn't Chester, it was Nolda. She's every bit as rancid about Naomi as he is, and they were both home that day."

"Weren't others here too?"

Glennis's face puckered in thought. "Vivian and Edward were in Boston that week for his nephew's christening, though she came back early for that awful séance party with her Talbot League crowd. I suppose Edward could have hoofed it back in secret, but really. Edward?"

Julia shrugged. She too found it hard to imagine either Vivian or Winterjay sneaking into Naomi's apartment to—what? Poison her? Cram tablets into her mouth? She hadn't had time to consider how Naomi's pregnancy altered the possible scenarios of how she had died, much less why or by whose hand.

"Let me think." Glennis settled back. "Russell stopped by that afternoon to see Chester and Nolda, but he couldn't stay for dinner. I don't think anyone else was here, except the help. I didn't even know Naomi and Alice were downstairs. But that's the problem, isn't it? We don't normally see who comes and goes from their apartment. I suppose anyone could have snuck in and killed her."

"Anyone with a motive," Julia said. "Let's concentrate on that, not opportunity. Who wanted her dead?"

"Chester. No wonder he couldn't wait to see her cremated."

Julia took a long swallow of Scotch. Her patience was thinned to breaking with Glennis's determination to whisk her brother off to the gallows. "He didn't resist the idea, that's true. But remember, it was Russell who suggested it."

"You're right. I'd forgotten. But that reminds me. On top of everything else, you'll never guess what I found in Naomi's journals."

Julia could jolly well guess. If she was right, it made breaking her own news easier. Glennis pulled Naomi's homemade diary from behind a stack of hatboxes on the floor. "You won't believe it," she said. "There's lots I couldn't figure out, but I know boy talk when I see it. I think she had a boyfriend, and he was a big secret. And do you know why?"

"Why?"

Glennis dimpled. "Because I think her boyfriend was Russell."

Julia did her best to look amazed.

"She calls him *R*, but with stuff about him being a lawyer and knowing him from way back, it has to be Russell. Can you even imagine? Russell's had a hundred girlfriends, and Naomi *never* seemed the least bit interested in any man. I always thought she might be, you know. It's just amazing. Russell and Naomi!"

In some sense Julia did not have to feign astonishment. The past few days had been so thick with surprises that she'd hardly had time to ponder Russell's admission that he and Naomi had been lovers. Glennis was titillated by her discovery, but Julia found it rife with painful implications.

Glennis's face clouded. "One problem, though. She never put dates on anything. I couldn't tell when stuff was happening. And the ink color changed a lot, like she only wrote now and then. The whole last half was just jottings, really, a few words or numbers strung together, not real sentences. The only actual names were Chester and Vivian, and hardly ever them. There was *R* for Russell and an *A*, I suppose for Alice, and a couple other initials now and then. I guess it was so personal she'd be the only one who needed to make sense of it."

Glennis closed the journal. "Do you think they were still at it, Russell and Naomi?"

"It's hard to say. What were her last entries about?"

"At the end it's just lists. I think they're about money. Like this." She showed Julia a litany of abbreviations interspersed with numerals and such commentary as *ask M. first, only fair!* and *half $ enough?* The pages were stippled with dollar signs, question marks, and exclamation points of all sizes, some underscored.

"She does seem preoccupied with money matters," Julia said. With excellent reason.

"Plus she changed her will."

That alone made perfect sense to Julia. It had been altered last October, the month Chester forced Naomi to accept his draconian terms. She must have resolved to ensure that at least in death she could control her own money.

"It's queer she didn't tell Russell, though," Glennis said. "Maybe she dumped him."

"Maybe."

Glennis frowned. The time had come. Julia freshened their highballs. "There's something else you should know. I only learned it myself this afternoon, and I hardly know what to make of it. Matters are more complicated than we imagine, Glennis. When I telephoned the office of that Dr. Greenbaum, the receptionist was quite tight-lipped, as I suppose she should be. But eventually I gathered that Naomi's appointment concerned, ah, female matters." Julia switched to the vague euphemism, remembering that Glennis digested information best in small doses.

"Naomi had womb trouble? I guess she was pretty old. That's not much help."

"Not womb trouble, not exactly. I'm sorry to put it so bluntly, but Naomi was seeing Dr. Greenbaum because she was pregnant."

As usual, the labored progress from confusion to understanding was visible on Glennis's wide face. Julia moved to sit beside her on the bed. "You must think me awfully thick," Glennis said. "I thought I knew at least my own family."

"Naomi was a woman of secrets. You can't blame yourself for not knowing what she kept hidden—from everyone, it seems." They leaned against one another, the mattress sagging beneath their weight. Julia held her glass to her forehead to cool its dull ache. Beyond the occasional crack of settling ice and fizzing soda, they heard distant raised voices, indistinct but agitated. Her mind was full with fragments that would not fit together. Naomi's life was more complex than she or Glennis had ever imagined, and the commotion downstairs suggested the rest of the Rankin family was coming to the same realization.

Glennis roused herself with a groan. "Do you think Russell was the baby's father?"

Julia had had more time to ponder that likelihood but was no less troubled by it. Russell claimed his intimacy with Naomi was long over. Why would he lie, if not to deny his role in her predicament?

Or in her death? Julia's stomach plunged. Russell would have had great incentive to see Naomi's body cremated, destroying the secret of her pregnancy forever. If Naomi had known of such darker streaks in his character, it would explain why she had changed her will without his knowledge. She would not have been the first woman to have feared a man she'd also loved.

Julia stirred, sickened at this plausible scenario. Was she wrong about the man? She liked Russell. Had she been a fool, taken in by his fondness for books and intimate candor? She rubbed Glennis's shoulders to disguise her own fidgeting.

"He'd marry her, though, wouldn't he?" Glennis said. "Unless he didn't know. But why wouldn't she tell him?" She shook her head. "I'm a dunce. None of this makes any sense."

"It's more than I can understand too."

"I bet Chester found out. I bet she refused to go to Arizona, or wherever those baby farm places are, and he decided to finish her off once and for all." Glennis's eyes fogged with tears. "Maybe he hounded her, roughed her up, boxed her good to kill the baby, and her too. Or maybe he told her she had to get rid of it. Handed her a poker and made her . . . I've heard about . . . it can kill you for sure. Oh Lordy. Even Chester couldn't be that vile, could he?"

Julia had witnessed appalling cruelty, physical and emotional, during those dark days in London when broken soldiers had returned to lives they could never resume. The mildest lamb could attack if backed into a corner. Chester clearly valued his family's illustrious name almost to obsession. But enough to subdue his own sister with such malice?

Logic intervened, a welcome comfort. "I don't think that's what happened. If she lost the baby, there'd be no mystery about how she died. There would be quite a lot of, you know, blood." Julia lowered her voice for the graphic word, but still Glennis slapped a hand across her mouth. "Much as Chester may have despised her, no, I can't see him doing anything so ruthless."

Glennis nodded a little, as much stymied as relieved. She licked her lips, intent on finding a new connection between Chester and Naomi's fate. "All right, so he telephoned her to meet him somewhere, put poison in her tea or something, then made it look like suicide. Clean and tidy—you can't say that doesn't sound exactly like him."

"Glennis, listen to me. Forget about Chester. It's time we took a hard look at the one person who's repeatedly lied to us."

"What do you mean?"

"Alice knows much more than she's admitted."

"Alice? You can't be serious. She loved Naomi. She's worked harder than anyone to keep Chester from sweeping her out with the rubbish."

Julia couldn't blame Glennis for resisting. She liked Alice too. "There are just too many inconsistencies. Remember the big calendar on Naomi's desk at the Union?"

Glennis nodded.

"I saw the note for the meeting on the night Naomi died."

"The one she made Alice go to instead."

"Yes. It was scheduled for eight thirty. Dr. Perry saw Naomi shortly after midnight, and he was certain—he said it twice—she'd been dead for at least eight hours. Don't you see? Alice wouldn't need more than an hour to get to the meeting. If she left the apartment before Naomi died, as she claims, she left several hours earlier than necessary. She may have gone somewhere else first, somewhere she's never mentioned. Or—"

Glennis calculated. "Or she was still there when Naomi died."

"Exactly. And another thing. Those anonymous threats someone sent us, like the notes Alice showed us?"

Glennis gave a reluctant nod, lower lip caught under her teeth.

"I found the typewriting machine that made them. It was hidden in Alice's bedroom."

"No. Impossible. Someone put it there to scare her off or make her look guilty. Alice would never send those threats." Glennis upended her empty glass over her mouth. Ice dropped against her teeth, splashing liquid onto her cheek.

"You must admit Chester's accusation isn't so rash. It's an awfully strong coincidence that Naomi should die in mysterious circumstances within a year of changing her will to provide for Alice."

There were more suspicions Julia might have confided, but they'd only provoke a new hailstorm of *why*s, which was the question she most struggled to answer herself. The new will gave Alice a strong financial motive for murder. She might have been jealous of Naomi's bond with Russell or believed he was distracting her from their work. Maybe she feared the scandal of Naomi's pregnancy would hurt the Union. Alice could have staged the suicide scenario, and she'd repeatedly revived the notion with her questions about the missing note. Suicide made Naomi a martyr to persecution, which served the Union's interests nicely. But Julia said none of this. More critical matters demanded answers first.

"Glennis, look at me. This is getting serious. We've stirred up a hornet's nest here, and things could get dangerous. Maybe we should let the police decide what happens next."

Glennis's fist bounced against the mattress. "I've told you. We can't. If we call the police, Chester will go straight to the superintendent, to the bloody mayor if he has to, and tell them I'm an excitable nincompoop. That would be the end of it, except he'd boot me down into that nasty apartment quicker than you could blink, and Archie would marry the next rich American he sees."

She twisted, knocking her knees into Julia's. "I know I've whinged on and on about Chester. I don't like him. I think he's tossy and evil. But I'm not imagining things. He's done everything he can to make Naomi disappear like some worthless nobody. And now he's going to get away with it, because we can*not* go to the police."

"Maybe not, but we can still ask Alice some hard questions."

Glennis rolled her eyes. "I don't see what good that will do."

"At least let's have another look around the apartment, when she's not there."

"Sneak in and snoop?"

"I suppose. She won't need to know. Tomorrow morning, when she's at work? The apartment's in your house, after all, and if Alice did have some role in Naomi's death, we're perfectly justified in poking around."

Glennis shooed away any moral qualms. The prospect of more snooping cheered her. "Or we might find something else, something Chester missed. Tomorrow's good, before he runs her out. Meet me here at ten, and we'll go down through the cellar when the kitchen's empty."

❧

It was late when Julia returned to Philip's apartment. She was glad it was dark, as it meant he was still out and their paths would not cross. She dropped the key in her handbag and stepped into a fragrance of gardenias thick as fog. Dwarfing the fine Jacobean table in the hall, another floral delivery waited, possibly more exuberant than the first.

There too in the deep shadows stood Philip and Mrs. Macready. She appeared to be leaving, a wool cape across her shoulders and one glove tugged smooth over her hand. Philip's back was to Julia. Jacketless, loose tie flung over his shoulder, he leaned one elbow into the wall, ear cupped in his palm. At Mrs. Macready's start, he turned. For the second time in a week, he and Julia gaped at each other.

Philip recovered first. "That stench is suffocating." He clawed through his hair, and the usual lock fell back across his brow. "Can't you just marry the poor Lothario?"

Julia started. She'd told Philip nothing of David, much less of his wedding intentions. She paled at her brother's eerily apt remark and then at his shrewd gaze observing her discomfort. She looked away and promised to move the flowers into her bedroom, though where they would fit, she couldn't imagine. A hasty glance conveyed the card's cabled message: *Monaco judge booked 9 November return Sunday next SS Majestic brother business over or not ticket waiting New York office your expiring David.* A small sound caught in her throat, and heat flared across her cheeks.

"Perhaps you intend to," Philip observed. "Just as well. Regardless, isn't it about time to take your plunder elsewhere? My apartment's no bower for aging fiancées."

"Philip!" His jaw flinched at Mrs. Macready's sharp reproof. He turned without a word and strode away down the dark hallway.

"Forgive him, Julia," Mrs. Macready whispered. "Lillian died a few hours ago."

Julia felt a pang of grief for the ill-tempered and impertinent but lively old woman. "I'm sorry to hear it, Philip," she called to his retreating back.

He ignored her, disappearing into the gloom. Another snub. Soon, soon, she reminded herself. Soon she'd be a continent away, beyond reach of his erratic moods.

Mrs. Macready sighed. "Think about it, my dear." She pulled on her remaining glove. "Please. I beg you. Think about it."

Julia stared at her. Think about what? The man's atrocious manners? Mrs. Macready lifted a finger to slowly brush her left ear.

And Julia understood. So simple and yet so astonishing. It made sense of everything, of his occasional rude disregard, his contorted postures, his always twisting to one side. That infernal peering. To what degree she couldn't be certain, but suddenly the explanation was plain as pudding. "He's deaf?"

"Only in one ear. But please say nothing. He wishes no one to know. He forgets himself, though; that's the trouble."

Julia felt doubly ashamed at her irritation. Philip hadn't spurned her sympathy, only failed to hear it. It was clear he loved his old aunt, in a rascally sort of way, and now she was dead. But his grief, however genuine, must be the least of Julia's concerns.

She reread the cable. *November 9* jerked the laces of the phantom corset squeezing her ribs. Expiring? Hardly. David's fingertips might trill a tabletop in exasperation, he might pace twice about his flat, but he no more *expired* than he *perished*. In three days his matrimonial intentions had progressed from blissful news to an appointment in Monaco. Julia still did not quite fathom his momentous decision—and certainly needed more time to respond to it—but he seemed to take her silence for maidenly hesitation, an obstacle to be swept aside with a declarative urgency many females might construe as charming devotion. Glennis would swoon flat at this cable; Julia was reduced to shallow breaths.

The harsh financial constrictions of her new life were beginning. Without money of her own, she would have to return on the ticket David purchased for her. Time to discover the treachery behind Naomi's death was running out. She was due to sail in six days.

CHAPTER 21

Night air that had felt mild when Julia returned from Glennis's was decidedly more bracing at three in the morning. Sleepless and a bit queasy in her bedroom hothouse of roses and gardenias, she swallowed two Spartans with quinine water, threw a shawl over her robe, and retreated to Philip's balcony. She sought fresh air and clarity. Instead, a numbing cold seeped through the folds of silk tucked around her legs as she stretched out on the chaise. Arms tight across her body, fists mittened in her shawl, she lay as restless under the stars as in her bed. When the shivering grew worse than her brooding, she gave up and returned indoors.

Remnants of a fire glowed in the library grate. Two crystal globes streaked with brandy waited on the trolley for Mrs. Cheadle to clear in the morning, and two ashtrays held the remnants of Philip's and Mrs. Macready's cigarettes, the stale odor of long hours together. Mourning Lillian Vancill? Planning ways to spend Julia's money? She switched on a reading lamp, poured some of Philip's Cointreau, and pushed the door ajar so she could retreat at the first sign of anyone about. She pulled down the Vale *Danaë* and stretched across the sofa. With two pillows behind her shoulders, she sipped the sweet liquor and hoped Ricketts's velvety black engravings would lure her thoughts far from New York and all its travails.

Three pages later she closed the book and balanced the glass on her breastbone.

Every hour pulled her closer to a new life. She hadn't sought marriage, but realistically, she would be foolish not to accept David's proposal. Or rather, to obey his instruction. Some women adored that sort of thing, but Julia bristled. He'd never addressed her like that before. As her lover, he had neither right nor need to concern himself with her affairs. Their lives were intermingled lines, not concentric circles. But as a wife without independent means, she'd be accepting terms, not dictating them. On the other hand, his demands would be few and hardly onerous. Marriage to David meant a future far from dire—it was boorish even to suggest it, considering Alice Clintock's and Naomi Rankin's meager lives and those of countless other women—but it was not the future she'd envisioned. That was what rankled. Philip's blasted lawsuit rendered her powerless to choose her own course. First Philip and likely soon David decided everything.

But not yet. Julia had six days left in New York, six days to steer for herself.

Christophine. Marriage to David would ensure that Julia could provide Christophine secure employment for as long as she drew breath, if necessary. For that alone she ought to be grateful for Helen Adair's quixotic divorce. Even if marriage were Julia's first step toward becoming the next Mrs. Adair languishing in Devon, she'd have the comforts of wealth, comforts that, as Glennis so cannily understood, could be considerable.

Julia's mind drifted to such consolations. She conjured a shopping list for Capriole: some shiny new fonts—the new Italian renaissance roman Morison spoke of and one of Fred Goudy's fat clownish designs for a joke—and a store of proprietary papers, maybe with a caprine watermark when she felt ready to announce herself so grandly, or a fresh batch of Cockerell's marbled papers for wrappers. With David's money she could indulge all that and more.

She gripped her glass. Yes, but only as long as Capriole remained a pastime, discreet and elite. He'd never allow (the term scalded) her to aspire to anything serious, anything that thrust her into the fray of public markets and critical scrutiny. However acclaimed her work might become, like most men, he would find such ambition in a woman distasteful, grasping and unseemly. She could feel his voice whispering hot censure into her ear.

Art, then. He'd indulge her lavishly in art. A small Kandinsky oil, perhaps, or one of Sonia Delaunay's panels. Julia dreamily transferred her favorite from a Soho gallery to her bedroom wall at home, above the blue velvet chaise, and admired its cheerful slices and cubes of color against the sunflower-gold walls. Wait. Her beautiful flat. She'd have to leave it. Julia swallowed more Cointreau. No, she would not think of that, not yet. Instead there'd be a tasteful house somewhere and gardens. And art. And books. Which of the pochoir French *livres d'artiste* would she seek out first? Something from Schmied, or a Brunelleschi, if it didn't cost the universe. Could David find her a few prints of Barbier's plates for *Le guirlande*, not too warm, within reason? There was the *Daphné* that Schmied would soon finish, reportedly too divine for words. Julia would melt for a copy. And a new bookplate by Janine Aghion. If her life was to be largely decorative, David's grandest ornament, she would make it shimmer. As Julia mused, her eyes rested on the portraits over the mantel.

Lillian Vancill gazed down, some private diversion buoying her mouth. Was she snickering from beyond the grave at Julia's efforts to gild her own cage? After just one hour in the woman's company, Julia could hear that cackle, a hearty hoot, nothing demure or spinsterish about it.

Julia's mind shifted to the photograph of Naomi Rankin, twined arm in arm with her friend, in easy peace with that unseen third intimate, the photographer. Had Russell Coates been behind the shutter that day? Naomi's expression was unguarded, even fond. Julia had no doubt that they were lovers. He'd spoken of it so candidly the other night, and yet he claimed he'd hardly seen her in recent months. Was that credible? He might want no one to suspect he was her baby's father. Or perhaps he welcomed the child, but she again refused to marry him. Would he have felt angry or betrayed enough to kill her?

Had he even known she'd been pregnant? Had anyone? That was key. Such knowledge might present powerful new motives and not only for Russell.

Julia rolled onto her side, lowering the book and glass to the floor. Glennis had said Russell had been to the house that Friday. He could have slipped downstairs or gone around outside to the basement apartment. On the other hand, Alice freely admitted she was there. Julia could find reasons to suspect either of them might be Naomi's killer. But they were merely the two she'd spoken with. Others' relationships with Naomi might be equally volatile. Philip said as much at the outset, and Glennis hammered on it at every chance. *Julia, you blessed dunderhead.* Had she focused on the obscure possibilities while ignoring the obvious ones?

She resettled onto her back, ignoring Lillian's smirk. Everything about Naomi's acute final illness suggested poison—death by toxic reaction, Dr. Perry had said—poison obscured first by the apparent morphine overdose and then forever by cremation. The immediate family, including both Winterjays, had access to her food. A delivery of soup from upstairs? A box of sweets? A pot of tea or coffee? It was lamentably easy. If Chester had discovered she was pregnant, would that have been the final straw pushing him to murder?

The Winterjays seemed more restrained, though Vivian had openly denounced her sister's politics. To a devoted champion of marriage, Naomi's pregnancy might be intolerable. According to Glennis neither Winterjay was at the house the day Naomi died, but murderers were often elsewhere when poison worked its deadly power. If anything, the couple's absence pointed more suspicion their way, not less. Julia turned over, then back. Every way she rolled she saw faces of those who might be murderers or who just as easily might not. She smacked the cushion.

"There's a cure for that, you know."

She jerked upright.

Philip stood by the door.

"Are you spying on me?"

"In my own library? Surely one's entitled to a bit of peaty solace at the end of a difficult day. You look like you could use a splash."

He fetched the bottle of whiskey, and she lifted her empty glass.

"I'm sorry for my bad temper in the hall earlier," he said, slumping into his chair by the fire. He too was in a dressing gown, securely belted this time. "No excuse for loutishness."

Julia received his apology with equally subdued silence. Philip observed this with heightened curiosity but wisely said nothing. Probing questions were the last thing she could abide. Let him think what he liked.

His head settled back into the worn dent of his chair. "Lillian's death caught me off guard, you see. Herself too, I imagine. We both thought she'd live for another eon, as she promised. She looked like a stick, but there was steel in her pins, believe me."

He gazed at the portraits above the mantel. "I wish you could have known her in her day. She was a rare old bird, quite extraordinary really. I always wondered if Lillian made herself tough to carry some of my mother's weight. My mother was like mended china, liable to come apart at a hard sneeze or slammed door. Can you imagine? If Lillian wasn't there to gallop me around the nursery on her back, I'd have busted my mother to pieces before noon every day."

Julia suspected his peaty solace had begun some hours earlier. He was speaking to her as a friend, possibly even as a sibling, too melancholy for his usual combative wit.

"Do you remember him?" he asked, eyeing their father in the portrait: proud and somber, chin out, hand firm upon Charlotte's shoulder as she held the infant Philip.

"Barely. A few glimpses through the balustrade, a Christmas dinner at which I couldn't eat. I don't recall he ever spoke to me more than a word or two."

"You were too young. What, six, when he died? He wouldn't have known what to say. I was seven or eight before we had anything resembling a conversation. He took me aside and said I should be a man and stop crying each time doctors came to see my mother. Babies cry, he told me, and girls."

Losing her mother at thirteen had been a horror. Philip had been even younger, just eight when Charlotte died. Julia groped for consoling words but found only a bromide. "At least you had him for comfort when she died."

"I had Lillian. Bless her cussed old bones. Milo shook my hand after the funeral. Man to man. I got another handshake when he returned two years later with your mother and, more or less"—he coughed— "you. I was dispatched off to boarding school within the week, I recall. He said it was time I saw something of the world. And Lillian was dispatched too, pushed out on her ear, really."

Julia was sorry about both rude oustings, but an apology would be as unwelcome as it was inappropriate. Neither was her fault. She thought instead of how she and Philip shared Milo Kydd's blood and until recently his money, but also they shared, it seemed, sorrow at never casting much of a shadow in the man's life. Which was worse? A handshake or nothing?

Philip pulled her out of these ruminations with a nod to the Vale *Danaë* on the floor. "You admire Ricketts?"

"Better than most of his ilk. Definitely more than Burne-Jones." Few of the English Pre-Raphaelites and their romantic brooding had ever much interested her.

He smiled. "The Kelmscotts were Milo's. Not to my taste either."

Julia cautioned herself. Best not to reveal a quickening interest. "You collect?"

"A bit. Work from the continent interests me more. I like my books either pure or lawless. Willy Wiegand or Apollinaire. Dufy's woodcuts for *Le bestiaire* could shrivel the socks off poor Ricketts."

She'd seen the stunning prospectus for Wiegand's Bremer Presse's new *Iliad* but knew little else about it. "I'm not very familiar with—" she began.

"I'd show you now, but I keep my anarchists in a private case down the hall." He smiled. "Not that kind of private case. Though Lord knows esoterica's about in droves these days, French postcards in twenty-dollar bindings. No, I merely try to shield la Cheadle's good Methodist mind. One glimpse of *Calligrames* would confirm her fears of my bolshie tendencies."

"Are you in the Colophon Club?" Julia said. "I spent an evening recently with Russell Coates and a rather boisterous set of members."

"I know it, and I know Coates," Philip said. "Solid chap, decent all through, but really, Julia. He's a Morley man."

Julia laughed, despite herself. The Morley interest was a mystery.

"Whatever you may think of me, and I shudder to imagine, I'm not that kind of joiner. The Grolier's airless as a bank vault, but Colophon's full of Babbitts with bookplates."

"Not so," Julia protested, laughing again.

He sat forward. "I should have picked a quarrel with you long ago. I suspect we've been missing no end of fun. How do you know your Kelmscotts and all?"

"I have an Albion," she said. "And an imprint."

"Good Lord!"

"Wait." She was on her feet and out the door. Half a minute later she returned with the solander case of Capriole treasures.

"You sly thing," he said when she showed him the daring new pressmark. "Gill plus Kydd equals Capriole. Stunning. I had no idea you were half so bold. Why didn't you show me this before?"

"I didn't think you'd be interested. More accurately, I expected you to mock it. Most brothers would find this rather shocking."

"Most sisters would die of blushes, and I might yet mock that—your *not* blushing. May I look?" He took up each of her books and handled them with care, assessing both design and execution. The Woolf interested him most, she was relieved to see.

"Trifles, but promising. I see you worked out the kinks with a few parlor tricks"—he nodded dismissively at Gerald's poems and *Gruff*—"and moved on to worthier fare. What's next?"

"I can't say. It may be crass of me to mention it, but private presses require means. Capriole's fling may be over now that you've pinched my money."

He looked at her with dismay untinged by guilt. "Nonsense. You're only a concoction or two away from poison in the Rankin affair. Plus there's that swain spewing lilies and roses. Marry his floral budget, and you're in business for life."

Their brief flicker of a pleasant conversation was over. "That's vile," she said, surrendering to a peevish disappointment.

"Better yet," Philip went on, "be a man about it, as it were. I'm serious. Oh, marry if you must, but make Capriole something to reckon with. Play with the boys."

"Fine presses rarely earn, Philip. You must know that."

"Naturally I do, but most are the playthings of indolent layabouts like me, producing books as fussy as they are. Orchids all. Thrust boldly, Julia. You've already breached a most manly of men's worlds. Don't stop there. Attack. Do everything they do but better. There's bracing new work out there dying for serious readers—have you read Amy Lowell or Richard Aldington? Lowell's twice your age, but she's the real ticket. I have a whacking good new pamphlet here somewhere by someone else you've never heard of. Hilda Doolittle, but she goes by initials." He went to the bookshelves near the door and dropped to his haunches. "Find something worth those fancy papers and foundry types, something eye poking and teeth rattling. Pack in a few engravings or drawings if you want. Make your books interesting, make Capriole a real publisher, and collectors like me will pay. Double even, for the sheer novelty of a woman printer. Imagine! Others will buy too, if the work's worth reading as much as owning."

"Don't think I haven't thought of this from every possible angle."

"Let me help if you're flummoxed. I can't compose a sonnet to save my life, much less a line of brevier, but I can goad. You or your poet quarry, whoever needs a prod. I'm a remarkably effective pest." *As you know,* his wry glance added.

"You want to help me, Philip? Tear up that awful arbitration judgment. Stop raining imminent poverty down on my head. If you'd left well enough alone last summer, I wouldn't need anyone's help. Capriole would be happily on course."

"Frivolous," he said, waving at *Gruff.* "Charming bric-a-brac, thoroughly silly."

"You called it promising. And at any rate it's private. I work to suit myself, not you or anyone else. That's the glory of a private press. I can print what I like, how I like, without pandering to the tastes of oafish buyers like you."

"Silly and frivolous," he repeated. "Why on earth would I heap further fortune onto you to produce self-indulgent baubles? Just as well you work a bit for your means. It might make you more discerning where those dollars go. Pounds, whatever."

"Philip!" The money was hers by *right.* Julia was no more required to deserve it than he was, just as she was now as entitled as he to cast a vote, no matter how careless or ill judged. "You're robbing me for my own benefit? Even to suggest it makes you a worse scoundrel than I—"

"Yes, yes," he interrupted from behind the drinks trolley, where he was still crouched, looking for the pamphlet he admired. "Scoundrel, devil, beast, yes, I know. I must have left it in my bedroom. Won't be two ticks."

He disappeared, retreating on bare feet down the long hallway to his quarters. Julia's shoulders fell back onto the pillows. How did he do it? Offer a glimmer of intelligent regard, display some spark of goodwill, lure her into hopeful trust—only to bash her with mockery? Why did she allow it to happen, time after time? It was bad enough to be tricked, worse to hear herself reduced to whining like a schoolgirl with sore braids.

Frivolous. Silly. Bric-a-brac. The barbs burrowed deep. Philip had a way of sharpening every blade of doubt already flashing in her heart. He was right. Savagely right. Capriole was a plaything, ambitious in its reach but self-indulgent nonetheless. She scorned his indolence, but wasn't that precisely what she resented losing, her own idle leisure? She'd lived all her life in money-lit radiance. Shadows now taught her the value of each dollar's tiny flame; what would she choose to illumine in her new dim world? It was a question one never asked while basking in perpetual sunshine. What vanity it was to weep for freedom without considering: Freedom from what? For what?

For Capriole money meant privacy meant whim. Money meant freedom from consequence and from judgment, which was little more than cowardice. Was her scramble for an independent income merely to protect herself from serious scrutiny? Wealth bestowed power and significance; those without it had to *earn* both. Money's endless opportunities and freedoms to choose—Biarritz or Cannes? Fortuny pleats or Poiret brocades?—made Naomi Rankin's choices poignantly stark. If Capriole was to be more than a fashionable parade of new chancery italics and naughty nymphs . . .

The heat woke her. Bright sun leaked through the draperies, and a fire burned in the grate. Green tartan wool blanketed her from toes to chin. Heaving it away, Julia saw the ashtrays wiped clean, the glasses washed and inverted on the trolley. Oh, please God, let it have been Mrs. Cheadle who'd covered up her sleepy disarray, not Philip. She stumbled to the mantel to see the time. Not yet nine. She slipped into her mules, pulled her mangled shawl about her arms, and hurried to reassemble her dignity. She was due at Glennis's in an hour.

⁓

Glennis pressed her ear against the heavy wood basement door and knocked. "Alice? Are you there? Do you mind if we come in? We need to finish up with Naomi's things." When no one answered, Glennis fitted a large key into the keyhole and heaved it to the left. The bolt slid back.

"I don't know why I'm nervous," she said. "I'm in my own house, and we do need to finish up our sorting."

Julia felt the same anxiety. She'd never sneaked into another person's home. Glennis stepped back to let Julia go first into the dark apartment. A weak yellow light shone from the living room window. A market basket leaned against the wall outside Alice's bedroom. They crept toward the light, careful to avoid the bulging basket.

Julia stepped on something small and rolled her instep to avoid crushing it, but at the sound of breaking glass, she sucked in a guilty breath.

Glennis crouched to peer at whatever lay beneath Julia's right foot. "Something white. Smashed to smithereens."

"Look." Across the floor lay more white beads. At the end of the hall, light came from the tall lamp beside the old rocker. The folded quilt cushioning the rocker was askew, bulging between the chair's tall back slats; someone was there.

"Alice?" Julia said. "So sorry. We're just here to finish up in—" Then she saw the leg stretched at a crooked angle toward the sofa.

Beads burst beneath her feet like pops of a tommy gun. Glennis arrived in a rush right behind her. Alice was sprawled in the rocker, her hips slid nearly off the seat. Both arms curled toward her throat and lay limp across her chest. Her head hung as if she were asleep or drunk.

219

Julia touched her wrist, and Alice lifted her head. Glennis gasped to see her livid throat, ringed with a purpling bruise. Alice's fingers crawled up to touch it, recoiled into weak fists.

"Quick, Glennis. A wet cloth. Cool water." Julia unbent Alice's hot fingers. "Can you breathe?"

Alice nodded and winced. Julia straightened Alice's arms and laid them in her lap. Glennis brought a damp dish towel and eased it against her throat. A sound rumbled from Alice's chest. Julia sent Glennis for a cup of water, then held it steady as Alice swallowed, at first in a blinking grimace, then again and again and again. "Run upstairs to telephone for a doctor," Julia told Glennis, hovering over her shoulder.

"No." Alice spoke with more air than sound.

"You're hurt. You need a doctor."

"No." Alice grasped Julia's wrist to pull herself up. She managed only a few inches, but with her shoulders less collapsed into her ribs, she looked more alive. Glennis gripped Alice under the arms to tug her another couple of inches upright. They helped her up to lie across the sofa and covered her with the quilt. Glennis fetched the uncased pillow from Naomi's bed, and Julia folded it to support Alice's blade-thin shoulders. She didn't look at Glennis for fear she'd see her own guilt mirrored there. Their stealthy plan to snoop around seemed a distant memory. This changed everything.

"What happened?" Julia leaned close. "Can you talk?"

Alice nodded, eyes closed. Several moments elapsed. "I was resting." She settled a hand against her throat. "Tight, burning." She spoke in a raspy voice between more sips of water.

"Did you hear anything?"

Alice's head moved. No. She wore the same wool dress she'd had on last evening.

"See anyone?"

Again, no.

Julia glanced at the front door: bolted. The attacker had probably entered and certainly left through the house. Not even Chester could disguise this as anything but a malicious attack, and suspicion fell squarely on the household. Only a fool would act so recklessly, and no one in this business was a fool. This was shrewdly done. However alarming the look of Alice's throat, her injuries were not serious. The attack was meant to frighten, to warn rather than to kill. The tremor of her hand against the quilt illustrated its success.

The more ominous question was why. To keep Naomi's money in the family? To scare Alice into forfeiting the new will? Or because Alice had lashed out with her one weapon, the assertion that she alone loved Naomi and understood her suffering? It was time for direct questions. They had to find out what Alice knew. Glennis gave Julia a poke, encouraging her with narrowed eyes to go on.

"Alice," Julia said, "this can't wait. You must trust us. We can't help unless you tell us what you know about Naomi's death."

"What really happened to her?" said Glennis.

Alice held the cloth to her neck, sipping and swallowing several more times. "So waspish," she said in a weak whisper. "That morning. Wouldn't tell me. Just walked out." She eased more water down her throat and patted the sofa cushion. "I found her here. Thought she had a headache. Didn't ask, even look. My heart was hard. Until, such sounds."

Her head sank into the pillow, but her voice grew stronger. "She was so pale. Hair sopping. Clammy. Barely breathing. I tried to help her but . . ."

"Someone poisoned her," Glennis said.

Alice fingered the loose skin below her jaw and moved her head slowly from side to side.

No? Not poison? "Alice, what are you not telling us?"

Another resisting shake.

"We know she was pregnant." Julia spoke bluntly.

Alice twisted her face into the pillow. After a full minute she said in a muffled voice, "So much blood. Blood everywhere. Her skirt was soaked through."

Shock buckled Glennis's knees, and she dropped into the rocker. "You mean she lost the baby?"

"Worse."

Julia's legs wobbled too. After her hours of crafting murderous possibilities, the truth caught her hard. It made no sense. How could Naomi, of all women, meet such an old, even banal fate? Despite her struggle for women's rights, in the end was Naomi just another poor and panicked victim of a knitting needle, a lye douche, a tincture of tansy or feverfew? Killed by despair, not malice? The most modern of women, undone by the most ancient of troubles?

"Blood everywhere," Alice repeated slowly. "Butchered. Torn stem to stern and sent home with nothing but a diaper, bloody wads of cotton. I've seen it before."

"How ghastly. I'm so sorry, Alice." Julia hated the feeble, inadequate words. Glennis only whimpered.

"I held her to the end, prayed to know what to do. I had to go to that meeting, but first I bathed her, got her into her fine underthings and a clean skirt."

Glennis's head swerved at the mention of Naomi's lingerie.

"To make it look like suicide," Julia said.

Alice refolded the cloth to find a cool patch. "To help the cause," she said. "People would despise her if they knew the truth. Call her a whore. It would destroy everything. Suicide would show how she suffered. How her own brother made life impossible. That her Union sisters were her only true family."

"And the note?" Julia said quickly, before Glennis could feel the sting of Alice's words.

Alice flinched and dropped her eyes. In barely a whisper she admitted, "A letter she wrote after he spelled out his terms. To share if things became unbearable. They did, and I wanted to shame him."

"And you placed the tablets in her mouth?"

"Too late, if that doctor's right."

"You expected to be the one to find her?"

Alice nodded. "So awful, seeing them here and that cloth he put on her head. Then when he said there was no note, I saw what he was up to but couldn't stop him."

Not without exposing her own deception. "So you typed up those threats and pretended they came earlier?"

"I wanted you to think he sent them. I wanted you to know how he tormented her."

"Who's the baby's father?" Glennis said abruptly. "I bet you know."

Alice gave a harsh sigh.

"Russell Coates?"

Alice weakly pushed herself upright. "He pestered her. She lost her good sense around him. But—I don't know." Her legs moved beneath the quilt. "I'm better now."

"Was Naomi wearing her gray cardigan that day?" Julia asked. It was a loose end, a detail in the winding down of their investigation, a distraction from the enormity of Naomi's awful but unintended death.

Alice thought. "I suppose. It was draped over the sofa, right here. I hung it in her bedroom. Why?"

"We found a café receipt in the pocket, probably from that morning. It doesn't matter now."

Alice stirred again, more forcefully. "I'd better go. Your brother will be angry if he finds me here," she said. "Will you help get my things together, Miss Rankin? In my room?"

"You bet. We'll get you to the Union, where you'll be safe." Glennis went to gather up the parcels in the hall and in the tiny bedroom.

As soon as she had stepped away, Alice gripped Julia's wrist to pull her close. In a low rasp she said, "I'm sorry I tried to trick you, but now you know everything, and I've betrayed my dearest friend. Can you do something for me in return? It's eating me alive." She listened for Glennis's return and hurried on. "Naomi would never go to a butcher like that. *Never*. We know doctors, brave, good doctors who help women weary half to death with too many children already. And, oh, the young girls . . ."

She leaned even closer. "She'd never let one of those other monsters near her body. Someone made her do this. Forced it on her, then dumped her here to die. As good as killed her."

Forced it on her? Were Glennis's accusations not so wild after all? "What do you want me to do?"

"Find out who did this," Alice said. "Who took her to be butchered. *Please*."

"Ready." Glennis returned, overstuffed cloth bags dangling from either hand. "I'll have George run us downtown in the motorcar."

Julia murmured a vague reassurance into Alice's ear as she helped her to her feet.

The story had taken a horrifying turn. Alice had been attacked by someone who feared what she knew. But which knowledge? Of the pregnancy or its gruesome termination? Or was there even more to the story, something Alice didn't know or was still hiding? The mystery of Naomi's death was not over. It had deepened alarmingly, like the bruises circling Alice's throat.

༄

While Glennis escorted Alice downtown, Julia went directly to Jack's office. He was generous with his time, sweeping her onto his schedule like a prized heiress rather than the penniless acquaintance she was about to become. She showed him the odd receipt from Naomi's pocket and told him of the shadowy hunch swirling in her mind. He understood it immediately and, better still, knew how to inquire for an answer. He made a series of short telephone calls before reaching a police detective in Mr. Kessler's office, to whom he listened with great care for nearly ten minutes, scribbling notes all the while.

"Pay dirt," Jack said when the call ended. "Your suspicion was not far off the mark, Julia. Turns out this isn't a receipt at all. Heacock is the street name of a disgraced doctor, a shady fellow named Weatherford who's been in all sorts of trouble with the law—illegal prescriptions, phony death certificates, patching up fugitives, and so on. Apparently he lost his clinic years ago and was sent to prison, but now he's back and operating on the lam. It seems this business about tea—"

He glanced at the paper. "*Black tea, no sugar, no milk, $40.14.* It's an address, a coded way of identifying where Heacock could be found."

"I wondered if it might be something like that."

"*Scrambled egg* is also a code, a crude one, for the service she received. Miss Rankin went to Heacock to end her pregnancy."

Julia relayed this information as benignly as she could to Glennis that evening over the telephone.

Glennis's voice shook. "I don't understand. Any of this. Why?"

Julia had no answers. Why terminate, and why go to Heacock? Naomi had already been seeing a reputable doctor to safeguard her pregnancy. If some drastic despair had changed her mind, she knew where to find clean, safe, and discreet help. Heacock was notorious for inflicting the opposite.

"*Why?*" Glennis demanded, her shrill voice vibrating across the wires.

"Do you remember the telephone call Alice says Naomi took that morning? The one that sent her rushing out of the Union in a foul temper? If Naomi decided to end her pregnancy, maybe the caller agreed to pay for it but only if he made the arrangements."

"Russell would never send her someplace grummy. But Chester would. He'd find the cheapest, nastiest doctor he could, just to cheese her."

Julia covered the mouthpiece and listened for sounds in the apartment. Philip appeared to be out, and Mrs. Cheadle was clanging pots in the kitchen. "*Paid in full*," she said, fingering the receipt. "That's all we know for sure. Someone either gave Naomi the money or more likely paid Heacock directly. Unfortunately, the only way to find out who sent her there is to snoop around at this man's clinic. It could be quite horrid and even dangerous, Glennis. You needn't come along. I have a tougher stomach than you."

As expected, Glennis howled her determination not to be left behind. They agreed to meet at Jack's office the following afternoon at three, by which time Jack hoped to have more information. It left the midday hours free for Julia's other urgent business, which she did not mention to Glennis, as it was every bit as disturbing and possibly as dangerous.

CHAPTER 22

"Yes, I understand I'm not on his schedule. I do apologize. But please, I need only a few minutes of his time." Julia softened her posture and smoothed every sharp edge off her words, trying to sound both deferential and helpless, but the secretary would not be moved. She studied her desk calendar's immaculate script detailing a succession of names, events, and responsibilities. Russell Coates's law practice was busier than Julia expected.

"It's important." Julia added a squeak of pathos to her voice, the sound, she hoped, of one who simply loathes causing trouble.

The woman tapped her needle-sharp pencil against the leather desk pad, clearly deliberating how best to be rid of her. She relented with a scowl and reached for the telephone. "You're due at the restaurant in twenty-five minutes, sir," she told her employer. "And a Miss Kydd is here to see you. Shall I schedule an appointment for her?"

She nodded at the reply and replaced the receiver. "Have a seat, Miss Kydd. Mr. Coates will see you presently."

But before Julia could turn to find a chair, Russell appeared. His coat was off, his tie loosened. He guided Julia into the office and closed the door. "What brings you here?"

The blinds were drawn, and folders lay strewed across his desk.

"I'm sorry to disturb you at work like this, but a great deal has come to light about Naomi's death. Can you spare a few minutes?"

He studied her face. It was the first time they'd seen each other close up in sober daylight, without the softening haze of liquor and smoke and vague desire. She met his gaze, eyes nearly level with his, alert, prepared.

"All right. But not here." He retrieved his jacket from behind the door. "Telephone Marchant to reschedule, Agnes," he told the secretary. "I'm stepping out. I'll be back in an hour or so."

The door closed on indignant reminders of other duties neglected.

Neither spoke until they reached the pavement three stories below. As the elevator descended, Julia fixed her eyes on the attendant's gold-braided collar and considered what she would say and how. Perhaps this had been a rash decision. It was certainly a hasty one. She'd spent the morning in a whirlwind of errands: sending telegrams, collecting her ticket for Sunday's sailing, and badgering Philip for a last installment of funds before Friday's meeting to complete the paperwork of his legal triumph. She'd telephoned Jack with instructions and, before her courage could fail, directed a taxicab to Russell's office.

It was another sultry autumn day. The street teemed with office workers slipping out for lunchtime strolls or coffees alfresco. Russell and Julia joined the throng heading west, toward Central Park. Another few minutes and they entered its oasis.

"What have you learned?" Russell asked as they passed noisy peanut and lemonade vendors, dodging the oncoming crush.

Julia stopped walking and was buffeted by three shopgirls, whose high-pitched tirades about poncy customers she could no longer abide, following close on her heels. They glared at her for an apology, without success, and marched on. Russell returned to her side. "This way," he suggested, and they headed for a narrower side path lined with benches, all occupied.

"Why were you so upset about Naomi's new will?" she asked.

They walked for several paces before he answered. "I'll presume this is relevant. As I told you the other night, I don't trust that Clintock

228

woman. I think she manipulated Naomi. Turned her away from lifelong attachments."

"Who benefited under the terms of the original will?"

Again he considered at length. "Since it's now void, I suppose I can tell you, as you seem to be acting as some kind of factotum for Glennis in this business." Julia accepted his pause for what it was, censure for her meddling, for extracting confidences under less-than-honest pretenses. She endured the burn across her cheeks and hoped it was sufficient penance.

"In strict confidence, of course. It was largely boilerplate." He coughed and said in a dry voice, as if reciting fine print, "Her estate would go to her children first, should she have any, then to her husband, should she have one, then to her surviving siblings in equal shares. Should they all predecease her, it would go to their children in equal shares."

"Any other provisions? For you, for example?"

"The grasping family lawyer, you mean? Yes, there was a sum designated for me, five thousand dollars, I believe. She stipulated the same for a particular college friend, for a few women she was close to in the party back then, and for her old nanny, who has since died. She hadn't amended the document in years."

"I'm sorry, but I had to ask."

"What's this about?"

Julia answered with another question. "You said the other evening that you and she were once lovers. What about in the past year or so? Were you still close?"

"As I told you, we saw each other fairly regularly since she moved back to New York and especially since she moved into the basement flat. It was easy to entice her out for a decent meal and good whiskey now and then, and she knew she could count on me when she needed to vent some steam. That flat was a prison, you know, with Chester and Nolda looming overhead. I was glad to offer a shoulder to rage against and to assure her that at least one social registry male didn't think she was poisonous. So, yes, we did become friends again. I like to think she was as pleased about it as I was." He nodded toward an empty bench ahead and asked if she wanted to sit.

Julia considered what she had to ask next and said she'd rather walk. It would be easier to concentrate on his answers. "Russell, I'm afraid this is very personal. I hate to ask such a thing, but it's vital."

He stiffened. "What?"

"Were you and Naomi still lovers?" When he did not answer, Julia turned to face him and asked the precise question. "Did you and she have sex last summer?"

"No." Sharp as a slap.

Did she believe him? So much suggested he was the baby's father, and yet he declared it impossible. Unless Julia could trust him, he was a viable, even foremost, candidate for Naomi's killer.

"I gather from the outrageous question that you've somehow learned her secret," he said.

It might be madness, but yes. She did trust him. For now. It was enough to proceed. "I know she was pregnant."

Russell stepped off the path to let a pair of schoolgirls pass. His face darkened. "What on earth possesses you to go marauding through Naomi's private life like this? Do you think it's some kind of game? I'm sorry, Julia, but I thought better of you."

"I'm sorry too, Russell, but I need you to trust me, just as I must trust you. Please. This gives me no pleasure either. A great deal is at stake." More than he could dream of.

He studied her for an excruciating length of time. "What do you want to know?"

"Whatever you can tell me about her pregnancy, for a start."

His glare lingered. At last, with a disgusted shake of his head, he resumed walking. "She called it her last and greatest surprise, although I doubt it would have been either. Chester would have called it a stunt, in that way he has of ridiculing everything she did."

"Were you surprised? Jealous?"

A faint color glowed above Russell's white collar. "Surprised, of course. Jealous, though? Not in the way you're insinuating. Our relationship hadn't been physical in some time, and it was never truly monogamous. Naomi believed women are entitled to the same freedoms of intimacy as men. She believed nature endows women to experience sensual pleasure as much as men. She wasn't wanton about it but not ashamed either."

The same freedoms of intimacy. So simple, so reasonable. If women and men enjoyed the same right to exercise a say in public affairs, shouldn't they be equally free to express and receive affections as they chose, including those most intimate? The principle was a cornerstone of the life that Julia strove for too. It was fair and just, and also woefully far from the custom of the land. Julia forced herself to concentrate on the matter at hand. "I realize this is another atrocious question, but it's important. If you weren't the baby's father, can you think who might be?"

He coughed in rough astonishment. "No. She refused to tell me. She'd hardly countenance the question, in fact."

"You must have some idea, though."

"I gathered only that it was a brief and unhappy encounter. When I tried to ask, she was furious, whether at me or herself or someone else I couldn't tell. The less said about it, the better, I quickly realized. I could only suspect the chap was someone she met in Albany last summer, just as I assumed an imprudent amount of alcohol was involved. I do know she had no intention to involve the fellow in her plans."

"Plans? Was it deliberate? Did she intend to become pregnant?" Julia had a friend in London with a two-year-old brother, evidence of her mother's sudden desire for another child before it was too late, a determination her friend termed "certifiably deranged." Spinsters with such a desire would face almost insurmountable hurdles from family, friends, church, and state. No wonder they invariably surrendered to a childless fate. Did Naomi hope to become a pioneering exception?

"Good Lord, no. She said the pregnancy was utterly unwelcome, the worst thing that could happen."

"An accident, then. Was it unusual that she took no precautions?"

Russell's jaw worked as he struggled for civility and composure. Julia grieved for what this interview was costing her in his regard, but it was a sacrifice she had to accept. "Quite unusual. She insisted on precautions. 'To keep the sexes equal,' she said. She had her own, ah, device—and believed every woman should have one, married or not. I can't think why she didn't use it. Perhaps it failed. Of course I couldn't ask. The issue seemed rather academic after the fact, not to mention judgmental."

"How did you first learn of all this?"

He expelled a great breath. "She was agitated about something last summer. In hindsight I realize it must have been that disastrous encounter, though at the time I had no idea what the problem was. At first she wouldn't discuss it, but about six weeks ago she confided that she was expecting. We had some mighty long talks about it, or rather, I listened as she argued with herself, back and forth, about how to proceed."

There was no need to elaborate. They both understood that options were few for women in Naomi's situation. All of them difficult, none of them happy.

"And then one morning she telephoned and asked to see me at once. I canceled a meeting and met her here at the park. We must have walked five miles as she laid out her decision." He glanced around. "On this very path, in fact. She was shaking, I remember, as much from nervousness as from excitement. She told me she'd decided to accept the child as a kind of gift. A blessing from disaster, she said."

"She intended to have the baby?"

"Yes, and to raise it herself, alone."

A pioneer indeed. "That was a brave decision."

"It was Naomi in a nutshell. She wanted to make an example of herself, show the world that women could raise children on their own, without either the financial support or respectability bestowed by marriage. It was time, she declared, to break the patriarchal grip on motherhood."

Julia could admire the breathtaking courage of it, but such a thing would spell disaster for any political ambitions. "Wouldn't that jeopardize her work? What about her hopes of running for senator in '26?"

They continued in silence for several paces. "I suppose you learned about that from her Union friends," Russell said. "Naomi would've admired your tenacity but resented like hell being the subject of it. But yes, that was paramount in her mind. Reconciling a baby to that ambition was no small challenge, as you might imagine."

"Even staunch radicals might not vote for a Hester with infant Pearl in full view." Julia thought of Philip's fierce old aunt Lillian, urging on La Follette and his bold reforms.

Russell smiled. "So I thought too. That conversation took another few miles. I finally persuaded her the only way she could hope to run a serious campaign for the Senate—that is, address any issue other than what everyone would call her promiscuity—would be to marry."

Ah. "You?"

His smile broadened. "I have my faults, to be sure, but there were worse candidates. We even laughed about it later, the nature of my 'proposal.' It was the political expediency that convinced her. We agreed to say we were secretly married last spring."

"Quite a compromise, given her views on the subject."

"Don't think I didn't tease her about it. 'A good launch,' I said, 'for a career in politics.' Not only the compromise but the pretense. That's all it was, of course. It would have been absurd—pointless and hypocritical—to harbor any romantic illusions of a conventional marriage. Oh, she was shrewd in her terms, all right, but in the end she agreed it could work. We both felt ready to devote our attentions to her child. Impending middle age, I suppose. We were planning to announce both the marriage and the child next month, once she felt confident the pregnancy was sound. By then it would have started to show."

"You were prepared for the usual snickers?"

"Of course, though I had an answer ready to quiet them. A friend of mine in Boston, a judge, owed me a favor. He signed a wedding license for us and dated it last April. I still have it, though I doubt I could bear to look at it now. I even convinced her to take my mother's emerald wedding ring, to wear once the baby became obvious, and a few other family baubles. So legally we were married for, what, six months. I suppose that makes me a widower now. Technically." His soft words disappeared in a long pause. "I trust you'll never repeat this? In the end it was only a scheme that never came to fruition."

They veered onto a new path lined with plump hydrangeas fading to silver and mauve. "You must have been devastated to learn of her death," Julia said to escape a haunting vision of that beautiful old ring hidden in Naomi's bedroom.

"I was eating breakfast when Chester telephoned. My God, what a day that was. And then the next day when he and Perry said she'd committed suicide, I could barely stay in my seat for wanting to rage at something, someone. Having to fathom such a thing and then discuss only how to hide it from the world. Every bone in my body hurt. I wanted it to be a vicious lie, an unspeakable hoax. How could she do such a thing? She'd been happier those last few days than I'd seen her in years. I couldn't imagine a more awful irony. After all she was giving up to make a new life for herself and that child. How far she'd come in accepting, even welcoming, that pregnancy. It was awful, Julia. You can't imagine the sick fury and guilt and grief I felt when the family only wanted to tidy over her death, render it sad but oh so tasteful."

She could imagine. The memory of Gerald's parents' picture-perfect decorum, the engraved notice of his "passing" they'd sent to important associates, still stirred the bile in her throat. Russell rolled his head in a great, bone-creaking circle. "There's always some devil of doubt to whisper your worst fears in your ear. I thought she'd suffered second thoughts, decided she couldn't go through with the charade after all. Maybe the prospect of life shackled to me made the bargain too onerous for her. At least Dr. Perry's news put those fears to rest. Though it was small consolation."

This was the moment she'd been waiting for. Julia stilled to replay every inflection of what she'd just heard. Was his sorrow genuine? She heard again the fears and grief he could never dispel. Yes. He did not know.

She turned. "Naomi didn't take her own life, Russell, but neither did she suffer a fatal illness." The truth's cruelty grew tenfold. "She died from an abortion."

Russell swiveled away. "Jesus God." His voice spiked in an explosion of shock. "She changed her mind? Without telling me? I can hardly believe it." He covered his eyes as the next thought dawned. "But that shouldn't kill her. Not these days."

Julia couldn't bring herself to repeat the grisly word Alice had used. *Butcher.* "It seems she died from a hemorrhage, likely an infection too. It was very badly done, probably quite cheaply."

"Damn her pride! She knew I'd help with whatever she thought best. I've told her a thousand times I'd give her the shirt off my back if she'd take it. No questions asked, ever. But money—Chester's restriction of it, I mean—was a kind of weapon for her. She used his meanness to get back at him. The more he cut her off, the more drama she made of her poverty. They were like demons, each with their teeth in the other's hide, refusing to let go or admit they were bloodied. It was madness, but I never thought it would kill her."

As painful as it was for him to think Naomi had changed her mind about marrying him and having the child, the suggestion that she'd been treated maliciously would be worse. Julia said nothing of Alice's assertions. They walked on in agonized silence.

At last he spoke. "How do you know this?"

"Alice Clintock told us yesterday. Glennis and I went downstairs to talk to her"—a bold elision—"and found her injured, barely conscious. After that family meeting the night before, someone tried to strangle her."

"What?" Pigeons scattered in a swoosh of mottled feathers.

"She wasn't badly hurt. But obviously someone wants to frighten her."

"Someone angry about the new will?"

"Perhaps. Or about putting the pills in Naomi's mouth."

"So it was her. I thought as much."

"She said Naomi would approve of the ruse, to call attention to Chester's abuses."

Russell made no reply.

"We think Alice was attacked that evening, not long after she ran out of the room. The apartment door and windows were bolted from the inside when we found her, which means her attacker got in through the basement."

"And you suspect me?"

"I thought very hard about you, yes. And her brother."

"This is too foul to contemplate," Russell said. "It's true Chester saw red wherever Naomi was concerned, and he can bluster with the best of them, but I can't believe he'd actually attack any woman like that, for any reason."

"Who then has access to the house and knows about the key in the pantry?"

"It's never been a secret. I've known where it was since we were boys. Certainly the family and staff know. And we were all there. You and Glennis disappeared, but the rest of us remained for some time. We all left the room at various times, I guess. Any of us could have slipped downstairs without being noticed. But what a thought. I can't believe it. I know these people, Julia. They fight with words, not physical violence."

A commotion ahead suspended their conversation. They entered a plaza filled with several throngs, each milling around a different person orating from a platform to cheers or catcalls. "Candidates," Russell explained. "Every lunch hour they're here, preaching to anyone who'll listen."

They circled the edge of the restless mass. Each speaker had a megaphone. How could anyone sort out one shouting voice from the next? The political hopefuls stood beneath placards announcing, in much patriotic swagger, their names and party affiliations. A few boasted simple slogans: "Clem's your friend." "Curtis won't hurt us." She recalled Willard Wright's curdling disdain for democracy, for its trust that the larger the aggregate of fools, the better the chance of collective wisdom.

The crowd thinned at one spot. At first Julia thought the platform there was unoccupied, but then a small poster bobbed above the hats of a dozen or so milling people. She recognized Fern Gillespie, one of the women at Naomi's Equal Rights Union. She held a megaphone with one hand and a placard with the other, pumping it up and down to the cadence of her cry. "ERA Now!" it proclaimed, the same as her repeated shout.

One of the watchers cupped his hands to his mouth and called out a vulgar epithet. Her chant did not falter. Another man imitated the way her squat body rocked as she poked her arm in the air for each thin-pitched "Now!" His fellows jeered with laughter, and a few joined in the mockery. Miss Gillespie kept her gaze fastened on the distant treetops. Her energy was clearly flagging, and the placard wobbled badly. She fumbled to switch hands, clutching the megaphone against her ribs under one arm while she transferred the placard pole to her other hand. It was a clumsy gesture, and the small crowd hooted its amusement.

"What's for supper, Mother?" one shouted.

"Leaflets *again!*" another complained in a pantomime of fork-fisted disgust.

"Who's minding the kiddies?" the first man demanded.

Miss Gillespie ignored them. Three women in brown coats, heavy for the fine day's warmth, stood close by and doggedly applauded. No one else seemed to be paying her any attention, more entertained by the antics of the men.

"ERA?" Julia asked.

"Equal Rights Amendment." Russell gave a short, cheerless laugh. "If you'd known Naomi, you wouldn't have to ask. With the Nineteenth Amendment passed, this is their next big push. A constitutional amendment to give women full equal rights under the law."

Julia recalled that Vivian Winterjay had mentioned it the evening of the gala. "I try to glance at a newspaper when I can," she said, "but that was the first I'd heard of it."

"Editors judge it a waste of ink, by and large. There's not a ghost of a chance it will go anywhere, but I suppose the WPA's in it for the long run, considering the sixty, seventy years it took to get the vote." He stopped. "Let's not go any closer. I don't want them to recognize me."

Such a blessing a good hat brim was. The shelter of one's own private shadow. "Fern Gillespie knows you?"

"Chewed me out once when I went to the Union to meet Naomi. Thought I was interfering, distracting her from her God Almighty work."

With a dismissive jeer the hecklers wandered on to skewer the next politician along the row. Most of Miss Gillespie's audience drifted away with them. She looked forlorn with only her three friends and a few passersby to witness, much less be persuaded by, her doomed message.

Russell and Julia turned away from the square's noisy cant. He bought a greasy sausage roll from a cart—she declined the offer—and they wandered toward the lake. They sat on a low rock wall circling an oak tree, far from neighboring picnickers.

"There was another pregnancy, years ago," he said. "We were both so young. Still in college. She was frantic with it, wouldn't hear of marriage. We couldn't tell her parents—her father was an iron-handed puritan who'd send her off to a nunnery to stew in shame until it was born. I sold some bonds my grandfather had left me, and off she went.

She never told me where or who helped her. The risk was just too great. We knew it was the only way—she was bound and determined to be a New Woman, you know, free love, independent, equal in everything. The thought of a husband and baby, especially at eighteen, horrified her. And she was right. That wouldn't be the Naomi I loved."

Love, Julia silently corrected him. Present tense.

"But we cried. Oh God, we cried."

They sat for some time.

"I'm sorry," Julia said. "I truly am."

Russell stood and offered his arm for the walk back to his office. "You're a brave one, Julia. I'll give you that. I can't think of many I'd care to hear this news from, but I appreciate your candor."

They walked past the mob reforming around a new assortment of candidates. Fern Gillespie was gone, her place taken by a man in an Uncle Sam hat haranguing on the perils of filthy papist foreigners taking American jobs.

"Life goes on," said Russell.

Three panting youths dashed past, goading each other with crude, exuberant taunts. Russell pulled Julia aside to avoid the sweat and spittle. His arm settled at her waist. It was a quiet, forgiving gesture. "Firuski will be in town again on Saturday, along with that Dwiggins fellow he can't stop raving about. He wanted me to ask if you'd be interested in a joint Dunster House–Capriole edition of an Archibald MacLeish piece he's been saving. If you're free for a drink to discuss it with him, perhaps you and I could have dinner after?"

The spent hydrangeas were lovely in the bobbing shadows of early afternoon. Julia had already declined an invitation from Beatrice Warde to attend the opening of an exhibit of fin de siècle title pages at the Met on Saturday. She admired the flowers as she separated the answer she wanted to give from the one she must. "I'm sorry, Russell, but I can't. I'll need to spend the day packing. It seems I'm sailing back to England on Sunday."

CHAPTER 23

The first thing Julia noticed when Miss Baxter ushered her into Jack's office later that afternoon was the look on Glennis's face. Jack bent over her right shoulder, finger pointing to the papers laid across the desk while she sat in his chair like a princess. Her smile to Julia signaled an alert, predatory pleasure, the unerring detection of a suitable bachelor who was not only interesting but attentive. An inventory of caution ran down Julia's spine. But for whom? She scolded herself: Who was she to judge who would or would not suit Glennis? Or Jack? Far stranger romances were commonplace. And as Glennis had clearly already calculated, a lawyer with good breeding and decent character working at a venerable downtown firm was nine-tenths of the way toward matrimonial prospect-hood. But if the fellow was also an artist?

"I was just explaining to Miss Rankin how we worked out the code of that note you brought in yesterday," Jack said, straightening quickly.

"It's terribly clever." Glennis arched her back. A pale starburst of fine hairs leaped from her head toward the dark wool of his jacket.

"Have you worked out the clinic's address?" Julia asked.

"Sergeant Warsinske did," Jack said. "His men have had trouble with Heacock before, so they keep an eye on what he's up to. He's been working out of Harlem the last few months. At least that's where the first direct contact is made."

"First direct contact?" Glennis widened her eyes in charming bafflement.

"The operation is split into two stages, which occur at different locations. The police suspect the initial overture is strictly verbal, likely through a network of intermediaries. The client gets an appointment slip like this one"—he tapped Naomi's dog-eared paper—"and is instructed where to take it. That is, they're told how to interpret the coded address. This apparently keeps their errand private from anyone who might come across the slip."

"I see. Thank you so much, Mr. Van Dyne," Glennis said.

Jack's auburn hair seemed to glow in her gratitude. "It's at that location," he continued, "where one actually meets one of Heacock's associates. Unless he's moved on recently, it's an ordinary apartment on West 129th. One goes there first to pay. Everything is strictly cash in advance. Someone there sizes up the situation, makes sure nothing's fishy. If all looks square, you're told when and where to find Heacock. From there it gets murkier. Warsinske doesn't have a fix on where he actually works. It probably changes a great deal."

"Well, it's this first person we need to see," Julia said. "We need to learn who set up and paid for his services."

"Julia thinks it might be the father," Glennis said.

"That's what I understand." Jack moved away from the desk and smoothed his tie. "I gather it's not uncommon for surrogates to make the arrangements. Give this to your driver." He handed Julia an address written in bold capital letters. "And tell him to take you as close to the entry as possible. This is not a part of the city you two should be wandering around in. Make sure he waits for you."

"Please. We're hardly bumpkins."

"I'm serious. If anything makes you uneasy, anything at all, stay in the taxi and go home. I can make time tomorrow to go there myself."

"Don't be absurd," Julia said. "We don't mind a little intrigue, do we, Glennis?"

Glennis seemed torn. She was eager for adventure but also loath to squander the offer of manly assistance. She nodded vaguely.

As they were leaving, Jack pulled Julia aside. He said in a low voice, "We're set for two thirty Friday. All the papers will be ready to sign."

Forty-eight hours until Julia would be stripped of her Kydd legacy. She gave a curt nod.

Jack hesitated. "There's something more I think you should know." Julia waited, watching Glennis dawdle near Miss Baxter's potted ferns. She wasn't sure she could bear much more, given the pained and reluctant tone of his voice.

"It was a shock to everyone," he said. "Lillian Vancill's will. Not that Philip was her heir but that her estate should be so sizable. Her death makes him a very rich man."

"Bloody hell!" Julia's outburst surprised them both. "Well, bully for him. *Two* new fortunes to wallow in."

"Julia, he had no idea. You saw how she lived. And besides—" He slapped his mouth.

"For heaven's sake, what?"

"He doesn't want you to know."

"Jack?" It was a well-modulated demand, but he refused to say anything more. Fine. She had no time for his games. She thanked him curtly and promised to return on Friday at the appointed hour. Just as well he wouldn't share whatever last foul secret Philip was harboring. Whatever it was, it could wait. More imminent concerns awaited her in Harlem.

❦

Jack was an old hen. As Julia stepped from the taxicab, she scoffed at his cautions. The street was busy with ordinary people doing ordinary things. Most passed without a glance, heading home with parcels of marketing or laundry, eager to start supper or rest their feet. It was nearly five. She hadn't thought about what hours Heacock's people might keep. She hoped it wasn't too late to see someone today.

Glennis froze halfway out of the taxi. Gripping the door handle, one foot on the pavement, she said, "Are you sure?"

Julia had to bend over to hear her.

"But, Julia, they're all colored. Every single person here. I'm not sure we should get out."

For pity's sake. There wasn't time for such nonsense. "Wait here then," Julia said and left Glennis cowering in the shadows of the locked taxi.

She climbed four flights of narrow stairs, each landing lit by a dusty bulb between two facing doors. At 4A she took out Naomi's appointment slip, readied herself, and rapped softly. Someone scrambled on the other side. Chin down, she gazed at the floor, presenting to the peephole a profile of chastened femininity. The chain clattered back, and a man in a collarless wrinkled shirt and brown braces eyed her. "You got an appointment? This is an appointment-only establishment."

His voice was deep but labored and wooden, as if he had struggled to memorize his brief line. His large frame blocked Julia's view of the interior. She held out the slip, thumb covering the date. He examined it, then her face, and stepped back into the apartment to allow her in.

The room held a small desk, two filing cabinets, and four mismatched wood chairs drawn into a semicircle. Another chair, surrounded by a sea of crumpled newspapers, was stationed beside the door, where this fellow apparently resided. The room was deserted, except for a gray-haired woman behind the desk.

She gave Julia a hard look. "No more appointments. We're finished for the day."

Julia crossed the room. "I'm afraid I'm not actually on your schedule," she began.

"Barney," the woman snapped, "what'd you let her in for? Can't you do one thing right? No appointment, nobody gets in. God help me, boy, sometimes you're worse than useless."

"She got one, Ma! I saw it. The little paper. Look." He pawed at Julia's hands. "Show her!" Fear ballooned his voice.

"Sorry, miss," the woman said. "Sometimes I swear he's too slow to catch a cold."

"A friend of mine came here for an appointment," Julia said quickly, "not long ago. I'm not here about that. I simply have one quick question."

The woman slapped shut the binder spread across her desk. "Out. No questions. Ever. Barney, get her out."

Barney licked his lips. A strand of slicked hair fell over his eye. He reached for Julia's arm. "But, Ma. She has—"

"Button your stupid flap, boy. Get her out. Now!"

Barney was no boy but a grown man at least ten years Julia's senior. He seized her wrist and tugged her toward the door. The distance was not far, but they covered it in fits and starts as she resisted, heels scraping across the dirty linoleum floor. He flung open the door and pushed her out. She dipped her left shoulder and knee in the semblance of a violent stumble and flung herself with a noisy thud against the wall. With her right hand she grabbed Barney's arm, pulling him toward her to ease her crumple to the floor. "Good heavens," she exclaimed.

"You all right, miss?" he asked, sinking to one knee.

"I'm not sure." Julia's voice was shaky but loud enough to carry into the apartment. She fumbled furiously in her handbag. "If you'll just be kind enough to help me up."

Shielded from his mother's glaring eye, Julia found what she sought and opened her palm to show him a pair of ten-dollar bills. From the bulge of his eyes, she guessed it might be half a month's wages or more. She gave him one of the bills. "If you help me, Barney," she whispered, "I'll give you the other one too."

His mother shoved back her chair. "Idiot! Get rid of her!"

Julia lolled against Barney, hooking her arm behind his neck as he righted her. He smelled of boiled pastrami. "Outside," he grunted, low but clear.

"Thank you." Her fingers lingered for a moment on the back of his hand, out of sight. Loudly she said, "Sorry to have troubled you, ma'am." The door did not close until she reached the landing below, and a coarse blasphemy struck the unfortunate Barney.

Julia sat in the taxicab across the street for a good twenty minutes, watching the building entrance. Glennis fidgeted the whole time, whining of criminals and savages. The driver snoozed, slumped against the window, cap pulled low. At last Julia saw Barney's mother leave. If a reflection off a passing motorcar hadn't briefly lit that angular face and thin mouth, she might not have spotted her. In a shapeless black coat and wide-brimmed hat pulled low, the woman easily disappeared into the crowd. She was well suited for her work.

Another ten minutes passed. Shadows pooled in the street. A steady snore came from the front seat. Had Barney's courage failed? Had he stung her, content to enjoy Julia's loss of ten good dollars? Surely twenty was enough enticement. He seemed willing to talk; Julia was sure of it. As she fretted, ten more minutes crawled by. Glennis fumed nervously, arms taut across her ribs.

Julia nearly sang out when she saw him. Barney stepped onto the stoop, looking in all directions. He wore an ill-knotted green tie and a brown tweed jacket over his braces. His hair was freshly slicked back. She imagined there would be a splash of some hideous shaving balm to contend with as well. She slid out of the taxi.

He saw her and trotted down the steps to the pavement. "Ma told me to sweep up," he said. "I can't be too long. She watches."

Julia took his arm. "We'll be quick, Barney. You're awfully nice to help me." Inside the building she spoke plainly. "My friend saw Dr. Heacock about three weeks ago, but the question isn't really about her.

I know who she is, naturally. I hope you can tell me who made the arrangements, who paid for the doctor's services."

He nodded, loosing several pesky strands of hair. "That depends."

Did he want more money already? Julia gave him an innocent smile. "On what?"

He stared dumbstruck, as if she were lit up large, a face on a moving picture screen.

"Barney?"

"On if you can find her papers."

"Oh yes. That would do it, I'm sure. Are the records upstairs?"

"Ma keeps them in her cabinet. Only, they're secret. She's the only one who reads them."

"Come on, Barney. Quick. Let's give it a try."

He mounted the stairs two at a time, turning at every landing to watch Julia hurry to catch up. Her shoes pinched, not made for such exertions. She hoped to heavens she wouldn't perspire. There was no time to get her frock cleaned before Sunday, and she loathed packing away soiled clothing. She slowed to a manageable pace. Barney simply took more time to gawk.

He groped across the dark office to switch on the desk lamp with an anxious glance at the drawn blinds. The chairs had been straightened and the newspapers tidied into a rough pile. He probably had little to do all day except peruse them, front to back and back to front, between clandestine knocks. "Sometimes she looks up here. She can see."

"You live nearby?"

He poked his thumb to the west.

"Let's hurry, then."

Barney took a key from under the desk, and Julia quickly unlocked the top drawer of the file cabinet. Her heart leaped when she saw bold surnames—*Adams, Bennet, Dingley*—printed across the tab of each file. This would be child's play. But in the second drawer there was no *Rankin*, no files at all between *Post* and *Swanson*. She tried *Pearsall*.

Nothing. She scanned the names again. *Negri, Pola. Pickford, Mary. Post, Emily. Swanson, Gloria.* False names, of course. Assigned or chosen, it made no difference. There was no way to find Naomi's file.

"Barney," Julia said, switching to a whisper at his frantic palm in the air. "They're made-up names. I can't find my friend."

"You sure?" He clutched the wadded ten-dollar bill in his fist. "You look in both places?"

"Both? Show me."

"These have names," he said, running his fingers down the top two drawers. "Those have numbers." He pointed at the bottom drawers.

"May I look?"

He unlocked the third drawer, and they crouched beside it. Across each file's tab was a four-digit number. The first was 0601, followed by another 0601, 0701, 1001, 1201, 1201, 1301, and so on. Inside each file appeared the false name: *Borden, Lizzie. March, Jo.*

Julia rifled through the numbered files. The first two digits increased successively, while the last two crept up, changing every fifty or so files. With Barney's eyes glued to her every movement, she turned her face away to think. What was the system? When it came to her, she vowed to kick herself later for being so thick. Of course. How simple. The appointment slip should have taught her. These were dates, inverted in the European fashion. 6 January, 6 January, 7 January, and so on. With a little cry that made Barney beam she pushed back to the 09s. 0509: one file labeled with the date of Naomi's appointment. The name beneath the number was printed in clear, schoolmarmish letters: *Pankhurst, Emmeline.*

Naomi. Who else would choose the name of the prominent British suffragist? It made a wan joke in the midst of such squalid despair.

A car horn blared in the street, and Barney jumped. "Hurry, miss."

Julia bit back a curse. There were only seven or eight lines written on a single sheet of paper, nothing intelligible. Medical information, perhaps. At the bottom was printed simply *Paid in Full, Cash.* This told her nothing more than what the appointment slip revealed. Watching her expression, Barney groaned.

She looked up into his broad face, creased with worry. "You've been awfully helpful, Barney. But this doesn't say what I hoped it would. I need to know who paid."

His chin sank to his chest, and she saw a smear of saliva on the top of his head, a remnant he'd failed to work through his thinning hair. It was as endearing as it was repulsive.

"Do you remember visitors, Barney?"

"Our ladies?"

"Yes. Do you remember the ladies? Or rather, who comes here to pay for them to see the doctor?"

"Yeah. I get to look at them as much as I want."

Julia could believe that. He'd surely memorized her features by now.

"Do you remember a visitor who came about Miss Pankhurst? A few weeks ago?"

He repeated the name three times, squinting in concentration. "I think so."

Julia slid the file back into place and closed the drawer. "Can you remember who it was, who paid for Miss Pankhurst's appointment? This is tricky, Barney. I'm not asking about Miss Pankhurst herself but about the person who paid the money. Do you remember?"

"Yeah, I think so."

"The person who paid? Are you sure you're remembering the right person?"

His gaze slinked to hers. "I remember. She had brand-new money. It made a pop when she counted it."

"She, Barney? It was a woman?"

"Yeah."

A woman. Julia considered the possibilities. Alice? Nolda Rankin? Vivian Winterjay? Someone from the Union? One of the Rankin maids? A secretary from Chester's bank? That would certainly fit with the crisp new bills. Of course Russell, or any other man, could have sent a female emissary for the task. It was hopeless. Nothing here would help identify the baby's father. It had been a long shot, and it had proved futile. Julia bit her lip in frustration.

Barney smoothed the damp bill in his palm. He eyed the door nervously.

She slipped the second bill into his jacket pocket. "I'm grateful for your help, Barney. Be sure to keep this for yourself now. Buy something special with it. We can go now, before she wonders where you are."

His eyes followed the money all the way to his pocket. "Don't you want to know her name?"

Julia subdued a flash of irritation. "I'm afraid Miss Pankhurst isn't her real name."

His face fell in confusion. "Not her. The other one."

"You know the name of the lady who *paid*?"

He nodded, a grin splitting his face.

"How do you know it?"

"I can read, can't I?"

Patience, patience, Julia reminded herself. "But, Barney, the names in the files aren't real names. And they're only for the patients."

"Not in the files," he thundered. "In the newspapers."

"You saw her name in the newspaper?"

He gave an exultant nod. "Pictures too. I seen her in my papers."

It was Julia's turn to stare.

"It was that Miss Rankin lady," he shouted, eager to please. "I remember 'cause she smelled real pukey."

"The lady who paid?"

"Yeah. *Yeah!* Her. That lady who made all the fuss about voting."

CHAPTER 24

Julia tapped on the taxicab's backseat window. Glennis squawked and unlocked the door, jolting the driver awake. Julia reported her disappointing discovery as they sped south.

"All that worry for a lousy fizz?" Glennis complained.

Exactly. Two precious days and twenty dollars Julia could ill afford to lose, merely to learn that Naomi herself arranged and paid for the fatal procedure. Alice did not know her friend as well as she thought. Apparently Russell's fears were closer to the mark: Naomi's defiant poverty was her undoing. By the time they crossed Fifty-Ninth Street, Glennis had cheered a bit, speculating that Chester had forced Naomi up those stairs. Regardless, they were no closer to knowing the baby's father or why Naomi had veered so dramatically onto the tragic course that cost her her life. Julia craved a sidecar. A shadowy plan was beginning to form, and she needed all the strengthening she could get.

$\backsim$

Shortly after eight the next evening, Julia watched the housemaid close the doors to the Rankin living room. The commotion inside suggested the Rankins, the Winterjays, and Russell were not amused at having been summoned again at short notice. Glennis's voice pierced the querulous noise. Her words were muffled by the thick oak doors, but the tone was clear: nervous, a bit too jolly. Something about very important travel arrangements for her wedding next April in Kent. The family's mood did not improve. Best to move quickly.

Julia and Alice were secreted in the butler's pantry. Alice fingered a white chiffon scarf wrapped loosely around her throat. She wore a dark felt cloche pulled low over her ears. Her eyes floated in the pallor of her gaunt face. "Ready?" Julia said. "Take a deep breath, and remember what you're going to say."

Alice took a few shallow breaths. "I know what I have to do."

Julia checked the hallway, saw it was deserted, and led Alice to the living room doors. They exchanged pinches for courage, and Julia pushed open both doors.

They were expecting stunned silence. But Nolda Rankin's immediate and guttural profanity surprised everyone. Her husband turned at it, astonished.

"Miss Clintock has something important to say," Julia announced.

Chester bounded from his seat toward Alice. "Get out of my house! There's nothing you can—"

She stood her ground and jerked away the scarf.

Julia blushed at this melodramatic touch, as it had been her idea, but it froze Chester. There was a tide of low exclamations. Vivian Winterjay stammered the obvious question.

"Someone attacked me," Alice said in a hoarse voice. "Tuesday night, after I left this room."

"Are you all right?" said Vivian, one hand comforting her own throat.

Alice laid a palm across the vivid marks. "Naomi was my dearest friend. For her sake I agreed to your demands for privacy. But now I'm frightened and exhausted." She labored to swallow, and Julia steadied her elbow. "I need to rest tonight; then I'll leave your house forever, Mr. Rankin. And tomorrow morning I'm going straight to the police with everything I know about Naomi's death. I see now it's the right thing to do."

"What do you mean?" Voices rose. "The *police?*"

"This is getting grim," muttered Russell.

Alice retucked the scarf around her throat and, ignoring the tumult, left the room. Julia turned to follow her out.

"Wait! Don't leave, Julia," begged Glennis, as usual a notch too loud, as she scrambled to grab her arm. "I need you here."

This time Julia would not be deterred. "I have to go, Glennis. The taxi's waiting. This is a family matter, and I don't belong here."

The last thing she heard as the door swung shut on the family's rising alarm was Glennis's wail as she plopped into the nearest chair. "Will somebody *please* tell me what's going on?"

$\curlyeqprec$

An hour later, the basement apartment was dark. Two bundles tied with string sat on the dining table, the last of Alice's things to be vacated in the morning. Only an occasional creak from the room above suggested the Rankins were still afoot, perhaps discussing plans for Glennis's wedding with redoubled urgency.

Glennis was crouched around the corner in the kitchen nook. Alice had safely barricaded herself in Naomi's bedroom. Julia waited in position, feigning sleep in the old rocker. Alice's long white scarf was now looped around her neck and trailed over the rocker's arm, the dark cloche slumped forward to hide Julia's face. On the low table near her feet sat a great china vase from Nolda's morning room. Should something happen, as they dearly hoped it would, Julia planned to kick out and knock it to the floor. The crash was the signal for Glennis to come running, making the loudest ruckus she could.

A click. The slightest of sounds. A current of musty air crept along the worn linoleum floor like a marsh tide. Julia's every nerve crackled. She clamped her lips together to stay quiet.

Fingers slid into the scarf's chiffon. Her stomach plunged. The fingers coiled, weightless, little more than a whiff of lavender talc, and she remembered, too late, to fill her lungs. With a fierce indrawn breath above her, the scarf tensed into a cord that bit across her throat. Her arms jumped as if yanked by a puppeteer, grasping helplessly at what loomed behind her. She kicked out at the table. The scarf went slack.

The vase hit the floor with a dull thud and rolled quietly under Julia's scuffling feet.

A second yank drove wet hisses from her throat. Pain flooded her skull. Colors swirled. She saw the tip of her mother's cigar glowing red. Christophine reaching through a gauzy curtain, weeping and hiccupping in her musical patois. Gerald's pink body: naked, shivering, unquiet. The flare of a hundred cigars, a furnace hot and loud.

Julia resented the lurch of distant muscles. The mind collapsed meekly into its fine understanding of death, but the body fought like the surly animal it was. Her knees rose up and drove both heels toward the floor. It was her last strength, and not entirely hers, gathered into one clumsy stomp, one chance of hitting the vase. Through the fiery roar in her head came a distant clatter.

"Stop!"

Or maybe some other word. But Glennis's voice, shrill as sirens. Yellow light blazed, and she appeared like a mad wraith, waving Chester's revolver in reckless loops. She uncorked a scream that would earn Madame Sosostris a handsome bonus. The scarf finally sagged.

Julia choked. With each heave of returning oxygen, vision crept out from under its red ooze, and thoughts revived into words. Her heartbeat receded back into her chest.

Glennis clawed at the scarf. "Get it off!"

Julia's hands rose to the base of her skull, rested limp for a moment, and removed the stiff collar hidden beneath the scarf. Stolen from Chester's wardrobe and reinforced with brass stays to appease worrywart Glennis, it had made all the difference, given Julia the extra moments to save herself. Relief washed over her throat, slick with perspiration and throbbing of nascent bruises. Colors would soon line her neck like some exotic duck's.

Glennis leaned close to peer at Julia. The gun still careened at the end of her right arm, in drunken surveillance of what remained motionless behind the rocker. Grateful tears swelled in Julia's eyes, and Glennis nodded solemnly to see them.

"Lord God Almighty!"

It was all Julia could distinguish in the torrent of voices thundering down the cellar stairs and past the wine reserves and the laundry basins and drying linens. It was a man's voice, but beyond that she couldn't discern.

"That's it. This has gone far enough." Russell's voice boomed.

Julia steadied the floor beneath her feet and stood, both hands gripping the rocker, to face him.

He was not looking at her. No one was. No one paled at her injured throat. No one exclaimed at the blood dripping down her calf, sliced by a shard of pottery. They saw only Vivian Winterjay, gloved hands still sculpted into loose fists. Her fingers, moments earlier coursing with chiffon, gripped nothing.

∾

"Darling?"

Vivian's blue eyes sparked at her husband's entreaty.

"What's going on here?" Russell demanded.

Glennis discovered the revolver in her hand and set it on the table. She ran to the kitchen for a glass of water. Julia clutched it with stiff fingers, the dented and twisted collar still dangling from her wrist. Each glide of cool water helped ease the fire in her throat.

"Wait." Nolda disappeared back into the dark cellar beyond the apartment door. Her steps pounded up the wooden staircase to the kitchen. The door at the top slammed shut, no doubt dispersing the servants huddled there. On returning she shoved home the bolt, locking the apartment door. "Keep your voices down. Those people have ears like rabbits."

Chester glowered at Julia. "Well?"

"I can explain everything." Julia's voice was a painful wisp. She lifted the mangled collar. "And I will. To the police."

Nolda made a choking noise and stumbled in a half circle before running for the commode and basin. A full blast of tap water couldn't disguise her retching. Chester flapped open a handkerchief and scrubbed it across his forehead and upper lip. "Can't you do something, Coates?"

Russell eyed Julia and did not answer.

"The police," Julia repeated between sips. "Unless you agree to honor Naomi's new will."

"That's blackmail." Chester's handkerchief dangled from his mouth like a costume beard. "Despicable. You'll bleed us dry. Hold us hostage. I won't do it. Something's wrong here. You tricked Vivian. I say go ahead, Miss Kydd. See what the police make of your vicious little games."

"It looks incriminating, Chester," Russell said. "I must counsel you to consider her terms. The story here could be worse than you imagine."

Nolda's sickness turned to waves of slurred weeping.

"The story is what you see, Mr. Rankin," Julia said. "Your sister attacked Miss Clintock Tuesday evening, and she tried again just now."

"Don't be absurd. Why on earth would she do that? You won't get away with this, whatever your scheme."

Winterjay held his wife's face tight against his breast pocket. "For pity's sake, Chester, think of Vivian. Think of Nolda. Think of the children. Nothing else matters. Let Miss Clintock have the money, if it means an end to this nightmare. Nothing is worth any more of our suffering."

From the cave of his chest came Vivian's first sound, a muffled wail.

"You *swear* you won't take any of this to the police or the newspapers?" Chester said.

"If you swear to honor Naomi's will, relinquish control over her money, then yes." Julia took another calming swallow. "And if you also listen to what I have to say."

His muttered profanity was assent enough. Winterjay rested his cheek against his wife's hair, stroking her back in restless gratitude.

"Mr. Coates as witness," Julia said.

"Fair enough," Russell said. "We need to get to the bottom of this. You owe us a great deal of explanation, Miss Kydd." He retreated toward the back wall, well away from the others. He hadn't yet met her gaze.

Julia accepted this with a nod. She noticed a stinging pain on her leg and saw a sticky mess of blood in her shoe. Glennis saw it too and fetched a cloth to wipe the wound clean. As its ooze slowed to a trickle, Julia's breathing settled, and she gathered her thoughts.

Nolda reappeared, silent and gray. Chester handed her his wadded handkerchief.

"When Alice—Miss Clintock—was attacked," Julia said, "I knew Glennis was right. She sensed from the start that Naomi's death was not what it seemed."

"You all thought I was potty," said Glennis, "but I knew she didn't accidentally take all those tablets. The idea was ridiculous."

"Whoever attacked Alice had something terrible to hide," Julia said. "The only way to learn what was to lure the assailant to come again. Alice's threat of going to the police provoked just that. But this time she—I—was ready."

"I knew it," Chester said. "A trick. Do you hear this, Coates? The girl's a lunatic."

"So I put on this collar under Alice's scarf and hat and waited, pretending to be asleep, as Alice was the other evening." The mangled collar testified to the consequences.

"Expecting me, I'm sure. As Glennis so brilliantly decided from the get-go."

"Not you, Mr. Rankin. By all accounts you quarreled constantly with Naomi and probably welcomed her death. But a stronger motive drove our attacker. Mrs. Winterjay was desperate to hide the truth about Naomi's death."

Vivian pulled away from her husband in a sharp breath. "Are you happy now, Miss Kydd? My life's a misery, and we're all in tatters. Just as Naomi wanted. She couldn't have done it, not without your help. You and Glennis and *her*." She jabbed a finger toward Alice. "You got her money. Wasn't that enough? Must you destroy her family too?"

Alice touched her injured throat.

Glennis barked out a high laugh. "You blubber about Naomi and Alice, Viv, but what about you? You tried to kill my friends."

"Your *friends*? Glennis! Open your silly eyes. If I'd let this Clintock woman go to the police and the newspapers, where do you think that would leave you and your precious Archie? He'd run the other way before you could blink. No man would want anything to do with this family. I couldn't let her destroy us. She forced me to act. Of course I hated it. But it was only a scare. She can moan till kingdom come, but that's all it was. Any doctor would say so."

"What about Julia? She'd be dead if it weren't for that collar."

Vivian dismissed this with a wave of her jaw. "You girls are fools, meddling in matters you cannot comprehend. I have no quarrel with Miss Kydd. It's her own fault if her stupid trick cost her a few bruises. Don't look so shocked and innocent. You knew exactly what would happen. How can you point a gun at my head, with that threat about going to the police, and not expect me to defend myself and my family?"

"Good God, Vivian," Russell said. "If you're so afraid of scandal, what did you think your arrest would do?"

"My arrest? Don't be ridiculous. Look at her. She's no more hurt than that Clintock woman was. I wasn't about to *kill* her, and besides, no one would ever know it was me. It was a mistake not to unlock the outside door the first time. I knew better tonight. With that door ajar, no one would dare accuse one of the family. Think of the people Naomi associated with. It would never have involved us."

Chester coughed in irritation. "Who cares about what didn't happen? I want to know why you girls cooked up this sneaky trap in the first place. We're still waiting for answers, Miss Kydd, and they'd better be good."

"Tell them," Glennis said.

"I guessed the truth," Julia said, "when I remembered there were *two* Miss Rankins active in the politics of women's suffrage. Naomi, of course, but also Mrs. Winterjay, before her marriage."

Except for the pink blaze across her cheeks, Vivian might have been a statue of stone.

"I discovered, you see, that it was Vivian Rankin, as she was well known in the newspapers years ago, who arranged for the abortion that killed Naomi."

CHAPTER 25

"No!" Vivian's denial was quick and fierce.

"*What?*" Chester and Winterjay exclaimed in unison.

"Performed by a butcher," Julia said. "Naomi lost a great deal of blood, and she likely suffered a deadly infection as well. Toxic reaction, Dr. Perry called it, though he assumed it was caused by an overdose of morphine."

"That's absurd," Chester said. "I found her myself. Not a drop of blood in sight. Perry will confirm it."

Julia silenced his doubts the same way she'd quelled her own, just before following Glennis and a shaky Alice out of the apartment the other morning. She untucked the afghan covering the sofa and overturned the center seat cushion. A huge brown stain confirmed that a significant pool of blood had saturated its fibers.

"God in heaven," Russell breathed.

Alice shifted toward Glennis for protection, in case the family's wrath again turned on her as they fathomed the scale of the suicide charade. But the stain drove their thoughts elsewhere, to a more visceral revelation: Naomi was not the woman they thought they knew.

Chester eyed the graphic brown patch. "You're saying Naomi was a whore, on top of everything else?"

"For pity's sake," Russell snapped. "She was your sister. Can't you for once see her as a human being, a grown woman with a mind and life of her own?"

"Who was subjected to a vicious assault by a notorious incompetent," Julia said. "Naomi suffered a violent, painful, lonely death."

"No! Stop saying—" Vivian's words dissolved as Winterjay pulled her against his chest.

He curled his shoulders to shield her. "Of course Naomi was human and entitled to her share of shortcomings, but she defied common decency in more ways than any of us can count. The Bible's heartbreakingly clear on this: as ye sow, so shall ye reap."

"Aren't you listening, man?" Russell said. "Spare us the sermonizing. Naomi would be alive today if your wife hadn't taken her to a butcher."

"Quiet!" Winterjay tightened his grip to hush Vivian's distress. "It's slanderous, what you're suggesting, and I won't stand for it. You owe Vivian—us both—a profound apology. You as well, Miss Kydd. You've made a thoughtless and hurtful mistake. I don't know what's going on here, but my wife is a gentle soul who would never knowingly harm anyone." He followed Julia's eyes to the scarf that had fallen to the floor. "Not without extreme provocation."

Julia wet her lips. "I'm afraid you're the one who's mistaken, Dr. Winterjay," she said. "A worker at the so-called clinic recognized your wife. He remembered her from newspaper photographs when she was fighting to defeat women's suffrage. He said she was the woman who made the arrangements for Naomi's 'service.' I confirmed it this afternoon, with an old photograph Glennis gave me." It had been one of several errands in Julia's long day, during which she had gained a new respect for the harried lives of police detectives.

"Stuff!" Chester spat. "The fellow's either a liar or an imbecile. No one would ever believe such a ludicrous story."

"It's not ludicrous," Glennis said, though she too had scoffed on first hearing it.

"Vivian didn't even know Naomi was pregnant," Winterjay said. "None of us did. How could we? We'd be the last people Naomi would confide in."

"That may be true. Nevertheless, your wife did know." Julia spoke boldly to cover her humming nerves. There were great patches of guess-work in her hypothesis.

Vivian squirmed free. Hair disheveled and face flushed, she glared at Julia. "What a keen little spy you are, Miss Kydd."

"What's this about, Viv?" Chester asked the question that shone from every face.

Julia turned to Vivian with the others for an answer, knees weak with relief. If more questions had been asked of her, she'd have fumbled badly. She didn't know the exact course of events, just enough to construct a plausible narrative. Now she hoped Vivian's righteousness would rise up and finish telling the story.

Vivian scanned the roomful of puzzled faces. With a sweep of her shoe, she kicked away the chiffon scarf. "Naomi is the villain here, not me. You can't imagine what I've had to endure these past weeks." She dragged her thumb across both cheeks. "This whole nightmare began with a perfectly ordinary morning. I'd come home a few days early from Boston to prepare for that dreadful Talbot League party. I stopped by here to borrow a punch bowl, and I saw the most curious thing. Naomi, on her knees in the garden, retching into the asters like a perfect peasant. I was astonished. What on earth was ailing her? I was about to ask if she needed help when a horrible, horrible thought occurred. It seemed impossible and yet appallingly plausible, considering Naomi.

"I was in torment the rest of that day. I couldn't sleep a wink all night. I knew her vile ideas about 'inconvenient' pregnancies. I knew exactly what she would do, and I had to stop her."

"You telephoned her at the Union," Julia said. "Asked her to meet you."

Vivian nodded. "We met for tea. She admitted she was expecting, just like that. Well, tempers were soon short, so I went straight to the point. I begged her to confront the father and insist he marry her. Give herself and the poor child a chance at a future with dignity.

"And you know what she said to me? She said, 'He's married, Viv,' with a strange look in her eye, and then she laughed, right in my face. I was aghast. I told her it was all the more important that she find a good home for the poor child, cursed with such a faithless father." Vivian clamped a hand over her jaw and shook her head. She twisted to retreat again to her husband's collar, as if that were the end of the story.

If only it had been. If only the sisters' conversation had stopped a minute sooner, before either could provoke the other and set in motion the day's fateful events. The family would be celebrating Naomi's pregnancy now, wishing her and Russell a long and happy marriage. Julia could not glance his way, could not bear to know if he was thinking of this too.

"There you have it." Winterjay stroked Vivian's head. "Just as I said. My wife would never play a part in Naomi's scheme. She abhors that abomination—we both do—with the deepest possible convictions. Moral, spiritual, ethical, legal. Nothing could ever alter that."

Did Vivian, shrouded inside his denials, stiffen at his protests? Was there a hint of disgust, a flinching recoil? However angelic a portrait of his wife Winterjay clung to, Vivian knew the truth, and—if her logic was right—so did Julia. She tucked her knuckles against her aching throat to steady her hands. It was time to play her last crucial card, a huge bluff. Everything depended on what happened next. "Naomi's pregnancy threatened more than your wife's principles, Dr. Winterjay. It threatened her marriage and her family."

"Complete and utter nonsense." He dismissed her remark with an easy smile. "Nothing about Naomi could possibly threaten us. That much I know for certain."

His calm conviction hung in the air. Julia was powerless. Only one person in the room could challenge his claim. Several seconds passed, but it felt like an eternity before Vivian reared back and flung off her husband's arms.

"You fool! You know *nothing*. She put me in an unbearable situation. She made me choose. Choose between honoring every principle I hold dear and defending my husband and my children. Saving your precious face!"

"*My* face?"

Her shoulders twitched in a brief shudder at his bemused skepticism. "At first I didn't understand it, the awful look in her eyes that shot straight through me when I asked about the father. There was contempt, oh, plenty of that, but also something else. Pity! *She* pitied *me*! As she sat there smugly refusing to listen to anything I said, it came crashing in on me. I felt such a fool, a mortified fool. It was not only me she was defying, but my husband. You, Edward! You!" She drove a feeble fist into Winterjay's ribs.

His arms fell to his sides, patiently making no gesture to defend himself from the bewildering outburst. "I don't understand . . ." He turned to the others with an embarrassed half smile, as if wanting to explain away her strange talk. His struggle between chivalry and confusion was painful to witness.

"Wait. No," he said slowly. "It can't be. Are you saying the baby was—"

"Yes. Yes. Yes!" Vivian's words pounded the short distance between their faces. "How can you be so stupid?"

"Good Lord. I had no idea." Winterjay looked about wildly. "How was I to know?"

"You? It was you? You had relations with . . ." Chester said, not so much a question as a slow comprehension of the unthinkable. Russell spread a hand across his face with a choke.

"Darling, please. I was lonely, miserable," Winterjay said. "It had been so long. You'd been in no condition—"

"My own sister? You couldn't be troubled to take your needs to some whore down—"

"Once!" Winterjay cut her short with an exasperated laugh. "One time. I swear just the once. I was in agony, you know—with you . . ." He nudged Vivian's jaw so she would look at him. "It meant nothing, darling. Nothing at all. Less than a dalliance. You were at the lake with the children. I saw Naomi coming home late one evening as I was leaving upstairs. She seemed worn, unhappy, so I took down a bottle of brandy to cheer her up. I swear that's all I had in mind. But then we had a few drinks, and nature took its course. That's all. I left sometime in the night. I swear until now I'd forgotten all about it."

Perhaps he had. This appalling candor squeezed Julia's breath no less than Vivian's strangling grip.

"For God's sake!" Anger burst from Russell. "Just another whore to you? Only more convenient? What kind of a monster are you?"

Nolda made a sharp sound. Her mouth went flat, lips pressed shut in bloodless fury.

Winterjay ignored them both. "She didn't resist, Viv. Not really. And believe me, she was no virgin. She may have been a spinster, but she knew what was what. And she was hardly one to simper about proprieties, not after all she did to flout them."

As if Naomi's will were a minor impediment to be brushed aside, rendered moot by his greater prerogative of need? What about the family's vaunted respectability? He seemed to consider only his own and deem it intact, as if Naomi's scorn for social norms absolved him as well. But she valued something much deeper, her right to act for herself, to accept or reject attentions as she chose. What about that? Had he dismissed that as mere feminine ruse?

Vivian's face tightened in disgust. "She said you forced her, showed me the faded bruises. Of course, anyone could have done that, but she told me details, intimate things she couldn't have known unless . . . Oh, I know you sometimes find comfort elsewhere, Edward. It's disgusting, but what can I do? She was so horribly convincing. I had no choice. I couldn't risk denying that the baby was yours. I had to accept she was telling the truth, that you had forced your attentions on her."

Winterjay shrugged irritably. "That's not fair, darling. Not at all. Yes, I was anxious for relief that night. I don't deny it. But she let me in, drank my brandy. Surely she knew how I was suffering. She must have known. Why else would she open the door to me?"

Julia could think of a dozen reasons. Others could too, judging by the uneasy shuffle of feet around the room.

Winterjay seemed to hear none of it. "Oh, she put up a tussle, as they do, but I knew her game. And sure enough, beneath that plain dress she wore underclothes as wanton as any whore's. When I saw that, well, what else was I to think?"

It was a rhetorical question, but Julia silently urged Vivian to answer it. There were plenty of reasons for Naomi's small luxuries beyond what his vanity supposed. But Vivian only glared at him. "I was furious, outraged. I begged her to go away somewhere quiet and discreet until the baby was born. I pleaded with her to let that precious infant answer some poor couple's prayers. It would have been only a few months, and I offered to pay for everything. But she wouldn't listen. She outright slapped the table as I spoke. She was ruthless, vindictive, just terrible!"

"Come on, Viv," Glennis exclaimed. "How can you put all the blame on her?"

Vivian spun on her heel. "Oh, I'm fully aware of my husband's stupidity in all this. But you heard him. Men are fools, pathetically weak fools when it comes to their needs. Naomi should have known not to encourage him. We women need to be the sensible ones, Glennis. You'll see soon enough."

A full two seconds elapsed before Glennis's eyes slid to Julia's. They were huge with disbelief. It was a hoary old caution, passed down from mother to daughter for generations. Did Vivian really believe the power to control what happened in the bedroom lay in women's hands? Or only the responsibility? That notion doubled men's license for pleasure while diminishing their lovers'. From some distant corner of memory, Julia heard her mother's laugh. She'd died before they'd spoken of sex, but hers would have been a different kind of counsel. She would have found the subject more merry than menacing.

Chester clapped impatiently. "All right, then. So Naomi refused to do the decent thing, and she paid a terrible price. Sounds like that's the grim fact of the matter. Hate to say it, but seems a fitting end for her, killed by the very wickedness she defended."

Chester's resolve to declare the business over made the hairs at the back of Julia's neck quiver. Once again he was dismissing Naomi's death by pronouncing her the architect of her own fate. Worse was the sight of Winterjay nodding sadly, and Nolda and Vivian covering their mouths in mournful assent. Julia wanted to shout, stamp her foot, do anything to break the spell. Chester's judgment, so smug and so self-serving, threatened everything she hoped yet to learn.

"Haven't you heard a word of this, any of you?" Russell's voice bellowed from the gloom beyond the lamplight. "Naomi died not because she ended her pregnancy but because a *barbarian* did it. Vivian took her to some wretch who used filthy instruments to gouge her open and—"

"No!" Vivian shrieked. Nolda swayed and bit down hard on Chester's handkerchief.

"What's wrong with you, man?" Winterjay said. "I don't know why everyone insists on veering so cruelly off the mark. Miss Kydd may be right about Naomi's wicked death, but you've heard my wife explain. She had nothing to do with it. She did everything she could to save that baby, to give some decent family the chance to adopt it, but Naomi would not be dissuaded. We all know her ferocious will."

His confidence was something to behold, as if his wife's moral conduct were a function of his character more than hers. To her horror,

Julia saw Chester and Nolda nod gratefully at this sanguine assurance of Vivian's innocence. She hurried to challenge it.

"Precisely the opposite is true, Dr. Winterjay," Julia said. "It was your wife who insisted on the procedure, not Naomi. Your wife made the arrangements."

He barely blinked, so quick was his dismissal. "That's preposterous. Impossible on every level. For one thing, Vivian wouldn't know the first thing about it."

"She would and she does. Last spring the *Woman Patriot* published a story vilifying the number of abortions in the city. I noticed the very issue in your home a few weeks ago. Earlier today I spoke with the author, Martha LeMay. She confirmed that Vivian questioned her recently about her research. The woman was only too happy to give me an earful about American moral turpitude."

Winterjay scoffed. "That can't possibly be true. The woman's mistaken or pulling your leg. I believe we've listened to enough of your innuendo and supposition, Miss Kydd. It's time you left this house. You've quite abused our family's hospitality. We took you for someone more honorable than you clearly are."

"Quite so," Nolda said fiercely, stepping forward to stand beside him. "This betrayal of our trust has gone on long enough. I must ask you to leave at once. You've sworn that what happened here will never leave this room, and we will hold you to it. Go. Now."

Nolda's imperious command nearly knocked Julia back a step. She knew all too well how egregiously she'd violated all protocols of courtesy. Her resolve withered, the floor beneath her feet changing to sand. She wavered, her next words melting fast.

A loud honking cough burst out from Glennis's lungs. She crossed her arms and jutted up both thumbs from the crooks of her elbows. They fluttered absurdly as if to signal *Don't stop now! Don't let her make you go!*

Julia could have kissed her friend for the comical surge of courage. She shifted her footing and held her ground. "I will leave, most gladly, as soon as you've all heard me out. You might dismiss my word, Dr. Winterjay, but what about your wife's? Why don't you ask her for the truth? Do you trust her to speak honestly?" It was another gamble. Vivian might lie to Julia, but to her husband? She who put such store in men's superior grasp of worldly nuance?

He gave a light laugh. "Vivian's honesty is above reproach. She'd never willfully deceive me. Would you, my dear?" He turned for her confirmation.

Vivian gave Julia a look of utter revulsion. She reached for her husband's hand.

"I tried, Edward. I tried desperately to reason with her. It's true she didn't plan to get rid of it. She had something even more vile in mind. She said she intended to have the child and raise it herself. 'Just pray the baby favors me,' she said. She actually laughed! It was monstrous, what she was planning. She would have wielded that child as a weapon over me, a weapon to shame and humiliate you, me, our children, and this whole family. I admit I've never felt such rage. So, yes, I did telephone Martha. She told me who to contact about someone to, to do it." Her head swerved in disgust.

Julia slowly let out the breath she hadn't known she was holding. Her guesswork held. Alice stifled a guttural sob, but no one else made a sound.

"My God," Winterjay breathed.

"No. Naomi would never agree to that," Russell said, edging his feet farther apart, as if preparing to defend the assertion by force if necessary. "Never."

"She was impossible as ever," Vivian said. "She's always been stubborn, especially when she thinks she can look down her nose at poor suffering mortals like me. Once I realized she was locked into her mad scheme, quite beyond all reason, I had to put a drop of laudanum in her tea." She peered frantically at the others, who only gazed back in silent shock. "Only a drop or two. To make her sleepy. I had to! What else could I do? You see my dilemma? She forced me."

Winterjay's face went hard and gray as Vivian's role in her sister's death became clear.

"Darling, please. You must understand. Of course I hated it. Everything about that business offends all that's sacred to me. It was awful! I had to go to a disgusting, squalid place in Harlem for instructions on where to find the reptile who would do it."

Wearing Naomi's sweater to protect her fine clothes. It was a small detail, but Julia slotted it into place.

"And I suppose she forced you to find the filthiest place possible?" Russell said.

Vivian's eyes filled with angry tears. "Don't you dare lecture me about moral niceties. I know about those other places, so fashionable, so tidy. Quick and simple they make it, hardly a bother. A spot of discomfort, then right as rain, back to normal. No worse than a toothache. Terribly modern. No, I couldn't allow that. She needed to understand the consequences of her reckless life. A woman *ought* to suffer for what she did."

"So you dragged her off, witless, to let that reptile gouge—" Russell choked.

"No!" Vivian screamed. "Edward, please!" She pleaded for her husband to meet her gaze, but he only clenched his jaw more tightly and turned away from her. She spun toward the others. "I couldn't do it. Even after all she did to torment and provoke me, in the end I couldn't do it. God tested me to the very brink of my endurance, but I finally found the strength to resist that awful temptation. I've confessed these terrible things so you'll understand the hell she put me through, the horror of what she did to me and my family. I swear by everything that's holy we never kept that appointment. I brought her home instead. The last time I saw her she was woozy but fine, resting right here on this sofa. I swear it."

Julia's heart collapsed into her shoes. She had banked on Vivian's principled honesty, trusting that she would take up the guilty narrative as Julia spooled it out to her. It had worked beautifully thus far, Vivian admitting everything as Julia had conjectured it. But if she lied now, balking at the last brutal scene, Julia had no way to prove otherwise. If Vivian claimed she'd left Naomi unharmed, the full story of those last hours would never be known.

Glennis gave another scornful honk. "That's a slick one. Sounds pretty and all, your high-minded morals kicking in just in time, but you would say that, wouldn't you? Seeing as how Naomi can't tell us what really happened."

"Glennis! Think. If I had harmed her, would I admit these terrible things? I swear I did nothing more than give her a muzzy head for a few hours. Ask our driver if you don't believe me. He stayed in the car with Naomi while she drowsed, and I went inside for instructions; then he drove us straight here from that disgusting place. Your gardener saw me helping her down the steps. Ask them. Did you think of that? Or were you too determined to fit me into your nasty scenario? Ask Mary, for that matter. She can tell you I was home that afternoon in plenty of time to get ready for that awful party."

Glennis pulled her mouth to one side. "I don't care. It still doesn't square. Naomi didn't die for no reason. All that blood didn't just pour out on its own, Viv."

"You think I wasn't shocked too? But when Chester told us she took her own life, I could understand it better than any of you, knowing her terrible shame. I thought most likely she meant to destroy only that poor baby. I figured she decided a child was too much bother after all. That would be just like her. Oh, I don't know. None of us does or ever can. It doesn't matter now. You've heard every last scrap of my part in this wretched business, and now that's the end of it, at least if this

Clintock person wants to see any of that money." Vivian gulped a deep breath of air, both hands calming her abdomen.

Julia rattled the empty water glass over her lips in search of something to ease the battering crescendo in her rib cage. It couldn't end like this, not at the very edge of truth. To her horror, she believed Vivian. Julia had made a frightful mistake. Her imagination had jumped too quickly from what she could prove—an appointment made—to what she could only surmise—the appointment kept. That mistake left her now with a throbbing throat and fading conviction.

But Glennis was right too. And Alice had insisted she'd found no instrument, no toasting fork or knitting needle, to suggest Naomi undertook the gruesome task on her own. Everything Russell said belied that possibility too. Either both were lying, or something else happened that day. Something Julia had overlooked entirely.

The room was suddenly crowded with two discoveries, not one: Naomi had died from a ruthless determination to destroy her pregnancy, and Vivian Winterjay was not responsible. The second revelation did not undermine the first but rendered it needlessly anguishing. Here among Naomi's family, lover, and dearest friend, all Julia had done was expose Naomi's agonizing death to those who would feel it most keenly. She brought them pain without any salve of understanding, much less justice. Worst of all, the person responsible—likely in this room—would remain forever unknown.

"I trust you're satisfied, Miss Kydd," Nolda Rankin said into the thickening silence. "Your sore throat's nothing compared to the injuries you've inflicted here tonight. You've hurt a good and honorable family with your deplorable insensitivity."

Vivian sobbed, spent of all anger. She turned to the consoling embrace of her husband, but he stiffened and stepped away. Nolda gave a soft cluck at this rebuff. "Vivian doesn't see your suffering, Edward," she murmured. "Always her own, never yours."

Julia stared, listening to Nolda try to soothe away the man's shock and pain. Her pulse began to thrum. What a colossal fool she had been. How many times had she witnessed that subtle touch, that tightly marcelled head bent in a private word for Winterjay, that small smile nuzzling at his back or sleeve or collar? It was the missing piece of the puzzle, and it had been in plain view from the start.

∽

Julia heard Glennis's voice leap in loyal protest of Nolda's criticism, but none of it distilled into words. Julia's own recollections clamored for attention. The mysterious story of Naomi's death was not a story at all, but a tangled sequence of furtive actions by different players for different reasons. Vivian had drugged Naomi, intending to get rid of the child she feared would destroy her family. Alice disguised Naomi's death as a suicide and fabricated threats to preserve her legacy as a martyr. Chester stole what he took for Naomi's suicide note to avoid a scandal. Each acted independently and at cross-purposes, yet each deception prompted another.

However ignoble and self-serving, each subterfuge was also ultimately ineffective. Julia had unraveled that tangled series of actions—driven by love, ambition, pride, and self-defense—but she'd missed the one deep malevolence that caused Naomi's death. Julia had never seen, until that moment, yet another powerful motive: jealousy.

"Naomi didn't change her mind," she said. "Neither was she mutilated on some wretched backstreet table. It happened right here. Didn't it, Mrs. Rankin?"

Nolda's eyes opened. They'd cooled into drowsy disregard, as if Julia were a chatty nuisance beside her at a salon, waiting for her nail lacquer to dry.

Chester's seize of air was so great that Julia braced for an explosion, but he released it in a hearty laugh. "Nolda! Going around the room now, accusing us one by one, is that it?"

"You promised to hear me out."

"How much more of this lunacy do we have to stand for, Coates? She's talking out of her backside now."

"I don't think we've heard the last of it, not quite yet," Russell said. "Go on, Miss Kydd—but our patience is wearing thin."

Julia nodded. Each moment the picture became clearer. Nolda idolized her brother-in-law. How many times had Julia witnessed her turn to Winterjay, not Chester, for answers, for comfort? Nolda's resentment must have been building for years. What agony she must have felt to witness Winterjay's affections toward not only Vivian but also Glennis and even Naomi, while her own yearning for his notice went unheeded. She would have sought nothing untoward, only the fond embraces and affectionate gaze he so readily bestowed upon the others. But she was married, and propriety erased her from his view. As another man's wife, she was no longer a woman to be cheered with appreciative regard. No wonder his admiring overtures to Julia the night of the Children's Aid gala had triggered such frosty resentment. Nolda hadn't been angry at Julia for breaching the Rankin family's privacy but for interrupting her rare moment alone with Winterjay, for stealing his interest.

Julia raced to formulate what must have happened the afternoon Naomi died. "Mrs. Rankin keeps a sharp eye on everything that goes on under this roof," she said. "She watches at windows, listens behind doors, always paying keen attention. Naomi was faint with laudanum that day. Vivian must have struggled to get her down those steps outside and into the apartment. Nolda wouldn't have missed it."

"That's your big discovery?" Chester said. "My wife runs a tight household? It's her duty to know what goes on under this roof."

"She came downstairs that day after Vivian left, let herself in through the basement door. Perhaps she was only curious, though I imagine she already suspected the truth."

Nolda, the daughter of a famous obstetrician, lifted her eyebrows. *Do tell,* the gesture said to Julia. *If you feel you must.*

"Yes, she realized the situation even then."

Winterjay edged away from Nolda's hovering touch. She folded her hands below her waist and sighed, a bored queen obliged to hear a complaint. *Burn the sofa,* she had demanded. Destroy the filthy thing—full as it was of Naomi's blood.

"The knowledge of Naomi's pregnancy stung like salt in an open wound," Julia said. "You remembered that night last summer, didn't you, Mrs. Rankin? Dr. Winterjay had been upstairs with you earlier, hadn't he? Probably restless, a little melancholy with Vivian away. You clearly prize his company above all else. Did you urge him to stay, hoping to lift his spirits, only to be brushed away? It must have pained you to see him slip back for a bottle from your husband's cabinet to take down here to share with Naomi. Did you listen at the cellar door or from the kitchen stairs? Did it pain you to hear her fighting him off, abusing the one man you most revere?"

Chester slapped his thigh in derision. "Utter rubbish. Nolda? Absurd." He babbled objections under his breath as the others listened for her reply.

Nolda smoothed her cuff. "He should have stayed with me. I'm the one who understands him. I see his worth more than any of you."

She met Vivian's bewildered gaze with raised, impatient eyebrows. *You failed him,* they chided. *I understand him, as you do not.*

"But he wanted Naomi's company, not yours," Julia prompted. "Never yours."

"And it was his downfall," Nolda snapped. "Yes, I listened that night. I feared for him, for what might happen to him, caught in this nasty lair of hers." She surveyed the room. "She had her ways, her slick little ways of arousing his lust. She lured him with her smutty ideas and godless talk, then treated him like muck. I heard everything. Not an ounce of feminine modesty in anything she said, some of it crude as a sailor, I'm sorry to say. How could he not be aroused by such rough talk and behavior? And then when he did what nature demands, you should have heard the names she called him. She had the cheek to curse him, the finest man she or any of us will ever know. She wasn't fit to wash his laundry, much less bear his child."

Julia fought to keep her face bland, her voice mild. Into the shocked silence she said with a knowing nod, "When you saw Vivian struggle to help her down to the apartment, you recognized your chance. If you acted quickly, you wouldn't need more laudanum to keep her quiet."

"Nolda can't tweeze a sliver," Chester protested. "Couldn't pop a blister to save her soul."

"You remembered stories you'd heard growing up, didn't you, Mrs. Rankin? Stories your father told of the desperate ways women tried to end their pregnancies. Stories you'd never forgotten."

"She's helpless as a jellyfish with any of that nurse-y stuff." Chester's bluster faded to a squeak.

Nolda stared at Julia for a long moment, then shrugged. "I did see them return, and anyone who knew what I did about Naomi's trickery could have figured out the truth behind that little drama stumbling down the steps. I understood at once. That baby would destroy Edward's career, his fine and important work. Naomi would have shamed him, shamed us all, every day that child drew breath."

"So you stopped her. You destroyed her child with such vehemence that you took her life as well."

There it was. The final piece to the grisly puzzle. Julia's heart was throbbing as if she'd scaled a steep rock face. She'd finally reached the truth, shaking but triumphant—if one could call anything about her task triumphant. Her words lingered in the stifling room until they disappeared under a crescendo of horror and disbelief.

Nolda, however, remained impassive.

"I, Miss Kydd?" she said when the room quieted. "On what grounds do you accuse me? I see no proof. You can badger my poor sister-in-law into spinning a tale that suits you, but you'll find I am less suggestible. Where is your evidence for this flight of ghoulish fancy?"

The words nearly tangled in Julia's throat, but she spoke them as calmly as she could. "The evidence is in your heart, your conscience. You know you left her here, bleeding and insensible. You took away your tool and your gruesome prize, and then you left her here to die."

Glennis caught hold of Alice's arm as she lunged forward with an angry growl. Vivian covered her eyes. Chester's mouth hung open, all resistance spent.

"I'm still waiting," Nolda said when Alice had been restrained and guided into a dining chair. "Your proof?"

Julia scoured her mind for something more to say, some way to pry from Nolda the only proof there could ever be. Ten more seconds passed.

"All right then," Nolda said. "You have none. Because the truth is that God took Naomi's life. Not me, not Vivian, not anyone in this room. God alone took her life. Her fate was harsh but just."

The silence was unbearable. Glennis gripped Alice by the shoulders. Russell pressed his forehead against the wall, the cords in his neck raising thin shadows in the lamplight.

"Oh, please," Nolda demanded, suddenly fierce again. "Naomi tormented us. Admit it. None of us is sorry she's dead. She brought nothing but trouble and pain to this family for years."

She reached for Winterjay's arm. He stiffened and clenched it to his side. She smiled and patted it instead. "It's time to remember what Edward told us. He said we must bury the memory of all she did to hurt us. He said we should console ourselves, take comfort in each other."

Somewhere upstairs a door closed. Glennis took a great noisy sniff. On either side of Russell's bent head, his palms pressed hard against the faded plaster, fingers wide, nails bloodless.

Vivian raised her head. "He's right," she said, her ashen face streaked and smeared. "I can't go on another minute like this. I'm sorry for Naomi's troubles and desperately sorry for what I did. I grieve for what you did too, Nolda. And I'm sorry we've all had to be exposed like this, our fears and our terrible failings. But that has to be enough. This suffering has to end."

How did she think it could end? Julia saw only terrible years ahead for this proud and loveless family. To protect Naomi's new will, she'd relinquished any chance of legal justice for Naomi's death, but it would not go unpunished. There would be little consolation here, less comfort. It took more than skillful oratory to summon such graces. Julia expected (or perhaps she only hoped) they'd do what the law could not: punish each other, possibly forever.

Vivian mustered the small, gracious smile Julia had first witnessed during that mutinous party a few long weeks ago. "I've struggled to forgive your foolish weakness, Edward, as you must now forgive mine. For our marriage and for our children's sake, we must put this awful thing behind us. Maybe now, at last, we can finally live at peace." Reaching for her husband's hand, she declared their ordeal over.

But Winterjay's arm exploded from his side. His elbow caught her below the ear, spinning her backward. "Don't touch me. You're vipers, both of you."

Glennis leaped to guide her sister's fall onto the afghan-shrouded sofa. Vivian wept as Winterjay strode from the room. His pounding steps up to the kitchen echoed like gunfire, in chilling counterpoint to her tiny frightened pants.

CHAPTER 26

At three o'clock the following afternoon, Julia sat in the reception lobby at Feeney, Churchman, Kessler, and Rousch, toying with the pale-pink silk wrapped loosely around her neck. Tucked beneath the brocade collar of her chestnut day suit, the slithery thing was anchored, more or less, by an amber cabochon. Julia rarely wore scarves because of that beastly slipping and sliding. Miss Baxter peered over her typewriting machine. She had already apologized twice for Jack's tardiness.

Philip waited in the opposite chair, a picture of calm preoccupation. Sketch pad across his knee, he skittered and swished his pencil in a rendering of the bowl of asters on the window ledge. He studied the flowers for an instant, then drew some droop or shadow, a bent petal or crowded leaf. His absorption suited Julia well. After a sleepless night, she felt weary and spent. For her as for the Rankin family, there was no true resolution, no clear and satisfying justice. Today's final reckoning with Philip felt equally flawed, and it weighed just as heavily on her spirits.

At the sound of Jack's greeting from the hallway, Julia cleared her throat. "Well, Philip," she said in a low voice. "Shall we end this sibling charade at last?"

Not even a blink. A few weeks ago, she would have fumed at the slight. Instead she touched his wrist to lift his head. "You should have told me," she said. "That you're deaf."

Philip frowned and sparked his fingers at his left ear. "A touch. Puny thing." He pressed a knuckle to his lips for secrecy. "But my vision is keen. I rarely miss a word. Don't give it another thought."

Jack arrived and clasped Philip's shoulder. He must know too. Of course there would be more thought, much more thought—but later. "Very sorry," Jack said. "A long telephone call I couldn't avoid. Ready?"

Philip rose and offered Julia his arm. "Shall we?" he said jauntily, as if they were returning for the next act of a vaudeville show. Somehow it seemed fitting, a last absurd gesture mocking the gravitas of the occasion.

They settled into the same chairs they'd occupied the morning they'd first parried arguments. Jack's desk was clear except for a single stack of documents: the tidy severing of all Julia's ties to her father and half brother. Jack reached for the papers. "The business at hand. At last."

Philip took out his cigarette case and offered it around. Julia didn't take one for fear her hand might shake.

"It's straightforward enough," Jack said. "In accordance with the partners' judgment, these papers transfer to Philip the accounts of Milo Kydd's estate that had been held in trust for Julia. With these documents, Julia, you renounce all claims to the estate. It seems harsh and unnecessary"—he looked sharply at Philip, who picked a fleck of tobacco from his lip—"but that's how your father's will is now construed. I'm sorry—"

"Isn't that a bit precipitous?" Julia said. She sniffled to hide the trace of hoarseness. "What about our codicil? The wager."

"What?" Jack jabbed the bridge of his spectacles to push them higher on his nose. "The judgment's made. Nothing you can do or say now will alter it."

"We agreed, and honor is honor. Philip, do you stand by your pledge?"

"My honor is as good as yours."

"Good," Julia said, "because it's resolved now, the mystery of Naomi Rankin's death." The words, that simple declarative sentence, were as ashes in her mouth.

"Brava! Cough it out. Am I to be merely rich or positively swish with it?"

"Philip, please," Jack said. "Be serious for once."

"Was I right?" Philip said, ignoring him. "No deadly concoctions after all?"

"No poison, no." Before Philip could crow, Julia added, "Nor was it suicide. Naomi Rankin died of a vicious attack to destroy her pregnancy."

He sat back. "My stars. Imagine that. There must be quite a story?"

"You're both still pledged to secrecy. Neither of you can breathe a word of this."

Philip assured her with a half wave.

She told them. She told them of the missing suicide note, the threats, Alice's deceit. She described the diary, the cryptic receipt, the attack on Alice, the discoveries with Barney. She described last evening's drama as lightly as possible. Neither man pressed her for details, fuming instead at her dangerous folly. Philip glared at her scarf. As if he would not have taken precisely the same risk.

"Naomi was drugged," Julia said. "Left powerless to resist an assault that left her dead. Glennis calls it murder."

"Did Mrs. Rankin confess?"

"No. But neither did she deny it."

Philip nodded thoughtfully. "Did Mrs. Rankin intend to kill her sister-in-law?"

"Probably not, though she showed no remorse. She claimed Naomi deserved her fate."

"I see. Tell me, if Naomi had inflicted the wound herself, with the same objective and same lamentable result, would you call it suicide?"

"Of course not, but—"

"Murder requires intent no less than suicide. Otherwise it's simply incompetence. I'm afraid Nolda Rankin's bloody hands are quite clean, technically speaking. An appalling metaphor and worse irony, but there it is."

"But you said yourself the most cunning murders often fall beyond the purview of the law. If a barber draws his blade across a man's throat with enough force to slit it open, would you shrug and call it incompetence? Would you give any surgeon, any policeman with a short temper and a billy club, carte blanche to—"

"Honest tools can serve an evil purpose."

"My point exactly."

"Note emphasis on purpose."

Julia spanked her handbag. It was all she could do not to shriek.

Philip had the decency to pale. "You're right. Enough pin dancing. If I recall correctly, I would prevail if you failed to prove it was murder."

"You insisted it was suicide. You were even further from the truth."

"Perhaps I misremember our precise language. It's possible we agreed on something more slippery. Neither of us was at our most serene at the time. I merely invoke the letter of the agreement, whatever the conversation's more general spirit."

"But—"

"I may, *however*," Philip continued, "be prevailed upon to accept your creative reasoning. Murder by malicious botchery—how can I resist the novelty of it? All right then, I concede." He launched a ridiculous sweep of his arm. "Hats off to the more devious mind. You win."

With that grand gesture he declared her the victor, the superior sleuth. The winner. *It's over*, a small voice in her head piped. At last. After weeks of wrenching worry, she'd finally achieved what she'd come for. What should have been a straightforward path had become a tortuous one, but she'd arrived—at a poor but redeeming end to both awful businesses, her usurped birthright and Naomi's terrible death.

Something in Julia's head soared off and zoomed about the room as she dared to fathom her triumph. She was again and forever free. She could marry David if she liked, but on her own terms. Or not at all. The jubilant notion wheeled and tumbled overhead like a drunken acrobat, a bee sozzled in honey.

"Tear it up, Jack," Philip went on. "The whole blasted thing, null and void. Poof." His fingertips sprang apart, dispelling Julia's weeks, months, of torment with a jaunty puff of air.

"How many times do I have to tell you—" Jack began.

"*Poof?*" Julia's bee faltered, her acrobat stumbled. "That's cavalier, considering the agonies you've put me through."

Philip paused in the process of lighting a fresh cigarette. "Julia, my dear, I don't want your money. Never did. It was Aunt Lillian, bless her soul, who insisted I pursue that balmy suit. She had it drawn up in my name and forced me at knifepoint—cake knife, but even so—to let it proceed. If I thought it had a ghost of a chance of prevailing, I'd have turned that flat little blade on her own finger, but honestly, I never thought it possible. No one was more surprised than I when those fools endorsed all that blather."

Jack slapped the desk. "Finally! At last a little truth. Good God, this whole business has been ridiculous from the start. Lillian pestered him like a rat terrier, Julia. She wouldn't leave him in peace until he agreed to let her contest the will on his behalf."

Bloody hell tenfold. An ocean would not suffice to distance her from this vindictive, horrid, spiteful man. "You stood to inherit a packet from the old lady, and still you'd see me denied?"

"Hardly a packet," Philip objected. "No one guessed that. And she did promise to live to a hundred."

"No wonder you goaded me into that wager. It meant nothing to you if you lost. Yet you would have me risk everything. This so-called concession is a sham. You've been laughing at me all this time. What a monstrous, monstrous man you are!"

Philip raised a forearm in mock alarm. "Mea culpa. Guilty as charged. But I only went along with the silly business for the chance to see you again. All those years of signing over sums made me curious about what had become of that spoiled, knock-kneed—yes, you were—ill-tempered urchin carting my name around on other continents. Once you got here and I'd had a good look, a mighty relieved one, I'll admit, I intended to denounce the old lady's flimflam at first crack, but then you turned out to be such a spanking fine adversary that, well, I couldn't resist. I had to keep it going a bit longer."

"This was all a great joke to you? All those things you said about me, about my mother, were froth, your idea of a fine amusement?"

"Perfect blather. Plausible objections, I suppose, but your claim seemed so secure I thought a bit of a dustup, an eyeball to eyeball, if you will, might make for good sport. You looked like you enjoyed it too, all those flashing eyes and ringing speeches."

"Enjoy it? Enjoy losing my independence? Enjoy my brother's rejection? And my father's? Having to risk everything to win back what you stole? You are unspeakably mad."

"Very possibly. But spare us the melodrama. You were never in the least danger. Even if you hadn't proven such a wily sleuth, I assume this Adair fellow has a bob or two. Besides, I'd always pitch in and give you—"

"*Give* me? That's outrageous! You were about to usurp my rightful inheritance, Philip. Any gift from you—drawn from my own money, no doubt—would be the very height of arrogant—" Julia choked at the ghastly echo of Naomi's situation and now Glennis's.

"What's going on in here?" Rousch loomed in the doorway. "Sounds like two cats on fire."

Jack scrambled to his feet. "There's some dispute about the judgment, sir."

"Stop wasting our time." Rousch pushed the stack of unsigned papers toward Philip. "You asked for arbitration, and you got it. The money's yours, Mr. Kydd, end of story."

Philip released an O of smoke. "I'm afraid circumstances have changed. I've been persuaded to drop the challenge. Sorry for the needless folderol and all that. We'll compensate you for your trouble, of course."

"Are you deaf, man?" Rousch said. "Our sole concern is the final execution of your father's will. He's our client here, not you. Sign the papers, both of you, and save your squawking for the street."

"But—" Julia and Philip protested in unison.

"Yes, sir," Jack said. "They're just about to, sir. We're almost done."

Reality blazed over Julia like a prison-yard beacon. She was so close, nearly there in her creep toward freedom under the cloak of their wager. She'd dared to imagine the new proofing press, the new titling fonts she'd buy with her reclaimed fortune. Now in a few blunt words, Rousch had exposed the futility of those hopes. The judgment was irrevocable: her father's will did not include her. The wager that had galvanized her last few weeks' effort was irrelevant. Nothing she'd learned had made, or could have made, any difference to her lost inheritance. She saw this now in searing clarity. Her cautious joy turned to cinders.

Rousch paused as he turned to go. "Oh, and best wishes, Miss Kydd, on your return to England. I understand you have a serious suitor. We'll look forward to wedding news within the year, as we reasoned would soon be the case. The best solution to your situation, I believe."

"Pompous ogre," Philip said as Jack pushed the door shut, a milder epithet than what rang in Julia's head. "You still won the wager, Julia. Your wits bested mine, for what it's worth."

For what it's worth. There it was, her meager prize, her only prize. What had her wits accomplished? She'd learned sleuthing was no game, no carefree romp of puzzle cracking. She'd achieved a measure of justice by ensuring Naomi's last wishes would be honored, but it had come at a great cost: a family in ruins, marriages torn, friends and lover freshly grieving. She'd brought to light the terrible truth of Naomi's death, but

Gerald's remained forever obscured by lies. Julia's cleverness could do nothing for that.

Philip resettled, flinging one leg over the arm of his chair. A turquoise sock gleamed at Julia. "I suppose we'll have to settle for a draw," he said. "Fair enough?"

She watched pigeons strut along the windowsills across the avenue. Any reply required too great an effort. So this was the true end. She felt limp, battered, flung from despair to victory to defeat to—what? She had no more fight left. Certainly no more wit. After all she'd done to defend what was rightfully hers, a draw was now the best she could achieve. Even that was a euphemism for whatever beneficence struck Philip's fancy. He'd slip her a nicely mollifying sum, enough to see her handed off comfortably into David's care.

Fair enough? It was what one said. There was nothing at all fair about this ending, but it would have to be enough. She was out of options. Life was always a draw: disappointments muted by triumphs tempered by obstacles eased by kindnesses. No ambitious Capriole agenda but no dreary bedsit either. Enough. She slid forward and extended her hand for the pen.

It was a daunting stack. She wrote her name on one sheet after another, and Jack laid them out across the desk to dry. They covered the surface in orderly rows, some nineteen pages, before she reached the end. She signed the final document and blew on the ink. "So be it. At last, the end of this awful business."

Thank God her voice was calm, her hand steady. Another few minutes and she could escape. Tomorrow. Not today but tomorrow she would begin to recalibrate, take the final, clear-eyed measurements of just what marriage would and would not allow of her.

Philip unscrambled his legs. "The end? Nothing will happen, daft girl, unless I sign as well."

"So get on with it." She thrust the pen at him. "Only a sadist would trifle at this point."

He sent another tremulous O of smoke into the air.

"Philip?" It had the shrill sound of foot stamping. "He's your friend, Jack. What madness is he up to now?"

"Why must you two always egg each other on?" Jack said. "You heard Rousch, Philip. Wink all you like, but what's done is done."

"Nonsense. Even if you shackle me to this chair for days and force my fainting hand to sign, I'll merely set up another monthly allowance, same as before only from my own ill-gotten estate. In fact, I'll boost it. Aunt Lillian ought to kick in something, for all the trouble she's caused."

The weary bee twitched. The acrobat made a wobbly somersault. Julia was too exhausted for more. Did he mean it? Resuming her present arrangement was not fair, but it could be enough. And yet. Was this another trick? More glib sport? She could bandy sham extravagance right back at him and better.

"Double it then," she said. "Triple it. But don't think you can ever compensate for what you stole, what we both know is mine by birthright. You're a poisonous cad. Fine, pay me dearly for this folly, but I'll never, ever forgive you."

"Poisonous? That's harsh. And you will, you know," Philip said. "I shall be a model citizen until you do. All these years, and I had no idea a sister could be so fun. I couldn't possibly sign you away. What about my lifetime supply of bookplates and calling cards? Maybe a volume of Lillian's bluest limericks? You need me to keep Capriole honest, steer you clear of any frightful *Rubaiyat*s or *Sonnets from the* bloody *Portuguese*. Bibliophiles everywhere will thank me. Why on earth would I sign all that away?"

Julia's head ached. Even if genuine, Philip's offer restored her options but presented a loathsome choice: Whose grip did she prefer on her purse strings, David's or Philip's? Appease one man's vanity or the other man's caprice? David would allow only the most safe and decorous production from Capriole, while Philip would pester her for anything but. David would soon wander off in search of his next Julia, leaving her to languish in peaceful comfort, if Helen's experience was anything to go by. On the other hand, with fresh coffers to plunder, Philip might use his money as marionette strings, making her dance (and print) to suit his every quirk and whim. Was it better to be a toy neglected or a toy worn to bits?

Let cynicism prevail then, once and for all. What folly to think she could escape the compromises even Naomi Rankin had accepted in the end, as Russell's hidden emerald ring attested. David too was a reasonable man. His demands—Julia's restrictions—would be few. She might still dabble in minor intrigues, print and bind as her (discreet) caprine whimsy moved. It could be enough. Like Naomi, she could not afford more. At last she could rid herself forever of everything Kydd and Vancill. *Julia Adair* had a stylish ring to it, after all.

"Just sign the wretched papers," she said. "I've been your plaything long enough. No allowance is worth a lifetime of your harebrained fun at my expense. Just sign and let me go."

Philip folded his arms across his chest, chin in the air. Though adults ten years apart in age, at the moment they might be feuding toddlers. If Julia had had something sturdy to hand, she'd have coshed him with it. Her bag was a trifle too dear to mash.

"Give me peace!" Jack expelled two cheekfuls of air and strode from the room.

He returned several minutes later to the same scene—not even a glance had been exchanged. Julia could match Philip in obstinacy any day of the week.

"You're both impossible." He thwacked two thick envelopes on his desk. "While you were stewing, Miss Baxter reminded me of these. Lillian Vancill's nurse brought them in. Apparently the old woman demanded they be delivered here in person. There's one for each of you, if you can drag your thoughts away from garroting each other."

Julia extended a gloved hand. "If I must." In truth, she was curious. What could the old lizard possibly have to say to her?

Philip tore his envelope open and pulled out two sheets folded twice and covered with a dense, wavery script in brilliant blue ink. He sighed and sat back to read.

Julia's held a tightly folded typescript and a brief note in the same blue ink. Without salutation, it read,

> *I've been a foolish old woman, Miss Kydd. I see now I was an even more foolish young woman. I confess with shame that I removed this from your father's library shortly before his death, for reasons I'd rather not disclose, but compelling ones, at least compelling to me. I apologize for meddling, then and now, and beg you to forgive the culprit, Lillian Lapham Vancill*

Julia unfolded the document in her lap. It was her father's will, dated March 8, 1906, a week before his death. The pages rattled like leaves in a windstorm as she searched for the pertinent phrase. She found it: *The remainder of my estate to be divided equally between my two children, Philip Vancill Kydd and Julia Jordahl Kydd . . .*

Julia tested her legs to be sure they wouldn't collapse like noodles beneath her, then stood with a sweep of her scarf. Philip and Jack watched mutely as one by one she tore in half each page she'd just signed. The pieces drifted to the floor.

"You can ho ho ho your cheeky largesse right out the window, Philip." She laid the resurrected will on the desk. "I'll merely collect what's mine and be on my way."

Both men elbowed closer to read it.

At last. At *last!* She neither needed nor wanted a penny of Philip's or Lillian's money. A more satisfying plan had begun to hatch in Julia's mind. Could Jack be persuaded to render a withering caricature of his friend to accompany some particularly baneful excerpt from Pope's *Dunciad*?

"My word," Philip said, flopping back in his chair. "Most curious, but there you have it. No wonder Lillian kept asking about you. She loved nothing more than a good fighter. Your charging off after Naomi Rankin's killer must have set the old girl's larcenous scheme on its ear. Here I thought she was wrestling with a fever in those last hours, but it must have been the tattered remnants of her conscience. Well, congratulations, my dear. Those French milliners shall dance their jigs, and I needn't miss Brahms's Second tonight after all."

He tapped at his right ear. "Side stall."

CHAPTER 27

With Philip out that evening, Julia was free to gather a few essentials from his guest quarters and make for the Seville Hotel. The next afternoon she returned to finish packing her trunks. She locked the bedroom door, even though Mrs. Cheadle had confirmed that Philip was away. This was serious work, and she needed to concentrate. Christophine had schooled her in what went where and how. "Your stockings with your smalls, Miss Julia." She had demonstrated while packing several weeks ago, lifting and replacing one neatly folded or rolled bundle after another. Julia was determined to avoid her housekeeper's dismay at opening the cases next weekend in their London flat.

Mrs. Cheadle knocked with a promised pot of coffee. When Julia opened the door to accept it, it was Philip who strode in, tray in hand.

"Don't worry," he said, "only one cup. No need for flight, you know. You're always welcome under my roof."

That was droll.

"It's high time to move my plunder, as you put it," Julia said. "I've imposed on you far too long. I'm sailing tomorrow afternoon and can't imagine ever returning. Your home is your own again and forever, Philip."

He balanced the tray atop a wicker wastebasket, as the bed, writing desk, dressing table, and nightstand were covered with luggage, clothing to be folded, or flowers. "I won't rest," he said, "until you believe

I'd never sign those papers. I may be a poisonous cad, but I'm no slink. I had no intention whatsoever to cheat you out of your inheritance. None."

"And yet you pursued the matter with zeal. Positive glee." Julia smoothed the wrinkles out of her clumsily folded pyjama trousers.

"What's the fun of having a sister if you can't give her a good dustup now and then? I hardly knew you, and then you turn out to be more full of beans than I am. It was too delicious to resist. I was weak, bored, brutish, whatever you like. But surely I've apologized enough."

"What was fun and games to you was frightfully serious to me. You jested with my *life*, Philip. I'll forgive you when there's an ocean between us."

He winced. "You wound me."

"Is nothing ever serious to you? You prattle on but understand nothing."

"You're wrong there." He sat on Julia's gabardine suit, laid across the bed. "I understand plenty. Too late."

She juggled rolls of lingerie in both hands, uncertain where to put them. She would not rise to the bait. Not anymore.

"It seems you're not my sister after all."

"Oh please!" Julia threw both rolls into the trunk. Not that horrid business about the missing marriage license. "Can't you leave me be? For the last time, the last bloody, bloody time, I'm as much a Kydd as you are."

"Not true."

Fury reduced Julia to nursery warfare. Pain shot up her wrist as she delivered a stinging slap across his cheek.

He rubbed his jaw. "A stunner, I'll agree, but true. Turns out you're more Kydd than I am. Milo's your father, all right," he said, "but not mine."

"*What?*" Julia sat hard beside him, squarely on her white chiffon evening frock.

"Seems Aunt Lillian ain't my aunt. She spent the winter before I was born in Charleston with my parents—helping, as spinster sisters did—but apparently she's the one who had the baby." Philip's face had become a perfect mask, lids lowered, nostrils taut, lips barely moving. Julia could only imagine the shock writ large across her own face.

"All hush-hush, you know. Milo and Charlotte returned triumphant, babe in arms. No wonder Lillian lived with us all those years. I had no idea. None. No one knew, apparently, until the old girl's confession plopped into my lap yesterday afternoon. Now you're the only other living soul to share her secret. I owe you that satisfaction."

Satisfaction? What was there to give Julia pleasure? She felt a stab of sorrow for withered old Aunt Lillian. How had she borne such a secret for thirty-five long years? Alone in that sweltering room with dusty relics of her only child, the son with whom she bantered and boxed, yet who knew her only as an eccentric batterymate. She'd sacrificed her own comfort to ensure his after her death. Why had she never revealed the truth? Perhaps the secret was too ingrained. Perhaps she'd feared the risk of Philip's resentment more than the chance for a closer bond. Frightful choice.

And Philip. What grief must he be feeling? To lose two mothers, after knowing one so briefly and the other, in a sense, not at all. Julia remembered her own weightlessness at her mother's death. Sorry was too poor a word for it. She covered his hand. He lifted hers, kissed it, and returned it to her lap.

New realizations dawned. "This mean we're not siblings?" she said.

"Not even remotely related. Joke's on me, it seems."

A rap sounded on the door. "The driver's here for your things, miss."

Julia jumped to her feet. "Thank you, Mrs. Cheadle. Please ask him to wait—five minutes."

She scooped up her lovely chiffon and pushed it into the trunk. Christophine would have to forgive the wrinkles. "I have to rush, but please, Philip, this is hardly a joke. I am sorry, truly sorry. Such a shock. Are you all right?"

He stood, folded her suit into neat thirds, and deposited it in the trunk. "I'll survive. We Vancills are a sturdy lot. You saw for yourself." He busied himself with folding and tucking, fastening hatboxes and trunk straps. Julia flew about the room, gathering lingerie, securing toiletries, and scooping the last of her jewelry into its case. She paused at her Capriole box.

Another knock. "He's rather impatient, miss."

"Yes, yes. Almost ready. Two minutes!"

The fellow's deep huff conceded one minute, nothing more. "Your secret is safe with me, Philip. I won't breathe a word of this to anyone. You've been an atrocious brother, but then I've been a pretty poor sister. How about we forgive each other and call it another draw?" In some ways, she was beginning to understand, she required as much forgiving as he did.

"Here." She gave him the Capriole box. "A token to remember me by. Juvenilia, mind."

The door handle turned, and Mrs. Cheadle's face appeared.

"I'm just coming now. Tell him—"

A burly fellow burst into the room. Philip drew Julia out of the way as the man latched and hoisted a trunk onto his trolley, pitched her toiletries case and three hatboxes on top of it, and careened out the door. Julia started after the lout, alarmed at the thud of bouncing leather, then turned back to Philip. "Agreed? Please?"

He flicked his fingers at her. "Of course. Scoot! Flee! Toddle forth!"

A crash in the hallway sent her swiveling.

"Oh, and Julia?" Philip caught her sleeve. "Best wishes with that swain of yours. I mean that. You may be losing a noisome brother but seems you might soon be gaining a florist's shop. I'm glad things have turned out well for you."

He set down the Capriole box and handed her a slim parcel from his inside breast pocket wrapped in brown paper. It was an octavo pamphlet of poems, simply bound in wrappers of green laid paper. *Hymen*, by H.D.: the book he'd searched for that night in the library. At first glance the printing was not too bad, the cover typography more attentive than usual, the title set in inline caps within a double-rule frame.

There wasn't time for all that she might say. Philip touched her throat, clucking at her bruises, and kissed her cheek. She clasped his shoulders lightly in return, then felt a surprising strength as his arms folded around her. He held her for a long moment.

It was the embrace she'd thought lost to her since childhood, sturdy and tender, more than a friend's and less than a lover's. She'd come to New York to collect her inheritance—hers by right, not charity—and to conclude an unhappy chapter of her life. Yet in the thump of his heart against her breast, she felt the offer of something deeply generous, the one thing Philip could give her, which could only be a gift: the intimate bond not of family but of an irony even sweeter—the secret that they were no such thing.

Yes, things had turned out well enough, if her luggage survived as far as the taxicab.

CHAPTER 28

The weather was raw. Clouds hunkered over the harbor, and a wet breeze swept leaves and debris into sodden corners. A line of black taxicabs snaked by the principal entrance to the pier. Harried travelers shouted and scolded, directing caravans of trunks and suitcases and hatboxes into the care of stewards and luggage clerks. The *Majestic* was sailing in three hours.

Standing at a large window inside the terminal, Julia turned up the collar of her coat and watched arriving passengers call to wayward children, linger over goodbyes, fret with last-minute instructions to porters, and edge forward with paperwork in hand. At last she saw her. Against the tide of travelers, Julia slipped through the double doors. Her quick embrace surprised Glennis, halting her in midsentence as she lectured the driver on the proper handling of her alligator-skin luggage.

Glennis beamed. "Julia! What a tickle! I can't believe I'm doing this. Deborah and I packed like fiends all night. What fabulous luck you scrounged me a ticket."

As she chattered, four large trunks were hoisted onto a luggage trolley, with as many smaller cases wedged in among them. Glennis thrust the large jewelry case she was carrying into Julia's arms and rummaged in her handbag to pay the driver, all the while ticking through the hasty decisions about what should go to her cabin and what to steerage. Her small mountain rumbled off to join the others.

"Funny, I knew this was the right thing to do as soon as you telephoned. I did think about it, I did"—she anticipated Julia's caution—"but I knew at once. That house is like a tomb. I had to get out of there. I'd never survive till spring. It's ghastly! Nolda hasn't come downstairs once. She'd kick my shins if she did, she's that sore. Chester's just as bad, touchy as a hedgehog."

She took back her case and clutched it, grinning like a princess on her birthday. "So I did it, Julia. Just like you said. When I told him I was thinking of sailing today and he started bleating again about my boo-hoo extravagance, that was it. I stood behind a chair so he couldn't smack me and did what you said. I told him he had to let me go, or I'd tell the papers what happened to Naomi. I said we'd changed the deal, murder being murder—oh, you should've seen his face! Either he forks over my allowance, I said, no strings attached, *and* Miss Clintock gets Naomi's dough, or I blab. I said it, just like that." As her arms were full, she gave Julia's shoulder a jubilant bump.

"Russell was there," she went on, "and he about gawked his eyes out at me telling Chester what's what, but he was a witness, and Chester knew I had him. So he ranted and spit and then went all tossy and ordered me to get on the boat and not come back. He yelled how he'd had enough, how he didn't care where I went as long as I did it pronto. Like it was his idea. Ha! You are brilliant!"

Julia laughed too. Gambits that turned out well could be quite amusing afterward. Thank goodness Russell had been there to hold Chester to account. Courage opened the door, but power (or threat) carried one through.

"So I huffed right back at him, 'Fine, if I must, I must,' and ran upstairs to pack before he changed his mind." Glennis shifted her armload and nuzzled Julia's elbow. "I'm so glad to get away from him, from all of them."

Julia asked if there was any news from the Winterjay household.

Glennis rolled her eyes. "I'll say. Not a peep from Viv, but Edward says he's moving to his club downtown. I heard him tell Chester he needs time to consider his future with a wife whose moral probity he can no longer trust." Glennis's chin dropped along with her voice in repeating the sanctimonious phrase. "He's even thinking of declaring her an unfit mother and taking the children to his sister in Boston. Rich, huh? I mean, sure, she treated Naomi like rubbish, but who is he to point a finger? None of this would've happened if he'd just kept his poker stashed. You know? Plus he swore he'd never again draw breath in the same room with Nolda. Chester harrumphed and all, but I think Edward means it. Serves her right, but what a prune he turned out to be."

Julia nodded. She recalled the tucked-away tearoom where she'd spent the afternoon of her birthday and the sight of Winterjay guiding a woman in navy linen to the hotel's elevator. He'd no doubt scoff to recollect it; hardly a comparable transgression, he'd say. Merely a discreet tryst: a harmless dalliance. That woman and surely others too accepted his carnal attentions—proof, he believed, of all women's acquiescence. The inference seemed ludicrous—given Naomi's resistance, which he'd ignored as so much coquetry—and yet commonplace. As difficult as financial freedom was for a woman to achieve, sexual freedom seemed even more elusive.

Glennis glanced over each shoulder and tardily lowered her voice. "It's just as bad at our house. The whole place is a blue funk. Nolda won't speak to Chester, and he *really* won't speak to her. He had her things moved into the old nursery upstairs, and when she screamed about it, he said she has to take her meals up there too." She giggled. "Isn't it a hoot? If ever there was a couple who needs to split, it's them, but they never will. Too embarrassing. Ha! Serves 'em right."

Julia listened throughout this storm of Rankin family news but said nothing. She felt none of Glennis's surprise, only a measure of that grim recompense one feels when those who cause suffering are in turn made to suffer. While not exactly justice, at least there were consequences for all that proud perfidy.

"Plus Russell's leaving," Glennis said. "He told Chester he has to go away for a while, to New Mexico, I think. Well, that absolutely did it. I never put much stock in him anyway. Archie isn't so bad. Now I just have to get back there and pin him down before someone else tries.

"Look." She balanced the case on her hip and tugged the glove off her left hand to reveal the small diamond ring Archie had given her in August, the ring she'd shown to Julia once and then kept hidden in her jewelry chest the entire time they'd been in New York. "It's kind of cute when you get used to it. I'm sure I can get something nicer later on. I cabled him yesterday to tell him to meet me. I hope he hasn't forgotten or changed his mind. Men can't do that, can they?" She laughed. "Well, I'll just have to dazzle him all over again. I can flirt pretty well when I want to, you know."

She wriggled her arm through Julia's. "This is going to be such fun. I'll get Archie to throw us a big party. You'll see what a good hostess I can be. Plus April isn't really very far off, and I need time to get a nice dress made and everything. We'll get you something dreamy too. And then there's sterling and crystal and all that. I have to tell the shops. You can help me choose. Oh, Julia, don't make that face. You can't say those things don't matter. People will talk, and anyway, who wants a hundred salad bowls and shrimp plates and beastly little pictures of terriers?"

Who indeed, Julia agreed.

"Just think, by next summer I'll be an old married lady. You'll see how fun it is and nail down that David of yours too, if I have anything to say about it. We can meet for tea at Claridge's, go to flower shows, wear hats the size of train cars. It'll be a scream. I'll start looking for a little flat in town near you, though I can't say anything about that until after I'm married. Archie won't mind." Her shoulders rose. "I can't believe this luck!"

Julia steered them into the correct line, where they slowed to a standstill. Glennis glanced about. Everywhere stood clusters of restless travelers, many sneaking peeks at their fellow passengers. Which might appear across one's dinner table? Which would amuse or annoy over morning croissants or late cocktails? Any attractive possibilities for that most delicious of pastimes, a shipboard romance?

She turned to Julia. "Where are your things?"

"I'm not going," Julia said, watching a nanny corral a small boy clutching a red balloon. "I'm staying in New York."

Glennis gaped. "But you can't. Julia, you can't. We're going back together." At the small shake of Julia's head, her voice went up an octave. "What about David? You'll break his heart!"

Heads turned. A bright-blue toque with a fan of ostrich tail feathers tipped in their direction, its occupant studying the ship's safety-instruction pamphlet.

Julia answered in the softest possible tones, grateful to be spared the much louder squeal Glennis might have made had she known a canceled wedding was involved. "His heart is quite resilient, I assure you. He'll get over me quickly."

"You are mad. Stark, raving loony. And what about your special maid, what's her name? Won't she be expecting you?"

"Christophine. I'll be over soon to settle my affairs and pack up our household. I'm staying on here just long enough to find us a flat. I'm at the Seville, so you can reach me there if you need to." Julia scribbled down the address and tucked it into Glennis's handbag. "Don't be glum. I'm doing what feels right for me. New York might be an amusing place to live after all."

"I know what's happened. You must have won that judgment business with your brother. Is that it? Did your inheritance come through?"

Julia smiled.

"Well, no wonder. You have all that money—"

"Not so much really. But enough."

"All that money and no bossy brother to parcel it out like some bloody reward for keeping mum about what a tosser he is. Holy Joe, I'd go for that too if I could get it."

A porter met them as they emerged from the clearing area. Glennis handed him her case and her papers, and they followed him up the gangplank and along a maze of corridors to the cabin. It was a pleasant space, with a starboard porthole. On the table waited a dozen red roses. Julia quickly found and removed the card. Another of David's grand gestures, obviously arranged before her telegram had arrived. "Look," she said brightly, "David wishes you a pleasant voyage."

Glennis made a sour face. "So this is your cabin." She looked around as if it were a soiled hand-me-down dress. "How could you do this to me? Now the crossing will be a big bore, and I'll have to stay with Archie's mother. She's a monster. She thinks I'm some damp flapper. She'll put the kibosh on everything."

"Stay at my flat," Julia said. "Christophine will help with anything you need." She wrote the address on another slip of paper and tucked it down beside the first, silently reminding herself to cable Christophine to clear the new paper shipments off the guest room bed.

A steward arrived with a silver ice bucket. He made space for it beside the roses and deftly opened the champagne. He glanced at a note protruding from his cuff. "Compliments of Mr. Adair, miss," he said to Glennis. He fetched a second glass from the trolley in the corridor.

"To fiancés," Julia suggested, toasting her friend. "May Archie make you very, very happy."

The answering smile was a very, very poor thing.

"I can't believe you're doing this to me," Glennis said, plopping into a barrel-backed chair. "I thought we were friends. I want us to be married ladies together. Can't you change your mind?"

"We're different, Glennis. I'm simply not the marrying sort, as I told you. I like my life the way it is."

"We're different, all right. You have your own money, all of it, free and clear." Glennis fidgeted with her ring. "I'd give Archie back this pokey thing in a heartbeat if I didn't need him to get Chester's mitts off mine. It's so flipping unfair."

"Glennis, listen. You don't have to marry Archie or anyone. Now that Chester needs to keep you quiet, he'll make sure you have plenty of funds to live on. Maybe not forever but for a few years at least. You can follow your own path too, decide for yourself if and when you marry. Lots of women do these days. You went to college. There must be things you'd like to do, hobbies or charities or work of some kind."

Glennis's eyebrows spurted up. "You mean like a *job*?"

"I mean whatever you'd find worthwhile, interesting. You could explore, take a class, try something new." Julia remembered the pleasure of her first printing and binding courses at Camberwell. Might Glennis experience the same novice's thrill? She tried to imagine Glennis squinting over a composing stick or scoring sheets with a folding bone, but the picture wouldn't form. No, they were different in that way as well.

Glennis sat back with a loud *ooof*. She took a gulp of champagne, pinched her lips to stifle the fizzy burn, and thought for several seconds. "Independence sounds all fine and jolly, but it only works when you're strong and clever like you. I'm stupid and silly and not even pretty. All I'm good at is shopping and going to parties—but not by myself. Archie may not be much of a wow, but at least I'd have him. I'd rather marry the old poke than have all the tra-la freedom in the world and be alone."

Julia set aside her glass and slid forward until her kneecaps rested against Glennis's. "Listen to me. You have a stout heart. You are fun and funny, and your laugh can outsparkle any diamond. You don't need glamour and posh long legs. You know right from wrong and say so, which puts you forever at the front of my book. Think what friends we've become this past month. You'll make oodles of new friends in London, once they see what a good person you are. Believe me. You are."

She stroked her friend's semi-engaged hand. "In six days you'll start an exciting new life. I'll make sure David invites you to his best parties, and by the time I join you in a month or so, you may even have a new beau, if you put your mind to it. You are a *very* good flirter."

Glennis smiled. She was.

"You can show me around the new clubs there just like you did here. And if Archie's still the ticket, well, then we'll shop for your trousseau."

Glennis's smile bloomed.

"And I'll dance at your wedding." It was a cliché, but Julia meant it. Of course she would. The freedom that meant so much to her had always terrified Glennis, and perhaps it always would. Even to Julia's ears her fine words of choice and independence had rung a bit hollow, given how close she too had come to marrying for convenience. Independence was a luxury, she now understood, secured with a steady income more than principled resolve. But money enabled other choices too, and Glennis's stretched out before her, including the married life she craved. Did she know how fortunate she was? How fortunate they both were?

Glennis refilled their glasses and hoisted hers high. "To trousseaus and weddings. And babies and parties and having a date for the rest of my life."

Julia drank to her friend's vision of bliss, however rosy. They settled back to enjoy the champagne, listening to the traffic in the corridor. Julia thought about Naomi and Alice and the countless other women whose fortunes, and choices, were far more circumscribed. In time she believed Glennis would think of them too.

A blast from the ship's horn warned visitors it was time to leave. Julia set down her glass and allowed herself a moment's fond regard of the roses. He was a lovely man. She would miss him. But he needed a wife. It was important for his business, for the way he liked to live. Thank goodness she would never have to be that idle woman squandering her days in Devon and Provence. Yes, David would be taken aback by her decision, possibly even wounded briefly, but Julia didn't doubt someone else, Lila French or maybe Sarah Wynchell, would make him the contented, absent wife he wished for. She expected word of it by year's end, spring at the latest.

They walked arm in arm back to the gangplank. "I will be happy for you," Julia said, "whether you marry Archie or someone else or nobody. All that matters is that you decide what's best, Glennis. I decide for me. You decide for you. But we're friends, always, no matter what."

On the deck they embraced. Glennis clamped her arms around Julia with her usual gusto, though this time it evoked the bond of their extraordinary past month together rather than a bruising determination to drag Julia along into her future. But when Glennis stepped back and seized her hands, Julia braced for another last entreaty.

Instead a fierce clasp crumpled her fingers. "No matter what," Glennis repeated firmly.

Julia turned to look up when she reached the pier. Glennis was leaning against the railing. She began to wave, arm sweeping like a matador's. Julia returned the wave and threw her friend a kiss. "Six days!" she mouthed. She sprang apart her fingertips to demonstrate the merest poof of time until Glennis's future could begin to unfold. Another bone-rattling blast sent people streaming down the gangplank. Other voyagers pressed against the railing, jostling Glennis, eager for the exuberant ritual of final farewells amid camera flashes and hurrahs.

Glennis would not be budged. She stood in her place, feet apart, face determined. With both palms she flung back a mighty kiss of her own across the roiling water.

CHAPTER 29

The next morning Julia arrived unannounced at the reception room of Feeney, Churchman, Kessler, and Rousch. She carried an envelope under her arm, a thin sheaf of Amy Lowell poems just received from Maurice Firuski over croissants in the café across the street. Eager as she was to read them, her long list of errands for the day demanded attention first. Miss Baxter eyed her skeptically when she refused to state her business. But when she put through word that Julia was waiting, Jack catapulted from his closet at the end of the hall.

"I thought you were on your way to Southampton. What's happened?"

With the office door firmly closed behind them, Julia explained the change of plan. He kindly said nothing of her jilted beau.

"I'd like your help," she said. "I've decided to stay. Yes, in New York. Manhattan. Philip may think I've gone balmy, but I'm not consulting him. I rather like this city, what I've seen of it, and surely it's big enough for both of us. I'm ready for a change. I'd like to give it a go and see what happens." Now that she had a bona fide brother, even an unrelated one, she was keen to repay his vexations. She was in considerable arrears.

"How can I help?"

"I need an agent to find me a suitable home. I'm fairly particular about what I'll need, which we can discuss later. There are a few other matters as well."

He pulled a notepad from his desk drawer and uncapped his pen. The tip of his tongue crept to his upper lip. "Julia," he said, "I must ask you something first. Willard Wright pesters me every time I see him. He wants to know the story behind Naomi Rankin's death. He's still got this cracked idea of writing detective stories, and he's hungry for material. Would you mind if I told him what you learned? I can hardly creep in and out of my building without him haranguing me about it."

Alarm shrilled Julia's answer. "Absolutely not. Never. Impossible. You're sworn to secrecy, Jack."

He looked miserable. "He won't stop hounding me. I suppose I could just insist there was nothing suspicious after all. He'll rant a blue streak, but eventually he'll have to accept it."

"A completely justified fib. The Rankins' privacy doesn't concern me, but others would be hurt if the story came to light."

He looked both relieved and ashamed. Why he let that odious Wright fellow torment him Julia couldn't imagine.

"I'll need your managerial talents," she said. "With my new accounts. I'd like to establish an endowment—an anonymous endowment, Jack, that's very important—to boost the wages of the women who work at the Empire State Equal Rights Union. Find out whatever Chester Rankin's bank pays its office employees and set the Union's wages fifty percent higher. Please do whatever you must to ensure the women have no inkling where the money has come from." The money would be welcome, she was sure, allowing Alice to devote more of Naomi's funds to Union programs.

Jack wrote steadily as she spoke. He looked up, expression sober but eloquent.

"What?"

He shook his head and slid the pad, lined with neatly jotted notes, to one side, uncovering the pile of recently opened mail he'd been reviewing when she'd interrupted. "I seem to recall Miss Baxter speaking highly of an estate agent her brother recently hired." He pushed his chair away from the desk. "I'll go see if she can recall the fellow's name."

It was practically laid out for Julia to see. The top sheet of Jack's morning mail was a handwritten note dated simply *Saturday.* It was signed with a flamboyant *P.* She listened for the sound of returning footsteps, heard none, and bent closer to read.

Feeling benevolent this morning, it said.

> *Old Lillian's largesse has addled my brain. If my fair sister should ask you to direct a portion of her new wealth to some charitable purpose—as I have a suspicion she might—please slap another ten thousand on it from Lillian's accounts. Strictly secret, promise me. I rather applaud the youngster's pluck, you know, even if she is so dashed exasperating.*

Julia read it again, more slowly. How many more facets to Philip's character had she not yet seen? How many more surprises might yet lie ahead? It was a dizzying prospect; she hoped for no more than one per day.

"George Aronson."

Julia jumped. Jack leaned in the open doorway, arms folded, and repeated the name. "The estate agent. I'll telephone him this afternoon and set up an appointment for tomorrow, if that suits your schedule."

She straightened and shook her head at the very idea of having a schedule. "Anytime tomorrow would suit." She wrote on his notepad the hotel address and telephone number where she could be reached.

He capped his pen. "Very well. I'll telephone later today. Anything else?"

"Just one more thing." She gathered up her gloves and handbag. "Would you happen to know how I might go about registering to vote?"

AFTERWORD

Although this is a work of fiction, and I have occasionally sacrificed strict historical accuracy for the purposes of my story, several minor characters are versions of real men and women, colorful players on the extraordinary cultural and political stage that was Manhattan in the 1920s.

Willard Huntington Wright was an erudite, often acerbic art critic who enjoyed a modest reputation in elite cultural circles. In 1925, at the age of thirty-seven, his health collapsed. He was forced to spend several months in solitude, recovering strength and sobriety. To endure the deprivation, he pursued the most lucrative enterprise he could manage, writing crime fiction for the readers he generally disdained, women and "the masses." Using the pseudonym S. S. Van Dine, he created Philo Vance, the first American amateur sleuth to truly ignite bestseller lists. Wright's first two novels—*The Benson Murder Case* and *The Canary Murder Case*—were hugely popular, their plots drawn from recent headline coverage of sensational Manhattan crimes. Other volumes quickly followed to meet the demand.

The cynical yet brilliant Philo Vance was soon famous for dazzling pedantry and solving crimes through psychological rather than forensic clues. There's no evidence that Wright modeled Vance and his devoted scribe Van Dine on real men of his acquaintance, but I have taken the liberty of imagining as much. I suspect such actual men, once freed from the distortion of Wright's misanthropic wit, might have had a wealth of interesting qualities Wright would scorn. Because he gave Vance a personal life nearly devoid of women, I felt compelled to ensure a female of extraordinary mettle in the life of the "real" Vance I imagined. An estranged half sister, perhaps. Or not a sister at all.

Although Wright's novels are set in Manhattan between the wars, they offer few glimpses into the fabled cultural energy of those decades. Vance's arcane tastes in book collecting, for example, bear little trace of the era's enthusiasm for private presses and fine bookmaking. Maurice Firuski's Dunster House imprint was a minor player in a thriving transatlantic market for beautiful limited editions of the sort produced by Julia's Capriole Press. Both Beatrice Warde and her enigmatic husband, though they separated in 1925, became significant players in the era's typographic renaissance, and by her death in 1970, Warde was hailed as the century's "first lady" of typography. I suspect she and Julia Kydd would be natural friends, given their kindred interests.

Rarer still in Wright's novels are glimpses of contemporary social and political turmoil. I've taken a different approach. Margaret Sanger, with her Clinical Research Bureau, staffed by Dr. Dorothy Bocker, was a well-known pioneer in the struggle for safe and legal birth control and women's health care. Similarly, although the Empire State Equal Rights Union is fictional, Alice Paul and the National Woman's Party were instrumental in gaining voting rights for women. They were opposed by, among others, Alice Hay Wadsworth (wife of James W. Wadsworth, New York senator from 1914 to 1926), president of the National Association Opposed to Woman Suffrage. The association published the *Woman Patriot* until 1932.

Finally, I've given Naomi Rankin political ambitions that were lofty but not unreachable. In 1932 Hattie Wyatt Caraway, a Democrat from Arkansas, became the first woman elected to the US Senate. Naomi's other great dream—an Equal Rights Amendment to the Constitution, assuring full gender equality under the law—remains unrealized to this day.

ACKNOWLEDGMENTS

Any first novel owes much to many, and mine is no exception. I'm grateful to the friends who've read evolving versions over the years, particularly my sister, Laura Bjornson, Emily Chamberlain, and Kathleen Thorne. Special thanks to Ellen Gruber Garvey, whose astute remarks breathed life into a draft I'd nearly declared dead, and to Susie Rennels for the insightful conversations that helped push the book to its final iteration.

Thanks to Claire Hicks, Lindsay Guzzardo, the late Sally Robison, Harriet Alexander, Cameron Snow, Nan Wooldridge, Abra Bennett, Babs Brownell, Suellen Cunningham, and Pat Speidel for early listening, reading, and encouragement. I'm also grateful to Woodleigh Marx Hubbard and Mickey Molnaire, who patiently plowed with me through assorted false starts and plot gaffes, and to LT Treviño Yoson and fellow writers Ruby Hansen Murray and Joyce Simons for advice, commiseration, and camaraderie.

I'm deeply grateful to my agent, Amanda Jain, for her enthusiastic skill in finding a good home for this book. I feel fortunate that her efforts led me to Lake Union Publishing. My editor Chris Werner, developmental editor Tiffany Yates Martin, Nicole Pomeroy, Haleigh Rucinski, Miranda Dunning, and the rest of the talented team have been nothing short of sterling.

Finally, I thank my husband, Paul Benton, for anchoring the essential "everything else" of my life, and my late father, Peter Beckman, for introducing me early on to the pleasures of good fiction. I may have groaned through every poem he intoned on car trips and every literary allusion he sprinkled over family dinners, but he gave me a deep love for language and the worlds it can create. This book is the result, and it's dedicated to his memory.

ABOUT THE AUTHOR

Photo © 2019 Keith Brofsky

Born near Boston, Marlowe Benn grew up in an Illinois college town along the Mississippi River. She holds a master's degree in the book arts from the University of Alabama and a doctorate in the history of books from the University of California, Berkeley. A former editor, college teacher, and letterpress printer, Benn now lives with her husband on an island near Seattle. *Relative Fortunes* is her first novel.